The Only Blue Door

The Only Blue Door

The Scottish novelist Joan Fallon, currently lives and works in the south of Spain. She writes both contemporary and historical fiction, and almost all her books have a strong female protagonist. She is the author of:

FICTION:
Spanish Lavender
The House on the Beach
Loving Harry
Santiago Tales
Palette of Secrets
The Thread That Binds Us

The al-Andalus series:
The Shining City (Book 1)
The Eye of the Falcon (Book 2)
The Ring of Flames (Book 3)

NON-FICTION:
Daughters of Spain

(all are available in paperback and as ebooks)

www.joanfallon.co.uk

JOAN FALLON

The Only Blue Door

Scott Publishing

ISBN 978 0 9576891 3 8
First published in 2013
Scott Publishing
Windsor, England

ACKNOWLEDGMENTS

My sincere thanks to my editors Sara Starbuck, author of the 'Dread Pirate Fleur' series of children's books and JG Harlond, author of 'The Chosen Man', for their invaluable advice and support.

The airline ticket lies on top of her bag where she cannot miss it, everything is packed and ready to go but still she hesitates. What will he think of her after all these years? Does he blame her? He has never said so in his letters, but then he never says much at all in his letters and, now that he is married, it's his wife, Adaline, who writes and gives her the latest news. Usually she tells her about the children and nowadays, the grandchildren too. Maggie sits down and picks up the last photo that her sister-in-law sent her, Billy, an old man now, sitting astride a brown horse, his hat awry. For a moment she thinks she can glimpse the child she used to know behind that grizzled beard and weather beaten face; the old pain of separation returns briefly but she tosses it aside. Better late than never, that was what her grandmother, a woman with a homily for every occasion, used to say. So many years, virtually a lifetime of separation, for what? The man in the photograph is looking at her; his eyes, which she knows are blue even though the photograph gives no hint of the colour, are kind; the skin around them is wrinkled from squinting into the sun and, she hopes, laughing. He is a man at peace with himself; he is not accusing her of anything.

Her hat, she must not forget her sunhat, she pads around the bedroom checking and rechecking her bag. She sets the alarm clock for six and places it by the bed, close at hand so she will hear it. She must not miss the flight; she has convinced herself that if she does not go this time she will never go and she will never see Billy again.

The Only Blue Door

PART ONE
LONDON
1940

'Ladybird, ladybird, fly away home
Your house is on fire and your children are gone
All except one and that's little Ann
For she crept under the frying pan'

Traditional English nursery rhyme

MAGGIE

'*Rat-tat-tat, who is that?*
Only Mrs Pussy Cat.'
The skipping rope flashes through the air, beating the ground in time to the girls' singing.
'*What do you want?*
A pint of milk.'
The words echo down the street, bouncing off the walls of the terraced houses where they live.
'*Where's your penny?*
In my pocket.'
And a plump little girl, her pigtails flying in time to the song, skips on.
Where's your pocket?
I forgot it.'
Now the girls' voices change key as they chant the last line.
'*Please walk out.*'
It's Maggie's turn now. As Greta jumps out, she jumps in.
'*Rat-tat-tat*' they begin again, seamlessly, tirelessly, their young voices carrying down the street.
Grace is whining now. Maggie can see the snot running down her top lip.
'Wipe your nose, Gracie. I won't be long,' she calls out, not breaking her rhythm.
'Come here Gracie, I'll help you,' says Ann, taking hold of the grubby handkerchief that is looped through the top buttonhole of the child's coat.
'She's got a real streamer,' she says, wiping her face carefully.

'She's had it all week. Come on, you're next.'

Maggie bounces out from under the skipping rope as Ann bounces in.

'Can't we go home now, Maggie?' Gracie whines.

'Five more minutes.'

'But why can't I play?'

'You're too small.'

'I'm not. I'll be 'free' soon.'

'Your turn Maggie.'

She takes the end of the rope from Mary and without a pause begins to turn it.

'Let's do "*Mother, mother*".'

'OK'

'*Mother, mother, I feel sick, send for the doctor, quick, quick, quick,*' the girls chant.

'Maggie. Tea time. Maggie.'

'That's yer mum,' says Mary.

'Gis the rope.'

Judy takes the rope from her and continues turning it.

'Come on Gracie, tea time.'

Maggie takes her sister's hand and they skip down the road together.

'*Send for the doctor, quick, quick, quick,*' sings Grace.

'That's what we'll have to do for you my girl if that cold don't get any better.'

Their Mum is standing in the doorway watching them, a broad smile on her face.

'Hello Mum. You look happy.'

'There's a letter from your Dad.'

'Oh goody. What's he say?'

'I thought we'd wait until we're all sitting down together and then I'd read it to you. Come on now, your Nan's waiting.'

'Is Nan here then?'

'Yes, she's just popped over to see how we are.'

'Did she bring any rock cakes?'

'Is that all you think about my girl, food?'

'Mum,' Grace says.

'What sweetheart?'

'I've got a headache.'

'Oh, my poor little Gracie, you are in the wars. Come here and Mum'll give you a cuddle.'

She bends down, awkwardly and picks up the little girl; she balances her on her extended stomach and carries her into the house. Maggie follows. The smell of toast and tea drifts from the kitchen down the passage. She closes the front door carefully behind her. Dad painted the front door just before he left for the fighting. He asked her what her favourite colour was and she said blue, so he painted it blue. It's the only blue door in the whole street. She likes that. When she comes home from school and turns into their street she can see their house straight away. All the other doors are brown. They line the street like ranks of soldiers dressed in brown uniforms, silently facing each other, and then there is their door. Blue. Blue like the sky.

Mum stands at the kitchen range, pouring the tea. Grace sits next to Nan at the kitchen table.

'Wash your hands dear before you sit down,' Mum says, without turning round.

'Hello Nan.'

'Hello there Maggie. What have you been up to then?'

'Playing.'

'How's school?'

'She's doing very well,' Mum answers for her, going into the scullery and taking a bottle of milk from the larder.

'Her teacher says she's one of the best in her class,' she adds putting the milk on the table.

'Well that's nice. You could teach that brother of yours a thing or two then.'

Nan looks up at Mum and asks:

'Has he settled down yet?'

'Billy's just a bit high-spirited,' Mum replies.

'Needs a father's hand, that's what he needs.'

'Mum, some more of our teachers have gone.'

'What's that Maggie?'

Mum cuts the bread into thick slices, one for each of them.

'Here Maggie, toast these will you.'

She hands her a long toasting fork, blackened with use.

Maggie opens the door to the range. She carefully skewers the first slice of bread onto the fork and holds it in front of the glowing coals.

'Still got the range going then,' says Nan.

'Well, the weather has been pretty cold for May,' Mum replies.

'I've never known a winter like it. Ice and snow. Even the river frozen over.'

'This is the last of the coal. Unless I can get some wood off old Alf when he next comes round, we'll have to do without.'

'It's going to be summer soon, Mum,' Maggie says.

'Let's hope so. I'm fed up with this cold weather,' moans Nan. 'It does nothing for my rheumatism.'

'Mr Hoskins and Mr Pitt have joined the army,' Maggie continues.

'Well, we all expected that to happen. Even teachers get called up.'

'Yes, but Mrs Holmes and Miss Skinner have gone too. They've gone with the evacuees.'

The heat from the range is making her face burn.

'Here, this bit's done.'

Maggie flips the toast onto the plate with her finger. It's hot.

'Did you say that more teachers have gone now?'

Maggie nods her head.

'Goodness me. There can't be many teachers left in your school,' says Nan.

'No, that's why Miss Bentley says that we can only go to school in the morning next week. Then the following week we have to go in the afternoons.'

'Well in that case you'll have to study at home. Don't think you're going to spend half the day playing in the street,' Mum says, passing Maggie some more bread.

'I could help you in the house Mum, or with the cooking,' Maggie suggests.

Maggie likes to cook. Last week they learnt how to make pastry and she has made cheese straws and jam tarts.

'That's a good idea Irene. You know, in your condition you should be taking it easy,' says Nan.

'I should cocoa. How can I take it easy with three kids and no man about the house?'

'Well, easier anyway. Maggie's a capable girl; she could be such a help to you if you let her.'

'Yes, I know. Maggie's a good girl.'

Mum smiles at Maggie and leans across to pat the top of her head.

'Or I could do the shopping, Mum,' she persists.

'Yes, now that's a thought. My back plays me up something awful standing in those queues.'

She turns to the older woman.

'Do you know I had to wait three hours yesterday for four eggs. I could have laid them myself in that time.'

She laughs. Maggie likes it when Mum laughs; it's like the tinkling of tiny bells.

'I see you managed to get some jam,' Nan says.

'No, that's left over from last year. The last of it, more's the pity. Don't tell me they're going to ration jam as well?'

Nan nods.

'Well, I don't know where I'll get the time to make any this year, what with the new baby and all, even if I can find the fruit to make it with.'

'I'll make some for you, Irene. Your Dad's planted goose-berry bushes in the back garden now. Makes good jam, does gooseberries.'

'What about his precious lawn?'

'Oh that's gone. It's 'Dig for Victory' now, all potatoes, cab-bages and gooseberries. He's set down a few lettuces for the summer too, and some onions.'

'Nan, did you bring any rock cakes?' Maggie asks, her impa-tience getting the better of her manners.

'I did. Look in here.'

Nan pulls out a battered sweet tin from her string bag and places it on the table.

'I was going to wait until Billy got home,' she says.

As though aware that his name has been mentioned, the front door crashes open and Maggie's brother appears in the doorway, looking for all the world like a Botticelli cherub that has lost his way and ended up in the rough and tumble of London's East End. His blond, curly hair is matted with mud and leaves, his shirt is ripped and blood drips down his leg from a cut on his knee. He hugs an equally muddy football to his chest as he stands there, regarding his family through enormous, round, blue eyes.

'Speak of the Devil. So where have you been then?' asks Nan.

'What's for tea?' is his only reply.

'Billy, what have you been up to?' Mum asks.

'Just playing footie. Hello Nan.'

He drops the football and sits down next to Nan.

'No, you don't my boy. You can get those muddy things off right away and wash your hands before you have any tea.'

'Mum, I'm starving.'

'Now.'

'But Mum.'

Mum glares at him.

'Go into the yard and wash yourself down. Then come back in here and I'll see to that knee. Maggie, go and get me the iodine, will you. There's a good girl.'

Sometimes Mum tries to be cross with Billy, but she never quite makes it. Nobody stays angry with Billy for long. Maggie puts the perfectly toasted bread on the table and goes upstairs. She likes to turn the bread towards the heat, toasting it gently so that it becomes an even golden brown all over, not black and burnt at the edges like when Billy does it.

She finds the iodine in the tin box under Mum's bed; the 'first aid box' she calls it. She straightens up and looks around the room. It's a pretty room; the walls are a creamy colour and there are brown curtains with cream flowers on them. She remembers Dad painting the room last year, before he joined the army. Mum made curtains to match but when the war started the warden came round and said she had to make some black ones as well, for the 'blackout'. Maggie helped Mum make black curtains for all the windows.

On the table next to the bed is her parents' wedding photograph. She picks it up and moves over to the window so she can see it more clearly. She thinks Mum looks beautiful in the photograph. She is a small woman, 'petite' is what Nan calls her. She wears a pale blue coat and a matching hat with a veil. She looks just like a princess. Her hair and eyes are brown, but you cannot see that in the photograph. She stands next to Dad, her arm linked into his, smiling at the camera. Dad wears a blue suit. She knows it's blue because it's still hanging in the wardrobe and smells of Brylcreem and cigarettes. He is a strong man, her Dad; even in his suit he looks like a prize fighter. He has sandy coloured hair and bright blue eyes. He told her that some of his friends in the army called him Ginger, Ginger Smith, but she does not think he is really ginger, not like the boy in her class who has bright red hair and lots of freckles.

Since Dad went away to fight in the War, Mum lets Grace sleep in bed with her. Maggie does not mind. It's better actually because now she has the bed to herself and does not have to worry about waking Grace every time she moves. Billy sleeps in her room, but he has his own bed. Nobody wants to sleep with Billy because he cannot keep still. All night long he tosses and turns and sometimes he dreams he is playing football and his legs jerk about. No, it's impossible to sleep with him.

She closes the door to Mum's room carefully behind her and goes downstairs. She can hear a different voice in the kitchen; it sounds like Mrs Kelly. When she gets back to the kitchen Billy is seated next to Nan, his face freshly scrubbed, and the tin of rock cakes is still unopened on the table.

'We're waiting for you,' Billy says, accusingly.

'Here's the iodine Mum,' Maggie says, handing her the tiny brown bottle, with its corrugated sides. 'Hello Mrs Kelly.'

'Hello there Maggie. And how are you today?'

'I'm fine thank you.'

'Cup o' char, Kate?' asks Mum.

'Please. I'm as dry as a bone.'

Mrs Kelly sits on the kitchen stool and pulls a packet of Player's Weights from her pocket.

'Want one?'

'No thanks. They make me feel queasy at the moment.'

'What about you Lil?'

She holds out the packet to Nan.

'Don't mind if I do.'

'Sorry about the tea. It's a bit weak; second time we've used those leaves.'

'It's grand. Wet and warm.'

'Nan?'

'All right, all right. Rock cakes.'

She pulls the tin towards her and opens it.

'Now, who would like one?'

Three hands shoot in the air.

'Shall we offer one to Mrs Kelly first?'

Three heads nod and they wait patiently while their visitor takes one.

'All right then. Eldest first.'

'That's not fair,' says Billy. 'She always gets to go first.'

'No, I don't,' Maggie protests.

'Now, now, no arguing.'

Nan offers the tin to Maggie then Billy and finally to Grace.

Maggie savours the taste of the crumbly cake, locates the raisins with her tongue and tucks them in the recesses of her mouth to enjoy last.

'Yummy, Nan,' Billy mumbles, his mouth still full.

'Looks lovely,' says Mrs Kelly, stubbing out her cigarette on the edge of the plate.

She carefully replaces the half smoked cigarette in the packet and turns her attention to the cake.

'Yes, very nice Lil. You haven't lost your touch, I see.'

Maggie likes Mrs Kelly. She has been their neighbour for as long as Maggie can remember and often sits in their kitchen, chatting to Mum and smoking. She is a plump woman, with a broad smile and always wears a big, yellow wrap-around apron with shamrocks on it and a green headscarf. She says green is a lucky colour for the Irish. Mum says that she came to England because the people in Ireland had nothing to eat. Everyone calls her Mrs Kelly although Maggie can never remember there being a Mr Kelly and when she asks Mrs Kelly about it, she just laughs and taps her nose secretively.

'Mum, what about the letter from Dad?' Maggie asks, as she finishes the last crumb of her cake.

'All right, now that we are all here and not worrying about rock cakes and the like, I'll read it to you.'

Mum pulls a creased envelope out of the pocket of her apron and opens the letter.

'*My dearest Irene,*' she begins.

Maggie sees her hesitate.

'*Maggie, Billy and Grace.*

I hope you are all keeping well and getting enough to eat. They are keeping us very busy out here. Just finished building a great big ...'

She breaks off and smiles at them.

'We'll just have to imagine what that was because the censors have been at it again.'

Two black lines obliterate whatever indiscretion Dad intended to tell them.

'Go on Mum.'

'*Pretty fed up with army food, I can tell you. I could do with a plate of your home cooking Irene. Tell your mum ta for the socks, by the way.*'

She falls silent and Maggie sees a solitary tear trickle down her cheek.

'Well, there's not much more, just that he loves you all very much and hopes to be home soon.'

'Kisses Mummy?' asks Grace, her eyes wide in anticipation.

'Oh yes, of course. '*And give Grace, Maggie and Billy a big kiss from me.*'

Grace puckers up her lips and closes her eyes in readiness. Mum leans across and kisses her forehead, then turns and hugs her other two children to her.

'Mum, you're squashing me,' complains Billy.

'Right come on now, let's clear away the tea things.'

'But where is Dad? Doesn't he say?' asks Billy, taking his plate to the sink and dropping it into the soapy water.

'No, of course not, silly. It's secret,' Maggie snaps.

'He would tell us if he could Billy, but the army have to keep their movements hidden from the Germans,' explains Mum.

'So they can surprise them like?'

'That's right.'

'I wouldn't tell anyone.'

'No, I know you wouldn't.'

'I wish he'd come home. He promised to let me wear his helmet.'

'Well, I don't suppose it'll be long now, sweetheart.'

'Johnnie Ferris's granddad's joined the army,' Billy continues.

'Don't be silly, he's far too old for the army,' Maggie says.

'He has.'

'I expect Billy means the Local Defence Volunteers. They've been asking for people to join up,' explains Nan.

'Yes, I heard the Secretary for War on the wireless, telling people to go to their local police station if they wanted to volunteer,' adds Mrs Kelly.

'Thousands have gone along, thousands.'

'What are they then Mum, these Defence Volunteers?' asks Maggie.

'They're men who can't fight in the army for some reason or other but they can help defend their country from home.'

'Old geezers,' adds Billy. 'They don't even have any uniforms, just stupid arm bands.'

'But why?'

'In case we're invaded,' Billy explains.

'Will the Germans come here then?' Maggie asks.

There's a tremble in her voice.

'No, of course not. It's just in case,' he says, reaching in and taking another rock cake. 'Why are girls so stupid?'

'But what would we do if they came to London?' insists Maggie.

'They won't come to London. Now stop it, Billy; you're frightening Grace.'

Grace is not even listening; she is busy picking the raisins out of her rock cake and lining them up on the table.

'Aren't you going to eat them?' Billy asks, about to take one.

'Mummy. He's taking my raisins,' Grace cries.

'Billy, leave her alone.'

'You said we shouldn't waste food,' he protests.

'I'm going to share them with Teddy,' Grace explains as she lifts her one-eyed teddy bear on to her lap.

'Any more tea in the pot gal?' asks Nan.

'Just a drop.'

Her mum tops up Nan's cup with the watery tea.

'Looks like nat's piss,' she moans. 'What about you Kate?'

'No, I'm grand. You've heard about Sally Kemp, I suppose?'

'No, what about her?' asks Mum.

'She and her kids have gone to the country,' Mrs Kelly says, relighting her cigarette and leaning back from the table.

'What, evacuated you mean?'

'Yes, the whole lot of them. Sent them to Wales or somewhere.'

'I think it's a good idea. Best to get the women and kids out of London,' adds Nan. 'I don't know why you don't go as well, Irene. The kids would love the country, lots of space to run around in, fresh milk, eggs. It would be great for them.'

Maggie looks across at Mum. She is tipping the tea leaves out onto a sheet of newspaper.

'I've seen them down at the centre,' she tells her mother.

'Who?'

'The children. They were all lined up, with labels on them and gas masks round their necks. The teachers were with them.'

Mum does not reply.

'You're never going to dry those leaves again?' asks Mrs Kelly.

'Why not? I'll mix them with some fresh and you'll never know the difference.'

'Lil's got a point you know. It would be much safer for you all in the country.'

'And you've got the new baby to consider,' adds Nan.

'No, we're staying here. What if Ronnie came back and we weren't here to welcome him? No, I want to be here when he gets home. This evacuation lark is all a waste of time anyway. The war will be over soon. No, I intend to stick it out in my own home. That's what Ronnie's fighting for after all, for his home and family.'

'But what about the baby?'

'He's going to be born in London, like the rest of them.'

'Well, you could send the children. Lots of children are going without their Mums. Then they would be safe.'

'Safe? They're safe here with me. I'm their Mum. No, no-one's going anywhere. This is our home and this is where we're staying.'

She stacks the wet plates on the draining board with such force that Maggie thinks they are going to break.

'I think it's time for bed. Maggie take Grace up to bed will you and you, young man can get yourself washed and off to bed too.'

'But I've just had a wash.'

'Now.'

'You going to read me a story Maggie?' asks Grace, holding up her arms to be helped down from her chair.

'Which one shall we have tonight then?'

'Billy Goat Gruff.'

She squeals in anticipation.

'Isn't that a bit frightening for bedtime?' asks Nan.

'No, she loves it. Come on now.'

Maggie takes her sister by the hand and leads her up the stairs.

'*Up the wooden hill we go,*' sings Grace.

'She's a happy little girl, that one,' says Mrs Kelly.

'Yes, she's no trouble. Luckily she's too young to realise what is happening.'

'So you've no idea when Ronnie'll be back?' asks Mrs Kelly.

'No, he didn't say very much in his letter.'

'There's talk of some of the men coming back from France,' Nan says. 'Maybe he'll be one of them.'

'Who knows.'

Maggie closes the bedroom door behind them. She feels a flutter of excitement in her stomach. What if they are right? What if Dad is coming home? How wonderful that would be. They have not seen him since New Year's Day. He came home on leave for Christmas. Ten whole days he was with them and then he left again. They all went to the railway station to see him off, even Nan. The station had been very crowded, full of soldiers and their families. Dad said lots of them were in his regiment. He recognised some of them and shouted out to them. One of the soldiers came over and Dad introduced them to him, one by one. He said:

'This is my mate George.'

Then he said:

'George, these are my children.'

Then George had shaken hands with each of them, very politely. She wonders if George will be coming home as well. A tear trickles down her cheek. It was nice to get the letter from Dad but she doesn't like it when the censors cut out all those words. It frightens her to think that they don't know where Dad is or when they will see him again. Mum says not to worry that they are not allowed to tell them everything about the soldiers' movements but Maggie can't help it. Despite what Nan said about the men coming home, she cannot get rid of this feeling that something bad is going to happen.

IRENE

'Come on, you lot, hurry up. We'll be late at this rate.'

'I'm ready Mum.'

'Where's Billy?'

'He's putting his shoes on.'

'Go and help him, there's a good girl.'

'Why are we going to church now Mum? It's too early for Sunday school.'

'The King wants us all to pray for the safe return of our soldiers, sweetheart.'

'Does that mean Dad too?'

'Of course it does. We want Dad to come back safely, don't we.'

Grace is listening too; she nods her head solemnly.

Irene bends down and buttons up her coat. Her youngest daughter looks a real picture. The coat is one Irene's mother made out of an old skirt; it's a light blue and matches her eyes perfectly. She knows it will not stay clean for five minutes, not a colour like that, but she does not care. For once she wants Grace to have something that is pretty rather than practical.

'Will Dad be coming back soon?' asks Billy.

He is wearing his Sunday best trousers and a clean white shirt. She will have to get that off him as soon as they get back or he will have it filthy in a minute.

'I hope so.'

'Johnnie Ferris says his Dad is in France. Is that where our Dad is?'

'I don't know Billy. It's possible.'

'Will everyone be praying for the soldiers?' asks Maggie.

'Mr Levy won't. He's a Jew,' Billy says.

'Mr Levy too. Everyone will be praying today.'

'But Mr Levy doesn't come to our church.'

'I expect he'll go to his own church.'

'It's called a synagogue,' Maggie informs them.

'That's right Maggie. Now come along, that's enough questions. We don't want to be late and have everyone looking at us do we.'

'No Mum.'

Irene ushers the children into the street and closes the door behind them.

'There's Mrs Kelly.'

'She's going the wrong way,' says Billy. 'Maybe she doesn't know we have to pray for the soldiers.'

'Mrs Kelly's a Catholic. She's going to another church.'

'Doesn't she go to St Matthew's then?' he asks.

'No silly, she goes to the "Lady of the Sumption",' explains Maggie.

'Not quite,' Irene says, smiling in spite of her agitation. 'Her church is called "Our Lady of the Assumption."'

St Matthew's is almost full by the time they arrive. Irene and the children slip into the back row and sit down. For once the children are subdued. She does not often bring them to church; she is not much of a believer. But she sends them to Sunday school every week without fail. If she is honest with herself, it was one way that she and Ronnie could be alone together without worrying that the children would hear them. Nowadays it's as much about getting an hour to herself as anything else. Maggie always takes them; it's not far to walk and there are no big roads to cross. She looks across at her eldest daughter. She is growing up very fast, almost twelve years old and tall for her age. She will soon be taller than her, although that would not take much doing. She smiles. Ronnie always refers to her as his 'little woman', with an emphasis on the little.

She was worried about Maggie when Billy was born. They had spoiled her, being their first and all, and to start with she was jealous of her new brother. Fortunately that did not last very long and she soon took to him. That was mostly down to Ronnie. He was marvellous with her, explaining how she was the eldest and how much they relied on her to help them with the new baby. She sighs when she thinks of her husband. Things must be very serious if the King is asking people to pray for the soldiers. She wishes she knew what was going on. There is so little news on the wireless. She has taken to leaving it on all day long, only turning it off when they go out or go to bed. She is terrified she will miss something important.

The service is starting. Everyone kneels. It's hard to hear the vicar from where they are, but she makes out the words:

'... for our soldiers in dire peril in France.'

Then the congregation begins to say the Lord's Prayer:

'*Our Father, who art in heaven ...*'

She mouths the familiar words and as she does so she has the sensation that she will never see her husband again. This awful war, what is it doing to them? Tears start to run down her cheeks and she can do nothing to stop them. She glances worriedly at her children, but they have their eyes tight shut and are concentrating on the words of the prayer. She pulls out a handkerchief and wipes her eyes.

For the next ten days Irene hardly strays from the kitchen. She has moved the wireless from the living room and propped it up on the windowsill, so that she can hear it better.

'Hello, anyone at home?'

'Hello Kate. Come in.'

Her neighbour pushes the front door open and comes in. She is followed by an old man. He hobbles in, supporting himself on a wooden stick. Kate drops a package wrapped in newspaper on the kitchen table.

'Hello Mr Ford. How are you keeping?' Irene asks.

'Not so bad Missus Smiff. Me rheumatism's been playing me up a bit lately, but I can't complain.'

'Sit down. I'll make us all a nice cuppa.'

She fills the kettle and puts it on the range.

'So what's this?' she asks, picking up the parcel.

'It's for you. I thought you could make a nice Irish stew with it,' Kate replies.

'For us? Kate you can't afford to spend your coupons on us. What is it, scrag end, neck?'

'It's whale meat.'

Irene drops the parcel on the table.

'Whale meat. Blimey. That sounds disgusting. You mean like blubber and that?'

'No, look at it. It looks fine and they say it's very healthy. And tasty,' she adds.

Gingerly Irene unwraps the newspaper.

'Mmmn. But what do I do with it?'

'Like I said, make a stew. It's just like beef they say, only tougher and sweeter.'

'Well, I suppose I could have a go. Better than horse meat, anyway. Maggie nearly had a fit when I came home with horse meat last week. She said she was going to become a vegetarian if I did it again.'

'Yes, well you can try it. See what it's like. It looks grand to me.'

'Why not. I'll stick it in the meat safe for now.'

'Good idea, it's turned a bit muggy today.'

Irene takes the whale meat into the scullery. It was nice of Kate to think of them; she is such a good friend.

'Don't say anything to the kids now, will you,' she adds, when she returns.

'No, of course not. Where are they by the way?'

'They're at school. Afternoons this week. And Gracie's having a sleep.'

A high pitched whistling breaks into the conversation.

'Right, let's make this tea, then.'

'The Prime Minister is going to speak to the nation this afternoon,' Mr Ford says.

He is wheezing.

'We thought we'd come round and listen to it with you.'

'That's fine.'

She takes down three china cups and matching saucers from the dresser and places them on the table.

'Bit posh today, aren't we.'

Irene laughs and pours out the tea. She likes nice things. They don't have a lot, but what they have she looks after and from time to time, she likes to use them. She is not like her neighbours, who keep all their best things in the front parlour and never use them unless there is a funeral or something of equal moment.

'Heard anything from your Tom?' she asks the old man.

'No, nothing.'

'He's in France, isn't he?'

'Yes, 42nd Division. What about your husband? Isn't he a sapper?'

'Yes, Royal Engineers. We haven't heard anything from him in ages.'

'Sounds as though things are pretty bad out there. We're getting ready for an invasion you know.'

'Really? That bad?'

She sips her tea to cover her fear.

'Don't you worry now, your Ronnie'll be all right, you see,' Kate says, patting her neighbour's hand.

Irene swallows; there is a hard lump in her throat.

'God, I hate this war.'

'Me oldest boy has joined this new LDV outfit. Sounds a bit of a shower, if you ask me.'

'What the "Look-Duck-Vanish" brigade?' Kate asks, laughing at her own joke.

'Do you mean Fred?'

Mr Ford's eldest son is in his forties. He runs the local newspaper shop.

'He says that they should be getting some weapons soon.'

'They've still got no guns? How can they defend the nation if they haven't got any guns?' asks Irene in surprise.

'He says they have to be resourceful. Some of them have got shotguns and handguns that blokes brought back from the trenches. I gave him my Turkish bayonet. Came from Gallipoli, that did. It'd put a dent in any Jerry.'

He slashes wildly at the air with his stick. The old man seems to be getting rather excited.

'Spot more tea Mr Ford?' Irene asks.

'Don't mind if I do.'

'Sarah Ferris says her husband is getting training. Some ex-soldiers have set up a training centre down near the docks; they're teaching them to shoot and make weapons. And they drill like proper soldiers and even learn sabotage techniques. I think it's grand,' adds Kate.

Mr Ford nods his head in agreement. His hand is trembling as he raises his cup to his lips.

'Hush. I think that's the news.'

Irene is at the wireless in a flash and turns it up to full volume.

'This is the BBC Home Service. The Prime Minister, Mr Winston Churchill will address the nation.'

'Come and sit down here, Kate.'

'No, I'm all right, thanks.'

They gather around the wireless; their faces tight with concentration as they strain to hear every word their new Prime Minister has to say. They listen to him tell of the success of Operation Dynamo, how he only expected to save no more than 30,000 of the beleaguered British Expeditionary Force and how, thanks to the efforts of the RAF, the Royal Navy and countless small boats, over 300,000 men have been rescued from Dunkirk. He continues:

'Wars are not won by evacuations. I am in no doubt that the last few weeks have been a colossal military disaster.'

'Will Dad come home now?' asks Maggie from the doorway.

'What are you doing here? Shouldn't you be at school?' Irene asks.

'No, our class was sent home because ...'

'Shush child, it's Mr Churchill,' says Mr Ford.

'Come here and sit down. You can tell me later,' Irene whispers.

The Prime Minister continues, warning the people that they must brace themselves for another blow:

'We are told that Herr Hitler has a plan for invading the British Isles.'

'Oh my God,' cries Mrs Kelly, grabbing hold of old Mr Ford's arm.

'Listen.'

'We shall defend our island whatever the cost may be. We shall fight on the beaches, we shall fight on the landing grounds, we shall fight in the fields and in the streets, we shall fight in the hills. We shall never surrender.'

Mr Ford struggles to his feet and salutes the wireless.

'God Save the King,' he croaks, tears streaming down his face.

They sit in silence, each lost in their own thoughts. Irene can feel her eyes filling up with tears. This bloody awful war. Well they are not going to let Jerry get the better of them. The thought of German troops marching through the streets of London makes her shiver.

'I think we need another cuppa,' she says.

She takes the kettle into the scullery to fill it up. So where is Ronnie in all this? She has listened to them talking about the British Expeditionary Forces, about rescuing men from under the noses of Jerry, about their French allies, about valour and heroism, but nobody can tell her what she wants to know. Where is her Ronnie? She looks out of the scullery window, as she has done a million times since this war began, hoping to see him walking down the street towards them. All she can see are a couple of stray dogs, rummaging around for scraps, and the milkman's horse waiting patiently outside number twenty-one.

'You all right Mum?'

'Yes, pet, I'm fine. Just thinking about yer dad.'

'But he'll come home now, won't he? Mr Churchill said they've brought the soldiers home in little ships.'

The hope shining in her daughter's eyes makes her want to weep even more. Well, maybe she is right, maybe he will soon be home. But then what? Where will they send him next?

'Come on Irene, let me do that.'

Kate takes the kettle from her and puts it on the range.

'No point getting worked up until we know exactly what's happening. Plenty of time for that later, begorrah.'

Irene smiles. Kate is so predictable. She always emphasises her Irishness when she wants to make her laugh.

'I know, it's just ...'

She glances at Maggie, who is opening her exercise books and spreading them out on the table.

'It's just the not knowing if he's alive or dead,' she whispers.

'I know.'

'He's a wonderful man,' Mr Ford says.

'Who?'

'Mr Churchill. If anyone can get us through this, he can.'

'I certainly hope so.'

'What was it your Ronnie did, before the war?' he asks, draining the last of his cup and peering at the tea leaves.

'He used to work down on the docks with his Dad but then he got this job at Perkins' Garage. He liked it there, the money was good and he got on well with the owner. Old Perkins said he'd keep his job open for him.'

Things had been easier in those days until Ronnie decided to enlist. She had argued that he was too old at thirty, that they wanted younger men but he said it was something he had to do. He had skills; he would join the Royal Engineers. He wanted to defend his country he told her, to defend her and the kids.

'That's nice of Mr Perkins. My poor niece is having a terrible time since her husband joined up. Six kids they've got and no money.'

'What about her husband's wages?'

'When she gets them. He's a real scoundrel, her Eddie. Doesn't care if she and the kids go hungry as long as he's got his fags and beer. Now her landlord is threatening to chuck them out because they owe so much rent.'

'That's terrible. Ronnie would never leave us in such a situation.'

'Yes, but your Ronnie is one in a million,' says Kate.

'Are we having another cuppa?' asks Mr Ford, extending his empty cup and saucer to Irene.

'Of course we are. We'll just let the tea brew a bit longer.'

She winks at Kate. This is the third time these leaves have been used; they will have to be thrown out after this brew.

It's only two days later that the news arrives. Billy sees him first. He shouts upstairs to tell her. She looks out of the window and watches as the boy leans his bicycle against the post box and wanders along the street looking at the numbers on the doors. When he gets to their own blue door he stops, checks the envelope again and knocks. She feels a tightness in her chest and is unable to move. Irene knows from the moment the boy's knuckles rap on her door that this marks the end of one life and the start of another. They will all remember that sound for a long time to come. She does not run to see is it good news or bad; her legs will not move. She lets Billy open the door and take the yellow envelope. She hears the voice of a young man, high and reedy.

'Mrs Smith?'

'Yes, that's my Mum.'

'Mrs Ronald Smith?'

'Yes.'

'OK son, give this to yer mum.'

She hears the door close and the sound of Billy's feet running down the passage.

'Mum, it's a telegram,' he cries, waving it in the air.

'Maybe it's to say Dad's coming home,' suggests Maggie.

She has Grace on her lap and is brushing her hair.

'Thank you darling,' Irene says.

She takes the envelope from him and slips it into the pocket of her apron.

'Come on Mum. Aren't you going to open it?'

'Yes, open it, Mum.'

She looks at the fresh, hopeful faces of her children and the tears begin to form in her eyes. She pulls out the standard yellow envelope and holds it against her cheek. The only other telegram she has ever received was on the day of their wedding; Ronnie's aunt May had sent it. 'To wish you a long and happy married life,' it said.

'Mum.'

Maggie is hopping from foot to foot in anticipation.

Carefully Irene takes out a knife from the kitchen drawer and slides it under the fold of the telegram. She can sense the children's eyes on her. She pulls out the folded paper and opens it.

'WE REGRET TO INFORM YOU ...'

The words stab at her heart as she tries to focus. The uniform printed letters dance in front of her eyes; she can hardly make out what they say.

'WE REGRET TO INFORM YOU THAT PRIVATE RONALD BRUCE SMITH HAS BEEN KILLED IN ACTION ...'

She struggles for breath. Her heart is banging so loudly she cannot hear what her children are saying. She thinks she will collapse.

'What's it say Mum?'

'Is he coming home? Is Dad coming home?'

'Mummy. What's it say?'

'What's the matter Mum? Mum? Is it about Dad?'

Irene lets out a long, agonised moan. Her legs give way under her and she grabs at the edge of the table to steady herself.

'What's the matter Mum?'

'Mummy, why are you crying?'

No, not her Ronnie, it can't be her Ronnie. Please God, let it be a mistake. But deep inside she knows it's no mistake. She looks at the anxious faces of her children; she has to be strong for them. She has to give them an answer.

'No darlings, Daddy's not coming home.'

The words are barely a whisper. She cannot hold back the tears.

'Don't cry Mummy,' says Grace, clinging to her mother's leg. 'Don't cry.'

The children crowd round her, each trying to comfort her in their own way. Maggie pulls out a chair so she can sit down.

Billy anxiously pats her hand and Grace climbs up onto her knee and puts her podgy arms around her mother's neck.

'Does he have to go to another war now?' asks Billy.

There is a lump in her throat that threatens to choke her; she swallows hard and says:

'No, darling, he's not going to go to any more wars, ever again.'

'So he can come home then,' says Billy, with a little skip of pleasure.

Maggie picks up the telegram from the table.

'No, silly, he's not ever coming home again.   He's been killed. Killed in action.'

She flings down the telegram and runs from the room.

'Maggie ...'

Irene does not have the strength to go after her daughter. She hugs her other children to her, rocking them back and forth like she used to do when they were babies. Billy is quiet now. Grace is crying. She tries to comfort them but she does not know what to say. What can she say? It just is not fair. Ronnie was a good man, a kind man; he was her husband. He was too young to die. And they are all too young to live without him. This bloody war. It's so unfair.

She lets them stay home that afternoon; she cannot bear to be alone with her sorrow. She feels that if she gives in to her grief she will never be able to pull herself out of it; it will devour her. Ronnie was her life. She does not want to live without him but these are his children and she must be strong for them. The only way she knows how to do that is to keep busy. She pulls out a pile of darning that she has been putting off for weeks and sets to with a fierce determination. She can hear the children talking in the scullery. Maggie has offered to make them all some bread and sugar sandwiches; the other two are sitting at the table watching her.

'What do you think it's like to be dead, Maggie?' asks Billy.

'How would I know, silly?   You have to be dead to know that.'

Billy thinks for a minute.

'Yes, but if you were dead then you couldn't tell anybody.'

'That's right.'

'So how does anybody know what it's like?'

'They don't.'

'Daddy's gone to Heaven,' says Grace.

'So how do they know about Heaven?' continues Billy.

'It's in the Bible.'

'But how did they know to write it in the Bible? Who told them?'

'The four aposulls,' chips in Grace. 'Matthew, Mark, Luke and John, Bless the bed that I lie on.'

'Apostles,' corrects Maggie.

'But who told them?'

'Billy, shut up for a bit. Here take your sandwich and don't make a mess.'

'Mummy will know,' adds Grace.

'No, don't ask Mum.'

'She's sad, isn't she?'

'Yes, she's sad about Dad.'

'I'm sad too,' says Grace. 'I want my Daddy.'

She begins to cry.

'Come on Gracie, don't cry. Here, let me wipe your nose.'

Maggie pulls out an old handkerchief and helps her sister to blow her nose.

'Look, I've finished your sandwich. See, I've cut it into quarters for you.'

'Thank you Maggie,' Grace sniffs.

Irene picks up the next sock and slips the darning egg down into the toe. She rubs her eyes to clear them so that she can focus; skilfully she threads the needle and begins to set up the web of threads necessary to fill the hole.

'Mum, I've made you a sandwich too.'

Maggie is standing in the doorway with a plate in her hand.

'Thank you Maggie. Leave it in the scullery and I'll have it later, when I've finished.'

'Mum, can I go out to play?' asks Billy.

'No, darling, not today. Why don't you go and play in your bedroom for a bit.'

'Mummy, is Daddy in Heaven?' Grace asks hesitantly.

'Yes darling, Daddy's in Heaven.'

'Like Bessy?'

'Yes, like Bessy.'

'But Bessy was a dog. Dogs go to Doggy Heaven,' protests Billy.

'Billy,' Maggie says, tugging at her brother's arm. 'Why don't you get out your toy soldiers?'

Irene sighs. Poor little mites. 'Killed in action' does not mean a lot to them. It will take Grace and Billy a few days to fully understand that they will never see their father again. Only Maggie appreciates the full horror of it.

'Mum would you like me to go round to Mrs Kelly's and ask her to come to see you?'

Irene looks up from her sewing. Maggie's eyes are red and swollen from crying. Irene stretches out her hand and pulls her daughter towards her, hugging her against her.

'Yes, that would be nice of you. Can you manage to tell her what has happened?'

'Yes, Mum.'

She strokes her daughter's hair.

'You're a good girl, Maggie. I don't know what I'd do without you.'

She kisses her forehead and says:

'Off you go then, but come right back.'

When her daughter has gone Irene puts down the darning, resting it on her swollen stomach. How big she is getting already. God, I hope it's not twins, she thinks as the child inside her gives a kick. That is all I need, another two mouths to feed. It's going to be difficult enough to feed all of us, as it is. She feels a surge of resentment against her unborn child. They should have tried to be more careful, but it was hard. Ronnie was only home for a short time. She thinks back to his last leave. It was so cold, even the Thames was frozen over. Most nights they went to bed early just to keep warm. She starts to cry again. Who is going to keep her warm now? Already she can feel the emptiness of a life without her Ronnie.

When she glimpses the khaki uniform walk past the window and stop at their door, her heart gives a skip and her first thought is that it's Ronnie, that there has been a mix-up and here he is, back on leave. She runs up the scullery steps and into the hall and has the door open before the soldier can knock a second time.

'Good afternoon. Mrs Smith?' he says politely removing his beret.

She cannot reply; the disappointment is so great it has rendered her speechless. She swallows hard and forces herself to say:

'Can I help you?'

'I'm sorry to bother you; you probably don't remember me. I'm George Wills, Ronnie's mate. We met once, at the railway station, last time we were on leave.'

'Oh yes, of course. How silly. Please come in.'

He has come to pay his respects. She leads the soldier into the front parlour.

'Please sit down. Can I make you some tea or something?'

She tries to remember if there is a bottle of beer left in the larder. Ronnie often liked a glass of beer when he came home on leave. The memory makes her eyes fill up again and she struggles to keep her composure.

'Tea would be great,' he says. 'If it's no trouble.'

'No, no trouble at all. I'll just put the kettle on.'

The young man sits awkwardly in the armchair. He seems to be too big for the room, all arms and legs. He places his kitbag on the floor beside him. It looks out of place next to the chintz covers on the chairs and the lace antimacassars that her grand-mother gave her.

'Won't be a moment,' she says, turning away before he can see the tears start to spill from her eyes.

'Come on Irene, this won't do. Pull yourself together, gal,' she tells herself, blowing her nose so hard it hurts.

She fills the kettle and places it on the range then takes down the remains of her precious store of tea. No way can she give this young man dried tea leaves. She takes two of her best cups and saucers and puts them on a tea tray then selects a couple of homemade biscuits to arrange neatly on the plate. Kate made them for the children. Gingerbread men. A little treat she said when she brought them round yesterday.

'Sorry to keep you waiting,' she says, five minutes later, as she pushes the door open with her hip.

'Here, let me help you with that.'

He is up and out of the chair instantly, taking the heavy tray from her and placing it on the table.

'My, that looks nice. It's so good to have a few home comforts at last.' he says.

She sits down opposite him. Inside she can feel herself trembling. It's the sight of his uniform and his raw masculinity that upsets her; the soldier smells faintly of sweat and cigarette smoke. It's the smell of a man in her house again. Only it's the wrong man; it's not her Ronnie.

'You've had a hard time?' she asks.

He nods.

'It's nice of you to come,' she says.

'Well, Ronnie and me, we had a pact. If anything happened to either one of us, the other would go and see that their family was all right.'

He pulls out a packet of Player's Weights and offers her one.

'Thanks.'

The soldier lights his cigarette but Irene puts hers to one side while she pours out the tea.

'Milk? Sugar?'

He nods to both.

'We were together through it all,' he eventually says.

A curl of blue smoke floats above his head.

'Right up to when Ronnie copped it.'

Irene swallows her tea. It burns her throat but she is hardly aware of it.

'Tell me about it,' she says. 'There has been very little news about what happened. We didn't even know that Ronnie was at Dunkirk. We just thought he was somewhere in France.'

'We were all up near the Belgian border with the French at first, then Jerry invaded Belgium, crossed into France and pushed us back. We tried to fight them off but they just kept pushing us back. Then we had orders to march on to Arras to attack the Jerry spearhead. That seemed to go well at first; we had them on the run but then they counter-attacked and we had to retreat to avoid being surrounded. The Germans were coming at us from all sides, forcing us back towards the coast. I think Jerry thought he'd got us then. We were cut off from the French, alone, marooned on the beaches.'

He stirs the sugar into his tea.

'It was chaos. You just can't imagine what it was like. There was mortar fire and black smoke everywhere. Jerry planes were strafing the road, gunning us down. Every five minutes we were jumping into the ditch for cover. I thought we'd never make it out of there. On top of that nobody seemed to know what they should do. We all headed for the coast, blindly, one following the other. Ronnie and I, being sappers, had a better idea than most how to survive. We left the road, cut across the fields and headed in the direction of the sea. We arrived at La Panne late one night. It was lovely, all quiet and peaceful like. We could have been in Scarborough, with the waves lapping on the beach and the moon shining on the sea. We slept in the dunes that night. Well, not so much slept as dug ourselves in and waited for morning.'

He swallows a mouthful of tea then continues:

'But we couldn't go anywhere; there was the sea between us and home. I remember Ronnie lying there, looking out at the Channel and saying: "Just across there is England. We're almost home, we can almost touch it." We were so close it seemed, yet so far.

Well, in the morning the sergeant appeared and told Ronnie and me to get to work building a jetty. They were sending boats to get us home. We could see some of them already, waiting off shore, with Jerry flying over, trying his best to bomb them out of the water. Our job was to help the poor bastards on the beach get out to the boats. Oh, excuse my French.'

He looks embarrassed at his slip of the tongue and hastily drinks some more tea.

'That's all right,' says Irene. 'Please go on.'

She lights her cigarette and watches the smoke drift across the room.

'Well, there were a lot of abandoned lorries on the beach, so we were ordered to fill them with sandbags to weigh them down and drive them into the sea, then we lashed them together and shot out the tyres to keep them steady.   You know, there's one good thing about us sappers, we're great at scavenging. We used anything we could get our hands on to make those blooming jetties. It was dirty work. The tide was out when we began but as it started coming in we were covered in oil and muck. God, it was hard work.   There were only about forty sappers left out of the one hundred and fifty that set out, so there was no time for slacking.   Besides which there were thousands of men waiting in the sand dunes and every day more were arriving.'

He stops, for a moment he looks as though he is back there on the beaches.

'Would you like some more tea?' Irene asks.

'Please.'

'So how did Ronnie die?' she eventually manages to ask.

He sighs.

'Ironic really.   He'd worked so hard helping others to get away, even rowing men out from the end of the jetty.'

He must have seen the puzzled look on her face.

'We had these small folding boats made of canvas, for ferrying stuff across rivers,' he explains, 'or when we had to blow up bridges. Pretty flimsy things, not at all suitable for the sea. Not stable you know.   Lots of them capsized and the men were drowned. But we had to give it a go, there was nothing else.'

He pulls out his packet of cigarettes.

'Like another fag?'

She shakes her head. Instead of upsetting her she finds it a comfort to hear about Ronnie's last days. She can visualise him there on the beach; amongst all that chaos he would be his usual practical, dependable self, she is sure.

'So, where was I? Yes. We'd been there for six days and still the men kept coming. You just can't imagine it. There were queues and queues of soldiers waiting to board the ships, any ship; they stretched back along the beach for miles. Sometimes the bloody Stukas would swoop down and strafe them. If a soldier was killed, the others just moved up and closed the line. There was no way anyone would give up their place in the queue. By then the beach was littered with their kit, helmets, weapons, all manner of things that had been discarded and there were dead bodies floating in the sea, being washed in and out by the tide. Some of them still had their packs on. But you took no notice of any of it. It was the living that mattered not the dead. We had to get as many troops off that beach and out to the ships as we could.'

He pauses, dragging hard on his cigarette.

'Then one day, our sergeant turned to us and said: "Right chaps. Now it's your turn. Get yourselves bloody out of here." So we did.'

He pauses and then adds sadly:

'I really thought we were going to make it.'

'Is that when it happened?' she asks.

'Yes. By then there were hundreds of small boats waiting off shore to rescue us.'

'Yes we heard the appeal for everyone with a boat to contact the Admiralty but we didn't know what it was about.'

'Hundreds of volunteers came to help. The boats, being smaller, could come in closer and pick up the troops in shallow water then take them out to the ships. Some of the bigger vessels didn't even bother taking them to the ships; they just took them straight back to England. We saw one fishing boat with at least three hundred troops on board. Squashed in like sardines they were.'

He laughs, dryly.

'Anyway Ronnie and I made our way to the end of the jetty and were waiting for our turn to get in a boat, when this bloody

Stuka came out of nowhere and made straight for us. That was when Ronnie copped it.'

He lifts his head and looks straight at her.

'He saved my life.'

Now she cannot stop the tears. She scrabbles in the pocket of her pinny for a handkerchief.

'What happened?' she manages to ask.

'It was terrifying. Jerry was heading straight for us. There was nowhere to hide. We were like bloody sitting ducks. Before I knew what was happening, Ronnie gave me a shove and I fell in the water. Went right down and the strafe of bullets passed straight over me. Ronnie and the others were mowed down where they stood.'

She cannot speak. For a few seconds she is furious with her husband. That was so typical of Ronnie, always thinking of others. Why hadn't he just jumped into the sea and survived? Why wasn't he here telling her this horrendous story instead of a young man she barely knew?

'I'm so sorry,' he says. 'I'm really sorry.'

Why is he so sorry? Because she has lost a husband and her children a father? Because he is alive and Ronnie is dead? She tries to check her bitterness. It's not his fault.

'Did he die straight away?' she asks.

'Oh yes, no doubt about it. He wouldn't have felt a thing. Just such a bloody shame.'

'Yes, a shame.'

The soldier looks uncomfortable; she is making him uncomfortable.

'I'll miss him. He was a bloody good mate,' he says.

She hears the door bang and footsteps in the hall. The sound of excited voices reaches them.

'That must be the children, home from school.'

'Well, I'll be off then.'

'Must you go?'

'Yes, I'm afraid so. I've got a train to catch. I'm off home to see the folks.'

'Yes, of course. It was so kind of you to come and see me.'

She feels numb.

'Well, like I said, me and Ronnie had an agreement.'

He picks up his beret and his kitbag and stands up.

'Do call in again if you're passing,' she says, opening the front door.

He holds out his hand.

'I will. Goodbye and thanks for the tea.'

'Thank you,' she says. 'And good luck.'

He hesitates.

'Oh, I nearly forgot. Here are some of Ronnie's things: his cap badge and a few photos.'

He pulls out an envelope and hands it to her. She stares at it, wanting to scream with pain. Is this all that's left of her husband?

MAGGIE

'Keep still, Maggie. I've nearly finished.'

Mum's hands rub the shampoo roughly into her hair.

'You're hurting me.'

'Don't be such a baby. If I don't get this right down to the roots we'll never kill the blooming things. There now, go and get on with your knitting. It's got to stay like that for at least twenty minutes.'

'To kill the blooming things,' echoes Billy.

'Enough cheek, young man. You're next.'

'But Mum I haven't got nits.'

'I don't care. I'm doing you all. I don't want any of those filthy things in my house.'

Maggie pulls the towel tight around her neck and picks up her knitting. She is knitting a scarf for the soldiers; all her class are making them. Mrs Archer, their teacher, says that when they are finished she will send them off to the soldiers in France. She pushes the needle into a stitch and carefully pulls the wool around it. It's very slow. Nan can knit really fast, she can even talk at the same time. The faster she knits, the faster she talks. She knitted a cardigan for Grace in just one day. It was nice when Nan was here. She stayed with them for weeks, ever since they heard about Dad. Now she has gone home to Islington because Granddad is ill.

'Mum, is Nan coming back to live here with us, like Nanny Smith used to?'

'I don't know Maggie. Maybe when Granddad is better. I could certainly do with her help when the baby arrives.'

'Our new baby will be here soon, won't he Mummy,' says Grace.

'Yes, very soon.'

'I hope it's a boy,' says Billy. 'Then he can be a Millwall supporter like me and Granddad.'

'Keep still.'

'Why was Nan angry with you Mum?' Maggie asks.

'She wasn't angry, not really.'

'Well, why?'

'She thinks we should leave London and go and stay with your Uncle Harry in Leeds.'

'Don't want to go to Leeds,' says Grace, with a pout.

'No, darling, neither do I. Come on, jump up here, it's your turn now.'

'But Mummy, that 'poo smells 'orrible.'

'I know, but the nits don't like it either.'

'Does it kill them?'

'Yes, bang, bang, you're dead,' shouts Billy, pointing his fingers at her head and pretending to shoot.

'Mrs Kelly's got an Anderson shelter in her garden,' says Maggie. 'Why haven't we got one?'

'Mrs Kelly's friend built it for her.'

'I've been in it. It's just like a play house. She's even got strips of lino on the floor and there're some beds in it. And you have to go down some steps to get in,' Maggie tells them.

'I'm going to ask Missus Kelly if we can play in it,' says Billy.

'Don't be silly, it's in case the Germans come. Anyway, she's got marrows growing on top of it.'

'Marrows. That's stupid.'

Billy sticks his tongue out at her and goes out into the yard. She can hear him firing at imaginary Germans.

'Billy, don't go far. I've got to wash it off in a minute,' Mum says.

'Or all your hair will fall out,' calls Grace, giggling.

There is a slight knock at the door and Mrs Kelly walks in.

'Oh hello Kate. Won't be a minute. Just washing the kids' hair.'

'Here, let me finish off for you. You look all in. Go on, sit down and put your feet up.'

'Would you? Oh that's kind. My back is fit to break. I'll be glad when this baby decides to make an appearance, I'm fed up waddling around like a barrel.'

'I'll help you with the baby, Mum. I like babies,' says Maggie

'I know you do sweetheart.'

'So come on now young lady, bend over the sink and we'll get rid of all that smelly shampoo,' instructs Mrs Kelly.

Maggie puts down her knitting and does as she is told.

The wireless is on; it's 'Sincerely Yours', Mum's favourite programme. Normally Mum likes to sing along with Vera Lynn; she knows the words to every song. But since Dad died Mum no longer sings; she just looks sad all the time.

'Mum, you like this one.'

They are playing '*It's a Lovely Day Tomorrow*'.

'Why don't you sing to us any more?' asks Maggie.

'I don't know darling. I just don't feel like it I suppose.'

Maggie knows what she means. Maggie feels the same. There is a hollowness inside her, not a pain exactly but an emptiness that will not go away.

'Come along, I'll sing it with you, but you'll have to help me with the words,' says Mrs Kelly.

She begins. Her voice is flat, not sweet and lovely like Mum's, but Grace and Maggie join in to help her. It's not easy with her head over the basin and her voice sounds different, sort of hollow and echoey. The song is all about hope and being positive Mum used to tell them. Poor Mum, she is too sad to be positive any more.

'So how are you feeling today then Irene?'

'Not brilliant. The doctor says I've got to watch my blood pressure. He says I'm to send for him the minute anything starts.'

Maggie was only nine when Grace was born but she remembers how ill Mum had been. Grace was born at home, in the bedroom upstairs, same as Billy. Nan and Mrs Kelly were there and Sarah Lind, the midwife but then the doctor came as well. He was very serious and sent Maggie downstairs. She remembers her Mum moaning a lot and then there was a loud scream, which frightened her. Then she heard the baby crying. When the doctor came downstairs he was wearing a striped apron, just like the butcher and there were bloodstains on it. He took something out of his bag and gave it to Dad, saying that it would make Mum sleep and that she had to stay in bed until the bleeding stopped. Dad gave him a pound note and shook his hand.

After that Nan stayed to look after them until Mum was well enough to get up because Dad was working at the garage and Nanny Smith had died. That was before the war. This new baby will be a war baby, Mrs Kelly says.

'I'll look after the kids for you. They can come round and stay at my place.'

'Can we go in the Anderson shelter?' asks Billy, who has come in to have the shampoo rinsed away.

'Yes, if we have to. I hope it won't be necessary.'

'Are there worms in there? And mice and spiders?'

'Don't like spiders,' Grace begins to wail.

'Billy behave yourself. Of course there aren't any worms in the shelter, or anything else for that matter,' Mum scolds. 'Now come on, keep still so Mrs Kelly can get to that mop of yours.'

'Wiggly, wiggly worm,' he begins to sing.

'Now stop that,' Mrs Kelly says.

She tips the basin of water over his head.

'Argh. That's cold.'

'Never mind, you'll soon warm up.'

She towels his head vigorously.

'Heard how your Dad is?' asks Mrs Kelly.

'He's all right. Just got to take it easy. It's his heart you know. But he will insist on continuing with his warden's work. Says he might as well as long as he's able.'

The chimes of Big Ben can be heard on the wireless. Maggie moves across to turn it up.

'*Here is the six o'clock news and this is Alvar Lidell reading it. The evacuation of British children is going smoothly and efficiently. The Ministry of Health says that great progress has been made with the government's arrangements.*'

She looks at Mum.

'Would you like a cuppa Kate?'

'Yes, but I'll do it. You sit there and listen to the news.'

'Both my friends Judy and Ann have been evacuated. Their Mum said it was the safest thing to do,' Maggie says, her eyes never leaving Mum's face.

'Well, that's up to them. You'll be fine here with me.'

'Yes, if Jerry comes we'll hide in Missus Kelly's shelter,' says Billy.

'They say all the railways stations are packed with evacuees. There're thousands of them,' Mrs Kelly tells them, drying her hands on the towel.

'Poor little souls, with their labels around their necks like so many parcels sent off to goodness knows where,' says Mum.

'Their teachers are going with them,' Maggie adds.

'Does that mean we don't have to go to school next week?' asks Billy.

'Nobody has said that your school is closed so off you go on Wednesday as planned, my lad. I didn't spend my valuable clothing coupons on some new trousers for you to play in the street in them.'

'Princess Elizabeth was on 'Children's Hour' today, Mum. We listened to it at school.'

'Was she, dear.'

'She says she and her sister feel sorry for the children that have to leave their mummies and daddies.'

'Can I go out now?' asks Billy. 'My hair's dry.'

'No, it's too dark, and anyway it's supper in half an hour.'

'What're we having Mum?' asks Maggie.

'Sprats.'

'Yuk,' says Billy.

'Father McNally was at King's Cross this morning with some of his orphan boys. They're going to families in Newcastle. He said he was at the station at five o'clock,' Mrs Kelly informs them, coming in with two steaming cups of tea. 'Here get that down you. There's nothing like a nice cup of char.'

'He's a good man,' agrees Mum, sipping the tea.

'Is Father Nally your Daddy?' asks Grace.

Mrs Kelly laughs.

'No child. He's the priest at our church.'

'But why do you call him Father?' asks Billy.

'That's what we do. I suppose he's like a Father to us. He helps people.'

'You don't go to the same church as us, do you Mrs Kelly?'

'No Maggie. I go to the Catholic Church down the road. Our Lady of the Assumption.'

'Why do you go there?'

'Because I'm a Catholic?'

'Are Catholics good people?' asks Billy.

'I like to think so.'

'I did a picture of Jesus at Sunday school,' says Grace.

She hands a crumpled piece of paper to Mrs Kelly. She has drawn a large circle with a smiling mouth, which she has coloured pink and around the circle she has drawn yellow lines that stick out like spikes.

'Why that's lovely Grace. What a clever wee girl you are.'

'That doesn't look like Jesus. Jesus has a beard,' says Billy. 'That's just a silly picture of the sun.'

'Billy, don't be horrible to your little sister,' Mum says. 'Maggie why don't you take Grace upstairs to play for a bit before bedtime.'

'All right Mum.'

'And you too, Billy.'

It's lucky that they have been sent home early from school. As soon as Maggie walks in the house she knows that something is wrong. Mum is leaning on the kitchen table; her skirt is soaking and clinging to her legs as though she has wet herself. She looks awful.

'Maggie, thank goodness. Run round to Mrs Kelly and ask her to phone the doctor for me. I think the baby's coming. There's some pennies on the sideboard for the phone box.'

She grabs her stomach and lets out a loud groan; Maggie thinks she is going to fall over.

'Do you want to lie down, Mum? Can I help you?'

She shakes her head and whispers:

'Just get Mrs Kelly. And hurry.'

She leans over and lets out another groan of pain. Her knuckles are white where she is gripping the table.

Maggie grabs the money and runs straight out to Mrs Kelly's house. She prays that she is at home. Maggie does not know what she will do if their neighbour is not in. She knocks and calls:

'Mrs Kelly, are you there? Please come quick; Mum's having the baby.'

The door opens.

'What's that pet?' asks Mrs Kelly.

'It's the baby. It's coming. You're to phone the doctor.'

She holds the pennies out to Mrs Kelly. Her hand is shaking.

'Right you are, Maggie. Let's do it right now.'

The phone box is in the next road, opposite the fish and chip shop. She stays outside, hopping from leg to leg as she waits for Mrs Kelly to finish. She does not know what to do, whether to run back to Mum or stay with Mrs Kelly. She feels she should be with Mum but she is frightened to go back alone.

'That's it. The doctor is coming right away. No need to worry now, pet. Run round to Sarah's and tell her the baby's on its way. I'll go and see how your poor mammy is getting on.'

The decision is made for her; she runs off in the direction of the midwife's house. Sarah Lind lives at the top of Hanbury Road and it seems to take Maggie ages to get there, even though she is running as fast as she can.

'Slow down, love. Anyone would think the house was on fire,' a man says as she bumps against him.

'My Mum's having a baby,' she calls back.

There is no time to apologise.

At last she arrives at the midwife's house; Mrs Lind is standing in her doorway chatting to the milkman.

'Mrs Lind, my Mum needs you, the baby's on its way,' she tells her. 'Can you come now?'

'I'll just get my bag, dear. Now you slow down; we'll be there in no time, I promise you.'

The midwife takes Maggie's hand and together they walk briskly back to the house. Maggie is impatient to get home but cannot make Mrs Lind walk any quicker.

'Don't worry, child. Babies aren't usually in so much of a rush to get into the world as all that. And why would they be, what with all this nasty war and no food for anyone,' she says.

At last they arrive at their house, with its blue front door. Maggie dreads what she will see inside; she lets Mrs Lind go in first. Mum is lying on the floor now, with a cushion beneath her head, watched over by Billy and Grace. Their faces are as white as Mum's and for once Billy has nothing to say.

'Oh Sarah, thanks for coming. I think it's on its way,' says Mum, panting heavily.

Her face is flushed and covered in sweat.

'The doctor'll be here any minute,' Kate adds.

'In the meantime let's get her more comfortable,' the midwife says, pulling back Irene's skirt and examining her.

'Ooooh,' Mum groans as the contractions return.

'They're getting closer,' she gasps. 'Oh I do hope it's not going to be born on the kitchen floor.'

Maggie thinks her voice sounds funny, as though she cannot breathe properly.

'Mummy, Mummy don't die,' Grace cries, tears running down her fat little cheeks.

'Mummy's not going to die, darling,' Mum says, panting harder than ever. 'Don't cry.'

'Maggie take the children upstairs, there's a good girl,' Mrs Kelly tells her. 'Now don't you fret Gracie, your mammy is going to be all right. It's just the baby, he's in a hurry to get into the world and meet his brother and sisters.'

Maggie ushers Billy and Grace out of the room. She is glad to be leaving everything to the midwife and Mrs Kelly. She feels she ought to stay with Mum but she is pleased that she has been given something else to do instead.

'Will we be able to play with the baby, Maggie?' asks Grace as she climbs up the stairs, pulling on the handrail.

'Yes, I expect so. It'll be very small at first you know, so you'll have to be especially careful.'

'Babies are smelly,' says Billy. 'They do their number twos in a nappy.'

He wrinkles up his face and holds his nose to emphasise his point.

'I don't have a nappy anymore, do I, Maggie?'

'No Grace. You haven't had a nappy for a long time. You're a big girl now.'

She remembers when Mum asked her to change Grace's nappy once; it was awful, all green and slimy. That's the worst part about babies she decides.

'What are we going to do?'

'Let's play I-spy,' suggests Billy. 'I'll go first. I spy with my little eye something beginning with ...'.

He look around the bedroom.

'S'

'Slipper.'

'No.'

'Sugar,' says Grace.

'No, silly, there's no sugar up here.'

'Socks.'

They guess and guess and in the end Billy says:

'Soldier of course.'

'What soldier?'

'Dad. He's a soldier.'

He points to the photograph by his Mum's bed.

'Yes, but he's not wearing his uniform, is he.'

'He's still a soldier. Anyway, I go again.'

'No, let Gracie have a go.'

The bedroom door opens. It's Mrs Kelly.

'The doctor is sending your mammy to the hospital. Do you want to come down and give her a kiss goodbye?'

They bundle out of the room and down the stairs. The ambulance man is helping Mum stand up. She seems calmer now and has stopped panting. The doctor is closing his battered brown bag and preparing to leave. He smiles at them. She likes Dr Brown; he has been their doctor for a long time. He came to see her once, when she had measles.

'Why is Mum going to the hospital?' Maggie whispers.

'It's just to be on the safe side, dear. No need to worry,' the midwife says.

'Bye Mum.'

'Bye-bye Mummy.'

'Goodbye sweethearts. Be good for Mrs Kelly now and I'll be back soon.'

'With the baby Mum?'

'Yes darling, with the baby. You think of some nice names for it while I'm away.'

'Have you got the case with the baby things Mum?' asks Maggie.

'Yes, it's here,' says Mrs Kelly.

Maggie takes Grace by one hand and Billy by the other. They follow Mum to the door and watch the ambulance man help her into the ambulance. The doctor waits until she is inside then climbs on his bike and cycles away. Billy waves goodbye but he doesn't notice him. All the neighbours have come out to see what is happening; they stand in their doorways, watching and chattering. Nothing happens in their street without the neighbours knowing, Mum says.

'Bye Mum, bye. Bye,' they chorus.

They watch until the ambulance turns the corner and disappears then go back inside. The house feels strange without Mum, quiet and empty. Maggie wants to cry but she swallows hard instead.

'Right, now kids let's get your things together then you can come home with me. I've got some eggs for tea,' says Mrs Kelly.

Eggs. They have not had eggs for ages. She hopes they can have them boiled with toasted soldiers.

'And I've made some jam tarts.'

'I like jam tarts,' says Grace.

'Yeah, they're my very bestest things,' says Billy.

'Good, so that's it then. Go and get your things and we'll be off.'

As they leave the empty house and close the front door behind them Maggie has the strangest feeling; things are about to change and not in a good way.

MAGGIE

Their new brother, all six pounds three ounces of him, enters the world the day before the first bomb of the Blitz falls on London, sending shock waves throughout the horrified country. Since then Mrs Kelly has been visiting Mum each day, bringing them back the latest news on her condition.

'The baby,' she says, 'is beautiful, just like your mammy but with a mop of red hair.'

'Like Dad,' Maggie says straight away.

'Yes, but he's a poorly wee mite,' she explains to them. 'Something is not right with his heart, so the doctors say that your mammy and the baby have to stay in the hospital a little longer than usual.'

Maggie wants to cry when she hears this, but she knows she must be strong; if she starts crying then Grace and Billy will start too.

'I know you're going to be very brave children,' Mrs Kelly continues. 'It won't be long until they are both home again.'

'Why can't we go and see her?' Billy says.

Maggie can see he is trying not to cry; his voice is quivering.

'They don't allow children in the hospital,' Mrs Kelly explains.

'But she's our Mum,' he wails and then the tears start to flow.

'The mothers and babies have to be kept quiet,' Mrs Kelly says. 'They're not allowed many visitors and certainly no children.'

'But we'd be as quiet as church mice,' he promises.

'I'm sorry Billy, there's nothing we can do about it. I'll go and see your mammy every day and I'll tell her you're missing her. It won't be long until she's home. You'll see, the time'll pass in a flash.'

'But ...,' he begins.

Mrs Kelly just shakes her head firmly.

'Now come along, wipe your eyes. It's time you were all ready for bed. Let's hope it's a quiet night tonight.'

Each night they put their coats on over their pyjamas and, carrying a candle, make their way to the bottom of the garden and climb down into the Anderson shelter. The first night Billy was very excited by the prospect of being underground but, after a few nights sleeping on the hard benches that serve as beds and listening to the sounds of bombs falling all around them, he has grown unusually quiet. Tonight he gets undressed slowly and dawdles over cleaning his teeth.

'Hurry up Billy. Mrs Kelly is waiting for us,' Maggie tells him.

Grace is already in her nightdress and slippers and has her teddy bear under her arm. Maggie helps her put on her coat and button it up.

'Right, are we all ready?' she asks. 'Let's go and see if Mrs Kelly has made us some cocoa?'

Mrs Kelly is waiting for them in the kitchen. She has a couple of blankets and a flask of cocoa. The children know the drill by now; they follow her along the garden path until they reach the mound that is the Anderson shelter. There is a moon tonight and it's easy to find their way, even without the candle. Maggie likes to look up at the moon but since she heard Mr Ford tell Mrs Kelly that a clear sky makes it easier for the planes to bomb them, it frightens her to see it as full and bright as it is to-night.

'Why don't you have a baby?' Grace asks Mrs Kelly as she pulls open the door to the shelter.

'Oh, I'm too old for that now,' Mrs Kelly replies.

They make their way into the shelter and squeeze inside. Mrs Kelly places the candle on a ledge and the yellow light spills around the room, bringing colour to their tired faces. Maggie deliberately does not look at the corners, still shrouded in darkness; Billy's taunts about worms and slugs don't seem so funny now that they are shut down here.

'Come closer, Gracie, Billy,' Mrs Kelly says. 'We'll snuggle up together and keep warm.'

They huddle together and pull the blankets over them.

'How about some cocoa?' she asks and pours them each a small cup of hot cocoa.

Maggie looks at Mrs Kelly's kindly face in the flickering candlelight. Her grey hair is tightly permed and held in place by a hair net and two kirby grips. There are not many wrinkles in her plump cheeks, only what Mum calls laughter lines. It suddenly occurs to her that Mrs Kelly does not wear a wedding ring; that seems strange.

'Mrs Kelly, did you get married in Ireland?' she asks, knowing that she would never have dared ask such a question if Mum was there.

'No child. I've never been married. I was going to. I was engaged and everything.'

'What happened?'

'Well, it was wartime, the last war. My fiancé was an Englishman; he was sent to France to fight and he never came back. I waited and waited and in the end I gave up.'

'My Daddy went to France,' says Grace quietly.

'Yes pet, that's true. Now drink up your cocoa and try to sleep.'

'If you're not married then why do we call you Mrs Kelly?' asks Billy.

'I don't know really. It was your mammy's idea. She said that Miss Kelly sounded like an old spinster, so she always told you to say Mrs instead. It doesn't make much difference to me.'

She laughs.

'After all, I am an old spinster.'

'Why didn't you go back to Ireland and marry someone there?' asks Maggie.

'Well all my friends were here, your Nanny Smith and your aunty Gladys.'

'Did you know Nanny Smith?'

This news surprises her; Nanny Smith died a long time ago. Maggie had been younger than Grace at the time; she hardly remembered her.

'Yes, she was my best friend. You know I've lived in this house nearly all my life. I was here when your Dad was born and when your Nanny died.'

All that Maggie can remember about Dad's mother is that she was very old and she always wore a long apron with big pockets on the front. Sometimes she would take a sweet or a biscuit out of one of the pockets and give it to Maggie.

'Are you as old as Nanny Smith?' she asks.

Mrs Kelly laughs.

'No, not quite,' she says. 'Although there are some days when I feel like it.'

'Why did Aunty Gladys go away?' she asks.

'She married your Uncle Harry and when he got a job in Leeds, she went with him.'

Maggie likes her uncle and aunty; every Christmas they send them a parcel with toys and nice things to eat. Mum says they can afford to do that because they don't have any children of their own.

'Aren't you lonely with no husband?' she asks. 'Mum is lonely since Dad died.'

'I know pet. Your mammy loved your dad very much. But I'm used to being on my own and anyway I have my faith.'

Maggie knows that she means the church. Mrs Kelly goes to church two or three times a week. She has told them that she lights candles for Mum and the baby, asking God to look after them. She even goes early Sunday mornings to arrange the flowers at the altar. She grows lots of flowers in her back yard so that she can pick them and take them to the church. Maggie had helped her pick some pink and white chrysanthemums last week. They looked lovely.

'Is Father Nally your friend?' asks Grace.

'Yes, Father McNally is everyone's friend.'

'He's nice,' Grace says, drowsily.

Maggie sees her tuck her thumb into her mouth. She'll be asleep any minute now, she thinks. She wonders what the new baby looks like.

'I'll take you to church with me tomorrow,' Mrs Kelly promises. 'Then you can help me do the flowers.'

There is a distant explosion and Maggie can feel the floorboards of the shelter shudder.

'Dear God,' Mrs Kelly murmurs then says:

'Let's say a prayer together for all the people of London.'

Maggie nods. She places her hands together and closes her eyes.

'Heavenly Father, protect and watch over your children tonight and save them from all harm. Our Father, who art in Heaven, hallowed be Thy name...'

Maggie and Billy repeat the Lord's prayer with her.

'Amen,' they chorus.

'Now I think it's time we tried to get to sleep.'

'Goodnight Mrs Kelly.'

'Goodnight Maggie, goodnight Billy. Sleep tight.'

Just as she promised, Mrs Kelly takes them to Mass with her the next morning. They go early so that Mrs Kelly can arrange the flowers before the service starts. Maggie finds the church very different to the one she goes to with Mum. Mrs Kelly keeps making the sign of the cross and she makes them all give a little bobbing curtsey when they enter the church. She knows lots of people in the church and they all come over to speak to her. They smile at the children and say how kind Mrs Kelly is to be looking after them while their mother is in hospital. After the hymns everyone goes up to the altar to receive Jesus's body, only it's not really his body, just a dry biscuit. Billy wants to go but Mrs Kelly says no, only Catholics can receive communion. Father McNally stands at the altar giving out the biscuits. He wears a long white robe and a gold coloured scarf. Mrs Kelly says the robe is called a cassock and the scarf is his stole. When they leave the church he is standing by the door smiling at everyone and shaking hands. He smiles at Mrs Kelly and asks her who her little friends are. Then he shakes hands with each of them and says he hopes to see them again soon.

After lunch Mrs Kelly tells them she is going to visit their mother again while they go to their Sunday School class.

'You'll be able to bring them home all right Maggie, won't you?' she asks as she leaves them at the church door. 'I've left the back door open and there's some bread in the larder if you're hungry.'

'We'll be fine, Mrs Kelly. Don't worry.'

Maggie does not like Sunday school; she already knows all the stories that the Sunday School teacher tells them and she gets bored. She and Billy are in the same class. He has his favourite stories, mostly ones that include some kind of violence, like Samson slaying the Philistines with the jawbone of an ass. One day he found the skeleton of a dead cat down near the canal and he brought it home. He hid it in his room for days until the smell alerted Mum and it got thrown in the dustbin. He wanted to remove its jawbone, he said. Then another day he refused to let Mum cut his hair in case it took away all his strength, like Samson. Grace is in the babies' class where they spend most of their time colouring pictures and singing songs. Grace's favourite song is '*Jesus Wants Me for a Sunbeam*'; she hums it all the time.

The teacher is halfway through telling them about Moses and how his mother put him in a basket and floated him down the river so that the wicked king would not find him and kill him, when the air raid sirens go off.

'Follow me children,' she calls. 'Quickly now. No don't bring anything with you, just follow me. Billy, don't run. Angela, there's no need to cry, just take hold of Susan's hand and follow me. Hurry up now.'

They follow her out of the room and further into the church. The babies' class is already ahead of them, making for the crypt. They form a long crocodile, all holding hands; some of them are crying. Maggie looks for Grace and sees her sandwiched between a girl with dark pigtails and a plump little boy, wearing odd socks. All the children are herded into the crypt and the door is securely closed behind them.

'Now children, I want you all to find a place to sit down. We'll be quite safe in here until we hear the all-clear.'

The teachers kneel down and begin to pray. Maggie makes her way across to Grace; she looks frightened.

'It's all right Gracie, we're all here together now.'

'Are we going to die? I don't want to go to Heaven,' she whimpers. 'I want my Mummy.'

The little girl with pigtails hears her and begins to cry.

'I want my Mummy too. I want my Mummy.'

'Hush now children. I know you're frightened but you must be brave boys and girls; this will be all over very soon and then we can go and look for your mothers,' the older of the two teachers says.

Maggie thinks she looks as frightened as the children.

'But my Mummy's in the hospital,' wails Grace. 'I want my Mummy.'

'Come over here Grace and I'll give you a cuddle,' says Maggie.

She has Billy tight by one hand and with the other she pulls her sister towards her.

'Why don't we all sing a song about Jesus?' suggests the younger teacher, who has blonde hair that she has pulled back from her face and tied in a bun. 'Which one shall it be?'

'*All Things Bright and Beautiful,*' says the boy with the odd socks.

'Right then, all together, "*All things bright and beautiful, all things great and small...*'

The childish voices rise and fall, creating their own special music in the darkened crypt. Outside Maggie can still hear the thudding of bombs exploding and the wailing of the fire engines. She is frightened. What is happening out there?

'That was lovely, now how about something else?' the bright young Sunday school teacher asks them.

'*Jesus Loves Me.*'

This is from one of the older children.

'All right. One, two, three. *Jesus loves me, this I know* ...,' the young teacher sings.

She has a clear voice that soars above them into the rafters. One by one the children join in. Grace does not know the words, so she just sings '*la, la, la.*' Suddenly there is a tremendous crash and the church is shaken to its very foundations. Maggie thinks the walls will come down, just like in that city in the Bible and hugs her brother and sister even tighter. The children start to scream and cry for their mothers. Everyone is too terrified to move. She can feel Grace trembling and Billy is crying, silent tears streaming down his face. The bomb sounds as though it landed very close.

'Don't worry,' she whispers to them. 'We'll be all right.'

'There now children, nothing to worry about,' the older teacher says, unconvincingly.

Her voice is cracking and she seems about to cry. They all sit in silence. Nobody feels like singing anymore. They just listen and wait to see what is going to happen next.

'Maggie, I'm cold,' whispers Grace.

'Are you, Gracie? Here put my cardie on for a bit.'

She takes off her cardigan and drapes it around her sister's shoulders.

'What's Mum going to call the new baby?' Billy asks.

Maggie can feel him shivering.

'Mrs Kelly says he's going to be called Leslie.'

'That's nice,' says Grace, snuggling closer to her sister.

'It's after Mum's Dad.'

'Granddad?'

'I'm called after my other granddad,' says Billy. 'William Ronald Smith.'

'And you, Maggie?' asks Grace.

'I'm not called after anybody that I know of; I think Mum just liked the name.'

'And me?'

'Oh you were named after Gracie Fields. She's a singer. Mum loves her, she sings all her songs.'

'I'm going to be a singer when I grow up,' Gracie tells them.

Suddenly there is a long, drawn-out wailing sound; they all know what it is. Maggie feels a wave of relief sweep over her. She stands up, pulling the others to their feet.

'There you are children, the all-clear,' says the teacher. 'I said we'd be all right, didn't I? I told you Jesus would protect us from harm. Right, line up at the door in double file. I think it's best if you collect all your things and go straight home now. Your parents will be worrying about you.'

The younger teacher unbolts the door and opens it. A shaft of sunlight breaks through the gloom; Maggie can see specks of dust dancing in the light, like little fairies. They must have been there all the time but they could not see them until she opened the door.

KATE

Kate Kelly stops in the doorway and looks back at her neighbour. Irene smiles and waves at her. She is looking tired but otherwise seems to be fine. The news about the baby is not so good though. Poor little mite, she will say a special prayer for him this evening. As she heads for the bus stop, she fingers the beads of her rosary.

If only things had been different she thinks, if Paul had not died. Would they have married? Would she have children now, maybe even grandchildren? Some nights she lies in bed and she can see him as clearly as if he were there beside her. Her mother said she should have moved on with her life, gone back to Ireland and married Patrick Heneshy. Maybe she was right, but it did not seem so at the time. Now Patrick Heneshy was dead, murdered in the Troubles, her parents were long dead and she rarely heard from any of her brothers and sisters. They felt she had betrayed them going off with an Englishman. She wonders where they are now. She was the only one to break away and leave Ireland; the others had stayed but she had wanted to see the world. She smiles wryly. See the world, that was a laugh. She had come to Bethnal Green and here she has stayed. And this is where she will remain; she is too old to be gallivanting anywhere else at her age.

The bus arrives, she sees her friend Rose sitting just inside the door and sits down next to her.

'Been to the hospital?' Rose asks.

'Yes. Irene Smith, you know, Lil's daughter, she's just had her fourth.'

'What, her that's husband's just been killed?'

Kate nods. She is not in the mood for a gossip; luckily she only has to go a couple of stops. Rose starts to tell her about the cousin of a friend whose husband has been sent to North Africa; she is not listening carefully enough and soon looses the thread. It does not matter; she does not know the people in question anyway.

'Bethnal Green,' the conductor shouts.

It's as though his words are the signal for the air raid sirens to start.

'Oh my God, not another air raid,' Rose cries as the high pitched whine starts. 'Thank goodness we're right beside the underground. Come on Kate.'

'No, you go Rose, I've got to get back for the kids. They'll be home any minute now.'

'But you'll never make it home in time.'

But Kate is already hurrying down the street towards her house. The sound of the siren is deafening her and now she can hear the drone of the bombers as they approach. She quickens her step. She is not so young any more; once she would have run all the way home without pausing for breath but now, with her hip problem and her bunions, it's all she can do to walk. She hears a bomb explode nearby; they are coming closer. The poor children, she hopes the teachers have had the good sense to keep them in the church. Not that they are safe anywhere these days. The bloody Germans seem determined to crush them all into the ground. They took away her Paul and now they are trying to get her as well.

'Our Father, Who art in Heaven, hallowed be Thy name,' she mutters, fingering the rosary in her pocket.

She is almost there, she can see her house in the distance. She quickens her steps. If the children are not there she'll go straight down to the shelter. Damned Jerries. She is desperate for a cup of tea but that will have to wait until the all-clear now.

'Almost there,' she murmurs. 'Almost home.'

There is a terrifying explosion, then silence and the world seems to be crashing down around her.

'Paul?' she murmurs.

MAGGIE

At first everything seems unchanged. They walk down the road that led from the church to the shops, then they turn up towards Hanbury Road. The fish and chip shop is gone. In its place is an enormous hole in the ground. Billy, who has been striding ahead, anxious to get back to Mrs Kelly's, stops and stares at it. Nobody speaks. Maggie takes his hand and cautiously they walk down Hanbury Road towards their own street and Mrs Kelly's house. Only it's not there anymore. They stop and look around them in bewilderment.

'Mrs Kelly's house is gone,' Grace says. 'Where's it gone?'

'And our house. Where's our house? They've all been bombed,' says Billy. 'They're all gone.'

The children are stunned. Maggie can do nothing but stare in horror at the scene before them. Their familiar street of terraced houses with their uniform brown doors is gone and in its place is an enormous pile of rubble. Maggie can see broken plates, cups, half a wall with its wallpaper torn and fluttering in the wind, an enamel sink, a bedstead, a chair leg, a tin bath mangled out of shape and piles and piles of broken bricks and stones. A chimney pot has landed upright and somehow miraculously remains intact. A chamber pot decorated with pink flowers lies smashed in dozens of pieces. All these images dance before her eyes like some terrifying collage of their lives.

'That's our front door,' says Billy, pointing to a splintered plank of blue, sticking up from the rubble.

He is crying. Their home is buried beneath the rubble, even their beautiful front door has gone. Without thinking she scrambles across the pile of bricks and mud and pulls at the blue-painted plank. It won't budge. She bends down and breaks a small piece from it and slips it into her pocket.

Grace feels abandoned and begins to wail: 'Maggie, Maggie.'

Maggie scrambles back to her and picks her up but the child refuses to be comforted. Seeing their house in ruins seems to be the last straw for Grace. She sobs and sobs.

'It's all right Gracie. Don't cry; it'll be all right. I promise.'

'Where's Missus Kelly?' cries Billy. 'She's not here. Where is she?'

'She'll be all right. I expect she's still at the hospital with Mum. Come on, we'll go and look for her.'

'Maybe she's in the Anderson Shelter,' suggests Billy. 'That's where she'd go if there was an air raid.'

'Of course. She might still be here.'

They pick their way along to where Mrs Kelly's back yard used to be but can see nothing but rubble. The air is thick with smoke and dust. There is no sign of the air raid shelter, no sign of the marrows, nothing. Her house resembles Grace's doll's house with the front wall removed; you can see into all the rooms. The floors have disappeared and the roof is gone; the house looks as though it's about to collapse. A wooden cross hangs lopsidedly on the remaining back wall.

'I don't think she can be here,' Maggie says. 'She'll be with Mum. Come on, I know how to get to the hospital. It's not far.'

She puts Grace down and the three of them set off as fast as it is possible, stumbling and tripping over the broken glass, bricks and chunks of mortar that block their path. Maggie cannot believe what she is seeing. It's a nightmare. Everywhere she looks there are ruined buildings, windows blown out, doors hanging off their hinges, huge craters in the ground where once houses or shops had stood. Their neighbours are foraging about in the rubble trying to save what few possessions they can. People are crying and moaning in pain; some are shouting curses at the men who did this to them, others are silent in their anger. The air is thick with dust and there is a strong smell of gas where the explosions have fractured the gas lines. The air raid sirens have been replaced with the whine of ambulances and the clanging of fire engines. The children pass some men in uniforms and tin hats who are pulling the body of an old man out from beneath the mound of bricks that was once his home.

'Is he dead?' asks Billy.

'I don't know. Come on, we must hurry,' she says.

She doesn't want to stop.

It takes them twenty minutes to reach the hospital. All the way there Maggie is repeating to herself:

'Dear God please don't let them bomb the hospital. Dear God please don't let them bomb Mum. Dear God ..'

Her prayers seem to have been answered. The grey facade of the maternity hospital stands strong and secure. She marches right up to the door and goes in. There is nobody about. Still gripping Billy and Grace by the hand, she walks down the corridor. Still there is nobody, no nurses, no patients and no babies. A heavy silence hangs over the place.

'Hello young lady, what do you think you're up to then?' a deep voice demands.

It's an old man with a warden's band on his right arm.

'We're looking for our Mum.'

'She's just had a baby,' offers Billy.

'Well, you won't find her here. You've just missed them. They moved all the mothers and babies out to Bushey this afternoon. Had to get them away from the bombing. Not safe here now, you know. There's an unexploded bomb in the next street.'

Maggie remembers noticing the police cordon as they passed. She shivers.

'But how will we find her again?' she asks, trying hard to hold back the tears.

'Now don't you worry your pretty little head about that my dear; it's only for a few days and then they'll be sending them home again. I expect she was too ill to go home just yet.'

'The baby has a weak heart,' Billy informs him.

'There you are then. Once they have sorted that out they'll be on their way again. She'll be back home with you in no time.'

'Maggie, I want to go home,' Grace begins to cry.

'That's right dear, you take your brother and sister home.'

'Our house has been blown up,' says Billy. 'We were at Sunday school.'

'Is that right? I'm very sorry to hear that. This afternoon was it? Pretty bad show that. Bloody Jerries.'

He peers down at them.

'Is someone looking after you?' he asks.

'Mrs Kelly,' Grace answers.

'You go back and tell Mrs Kelly that your Mum is safe and she'll be going home soon.'

They turn and make their way back to the hospital entrance. What are they going to do now?

'Maggie, where's Bushey?' ask Billy.

'I don't know Billy, somewhere where there're no bombs, I suppose.'

She feels the tears filling her eyes and blinks hard.

'Maggie I's tired,' says Grace, slipping back into her baby lisp.

'Let's sit down for a bit then.'

They sit together on the steps that lead up to the hospital entrance. Nobody speaks. Maggie does not know what to say. She knows that the others are waiting for her to tell them that everything will be all right but it does not feel as though it will be. She wonders if anything will ever be all right again. If only they could find Mum. She would tell them what to do.

A policeman comes round the corner on his bicycle, his bell ringing frantically. Normally, at the sight of a bobby on his bike, Billy would have jumped up, but today he just remains sitting by her side. He looks as though he has had all the stuffing knocked out of him. Maggie too feels numb. What should she do? She has no idea. She cannot think.

'Do you think Missus Kelly will be looking for us?' Billy asks at last.

'She might be. What do you say, shall we go back and see if she's at her house?'

'Mrs Kelly's house is bombed,' says Grace.

'She might be looking for things,' says Billy. 'Like those other people.'

'You're right. Come on let's go back and see if we can see her. We can't sit here all day.'

Maggie is getting worried. It will be dark soon. She has no coat; she left it at Mrs Kelly's house and now she is feeling cold.

'Are you all right Gracie? Do you think you can walk all that way back to Mrs Kelly's house?'

Her little sister smiles and takes her hand.

'I's fine, Maggie.'

'Good, come on then.'

They trudge back, through the ruined streets and derellct houses. They pass few people and those they do see are intent on their own business; they don't even notice the three grim faced children, walking hand in hand. They are invisible amongst all this chaos and destruction.

When they arrive back at Stanlet Street, Maggie is half hoping that everything will be all right, that maybe they have made a mistake and it was not their street that has been razed to the ground, but another one. But there is no mistake. Although it's difficult to recognise anything that was there before, nevertheless this is where they lived and someone has just destroyed it.

'I can't see Missus Kelly,' says Billy.

They walk past their own house and down as far as hers. There is no sign of any life.

'Billy take Grace's hand and just wait here a minute,' Maggie says.

'Where're you going?'

'I'll just be a minute.'

Before he can protest she is clambering over the pile of rubble that was once Missus Kelly's house. Amongst all the dirt and debris she has seen it, her plaid coat. She pulls away the bricks until she has it free. It's covered in dirt but otherwise seems all right. She gives it a good shake and then makes her way back to her brother and sister.

'That's your coat Maggie,' Grace says, in amazement.

'Yes.'

'And there's Teddy.'

She points excitedly to where a tiny furry arm is sticking up out of the debris.

'So it is. Well spotted Grace. Stay there and I'll get him for you.'

She thrusts her arms into the sleeves of her coat and buttons it up then clambers back over the rubble and digs out the unfortunate teddy bear.

'Is he hurt?' Grace calls to her.

'No, he's fine.'

Maggie dusts him off and straightens his scarf.

'We'll give him a brush and he'll be as good as new.'

Grace clasps him to her.

'You're a naughty teddy; I told you to come to church with us,' she scolds. 'Now you stay with me and don't get lost.'

'Did you see Missus Kelly?' Billy asks.

'No,' says Maggie.

Nobody could be alive under there.

'Here what are you lot up to?' a gruff voice demands.

A man in a fire fighter's uniform comes over to them.

'You can't go clambering about over there; it's far too dangerous. Could be a gas leak and then if that goes off, we'll all go up.'

Instinctively Maggie pulls Billy and Grace back, away from the rubble.

'We're looking for our friend,' she says.

'Missus Kelly,' Billy adds.

'Well, you won't find her in there. There's no-one left alive in there, I can tell you. Caught it straight on. Not a chance.'

'But she has an Anderson shelter,' Billy tells him.

The warden looks at them. Grace is crying; they are all shivering.

'Sorry kids. Even if she was in the shelter she wouldn't have survived a direct hit.'

'If anyone was still alive, where would they be?' asks Maggie.

'Down at the church hall. They've taken all the wounded down there for now. If your friend's alive, that's where she'll be.'

'I know where that is,' Maggie says. 'Mrs Kelly used to go there to her WVS meetings. Come on.'

She grabs Grace and Billy by their hands and pulls them off in the direction of the church hall.

'Thank you,' she calls back to the fire warden, who does not reply.

He is already moving on down the street. Once more they are invisible.

It's not far to the church hall. As they turn the corner they can already hear the groans and cries of the wounded and frightened. The tiny hall is packed with people, some lie on the floor, others are propped up against the wall and some wander around with blank, hopeless faces. Maggie cannot see anyone who looks like Mrs Kelly. She goes up to a woman in a nurse's uniform and asks her:

'Do you know Mrs Kelly? She's our friend and we're looking for her.'

'No dear, don't know any one of that name.'

'Her house has been bombed,' says Billy.

'Well, she might be here. Have a look around, but don't get in the way.'

They wander up and down but cannot see any sign of her.

'That's Missus Kelly's friend,' Grace suddenly says.

'Where?'

'That lady. She was in the church,' explains Grace.

'Oh what a clever little girl you are, Gracie.'

Maggie heads across to the woman. She is about the same age as Mrs Kelly and wears a brown coat and a printed head scarf. She is holding the hand of an old man, who is shaking badly.

'Excuse me. We're looking for Mrs Kelly. Do you know where she is?' Maggie asks.

The woman looks up. The man is unaware that they are there. Maggie sees that he is crying.

'Kate Kelly?'

'Yes.'

The woman's eyes fill with tears.

'She was caught in the bombing today.'

'No, she was going to the hospital to see our Mum.'

'I don't know nothing about that. Her house caught it full on.'

'But she had an Anderson shelter,' says Billy.

'Lot of good that did her.'

'Do you mean she's dead?' asks Maggie.

'Yes child, dead and gone to heaven. If ever anyone deserved to go to heaven, it was Kate. She was a good Christian woman.'

'She's a Catholic,' says Billy.

Maggie feels numb. If Mrs Kelly is dead and Mum is in Bushey what are they going to do? Who can she turn to now? She feels frightened and alone. There seems to be nobody to help them; everyone has their own problems. Nobody has time for three homeless children. What can she do? How can she look after Billy and Grace on her own? She can feel tears fill her eyes and blinks them back angrily. Whatever happens she has to be strong.

The woman turns back to the old man. She holds a cup of tea up to his mouth but he does not drink it; he cannot stop shaking.

'What shall we do now, Maggie?' asks Billy.

'I don't know but there's no point staying here. Come on.'

'I'm hungry,' wails Grace.

'So am I. Missus Kelly always gives us jam tarts on a Sunday,' says Billy.

The thought of no more Mrs Kelly and no more jam tarts is just too much for Billy and he breaks into loud, harsh sobs.

'Come on Billy. It's not that bad. We've just got to find someone to look after us until Mum gets home.'

'We could go to Nan's.'

Maggie is not sure how to get to her grandparents' house. She knows it's somewhere in Islington and that you have to get on three different buses to get there, but she has no money for the bus fare. Besides, what if they get lost? What if they get there and Nan's house has been bombed too? No, she decides, it's best to stay here where Mum can find them.

'We have to be here for when Mum gets home,' she says.

'Father Nally will help us,' Grace says.

'Father McNally,' corrects Billy. 'Yes, Missus Kelly said he was a friend of everyone. Maybe he'll be our friend.'

'I think that's a good idea Grace. You're full of good ideas today, aren't you. Come on, we'll go to Mrs Kelly's church and see if Father McNally is there.'

The church is in darkness when they arrive but the big, wooden doors are unlocked. They are heavy and creak loudly as Maggie pushes them open

'We'll wait inside the church until he comes,' says Maggie. 'We can lie down on the pews.'

'It's scary,' says Billy.

Maggie agrees with her, but she knows she has to be brave so instead she says:

'Mrs Kelly's says this is God's house, so we'll be safe here. His angels will protect us.'

'I like angels,' says Grace. 'They've got wings, like fairies.'

'It's cold,' Billy complains.

'Let's cuddle up together and then we'll be warmer.'

She is glad she found her coat, she buttons it up to the neck and tucks her hands into her pockets. A tiny prick on her finger reminds her of the piece of blue wood she took from the door. She holds it between her finger and thumb and rubs it gently. She must not lose it. As long as she has it she knows their mother will be able to find them.

'What if he doesn't come tonight?' asks Billy.

He is shivering.

'He'll come. Don't you remember, Mrs Kelly always went to Mass at six o'clock.'

His face brightens and he says:

'Yes, cos Mum used to say Mrs Kelly should stay at home with us and listen to "The Hi Gang Show" but she always went to church instead.'

'Hi Gang,' chirps Grace.

'Hi Ben,' Billy replies.

They laugh.

'That's my favourite programme,' says Billy.

'So you see he'll come to do the Mass,' says Maggie. 'And well, if he doesn't, we'll just have to sleep here tonight.'

As she says it Maggie gives a shudder; the idea of sleeping in the church, even if it is God's house, frightens her. There are dead people in the cemetery; she saw the gravestones as they came in.

'The Germans won't get us here,' says Billy, snuggling closer to his sister.

They must have fallen asleep because the next thing Maggie knows is that someone is shaking her by the arm.

'Wake up child. What do you think you are doing in here?'

Maggie sits up and rubs her eyes. Her mouth feels dry and her arm hurts. She must have been lying on it.

'Uh, we want to see Father McNally,' she whispers. 'We want him to help us.'

The woman is a small, dark haired woman and she speaks a bit like Mrs Kelly. She looks at them for a moment then says:

'All right. Stay here and I'll see if he's arrived yet.'

Maggie stands up and stretches; she is cold and stiff. Billy and Grace are still sleeping. Billy is stretched out across two faded kneelers, his arms flung open and Grace is curled up in a ball next to him. She decides to let them sleep a little longer. It seems to be taking a long time to find Father McNally and Maggie can feel herself getting drowsy again. Then she hears footsteps and whispered voices; she looks round. The priest is coming down the aisle towards them, his robes billowing around him like a huge black cape; the woman trots behind. When they reach Maggie they stop and look down at her.

'Well I never. You're the children that were with Kate Kelly this morning aren't you?' he booms.

Maggie nods. The sound of his voice wakes the others. Billy sits up, rubbing his eyes and Grace starts to whimper.

'Shush Gracie, it's all right. It's Father McNally.'

'So what are you doing here? Where's Mrs Kelly?' the priest asks.

He sits down on the bench beside them.

'We don't know,' Maggie replies. 'We were at Sunday school when the bombs came, then when we went home we couldn't find her.'

'Stanlet Street was bombed,' whispers the woman.

'Mrs Kelly's house is gone,' Grace says.

'And our house,' adds Billy.

'Mrs Kelly had a Ansen shelter,' Grace volunteers.

'What about your parents?'

'Mum's in the hospital   We went there but they have all gone,' Maggie says. 'They moved them somewhere safer.'

She is close to tears but bites her lip so that she won't cry.

'And your Dad?'

'He's dead,' says Billy. 'He was killed in France.'

'My goodness.'

'You poor little lambs,' the woman says, bending down and giving Grace a hug.

'So, what are we going to do with you, I wonder,' Father McNally says.

He stands up.   People are beginning to arrive for the six o'clock Mass.   They crowd down the main aisle; some look across curiously at the children.

'Take them along to the vestry for now Mrs Biggs and we'll decide what to do after Mass,' he tells her.

They follow the woman through to the vestry.   It will be all right now, Maggie is sure.   Father McNally will help them find their mother. They are safe now.

IRENE

The journey to Bushey takes hours. They are all bundled into an old coach that, by the look of the worn seats and scratched paintwork, has seen plenty of years of service. There are about twenty of them in all, nine mothers and their babies and two hospital staff. They have only sent an orderly, an oldish man, maybe fifty, she thinks and a midwife to look after them. The rest of the nursing staff have been transferred to the district hospital to help with last night's casualties.

She looks around the bus; what a sad little group they are. One woman only gave birth a couple of hours before and she half lies, half sits on the back seat with her newly born baby next to her, wrapped in a hospital blanket. The rest sit staring out the windows at the devastation that surrounds them. She knows most of them by name now because she has been there for over a week. Apart from one woman in her forties, Irene is the oldest there. She feels old and tired beside all these young mothers, many of them having just had their first child. Maybe it's the thought of having to face life on her own that makes her feel so exhausted; bringing up four kids is not going to be easy.

'Everyone all right?' the midwife calls down the bus.

'There's something wrong with my baby,' a young girl, no more than sixteen, replies. 'He won't stop crying.'

The midwife lurches to the back of the bus.

'You need to change his nappy, dear. The poor little mite is soaked.'

'Here, I'll help you,' says Irene.

Leslie is fast asleep, wrapped up in her coat on the seat beside her. Gently, so as not to disturb him, she moves across to the seat opposite the girl.

'Did they give you some Vaseline to put on his bottom?'

'Yes, I've got it here.'

The girl pulls out a cloth bag and empties it onto the seat. Irene picks up the baby.

'He's a lovely little chap.'

The girl begins to cry.

'She's a girl.'

'Even better.'

'They won't let me keep her,' she wails. 'My dad says I'm too young. He says she has to be adopted.'

'Oh my dear, I am sorry.'

She notices that the girl has no wedding ring. Gently she unwraps the baby from its swaddling of hospital sheets and removes the soggy nappy.

'I'm going to that Mother and Baby Home in Stepney,' the girl explains. 'They take care of everything for you.'

She sniffles, dragging her sleeve across her face to wipe away the tears.

'Mum says it's for the best.'

Irene looks at the baby. She has stopped crying and is gurgling happily.

'I expect your mum's right,' she says.

She looks across at her own new baby. Poor little Leslie. What a start to life he has had: no Dad and a weak heart and there is not much she can do about either.

'Do you know where we're going?' the girl asks.

'Not really. All I heard was something about a maternity home in Bushey. It's just for a while, until we're fit enough to go home.'

'I've got to stay in the Mother and Baby Home until the baby's six weeks old,' the girl says.

She starts to cry again.

Irene closes the nappy pin carefully and rewraps the baby in her sheet.

'There you are, one clean, happy baby. Maybe she'd like a feed,' she suggests, handing the baby girl back to her mother.

The girl looks down the bus. The orderly is sitting at the front chatting to the driver. She lifts her blouse and pulls out her breast. The baby greedily attaches herself to the swollen teat.

'You're right, she is hungry.'

'Babies are always hungry. Will you be all right now?'

The girl nods.

'Thanks.'

'That's all right.'

Irene moves back to her seat; Leslie is still asleep. He is a good little chap, so like Ronnie to look at, except that his skin has a bluish tinge to it. The doctor says that is because he is not getting enough oxygen; his heart is not strong enough to pump the blood round his body. It has a leaky valve or something. She was so upset when he told her that she did not take everything in and now she wishes that she had asked him more questions. All she really understands is that Leslie cannot go home yet; he is still too weak. The doctor said he would probably have to go to the Great Ormond Street Hospital to have an operation once he was a bit stronger. Poor little mite, he is very small to have an operation. And how is she going to pay for it?

In the meantime they are going to Bushey to get away from the air-raids but for how long? And what about her other children? Will Kate be able to cope with them? Her friend has told her repeatedly not to worry, that she can manage just fine, but it's a lot to ask of her, after all she has never had any children of her own. She should have sent the kids to her mother's but Kate had insisted. She said it wasn't fair to give Irene's mother more work when she had enough to do, looking after Irene's father. After all it was only supposed to be for a few days.

The bus lurches to a stop. There is a convoy of army lorries crossing ahead of them; she can see the khaki uniforms of the soldiers packed in the back. For a moment her heart gives a leap of excitement then she remembers that Ronnie is dead; he is not one of those laughing young men leaning out to get a glimpse of the pretty women in the bus. A black cloud of despair settles over her. This dreadful war, it's taking everything from her.

The convoy passes and the bus continues on its way north. They are heading for Islington and the A1. She wonders if her mother is at home. All she has to do is tell the driver to stop and she could get off and walk to her mother's house; it's not far. She looks at her little son, sleeping peacefully beside her. No, she will stick it out for him; he deserves the chance of a better life.

The streets they are passing through have obviously been bombed quite recently and she looks at the devastation and shudders. A heavy pall of dust hangs over everything and the acrid smell of burning still floats in the air. People are scurrying about in the rubble, trying to salvage what few possessions they can. There is a bleakness in their faces that she feels reflects her own feelings. Only one thought is in people's minds these days: how to survive the war.

She looks across at the young girl opposite her; both mother and baby seem contented now. She feels a wave of sympathy for her. That could so easily have been her; she had not been much older when Maggie was born.

She met Ronnie at a dance the year she turned sixteen. It was the first time she had been to a dance. Her Dad was always very strict about what she did and where she went, but once she had left school, he had been forced to allow her more freedom. She had gone to the dance with Belle and Ruth, her best friends. The three of them went everywhere together, inseparable since schooldays. That was until she met Ronnie. She liked the look of him straight away and they started courting almost immediately.

She had been a pretty little thing in those days, or so everyone told her; her nose was small and turned-up, there were dimples in her cheeks and she had straight, even teeth. She sighs and her tongue automatically feels its way around the gap left by the three missing molars. It was the babies they said, took all the goodness out of your body. She used to roll her long, brown hair up, away from her face and fix it in place with clips. Belle said she looked like Ida Lupino. Ronnie never commented but, when they were alone, he liked to remove the hair clips and let her hair cascade down onto her shoulders. Again she sighs. Well, she has no time for anything like that now.

The bus is moving more quickly now. She picks Leslie up and holds him steady against her chest. She can see the grim outline of Holloway Prison dwindling away to her right. They are moving into new territory. She has never been so far north before. The scenery is changing; there are more green spaces, trees and parks. She wonders if they are nearly there.

Ronnie got on well with her family, especially her two older brothers. They were all pleased that she had a steady boyfriend. Her mother said it would quieten her down a bit, although Irene never really understood what she had meant by that remark. Everything had been fine at first; he came round to take her out dancing every Saturday night and on Sundays they would go for a walk in the park. She was working in the Co-op then, on the cash desk and her only free time was Sundays. She earned one pound ten shillings a week, gave a pound to her mother and kept the other ten shillings for herself. Life seemed perfect. Then she found out that she was pregnant. What a bombshell that had been. She did not know who to tell. In the end she confided in Ruth, who convinced her that she would not be able to keep her condition a secret for long and that she should tell her mother as soon as possible. Of course then her mother told her Dad. Well, that was that. The following Sunday Ronnie was summoned into the front parlour and told that he had no option; he was to marry her or else. To give him his due, Ronnie had been quite relaxed about it.

'We were going to get married anyway,' he told everyone.

So they were married, quietly, hoping no-one outside the family would realise she was in the family way. It had been winter so she had worn her blue coat, a cavernous thing of fine tweed, to hide her swelling belly. Ronnie had been wonderful. She was so proud of him. He looked very handsome in his new blue suit with a carnation in his button hole.

They could not afford a honeymoon, but her parents paid for a bit of a party at their local pub. Ruth and Belle were invited and a couple of Ronnie's mates from the football club, but otherwise it was just family. Later he took her back to his parents' home in Bethnal Green. She has been there ever since.

'Not much further ladies,' the bus driver calls back to them. 'We'll soon have you all tucked up in bed again.'

She sees him turn round and smirk at them.

It was not easy living with Ronnie's parents, but they could not afford a place of their own and there was no room at her parents' house. Still, Ronnie's parents were very kind to her. They were much older than her mother and father and Ronnie was their only child. As his Dad said at the reception, they were pleased to have gained a daughter after all those years. When they told them about the baby, instead of being shocked as she had expected, they were delighted to learn that they would have a grandchild so soon. They gave them Ronnie's old room and later let them use the spare room as well. Those were happy days, before the war.

That dragging feeling of loneliness settles on her again. She moves her son to her other arm and holds him closer to her chest; he continues to sleep, rocked by the motion of the bus.

St Margaret's Maternity Home is a converted Victorian mansion, with high turrets and a red brick facade. The bus trundles up a winding drive that leads them through an overgrown and neglected garden to where a welcoming committee of fresh faced young women in blue uniforms is waiting for them. With the minimum of formality they are all escorted to the maternity ward that has been allocated for them.

Their room is long and airy; its windows looking out over the gardens. Her bed is at the far end, close to the bathroom. What a relief she thinks as soon as she sees it; she will not have to creep down the length of the ward in the night when she is caught short. The young girl, whose name she has by now discovered is Jane, is given the bed opposite. She does not seem to have recovered her spirits and lies down immediately, burying her face in her pillow.

Irene places her baby in the cot beside the bed. He is beginning to stir; he will want feeding soon. There is a blue and white hospital nightdress laid out on the bed. Carefully she removes her clothes and puts it on. It seems ridiculous going to bed in the middle of the day when she is neither tired nor unwell. Still that is the procedure and she does not dare argue with the midwife who has only just barked out her orders to the newcomers. Anyway she might as well get as much rest as she can. God knows she will get little enough of it when she goes home.

There is a sudden commotion at the far end of the ward. It's the doctor, followed by an entourage of eager young nurses. He moves from bed to bed, dispensing news, some good, some bad. Two of the women are told that they and their babies can go home, another that her baby has not survived the night. He stops in front of Jane's bed and looks at her disapprovingly. Irene hears him tell her brusquely that she can leave the next day; there will be a bus to take her to the Mother and Baby Home in Stepney. She can see Jane's face looking up at him; it's white and tearful. Poor girl, she is not much more than a child herself. She cannot imagine what it must be like to give away your child; the mere thought of it makes her stomach turn to water. She thinks of her own little family. What will they be doing now? Maggie and Billy will probably be at school. And little Gracie? She smiles as she thinks of her beautiful little daughter. She will be at home with Kate.

The doctor turns and comes across to her bed. His manner softens as he approaches her; now he is all smiles. What a difference a wedding ring makes, she thinks.

'Mrs Smith, how are you today?'

'I'm fine doctor. Can I go home now? It's been ten days already. I need to get back to my family.'

'Just a few more days Mrs Smith. I realise that you want to get back to your children but right now this little chap needs you more.'

'I thought he was going to go into hospital?'

The doctor nods.

'He must have an operation just as soon as he's strong enough. The problem is that I'm having trouble finding him a bed. Great Ormond Street was bombed last night; all their patients have been transferred to other hospitals. I'm trying to get the Evelina to take him but it may take a few more days. You will just have to be patient my dear, after all, there is a war on,' he adds.

As if I don't know, she thinks, and once again a wave of self-pity sweeps over her and tears fill her eyes.

'This must be costing a fortune,' she says 'How can I pay for it all?'

For a moment he frowns at her then says:

'We'll worry about that once the baby's better.'

'Is there any way I can get in touch with my family?' she asks, her voice breaking as she struggles to hold back her tears.

'Sister will help you with that,' he says. 'Now, now, chin up my dear.'

He picks up his clip board and moves on to the next patient. The nurses follow him.

'You going home?' Jane calls across the ward.

'Not today,'

'I'm leaving tomorrow,' she says.

'Yes, I heard.'

'I'll miss you. It's lonely with no visitors.'

'Maybe your Mum will come to visit you at the Home.'

'No, I don't think so.'

'What about the baby's dad?' Irene asks.

'He's in the navy. I don't expect I'll hear from him again.'

'Does he know about the baby?'

'No, I couldn't get in touch with him. Didn't have his address or nothing.'

Maybe her mother is right; maybe it is for the best. After all, how can this scrap of a girl bring up her baby on her own?

'I thought of writing to his ship, but I only had his first name and I was too embarrassed to do it.'

'Mrs Smith, Doctor says you want a word with me.'

The ward sister stops by her bed.

'Oh yes, Sister. The doctor says I can't go home yet and I need to get in touch with my family. They don't know where I am.'

'Oh I'm sure they do. We left clear instructions at the hospital that all visitors were to be informed of their families' whereabouts,' she says in a matter-of-fact voice.

'But no-one's been to see me for days now.'

'I expect they're busy.'

'But you don't understand, my friend is looking after my children. She promised to come and see me every day. I know she wouldn't break her promise.'

'Is there any way we can get in touch with her?'

'I don't know. She lives next door to me, her house is in Stanlet Street, in Bethnal Green.'

'I'll see what I can do but I can't promise anything. Don't worry, I expect you'll be going home in a few days anyway.'

'What about my mother, couldn't somebody get in touch with her?'

'Write down her address and I'll give it to the almoner. Maybe she can help.'

'Oh thank you.'

Hurriedly Irene scribbles her mother's name and address on a piece of paper and gives it to the Sister.

'Now I can't promise anything, mind you.'

As she moves away, the woman in the bed on Irene's left speaks.

'You're from down near Hanbury Road, aren't you? I thought I'd seen you before. My Sam says there's been dreadful bombing raids every night this week. Maybe your friend's got caught up in that.'

'Did he say where exactly?'

'No, just somewhere in the East End, but I think Bethnal Green was one of them.'

'Oh my God, no.'

'Well now, don't take on so; I might have that wrong. Maybe it was Stepney or Hackney. I'm sorry I wasn't listening all that closely. Look, he's coming to see me again tonight. I'll ask him then.'

Irene does not answer. She rolls over onto her side and buries her face in the pillow. This awful war, it's destroying them. What has happened to her children? Where are they? Are they all right?

MAGGIE

They follow Father McNally through the damp, dark streets. The Blackout means that there are no street lights and no light from any of the houses. It's hard to see where they are walking; even the stars and moon are hidden behind dark rain clouds. She would like to take hold of the priest's robe but she is frightened to do so, besides which, both her hands are occupied holding on to Billy and Grace. So she drags them along as fast as their legs can manage, trying to match the priest's long strides.

'Come on Gracie, keep up, it's not far now,' she whispers encouragingly.

'You're squeezing my hand,' complains Billy.

'Sorry.'

She relaxes her grip slightly. The air is heavy with the smell of cordite and dust and there is a fine drizzle that soaks her hair. The priest is striding ahead, oblivious of them, his head down, his black robes billowing around him. Maggie shivers with cold despite the scarf that Mrs Biggs has given her.

'Where are we going?' asks Billy.

Maggie can sense that he is close to crying again.

'Father McNally is taking us to the nuns. They'll look after us until we can find Mum.'

'Will we have some supper?' asks Billy.

'I hope so.'

The mention of food makes her stomach rumble. None of them has eaten anything since lunchtime; it seems such a long time ago.

'Maggie, aeroplane,' whispers Grace. 'Is it going to bomb us?'

She squeezes Maggie's hand; she is trembling.

'It's not a plane, silly,' says Billy. 'It's just an old lorry.'

As he speaks a black shape hurtles around the corner and drives past them, throwing up a spray of cold water.

'Hey, I'm soaked,' Billy cries out, pulling away from Maggie.

'Now, now children, calm down. We don't want the nuns to think you're badly behaved now, do we,' Father McNally says, giving them his attention at last.

He stops and peers down at them.

'Well, we're here now. You'll soon be out of this dreadful rain and warm and dry in no time.'

Maggie fancies he is smiling at them but she cannot see his face in the dark. She takes Billy's hand again.

Directly in front of them is a big wooden door. Father McNally reaches up and pulls hard on an iron chain. A loud ringing can be heard echoing through the building.

'Is this where the nuns live?' she asks him.

It's a grim looking building.

'Yes, my child. This is St Margaret's Orphanage.'

An orphanage. Her stomach turns over. She knows what orphanages are; they are for children with no parents.

'But ...', she falters.

'Don't worry child, this is just until we can find your mother. The nuns are very kind; they will look after you.'

As he speaks, the heavy door swings open and she can see the figure of an old woman wearing a nun's habit. Maggie does not think she looks very kind; she looks like a witch. Her hair is scraped back into her white cap but the rest of her clothes are long and black. Although the nun smiles when she sees Father McNally, her eyes are cold when she looks down at them and her lips are compressed into a thin tight line.

'Good evening Sister Mary.'

'Father McNally, come in. What brings you out on such a dreadful night?'

'Is the Mother Superior at home?'

'Yes. She was in the chapel, but I think she has finished her devotions now. I'll go and get her.'

She opens the door just enough to allow them to pass through, then lets it close behind them with a clang. She does not seem very interested in the children; she does not ask him who they are.

'Please have a seat Father. I'll be right back.'

Father McNally removes his wide brimmed hat and brushes the raindrops from it. He sits down on a long bench and motions for the children to do the same.

Maggie feels nervous. She looks around her. The room is cold and bare except for the bench on which they are sitting and a large wooden cross that hangs on the wall. The smell of boiled cabbage floats up from somewhere in the recesses of the building. She thinks she might be sick. Grace is squeezing her hand so much it feels as though her circulation is being cut off.

'It's all right Grace,' she whispers and loosens the little girl's grip on her.

She can feel her sister trembling, so she puts her arm around her and pulls her closer. Billy sits down on the bench and says nothing but his blue eyes are wide with fear.

After a few minutes the nun returns.

'The Mother Superior will see you now Father,' she says and motions for him to follow her.

'Just wait here children. I won't be long,' he tells them.

Maggie nods, she does not know what to say. She knows the priest is trying to help them but she cannot shake off this feeling of dread. Everything in her body is telling her to get up and run away. But where can they go? Grace is too small to wander around the streets in the dark and anyway the wardens would only pick them up and take them to the police station. Maybe it's best to stay here with the nuns, for now. But will Mum be able to find them?

She gets up quietly.

'Stay here. I'm going to see what's happening. Billy, take Grace's hand and don't let go of it until I get back.'

Billy opens his mouth to protest, but Maggie gives him a look that says, don't you dare.

She creeps down the corridor in the direction taken by Father McNally and the nun. After a few moments she can hear voices. She moves closer to the door so that she can hear better.

'We don't have any room for more children.'

'It's just for a night or two.'

'And you know we don't take boys.'

'But Mother Superior, he's only ten, and quite small still. I thought you took boys up to ten years old.'

'That was before, when we had plenty of space. It's just impossible now. There are so many orphans.'

'Their mother's in the hospital; she'll be home any day now.'

'What about the father?'

'Killed in France.'

There is silence.

'So that's settled then,' Father McNally's voice booms.

'We'll do what we can, Father, but remember it's only for a few days.'

Maggie sees the door handle move, but before the door can open she turns and races back to the hall. Billy and Grace are still sitting on the bench, looking even more worried without her there to protect them.

'What's happening?' Billy whispers.

'Shush, they're coming.'

She slides into place beside him just as Father McNally and Sister Mary reappear.

'Right now children, come along with me,' the nun says.

They stand up and look at Father McNally.

'That's all right children, do as Sister Mary says. You can stay here for a few days until we can locate your mother.'

'Will you come back to see us?' Maggie asks, a tremble in her voice.

The priest smiles.

'Maybe, my child. We'll see. Now you be good and do as the sisters tell you.'

He raises his hand and makes the sign of the cross.

'God bless and keep you.'

The nun gives a little bob and mutters:

'God bless you too, Father.'

She pulls back the bolt on the heavy door and lets the priest out into the black night. As the door swings shut Maggie feels a shiver run up her back. She reaches out and takes her brother and sister by the hand again. The nun regards them coldly.

'This way.'

They follow her along the corridor and into a large room with long tables and benches.

'Sit down there and I'll see if I can get you anything to eat. The kitchen's closed now, but I'm sure I can find you something.'

Obediently they sit at one of the tables and wait. After a few minutes the nun returns with a tray carrying a plate of bread, some jam and three mugs of cocoa.

'That's all there is,' she says as she places it on the table.

'Thank you,' says Maggie.

She takes a slice of bread, spreads some jam on it and cuts it into four pieces before passing it to Grace. Billy helps himself.

'Mmn, this is nice,' he says.

'Don't speak with your mouth full,' the nun snaps.

Maggie chews her bread slowly; her throat feels dry and it's hard to swallow. She tries drinking the cocoa but it's very hot and there is no sugar. The nun is watching them closely. Maggie wants to cry. She wishes Mum was there.

'If you've finished I'll take you to your room.'

They all stand up.

'No, not you. You wait here boy.'

'Can't he come with us? He's our brother,' protests Maggie.

'No, he can't. He can't sleep in the girls' dormitory. I'll make a bed up for him in the pantry.'

At this news Billy turns pale. He is biting his lip and looks as though he will cry.

'Now come along, there's no need for that. You'll see your sisters in the morning.'

'It's all right Billy. We won't be far away. We'll see you at breakfast,' says Maggie, giving her brother a squeeze.

'But I don't want to be on my own,' he whispers.

'Stuff and nonsense. Just stay here until I get back. Now come along girls, I haven't got all night.'

'Can't we sleep with him in the pantry?' asks Maggie. 'We'll be fine together.'

Sleeping in the pantry does not sound like a very inviting prospect; their own pantry had a stone floor and was cold and damp.

'It will be just for one night,' she adds. 'We've never been apart before, you see.'

The nun looks at them and hesitates,

'Holy Mother give me patience. Well, just for tonight, until we can make other arrangements for you. Stay here and I'll go and get some blankets.'

She returns a few minutes later carrying blankets and sheets which she places in front of them.

'Now take these and follow me. And don't make any noise.'

They pick up the bedding and follow the nun back down the corridor and into a small room that reminds Maggie of a doctor's waiting room.

'Is this the pantry?' asks Billy.

The nun glares at him.

'No. This is the Mother Superior's sitting room. This is where she comes to be alone and contemplate.'

Maggie does not think it looks very comfortable for a sitting room. There are no easy chairs like there had been in their sitting room at home and no ornaments but there are some paintings on the walls. She looks closely; there is one of baby Jesus sitting on his mother's knee and another of Mary wearing a blue dress and smiling. She likes the paintings. They make her feel safe.

'Now this is where you'll sleep tonight. If you'd like to go to the bathroom you can come with me now.'

Maggie passes the night fitfully; Grace sleeps like the baby she is, her thumb tucked into her mouth and curled into a ball, while Billy tosses and turns. Occasionally she hears him give a slight whimper in his sleep. The floor of the sitting room is hard but at least they are warm and dry; it's better than sleeping in the church she decides.

It's still dark when the door opens and a young girl in a grey dress comes in to wake them. Her hair is cut short and sticks out unevenly from her head. She smiles at them pleasantly and tells them to get up and follow her.

'Fold your blankets first. You'll have to take them back to the dormitory, later,' she instructs them.

'Where are we going?'

'To the refectory.'

She waits until they are ready and then sets off. Maggie takes Grace's hand and pushes Billy ahead of her. He is still half asleep and grumbles to himself as he trails behind the girl.

'Get a move on Billy; we don't want to be late,' she whispers.

'I'm tired,' he moans.

The girl walks very quickly and Grace has a problem keeping up.

'Excuse me,' Maggie says.

The girl stops and looks at her.

'Do you live here?' asks Maggie. 'Are you an orphan?'

The girl turns away and carries on walking.

'Hurry up. Sister Theresa will murder me if we're late for breakfast,' she says.

At the mention of breakfast Billy's face brightens and he begins to walk more quickly. The girl takes them back to the room they had eaten in the night before but now it's full; there are row upon row of girls, all dressed in the same coarse grey material as their guide, all seated in silence. It's obvious that the girls have been waiting for them to arrive.

'At last Brown. Where have you been, giving them a tour of the premises?' asks a tall nun who is standing on a dais at the end of the room. 'Sit down quickly now. It's already ten past seven.'

They squeeze in at the end of one of the benches and sit down.

'Let us say Grace,' the tall nun says.

Her voice is deep, like a man's.

As one, the whole assembly stand up and bow their heads. The tall nun makes the sign of the cross and begins:

'*Bless us, O Lord, and these Thy gifts which we are about to receive from Thy bounty, through Christ our Lord, Amen.*'

Then the girls sit down again. Maggie thinks it's strange that nobody is speaking.

'Why isn't anyone saying anything?' she whispers to their new companion.

'Shush,' the girl hisses fearfully.

'Brown is that you talking?'

'No Sister Theresa.'

'Stand up. Now you will remain standing throughout breakfast.'

The girl scowls at Maggie.

Two girls from each table go off in the direction of the kitchen and return carrying the trays of food. A bowl is placed in front of each child; they contain what looks like watery porridge. Now Maggie is frightened to move. She looks around her; nobody is touching the food. They all sit, heads down, waiting. She feels Billy's hand reach for the spoon and places her hand on his leg to stop him. This is a very strict place. They will have to be careful.

Once all the bowls have been brought out from the kitchen and the waitresses have sat down, the nun says:

'Now you may eat.'

There is a clatter of spoons as fifty girls attack their porridge eagerly. Maggie cannot understand their enthusiasm because, as far as she can tell, it tastes of nothing at all. Even Billy seems reluctant to eat it. She nudges him, indicating that he must eat it all. The girl referred to as Brown has not been given any porridge. She is standing motionless, staring ahead of her. She is the same age as Maggie. Maggie thinks she looks nice. She feels sorry for her standing there in front of all the children.

'Maggie, I don't like this soup.'

Grace's clear little voice rings out across the dining room. Maggie sees everyone turn and look at them.

'Who was that?' Sister Theresa snaps.

Maggie lifts her hand nervously.

'I'm sorry, it was my little sister. She's only three, she doesn't understand.'

The nun walks towards them, stopping a foot away from Grace. Maggie thinks Grace is going to cry; her eyes are wide and shiny. Any moment tears will fall.

'What is your name child?' the nun asks.

'Gracie. I'm 'free',' she replies.

'Well, Grace, we have a rule here that we don't talk at meal-times. Do you think you can remember that?'

Grace nods her head vigorously.

As the nun turns away her hand brushes against Grace's blonde curls.

'Sit down Brown,' she snaps. 'I'm tired of looking at you.'

The girl slips back into her seat. Maggie pushes Grace's half-eaten porridge across to her. Before the nun can resume her place on the dais, the girl has eaten it and pushed the bowl back again. She smiles at Maggie.

At a signal from the nun the girls stand in unison and file out of the dining room. Maggie notices that some girls remain to clear the tables and others have started to sweep the floor. Their guide motions for them to follow her. Once outside, she stops and says:

'We have to do our chores now.'

'I'm sorry I got you into trouble,' Maggie says. 'I didn't realise. I've never been anywhere where you couldn't talk at break-fast-time.'

'It's not all the time, only when Sister Theresa is on duty. Most of the other nuns let us talk as long as we don't make too much noise.'

'Well, anyway, I'm sorry.'

'Don't worry. That old cow doesn't like me anyway. If it hadn't been that, it would have been something else. My name's Elsie, by the way.'

'Hello Elsie. I'm Maggie and this is Billy, and ...'

'I know, Gracie.'

She pats Grace on the head.

'She's very sweet. Old sourpuss thinks so anyway. I've never seen her smile before. Didn't think she was able to.'

'What do we have to do?'

'I'm in charge of wets today. You can help me.'

'Wets?'

'You'll see. First we have to take Billy out to the gardener then we'll pick up your blankets.'

Billy is deposited, rather reluctantly, with the gardener and set to sweeping up the dead leaves that cover the back lawn. Then Maggie and Grace follow Elsie up to the dormitories.

'There are two dormitories, one for the younger girls and one for the older ones. We have to clean the first one.'

'Don't the girls have to make their own beds? I always make my bed at home.'

At the thought of home, Maggie feels a tightening in her throat. There is no home now; it has gone, bombed out of existence. She wonders if Mum knows about it yet. Will someone have told her what has happened to Mrs Kelly? She will be worrying about them, Maggie is sure; she will probably be trying to come for them right now. She hopes that Father McNally will find her soon and tell her that they are all right.

'Yes, we all make our beds. What you and I have to do, is change the wet ones. Then we have to scrub the floor.'

She points to a sodden sheet on a nearby bed.

'I'll go and get some water while you strip the wet sheets off the beds.'

'How many are there?'

'Depends, usually there're about ten, but there may be less today because Sister Alice was not on duty last night.'

'Sister Alice?'

'She's awful, worse than Sister Theresa. If she catches anyone wetting the bed, she makes them strip off and beats them with a ruler.'

Maggie cannot speak. What if Grace wets the bed? She has done it before but Mum has never been cross with her.

She starts pulling at the wet sheets. The smell is awful.

'Drag them into the middle of the room and we'll take them down to the laundry together.'

'I'll help you, Maggie,' pipes up Grace.

'No. Don't touch those smelly sheets. Go and sit over there and tell us if you see anyone coming.'

Elsie looks at her in surprise.

'It's unhygienic,' Maggie tells her. 'Grace is only a baby, after all.'

'I think you'll find that the nuns have a different view. Everyone here has to work for their keep.'

'We're only going to be here for a few days, just until they find our Mum,' Maggie explains.

She wants to keep repeating these words; only then can she continue to believe them.

'All right, well here's the water. Now you have to wash down the plastic mattress and when it's dry we put a clean sheet on it. I'll start over there; you do this one.'

The two of them set to work.

MOTHER SUPERIOR

The Mother Superior sits down heavily in her big, leather chair. Just lately her back has been giving her a lot of trouble; if only there was something she could do about it. She spoke to the doctor when he came to give the girls their annual check-up but he said it was just old age; there was nothing to be done. She should have retired by now; she is after all nearly seventy but the Bishop has asked her to carry on until the war is over. So she has prayed for relief from her pain but it seems that God has decided that this is to be her cross and she must bear it alone.

There is a knock on the door.

'Come in.'

Two nuns enter.

'Good morning Sisters. What can I do for you?'

'Good morning Mother Superior,' they chorus.

The Mother Superior motions for them to sit down.

'Well?' she asks.

'It's about the new children.'

'We really don't have any room for any more children.'

'We are only supposed to take forty girls and already we have fifty.'

'With the new ones, it'll be fifty-two.'

The two nuns prattle on; it's enough to give her a headache.

'I am quite aware of how many children we have, Sister Magdalene,' she says.

'And the boy.'

'What do we do with the boy?'

'We can't cater for boys.'

The Mother Superior sighs.

'So what do you suggest we do, Sister Lilian?' she asks.

The two nuns look at each other and hesitate. The Mother Superior waits for a moment then asks:

'Well, what do we know about these children?'

'Only what Father McNally has told us.'

'Their father was killed in the war and their mother is missing.'

'So who has been looking after them?' the Mother Superior asks.

'A Mrs Kelly, one of Father McNally's parishioners.'

'And where is she?'

'She's dead. Her house was bombed the other night.'

'And the children's house?'

'Bombed as well.'

'What do we know about the mother?'

'Very little.'

'So it's possible that she's dead too?'

Both nuns nod.

'Any other family, grandparents, aunts?'

'We don't think so, otherwise the children would have been with them rather than Mrs Kelly.'

'True.'

'We just don't have any room for them,' repeats Sister Lilian.

'Well, maybe we could send them up to Pontefract, to the Sisters of Mercy. That would get them out of London and away from the bombing,' the Mother Superior suggests at last.

'We considered that but the Sisters of Mercy say they are already overloaded.'

'It's the evacuees, you see.'

The Mother Superior nods.

'St. Mary's in Wexford?'

'The same.'

'Well Sisters, what do you suggest?' she repeats.

Her back is killing her. She desperately wants to get up and walk in the garden for a while.

'What about the Crusade of Rescue? Maybe they could take them?' Sister Magdalene asks.

The Mother Superior shakes her head.

'They might but it takes a long time to organise. What do we do with them in the meantime?'

Sister Lilian hesitates then says:

'My cousin works for the Government, with the Children's Overseas Reception Board. She says they are always sending ships to Australia or Canada, with homeless children on board. We could send them there.'

'Send them to Australia?' the Mother Superior asks.

'The Poor Sisters of Nazareth have some excellent orphanages in Australia.'

'And the children would grow up in a wonderful climate, with lots of good food.'

'They'd be safe from the bombing.'

'And would have a wonderful opportunity for a new life.'

'I don't know. It's a long way to send them. The journey could be dangerous,' the Mother Superior replies.

'It's more dangerous for them to stay here.'

She looks at the nuns. Their faces are shining with enthusiasm. Obviously they think this is a wonderful plan. Well, maybe they are right. She can see the possibilities in what they are proposing. If only the pain in her back would let up for a moment she would be able to think more clearly.

'How do you know if there are any free spaces?' she asks.

'I can find out.'

'So what if we do send them to the Poor Sisters of Nazareth, what about the boy? They won't take the boy.'

'We send him to the Christian Brothers. They have a farm school in Western Australia.'

'He'd learn a trade.'

'And they'd all be brought up as good Catholics,' adds Sister Magdalene.

This final argument makes sense; it's her duty, as Mother Superior, to ensure that all the children that come into her care have a decent Catholic upbringing. It seems that the nuns have come up with a perfect solution.   After all, the children are probably orphans; they certainly are destitute and homeless.   They will have a much better life in Australia.

'Very well, Sister Magdalene, ring the Sisters of Nazareth in Melbourne and see what they can arrange.   Sister Lilian, get in touch with your cousin and ask her if she has room for three children on the next voyage.   I'll speak to Father McNally.'

'Thank you Mother Superior, we'll get on to it right away.'

JEREMY ACTON-DUNN

Ever since they opened in June, the London offices of the newly formed Children's Overseas Reception Board has been inundated with requests from distraught parents to send their children overseas. Now the war at sea is threatening their plans.

'Close the door on your way out, Miriam,' Jeremy Acton-Dunn tells his secretary, as he sits down at the end of the meeting table.

In his boss's absence, he is the Chairman today.

'Right now, Jeremy, what's this all about?' asks Archie, a tall, military looking man in his early sixties.

'Sir Percy asked me to call the meeting; he's worried about how things are going.'

'Where is the old sod, anyway?' asks Dickie.

'He's had to go to a funeral.'

'A funeral? Well, what's so bloody important that it can't wait until he gets back?'

Dickie is grossly overweight and whenever he gets agitated he begins to sweat profusely. Now he takes out a large, white handkerchief and mops his forehead vigorously.

'It's not exactly that, it's well,' Jeremy hesitates. 'He just wants us to discuss a few things before he gets back. You know, try to clarify a few objectives and that.'

'All right, well spit it out. I, for one, haven't got all day.'

He folds the handkerchief and puts it back in his pocket.

'OK. It's like this,' Jeremy continues.

He looks around the table. He knows his colleagues well; they worked together in other departments before the Children's

Overseas Reception Board was formed. At least two of them, Dickie Conway and Archie Pennington-Smythe, have been working in child migration for some years. Archie certainly is convinced of the value of their work. Only Victoria Bell is new to child migration; she has been seconded from the Health Department, where she was involved in the evacuation of children from inner city homes to the countryside. He takes a deep breath and says:

'As I'm sure you know, Churchill doesn't approve of what we're doing here.'

'Hrmmph.'

'He says it's too dangerous to send unprotected children across the sea during wartime.'

'Well, what else are we supposed to do with them? Leave them here to get bombed to smithereens?' asks Dickie.

'It's the U-boats, they're a menace to shipping. Ever since the *"Volendam"* was torpedoed last month, the government has been jittery. If another boatload of children goes down they think people will blame them.'

'There were no fatalities,' interjects Victoria, from the far end of the table.

'That's true, but we may not be so lucky next time. We have to think of the children; they are our priority.'

'But what about the parents? They're the ones who are keen to send their children away. We've had over 200,000 applications since June,' says Archie.

'It's amazing. I can't understand why parents want to send their children halfway across the world on their own. You'd think they would want to keep them here, with them,' comments the woman. 'Why don't they just send them into the country with the evacuees?'

'But what if there's a German invasion?' continues Archie.

'Yes, Archie's right, I'm sure they feel it's for the best. My own children have gone to South Africa to stay with their grandmother,' he tells them. 'My wife is heartbroken but we know it's the safest thing for them.'

'Don't you miss them?' she asks.

'Of course we miss them but at least we know they're safe,' he repeats.

'Most parents know it's for the children's own good. They get a magnificent new start in life, they're safe from the war and they're well looked after,' adds Dickie.

'I suppose so, but most of these applications are from wealthy families,' she continues.

'If you can afford it why shouldn't you pay for your children to go to safety until the war's over,' replies Dickie. 'I know I would, if I had any kids.'

'It's not just rich kids, you know. We're trying to do the very best for all the children. What sort of life would some of them have if they stayed here? Many have lost their parents, lost their homes and a lot never had very much to start with anyway. Come on, Victoria, you've seen the squalor that some of these kids come from. A new life in Canada or Australia's far better for them,' Archie says.

'I think that smacks of nineteenth century ethics, better to cut their ties with poverty than leave them with their families.'

Victoria's voice has risen an octave. Jeremy hopes she is not going to be difficult over this.

'Well, maybe that's the only way for some kids. Even without the war, what future have they got here?' he asks.

'Whereas?'

'Whereas in Australia they can build a new life.'

'Nothing to do with the fact that the colonies need manpower?' she asks.

What is this woman getting at? She is becoming irritating now.

'Of course, but we must be realistic. Canada and Australia need people but they want British people,' he tells her.

'Good British stock.'

'Now you're being ridiculous; you make it sound like cattle rearing.'

'And even better if they're children, easier to train, more adaptable and long working lives ahead of them.'

'It's not like that. We're trying to help these kids,' Archie interjects.

'Voluntary agencies have been sending children out to the colonies for years. By and large the schemes have worked well,' adds Dickie. 'We wouldn't be doing it otherwise.'

'Besides which, it's not as though they're just dumped off in a strange country with no back-up. In Australia for example, as you very well know, they come under the guardianship of the Commonwealth Minister of the Interior,' Archie reminds her.

'So what does Sir Percy want us to do?' asks Rupert, looking at his watch impatiently.

So far he has been silent on the subject. Rupert Barnes is a retired naval officer and is only there because Churchill feels that there should be some military presence at the meetings. At first Sir Percy objected to this addition to his team but the Prime Minister was adamant. Personally Jeremy feels it's just to make the old boy feel useful.

'Well, he thinks we should listen to Churchill. There's no naval protection for any of our liners now; they just can't spare the ships for the convoys. He thinks we should put the overseas emigration of children on hold until after the war.'

'Well, if that's what Winnie wants, I suppose that's what we'll have to do,' Archie says.

'But is it feasible?' asks Dickie.

'I don't see why not. We don't really have any option.'

Dickie gives an exasperated sigh and pulls out a packet of cigarettes.

'How does that leave us now?' asks Jeremy.

He turns to Victoria. She is consulting the sheaf of papers on the desk before her.

'Well, the "*City of Benares*" has just left for Canada and we've got two more ships ready to sail. "*SS Castle*" leaves for Canada on the thirteenth; it's got a full manifesto,' she says, reading from her notes. 'And the "*SS Orinoco*" is due to sail on the sixteenth to Melbourne.'

'Right, well then, we have no choice but to go ahead with them,' says Archie.

'Is the "*Orinoco*" full?' asks Jeremy.

'No, I don't think so. Most of the children on our waiting lists are bound for Canada; there're not that many for Australia.'

She flicks through her papers.

'Yes, at the moment there're only sixty children on the "*Orinoco's*" manifesto but it's quite possible that they may add some troops at the last minute. The last ship we sent to Australia had five hundred troops bound for Singapore.'

'Well, let's see if we can round up a few more kids for the voyage. It could be the last chance any of them will have to get off this island. Get in touch with the Overseas Settlement Board and see if they have any children waiting to go to Australia,' he tells her.

'All right Jeremy, I'll see what I can do.'

'What about the orphanages,' suggests Rupert.

'Yes, good idea.'

He turns to Victoria.

'Best to speak to Catherine Smart, she liaises with all the voluntary agencies: Barnados, the Catholic Emigration Association, the Salvation Army and all that lot.'

'All right.'

'What type of child is on the list at the moment? We need a good mix, you know,' Dickie reminds them.

Victoria studies the names carefully.

'I'd say, by looking at their schools, about half are from well-to-do backgrounds and the rest are working class or lower-working class. Mostly C of E but, by the look of the names, there are a few Jews and a handful of Roman Catholics. I can check if you want.'

'No, just a rough idea is all we need.'

'All English?' asks Dickie.

'No, we've quite a few Welsh and some Scots, also three from Northern Ireland.'

'Ask Catherine to try the Roman Catholic orphanages first, to see what they have.'

She scribbles something on her notes.

Jeremy looks down at his agenda.

'The next item is to do with staffing. Have we got a full complement of staff for each of the ships?'

'Yes, the usual ratio on "*SS Castle*", one escort for every fifteen children.'

'Doctors, nurses?'

'Yes.'

'Who do you have as the clerical escorts?' asks Dickie.

'Your old friend, Father Michael, a couple of his curates and two C of E chaplains. Oh and there's also Rabi Katz.'

'Father Michael must have done that crossing now at least twice.'

'Yes, this'll be his third trip to Canada.'

'What about the "*Orinoco*"?'

'No, I've still to finalise that.'

'Of course, best to wait until you see how many children you've got first.'

She nods.

'Is that all Jeremy? Only I'm supposed to be interviewing some new escorts at eleven.'

'Yes, you run along. We've just about finished anyway.'

'So that's agreed then; there's to be no more sea evacuees until further notice,' says Archie.

'That's what it looks like. Sir Percy will fill in the details when he gets back.'

'Right, well we'd better get these last two ships on their way as soon as we can before they put the block on them too.'

Jeremy gets up and opens the window; a pall of cigarette smoke hangs in the air. He flaps a newspaper, ineffectually; damn Dickie and his foul Egyptian cigarettes. Now that the others have left he can get on with his report. He sits down at his desk and opens the file of papers before him. Churchill wants a detailed report of their activities. He has all the statistics in front of him: three thousand children evacuated to the colonies between July and September, a good achievement by any standard. But how can he explain to their new Prime Minster the real success of the venture, three thousand young lives saved, three thousand opportunities for a new life. Some of these children, his own, for example, will return, but many will stay. They will take the British blood line to the colonies and ensure that the Commonwealth remains British in more than just name.

Now Churchill wants them to stop sending children overseas. Too dangerous, he says. Jeremy thinks about the *Volendam*; true there were no casualties but there could have been. Three hundred children had to abandon the ship after it was struck by a torpedo and take to the lifeboats. They were adrift in the Atlantic, prey to any passing U-boat, until they were rescued. They had been very lucky.

What does it mean for the future of CORB? Will they be disbanded or continue processing the hundreds of thousands of applications that they have already received? Will their work continue when the war is over? Surely the government must recognise the importance of what they are doing. After the war there will be even more need to find homes for the thousands of war orphans that will be dependent on them.

He moves the photograph of his children so that he can see it better. It's true what he told Victoria, he does miss his children. It's strange, he does not know why he feels their absence so keenly. After all both boys have been away at boarding school since they were eight years old. Maybe it's the distance, knowing that there is an ocean between them now, maybe it's the feeling that his family has been split in two, maybe it's because Penny cries whenever he mentions them. The thought of his wife's pain makes him sigh. He has tried to explain to her that there is nothing he can do; there is a war on. He suggested she go with their sons to South Africa, but she refused to leave him; her place was here in England, with her husband, she said. Now he hardly sees her either because she is working at some secret establishment in Bletchley Park. The war has disrupted all their lives. He picks up his pen and begins to write.

MOTHER SUPERIOR

There is a sharp knock on the door. The Mother Superior looks at her watch; it's only ten thirty. Who could be interrupting her devotions at this hour? Slowly she pulls her heavy body up from the kneeler, genuflects towards the cross in front of her and goes across to her desk. Every step is agony.

'Come in.'

'I'm sorry to interrupt you Mother Superior but there is someone here from the Children's Overseas Reception Board to see you.'

'Very well, Sister Magdalene, show them in.'

A moment later the nun returns with a young woman in a brown suit. She carries a battered briefcase under her arm.

'Good morning Mother Superior,' says the woman, extending her hand.

The Mother Superior nods, motioning for the woman to sit down. She is not going to get up just to shake hands.

'My name is Catherine Smart. I'm from the Children's Overseas Reception Board and I'm here to discuss the arrangements for ...'.

She pauses, opens her briefcase and extracts a sheaf of papers.

'Maggie Smith, William Smith and Grace Smith. All one family I take it?'

The Mother Superior nods.

'If I may, I thought it might be appropriate to tell you something about our organisation first.'

Once again the Mother Superior nods. She hopes this is not going to take long. The woman continues:

'We, at the Children's Overseas Reception Board, take great pride in the work we are doing. Since we were set up in June we have sent many hundreds of children out to the Dominions. However unlike religious charities, such as your own and Barnados, we don't place the children in orphanages. Most of our children have parents and homes to return to when the war is over, so we find foster families to look after them until then. Our main objective is to help parents send their children to safety. Many parents nominate the homes that they want their children to go to, either to friends or relatives, but, for those who don't know anyone, we make the arrangements. Of course, the children are always placed in individual homes, never in an institution. And, in the case of families, we endeavour to place the children close together and we never expect a child to have to share a room with someone they don't know.'

'These children don't have any parents,' says the Mother Superior.

She thinks the woman sounds rather smug.

'Yes, that has been pointed out to me. I think in their case we can make an exception. Sister Lilian has told me that someone from the Sisters of Nazareth will meet them at Melbourne, so I suppose all you need from us is their passage to Australia.'

'Yes, that's right.'

'I will have to make sure that all the paperwork is in order. Normally there is an official reception for the children at the port of arrival and then they stay in a hostel for a few days while the final arrangements are made. I will need to know who will be collecting them so that I can inform the escorts. You understand we can't hand the children over to just anyone.'

'I would hardly call a Sister of Nazareth, a woman who has dedicated her life to God, just anyone.'

'No, no, of course not, Mother Superior. I did not mean that for one moment but you see, we do have our rules. We must think of the children.'

She hesitates.

'I assume these children are Catholic?' she asks.

'Of course.'

'Good, I just needed to check.'

'When can they leave?'

'The ship sails next week but first there are certain procedures to go through.'

She pulls some more papers from her briefcase.

'I will need their school reports, recommendations from their teachers and parental consent.'

She looks up.

'In this case, as the parents are both dead, I take it you will be in *loco parentis*.'

'Naturally.'

'Now, what else? Yes, the children need to undergo a thorough medical examination. We can arrange that if you wish?'

'No, there is no need. We have our own doctor; he visits all the children regularly.'

'Fine. Now, one more thing, about their clothes. We will provide the children with new clothes for the journey. These will be given out to them at the hostels before they embark, so there is no need for you to concern yourselves about it. Some of the children come from very deprived backgrounds,' she adds. 'We want to be sure that they are adequately clothed.'

'Of course.'

'Well, I think that is all. The ship embarks from Liverpool on 16th September. I will have their train tickets sent around as soon as possible.'

'Thank you.'

'If you can let me have all the completed paperwork back before they depart.'

'Of course.'

The woman closes her briefcase and stands up.

'Thank you for your time, Mother Superior.'

'Thank you, and God go with you.'

She waits until Catherine Smart has closed the door behind her then bends down and unlocks the bottom drawer of her desk. She takes out a half-empty bottle of British sherry and a small glass, then pours herself a measure. The sherry is warm and comforting as it slides down her throat. Carefully she wipes her lips and replaces the bottle and the glass.

There is a light tap on the door.

'Come in,' she says, sliding the drawer closed and turning the key.

'Is there anything you want me to do, Mother Superior?' asks Sister Magdalene.

'Has that woman gone?'

'Yes, Mother Superior.'

'Good. Take these forms to Sister Theresa and ask her to write up recommendations for the three Smith children, and to complete these school reports.'

'But they haven't started attending the school yet.'

'That doesn't matter. Sister Theresa can make some assessment of their abilities. What else can we do? Their own school is probably closed or bombed.'

'Very well Mother Superior.'

'And telephone Doctor Hardy. Tell him I need him to come and examine three children tomorrow morning. Tell him it's urgent.'

'Very well, Mother Superior.'

'And Sister Magdalene.'

'Yes, Mother Superior?'

'I don't wish to be disturbed again today. Is that clear?'

'Yes, Mother Superior.'

MAGGIE

They have been in the orphanage for three days now and still there is no news of Mum. There is nobody she can ask; she is too afraid of the nuns and Father McNally has not been back to see them. She thinks about running away to look for her but even that seems impossible now; the main door is locked and bolted and most of the time she is separated from Billy and Grace. There is no way she can leave without them. Billy spends most of his time working in the garden with an old man called Sid and Grace has been taken off with the babies. Maggie's day is divided between helping in the kitchen and joining the other girls at prayers in the chapel. The only time she sees her brother and sister is at mealtimes and then, because Sister Theresa is still on duty, they are unable to talk. She has to content herself with squeezing Billy's hand and giving Grace a surreptitious hug. So, when Elsie tells her that she is wanted in the Mother Superior's office, her heart gives a leap. Perhaps at last there is some news of Mum and they can all go home.

She knocks timidly at the door.

'Come in,' says the Mother Superior.

She opens the door and peers into the room. Her brother and sister are already there, standing by the wall; the Mother Superior is sitting behind her desk and Sister Magdalene is standing beside her.

'Come in child, and shut the door behind you.'

Her legs feel weak, but she forces herself to move forward and stand beside Grace. She takes her sister's hand and gives it a squeeze.

'No need to look so frightened, child. We have some good news for you,' says the Mother Superior.

So it's true. They have found Mum. Now they can all be together again.

'You are going to go on a lovely holiday. All three of you. You are such lucky children. Do you know where you are going?' asks Sister Magdalene.

The nun leans forward and smiles at them; her teeth are stained and uneven. Her breath smells of rotten eggs.

Maggie shakes her head dumbly. What does this have to do with Mum? Are Mum and the baby going on holiday too?

'You are going to Australia.'

She stares at her in disbelief.

'That's a long way,' Billy says. 'That's the other side of the world.'

He looks frightened. The nun ignores him and continues to look straight at Maggie. Her breath is unbearable.

'Australia is a big country where the sun shines all the time and it's never cold. You will have lots to eat and you'll be able to see kangaroos and wallabies,' continues Sister Magdalene.

'I want to see the wababees,' says Grace, suddenly losing her shyness.

Maggie knows exactly where Australia is; Miss Jennings taught them all about it. She remembers going to the zoo with her class, a long time ago, when Billy was just a toddler. They had seen the kangaroos and the wallabies. She knows all about Australia; she knows it's a long way from London.

'What about Mum?' she asks. 'Will she come to Australia too?'

Sister Magdalene looks at the Mother Superior who gives her a slight nod.

'No child,' she continues. 'Your mother will not be able to go with you. Your mother is in Heaven.'

Maggie feels the ground sway beneath her feet. What are they saying? Mum is dead? You could not be in Heaven unless you were dead. She cannot be dead; she is in the hospital with the baby. It's a lie.

'No. That's not true. I don't believe you. Mum can't be dead. She's with the baby. She wasn't in the bombing; she was safe in the hospital. She's not dead. She's coming back for us. She's coming to get us. She's not dead,' she repeats.

She begins to cry and cannot stop. It's as though all the anxiety, fears and frustrations of the past few days are spilling out of her. She knows Billy and Grace will be upset seeing their normally strong sister collapse in front of them but she cannot help herself. She cannot take any more.

The Mother Superior motions to Sister Magdalene, who comes round from the other side of the desk and stretches out her hand to Maggie.

'Now, now child, don't cry. Your mother is in Heaven with Jesus. She will be looking down on you and asking Jesus to make you strong.'

Billy and Grace are crying now.

'My Daddy is in Heaven,' sobs Grace.

'So Mum's with Dad now,' adds Billy, through his tears. 'They're both in Heaven.'

Maggie finds it hard to speak. Her mind is in a turmoil. What if it's true? What if they are really orphans now? How will they manage? Eventually she asks:

'What about the baby? What's happened to the baby?'

She wipes the tears from her eyes with the back of her hand. Suddenly she is worried that the baby has been abandoned, like them. If Mum really is dead, who is looking after the baby?

'Sister Magdalen,' the Mother Superior says and the nun produces a handkerchief from the folds of her robe and hands it to Maggie.

'Now wipe your eyes child. You and your brother and sister are going to a wonderful new life in Australia. You are very lucky children; don't you realise that? No more bombs, no more war. You are going to a lovely country with plenty of sunshine and good food to eat.'

Billy and Grace nod, but Maggie cannot answer. This is too much to bear. They can't lose Mum as well; she longs for her to be there with them. She sobs uncontrollably.

'You can go now, children. I'll speak to you later when you've got better control of yourselves,' the Mother Superior says, waving her hand to dismiss them.

'But the baby?'

'Go now.'

Maggie grabs hold of her brother and sister and leaves. She wants to run away from the orphanage and never stop running but that is not possible. As soon as the door shuts behind them Billy is sent back to the garden and Grace is whisked away by Sister Magdalen. Where could she run to without them?

She does not feel able to return to the kitchen, so instead she creeps into the dormitory. It's forbidden to go into the dormitory during the day but Maggie does not care; she is not going to be here for much longer anyway. She lies down on her bed and cries, her shoulders heaving with the violence of her sobs. Why is this happening to them? It just is not fair. First Dad, now Mum, it can't be true.

'Maggie, whatever's the matter? Have you been beaten?'

It's Elsie.

Maggie feels her friend's hand on her head, stroking her hair gently.

'There, there. Tell me what's the matter.'

At first Maggie cannot bring herself to say the words. Each time she tries to speak, she begins to cry again. Elsie waits patiently and continues to stroke her hair. At last she takes a deep breath and tells her new friend what the nuns have said.

'Oh you poor thing. So you're an orphan now, just like me.'

'It's not fair.'

'Tell me about it. I've been here since I was two. I've never known a home life and can't remember my Mum at all. At least you've got your brother and sister. I had a brother once but they sent him away to an orphanage in Ireland. I haven't seen him for ten years.'

Maggie is so surprised at all these revelations that she stops crying and sits up.

'I didn't know that you had a brother.'

'His name is Reg. I don't know where he is now; he might as well be dead for all I know.'

'I'm sorry.'

'Don't be. I'll be out of here in two years, just as soon as I'm fourteen.'

'They're sending us to Australia.'

'What, really? You're the lucky ones then. Lots of sunshine and plenty to eat. No bombs. Lucky beggar. I wish they'd send me.'

'Do you really think so?'

'Yes, can't be worse than living in this dump.'

'But we won't know anyone there.'

'Well, who do you know here?'

'There's my Nan.'

'You have a Nan? Where does she live?'

'I'm not really sure, but somewhere in London.'

'So why don't the nuns send you back to her?'

'I don't know. I'm frightened to say anything in case they tell me she's gone to Heaven too.'

A loud ringing warns them that it's time for lunch.

'I'm not hungry,' Maggie says.

'Well, you can give yours to me; I'm starving. Come on or we'll both be in trouble.'

The next morning, straight after prayers, Maggie is summoned to the sick bay. Billy is already waiting outside; he is sitting on the floor with his head on his knees.

'Billy, you all right?'

'They said I had to wait here for the doctor.'

'Yes, me too.'

Her brother is looking peaky. There is something different about him; he seems to have lost his usual bounce. Then she realises what it is; he is no longer pestering everyone with his endless questions. She has never known him to be so quiet. Even when he had mumps and his throat was red and swollen he managed to chatter away to the doctor.

'Maggie, do you think they'll split us up?' he suddenly asks.

'No. They said we were going to Australia together.'

'But they keep on about me being a boy,' he sobs. 'The gardener says I shouldn't live here. He says I should be with the Christian Brothers.'

'I don't expect it has anything to do with the gardener where you live.'

'I don't want them to split us up. I don't want to be on my own.'

She has never seen Billy so anxious before. She puts her arm around him.

'Don't worry Billy; we'll stick together, I promise.'

'Ah, there you are.'

A man in a white coat has arrived. He has a grey, handlebar moustache and twinkly eyes. Sister Lilian is coming up the passage behind him, leading Grace by the hand.

'Right, let's have a look at you then.'

He opens the door to the sick bay and ushers them in.

'All right now children, take your clothes off. Just leave your vests and knickers.'

Maggie feel uncomfortable undressing in front of him but she does as she is told then helps Grace to undo her buttons and remove her dress.

'I'll take the oldest one, first Sister,' the doctor says.

Maggie steps forward.

'Right, young lady, how old are you?'

'I'm twelve, sir.'

He writes something on his pad then looks at her.

'And have you started your periods yet?' he asks.

Maggie feels herself blushing. She looks down at the ground and whispers:

'Yes.'

'Speak up, child,' barks Sister Lilian.

'Yes, doctor,' Maggie repeats.

'Good. Now, have you or your brother and sister had any of these illnesses: measles, chicken pox, scarlet fever, TB, shingles?'

'We've all had the measles, sir, and Grace has had chicken pox.'

She has not heard of the other illnesses.

'And your brother?'

'No, sir.'

'What about diphtheria, mumps, whooping cough, polio?'

She remembers that, when she was six, there was a girl in her class who was ill; the teacher said she had diphtheria. She had to stay at home and nobody could visit her. Later she heard Mum telling Mrs Kelly that the girl had died.

'A boy in my class had polio,' interrupts Billy.

'We all had whooping cough last winter,' says Maggie, 'and Billy had the mumps.'

'Have any of you been vaccinated against diphtheria?'

'No.'

'Right, well we'll do that now. Please get the vaccines ready Sister.'

He scribbles some notes on his pad then picks up his stethoscope and comes across to Maggie.

'I'm just going to listen to your heart. Now take a deep breath.'

The stethoscope is cold and she wants to giggle. The harder she tries to control it the worse it becomes. It's like water bubbling up inside her and bursting to get out.

'Stand still child, how can the doctor do his job if you keep wriggling about like that,' snaps the nun.

'That's all right, I'm finished now. Just open your mouth and let me look at your teeth. Ah, not bad. Now your eyes.'

He leans forward and shines a bright light in her eyes. He smells of peppermint.

'Try not to blink. Good. No problems there. Now your hair.'

He takes out a comb and begins parting her hair.

'Excellent, no sign of head-lice. All right, that's you done. You can put your clothes back on now.'

While Maggie is dressing the doctor examines Billy and Grace.

'All fine, very healthy children for orphans,' he says to Sister Lilian.

'They have only just arrived.'

'Off to Australia I hear, what lucky children. I wouldn't mind a few weeks in Australia, lots of sun and sand.'

He smiles at them.

'Just the vaccinations now then you can go back to play,' he says.

Sister Lilian frowns at the mention of play.

'They have their duties to do then school,' she corrects him.

'Oh sorry,'

He looks at Maggie and winks.

'Right, roll up your sleeve please. This may hurt a little but it'll soon be over.'

The needle is very long and looks sharp. Maggie shuts her eyes and grits her teeth together tightly. It's very painful and afterwards it stings where he vaccinated her.

'There all done. Hold that on it for a bit until it stops bleeding. Right, next.'

Grace has started to cry.

'I'll go next,' says Billy. 'I'm not frightened.'

'Good lad.'

When it's Grace's turn Maggie offers to let her sit on her lap, so that she can put her head on her shoulder. It makes little difference, Grace screams and kicks and in the end Sister Lilian has to help her hold Grace still, so that the doctor can vaccinate her.

'There, there, Gracie, it's all over now. Hush now,' she whispers in her ear.

But Grace is only three and does not understand; she continues to sob and sob.

'Here, young lady, would you like a sweetie?' the doctor asks.

He holds out a sweet to Grace but she pushes his hand away, knocking the sweet to the floor.

'No,' she shouts.

Maggie has never seen her in such a temper. She is frightened the doctor will get angry and then Sister Lilian will take Grace away and punish her.

'Hush Grace. That's not very nice now, is it,' she says.

She bends down and picks up the sweet.

'Thank you doctor. I'm sorry. She's still a baby, you see.'

'Keep rubbing her arm; the soreness will soon go,' he says.

He does not seem to mind Grace's tantrum.

'Well, that's that then. I'm finished here now.'

He takes off his white coat and hangs it over the chair.

'Thank you Dr Hardy. I'll see you out,' says Sister Lilian. 'We'll see you next month then?'

'Naturally.'

She turns to Maggie and Billy.

'You can go back to your work now,' she says. 'Grace, you come with me.'

The next morning the children are told to have a shower after breakfast. They don't have to do their usual chores.

'You're so lucky,' complains Elsie. 'Now, I'll have to work twice as hard if you're not here.'

'And having a shower on a Friday. We all have to wait until Sunday. Sunday's bath-night,' adds a thin girl called Lucy.

'Maybe they're leaving today,' suggests one of the others.

She looks at Maggie wistfully.

'I wish I was going to Australia.'

'I wish I was going anywhere, so long as it was away from here,' says Elsie.

She rubs her leg absentmindedly.

'What's wrong with your legs?' asks Maggie.

There are thick red wheals across the back of both legs.

'Sister Alice.'

'What do you mean? Did she hit you?'

'I just can't get the hang of long division. She says it's easy, that we're just being lazy, but it's her. She's a blinking awful teacher. Nobody understands what she says.'

'So she hit you?'

'Not just me, Megan and Susie as well. We had to stay behind and she walloped us with that ruler of hers. God I'll be glad when I can get out of here.'

Sister Lilian is standing by the showers when they arrive. She has some towels in her arms.

'Hurry up now children. Strip off and get in the showers. Not you boy. Go and wait outside until I call you.'

They strip off their clothes; even Grace looks embarrassed removing her clothes under the watchful eye of the nun. They have never had a shower before. Saturday night was always bath-night for them, when Mum would drag the old zinc bath in from the yard and fill it with hot water. They usually went in rotation: first Grace, because she was the smallest, then Billy, then Maggie. Sometimes, after they had gone to bed, Mum would add some more hot water and get in herself.

'Come along. We haven't got all day.'

Maggie edges forward carefully. The water looks cold. She stretches out her hand tentatively.

'If you don't hurry up, you'll feel my hand across your bottom,' the nun snaps.

Maggie takes a deep breath and steps under the shower. It's not very warm but neither is it freezing.

'Come on Gracie, here take my hand.'

The sisters stand under the shower together; Maggie picks up the soap and begins to wash Grace's hair. It's hard to make it lather. Maggie feels miserable. She wants Mum so much.

At two o'clock the three of them are standing on the platform at Euston station. Around each of their necks hangs a gas mask and a large brown label with their names written in capital letters. Sister Lilian has accompanied them to the station. She has told them to stay where they are and not to move while she makes some enquiries about their train.

They are not the only children waiting on the platform. There are groups of evacuees, similarly decked with gas masks and labels, their meagre possessions clutched to their chests, while their teachers read out a list of their names.

'Not more evacuees', a woman says, as she shoulders past them. 'Poor little souls.'

'Are we vacuees?' asks Grace.

'I suppose we are,' Maggie says.

Billy is playing with his label, it says WILLIAM SMITH.

'Don't do that Billy; it might come off,' she tells him.

'Then we won't be able to find you,' Grace says.

'Mum didn't want us to be evacuees,' he says suddenly. 'She said she didn't want us to be like blooming parcels.'

'Well, Mum's not here now, is she,' Maggie says.

The wind is blowing a cold, fine rain along the crowded platform, soaking people's coats and making them huddle together. It falls on the caps and hats of the schoolchildren, trickling down their necks and onto the collars of their winter coats; it makes the soldiers swear and stamp their feet, impatient to board the train; it drips from the umbrellas of tired businessmen, newly discharged from the station refreshment bar, smelling of stale beer; in a sudden gust it catches the black shawl of the old woman who sits by the turnstile with a large wicker basket in front of her.

'Lucky heather, boys,' she sings out to the soldiers as they pass her. 'Buy some lucky heather.'

'We need more than bloody heather if we're going to win this war, dear,' one soldier calls back to her.

He drops a threepenny bit into her hand and thrusts the soggy sprig of heather into his cap.

By now the rain is running down Maggie's neck but she hardly notices it; she is far more interested in all around her. The last time she was at a station was to wave goodbye to Dad. She stares at the soldiers as they go by; maybe one of them is Dad's friend, George.

All at once people begin to pick up their bags and shuffle towards the edge of the platform. The train is coming; she can hear a rumble in the distance.

'Right children. Here's your train now,' says Sister Lilian.

She holds a battered umbrella over her black habit.

'I have your tickets here. Now look after them child. Give them to the ticket collector when he asks you for them. Otherwise don't speak to anyone. Is that understood?'

She hands the tickets to Maggie.

'You have the sandwiches?'

'Yes, Sister.'

The train pulls into the station, enveloping everything in a cloud of steam and smoke. The noise is deafening. Sister Lilian seems to be saying something to them but Maggie cannot make it out. Then she is gone. The children don't move. Hundreds of people are surging towards the train, doors are opening and banging closed again as one wave of people alight and another attempt to board. What should she do? She slips the tickets into her coat pocket and grabs Billy and Grace by the hand.

'Come on, let's follow those children,' she says.

They tuck in behind a crocodile of school children and climb aboard. They have never been on a train before. They had seen plenty of them, whistling and steaming across the railway bridge in Bethnal Green, but that was as close as they had got. Now she does not know what to do. Where do they sit? The train is very full; all the seats have been taken and people are even sitting on the floor. She pulls her brother and sister further through the train until at last she finds a free seat.

'This'll do. We can squeeze in here. What do you think?'

'I'm tired Maggie,' says Grace.

'All right Gracie, I'll sit here and you sit on my knee. Billy you sit on the floor.'

'But it's hard.'

She takes off her coat.

'Fold this up and sit on it, then you'll be more comfortable.'

The boy sits down with his back against the seat.

'All right?'

'S'pose so.'

'It's not for long.'

'Where're you kids off to?' asks one of the soldiers, sitting across the aisle.

'Stralia,' says Grace.

The soldier laughs.

'Well, I'm not sure if this train goes all the way to Australia, love.'

'We're going to Liverpool to get a boat,' explains Maggie.

'That's very brave of you. Where's your Mam and Dad?'

'They're dead,' says Billy. 'We're orphans.'

'I'm sorry to hear that. My Mam's dead too.'

'Is she in Heaven?' asks Grace. 'Our Mum and Dad are in Heaven.'

'Yes, I expect she is.'

'Hey Alec, want to play cards?' asks the soldier sitting next to him.

'Yes, why not.'

He turns back to his companions.

'Maggie, I'm hungry,' Billy informs her.

She opens the packet of sandwiches and breaks off a piece of bread.

'Here, that's all you can have for now. These have to last us until we get to Liverpool.'

'What do we do when we get there?' he asks, cramming the bread into his mouth.

'Sister Lilian says that someone will meet us at the station and look after us.'

'I hope they give us some tea, because it'll be teatime by then, won't it?'

The children doze. Maggie wakes with a jerk and a sense of panic each time the train stops at a station. At Crewe the old woman sitting next to the window gets off and Maggie moves across, letting Grace have the aisle seat to herself.

She is sleeping, dreaming of walking around the zoo, holding Dad's hand. There are penguins and Billy is trying to feed them with a piece of bread.

'No, silly, they only eat fish,' she says to him and with that the bread turns into a wriggling goldfish.

Something is wrong. She turns restlessly and stretches out her hand, automatically feeling for Grace. The seat is empty; she is not there. In an instant Maggie is awake. Billy is still fast asleep, stretched out on a pile of coats across the aisle, but there is no sign of Grace. She feels her stomach turn to water. Where is she? She is on her feet now.

'Grace, Gracie,' she calls, looking desperately up and down the train.

Then she sees her; just disappearing through the door at the end of the carriage she glimpses a flash of blue and a tousled blonde head. A man has her by the hand. Maggie starts to run.

'Hey, what's the matter, love?' asks one of the soldiers. 'Train on fire?'

'It's my sister. She's gone. That man's got her.'

She is almost in tears now.

'What's that?'

The soldier and his mate are on their feet and ahead of her.

'Don't worry love; we'll get her. He can't get off yet; the train doesn't stop for another half hour. You stay here with your little brother.'

She looks back at Billy. What should she do? She ought not leave Billy. If she goes after Grace and then Billy disappears too ..., the thought is too awful to bear.

'They're right love; you sit down and wait. They'll find your sister for you,' says the woman sitting opposite.

'No, I have to go. Please, if he wakes up, would you tell him I'll be back in a minute. I have to look for my sister; she's only three you know. She's just a baby.'

She can feel the tears running down her cheeks now.

'Of course I will love. Don't cry; it'll be all right. You run along then.'

Maggie pushes open the door at the end of the carriage and makes her way into the next part of the train. There is no sign of the soldiers and no sign of Grace. She squeezes past people standing in the aisle and hurries as fast as she can, stepping over the sleeping bodies until she comes to the next door. This time when she clambers across into the adjacent carriage, she can see them. Grace is crying and one of the soldiers has a middle-aged man by the collar.

'Gracie, Gracie, it's all right now. I'm here, everything's all right now,' she calls, hurrying towards her sister.

'He says he was just taking her to the toilet,' the soldier explains.

'Bloody pervert. I'd like to knock his block off,' says the other soldier.

'I haven't done anything. I was just trying to help,' the man protests.

'Oh yeah?'

'She wanted to go to the toilet and her sister was asleep. I was just trying to help,' he repeats.

'Yes, well you can tell that to the police. Bloody conchie.'

Maggie thinks the man is going to cry; his face crumples up and he seems about to collapse. Only the soldier's firm grasp prevents him from falling to the floor.

'Now, don't take on so,' the other soldier says, turning to Maggie. 'Take your sister and go back to your seat. We'll see to this bloke; he won't trouble you no more.'

She grabs Grace and hurries back to Billy. He is in the same position, undisturbed by the commotion going on further along the train. This time she puts Grace in the seat by the window then gently pulls Billy up and pushes him in next to her. She sits down beside him, her feet sticking out into the aisle and sobs quietly to herself. This is what she should have done first of all, put them on the inside where they were safe, where she could protect them. She leans back and closes her eyes.

The next thing she knows the train is stopping. The station announcer is saying 'Liverpool Station' and everyone is bustling about, grabbing bags and coats and making for the exit. Grace continues to sleep but Billy is awake. He sits up and puts on his coat.

'Are we here, Maggie?' he asks sleepily.

'Yes, this is where we get off,' she tells him.

She wakes Grace gently and dresses her in her coat and scarf. Then the children sit and wait until most of the people have left the carriage before getting off. The crowds disperse quickly and the platform at Liverpool Station is soon empty, save for a few bedraggled children. They stand next to them and wait. It's just as Sister Lilian promised. It only takes a few minutes for their escort to find them; she is a rosy faced woman called June.

'Hello children. I hope you had a good journey,' she says.

She takes out a list of names and checks that they are all present. As she passes Grace, she bends down and strokes her hair.

'What's your name, sweetie?' she asks.

'Gracie. I's free,' she lisps.

Then June tells them that they are sea evacuees and she will look after them until they arrive in Australia. There are fifteen of them in total. Maggie notices that they all look as frightened as Billy and Grace. June makes the children line up in a double file and takes them to an old bus that is waiting outside the station, other sea evacuees are already seated in it. June's group are the last to arrive; they climb aboard and the bus immediately sets off for the hostel.

Half an hour later they pull up outside an old brick building. It's a secondary school; Maggie can see the name on the gate: High School for Girls, Fazackerly. She wonders where the girls are today while all these children are encamped in their school. Have they been evacuated too?

'All right children, just line up here in double file. The bus driver will get your cases out for you,' June tells them.

Maggie has Grace by the hand and she pushes Billy ahead of her, where she can keep an eye on him. He stands next to a tall boy with fair hair. They wait patiently in line while the driver piles the suitcases on the pavement and then drives away. June tells the children to collect their luggage and follow her into the school. Maggie feels awkward; they don't have any luggage to collect. The escort leads them into a large room that, from the wall bars and ropes that hang from the walls and the parallel bars tucked in the corner, seems to double both as a gymnasium and an assembly hall. Now, it turns out, it's to be their home for the next two days. There are already about forty other children in there. Someone has given them mattresses and they sit there, their cases beside them, waiting to be told what to do. They all turn to look at the new arrivals. Maggie feels embarrassed to have so many eyes staring at her but Billy just grins and says:

'Hi, I'm Billy and these are my sisters.'

June smiles at him and says:

'Just wait here for a moment children, while I find out where you are to go. Then you can go and meet the others.'

She goes across to speak to a young man at the end of the hall. When she returns she is smiling.

'Well, children, let's get you settled in first then we will go and have something to eat. Follow me.'

They all brighten at this news and follow June as she allocates them their individual spots. Maggie and her brother and sister are given one large mattress to share; they sit down on it and wait. There seems to be a lot of waiting to do, Maggie thinks. Grace is tired; she is grizzling to herself quietly. Maggie knows she will soon be asleep. She makes her lie down on the mattress and puts her coat over her. Already Billy is getting impatient; he wants to meet the other children. He edges across to speak to a boy of about his own age, who is playing with some cigarette cards. Maggie leans back against the wall and looks around the room. She is glad they will not be staying here long; it's noisy and not very warm. Some of the children are crying.

June comes back. She carries a sheaf of papers with her, checking who is who and where they should be. Now she comes up to Maggie.

'I see you don't have any luggage,' she says.

'No. All our things were bombed,' Maggie explains.

'You poor things, I'm so sorry,' June says. 'We have some clothes here for you. We can't have you going all the way to Australia in just the clothes you stand up in, can we.'

She smiles at them.

'As soon as you've eaten, I'll take you over to get you all kitted out.'

The two days pass quickly. The women from the Women's Volunteer Services give them new clothes and suitcases to put them in. They want to take away their old clothes but Maggie insists on keeping her plaid coat. She has to have something of her old life. Once again they are inspected by the doctor and declared healthy enough for the voyage. The escorts are with them all the time and make sure that each day they have some exercise; they push the mattresses to one side and play games in the hall. Usually it's some sort of team game, like relay races or ball games. Maggie finds a skipping rope and gets some of the girls to join her in skipping games but Billy and the boys prefer to kick a football around. The food is good and plentiful and they eat well; at night they sleep fitfully on the lumpy mattresses, but all this time nobody mentions Mum.

At last they are told that it's time to leave. June comes bustling in one morning and tells them to collect all their belongings and line up.

'What's happening?' one of the older girls asks.

'We're going to the docks,' June says. 'It's time to board the ship.'

'Are we going to Stralia now?' Grace whispers.

'Yes, dear. Now go and line up over there with the other children.'

Maggie looks round the room. All the children are subdued. No-one has much to say and for once the endless burble of childish chatter ceases. She picks up Grace's suitcase as well as her own and tells Billy to grab Grace's hand; they wait for June's signal and then follow her to their bus.

Maggie is nervous. She pushes Billy and Grace into a seat and squeezes in beside them; they cling to each other, hands entwined.

'I don't want to go to Stralia,' Grace says.

'Shss, Gracie,' Maggie whispers.

'I want my Mummy.'

She starts to cry.

'Mum's in Heaven with Dad,' Billy tells her.

Maggie does not know what to say. She is frightened and hugs her brother and sister tighter to her. What if the nuns were wrong, what if Mum is not dead? How will she find them if they are in Australia? She might think that they are dead; she might think that they were killed in the bombing. Then she wouldn't bother to look for them. Maggie wonders if she should mention her fears to June.

The bus splutters to a start and rattles off towards the docks. As she watches their temporary home recede in the distance, Maggie suddenly does not want to leave it. They pass through narrow cobbled streets of red brick houses, untouched by the bombs. Housewives stand in the doorways, their arms folded over their pinnies, just like they did in Stanlet Street and watch the buses go past. Why can't they stay here? This seems to be a safer place than London. Why do they have to go all the way to Australia? As they turn a corner, a ship looms up before them, enormous against the skyline; it dwarfs everything around it. They have arrived. Heavy iron gates swing open and the buses drive through into the docks. She has never been anywhere like this before; dozens of people scurry to and fro, moving cargo from the ships into the huge warehouses that line the water's edge. There are warships in the harbour, some so close she can read their names and others, dim outlines further off shore. She smells burning coal and diesel fumes, the salty aroma of rotting fish and other earthy smells that she cannot identify. A sudden crash makes her jump but it's only a crane dropping its load on the dock. She turns her attention back to her brother and sister; they are both white-faced and silent. Tears stain Grace's face and Billy is gripping her hand.

'It's OK,' Maggie says. 'The lady will look after us.'

The buses stop one behind the other and all the children get out and line up in double file on the dock. Some of the escorts are dashing around, checking that no-one is missing and she can see a sailor, standing by the gangplank, guiding the children on board the ship.

'Is that our ship? The Or-in-o-co,' Billy asks. 'It's gi-norm-ous.'

June counts off the children on her list, tapping each of her charges gently on the head as she passes them. When she reaches Grace she stops and bends down.

'Hey, no need for tears little one; you're going on a lovely journey,' she says to her then she turns to Maggie.

'Let me take her suitcase. You can't manage both cases and hold on to her.'

Gratefully Maggie relinquishes her hold on Grace's case.

'Thank you,' she says.

Slowly they follow the other children up the gangplank.

'Keep close to me Billy. Don't wander off,' she warns her brother.

She can see he is fascinated by everything around him and gradually his curiosity is overcoming his fear. Any minute now he will be off exploring.

At last they are on board and line up on deck to watch as the *SS Orinoco* slowly steams away from the harbour. They stand there, with their new luggage at their feet, gazing in wonder as the port of Liverpool expands before their eyes. It's a panorama of docks and jetties, cranes and ships, towering stacks of cargo waiting to be dispersed, dockers and stevedores, sailors, soldiers about to embark, others disembarking, passengers for the New World clutching their passports like talismans. Strange noises and exotic smells float across the ever widening stretch of water towards them. Despite her fears, Maggie begins to feel a thrill of excitement at the prospect of a sea voyage and Billy, she is happy to see, is once again bouncing with all his old vigour. Two days in the hostel with plenty of food to eat and other boys his age have restored his equilibrium. Now an incessant stream of chatter flows from his lips. He has already picked up the jargon of life at sea.

'This ship is called the *Orinoco*,' he informs them. 'I saw it painted on the side. You don't say left and right on a ship you say port and starboard. Do you think the captain will let me go up on the bridge?'

Then a moment later, he asks:

'When will we get to Australia? Will we go straight there or will we stop at other ports?'

She does not bother to answer him; he does not really want answers. He is too excited.

'What are those birds? Look they're following the ship. Are they looking for fish? Maggie, why is that boat pulling us along? It's much smaller than us. How can it do that?'

And on and on, Billy is his old self again. While they were in the hostel, he made friends with one of the other boys and now he hurries over to chat to him. Maggie is glad to see him so animated once more. Grace, on the other hand, is not happy. She clings to Maggie and constantly wails:

'I want to go home. I want my Mummy. Don't like this boat. I want my Mummy.'

Nothing can console her, nothing Maggie says or does can stop her crying. She hugs her little sister to her; they have been through so much together and now this is the final straw for Gracie. She is so small, dwarfed by the size of everything around her.

As the ship steams away from the coast, Maggie can no longer see the port in any detail; it recedes into a blur on the horizon. The waves are higher now and break against the ship's prow in cascades of white foam, while the wind, suddenly colder and stronger, whips around them, making her shiver.

'Come on Gracie, let's get out of this wind and find somewhere warmer.'

She turns away from her lookout spot to seek shelter from the stinging spray. A shout goes up and the tugboat is released; with a final toot of its klaxon, it turns and heads back for Liverpool. She watches it go. They are on their own now and heading out to sea.

IRENE

They are taking her and the baby to the Evelina Hospital in Southwark. The doctor came and told her this morning; he was very pleased with himself. It had not been easy to get a bed for the poor little chap, he said, but they hoped to operate in a couple of days.

She hugs her son to her breast; he is so tiny. How could someone so small survive such a major operation? She will not be able to bear it if anything happens to him as well. She yawns. The last few nights she has not been able to sleep. Leslie has been very restless lately and each night she has been up and down seeing to him. Normally the nurses see to the babies during the night but the maternity home is so short staffed that the mothers have to do the night duty as well as the day. She does not mind; she loves holding her little son. If only Ronnie could see him, he would be so proud. The thought of her husband makes her sigh. She can feel the tears starting again. It must be the breast feeding that is making her so weepy. She will have to get a grip of herself; she cannot have the children seeing her crying all the time. If this goes on she will have to go to the doctor and ask him for a tonic. Maybe that is what she needs, some Sanatogen wine or a few glasses of Guinness. Ronnie always swore by Guinness.

'Put's iron in your blood,' he would say and Kate would agree with him.

Irene has never really liked the stuff, too bitter for her. Her usual pick-me-up is the dependable cup of tea.

'We're almost there love,' the ambulance driver says.

'Just another five minutes.'

She feels her stomach churning. The thought of leaving her son in the hospital frightens her, but what else can she do. She must find out what has happened to the other children. And Kate, what on earth can have happened to Kate? She does not want to think of the possibilities but she knows she must. As soon as she has Leslie settled she will get the bus home and see for herself what is going on.

She does not feel optimistic. As she looks out of the ambulance window she can see nothing but devastation; the Blitz is taking its toll of London and Londoners. According to the wireless there are hundreds of displaced people in the city.

'This is awful,' she says to the driver.

'There was another air raid last night,' he said. 'Must have been nigh on five hundred bombers came over. They were at it all night.'

'How can anyone survive in all this destruction?' she asks.

She is thinking about Kate and the children.

The ambulance driver does not reply; he just shakes his head. They pull into the hospital grounds and he drives up the Admissions entrance.

'Here you are love. Just sit tight for a minute and I'll help you down.'

He goes round to the passenger door and takes the baby from her while she clambers down.

'Thanks, I'll be all right now.'

'Right then. Well, best of luck, little chap,' he says, patting Leslie on the head. 'Don't you worry love, the doctors here are the best there are.'

He climbs back into the ambulance and drives away. Irene puts her bag over her shoulder and adjusts her hold on the baby. She takes a deep breath; there is no alternative. This is for the best.

It hurts to leave him behind. She should be with him. It's not hospital policy, is what the nurse has told her. Come back in the morning. They will look after him and she is to return each day to feed him. They want him to stay on mother's milk. She agrees that it's much better for him; his constitution is too weak for powdered milk. So every night she is to express her milk and take it in to the hospital the following morning. She walks to the bus stop and joins the queue.

'Going far love?' a woman asks her.

She has two shopping bags filled with kindling.

'Bethnal Green.'

'You want the number twenty-one then.'

'Thanks. Is it due?'

'Should be here by now, but you can never tell these days. There's been such a lot of damage to the roads, what with the bombs and all.'

Irene nods. It's amazing that life goes on, despite all the destruction. She sees the bus come round the corner and feels a wave of pride for her city and its people. Despite the Blitz the buses are still running. When the bus stops she climbs aboard; the bus is full.

'Here, have my seat, love,' an old man says.

She feels that he needs the seat more than she does but smiles and thanks him then sits by the window.

The momentary warmth that she experienced on seeing the familiar red bus turn up on time soon disappears as she gets closer to Bethnal Green; she can hardly recognise the place. The buses might still be running but where are the houses?

'Bethnal Green,' cries the conductor.

'This'll do me,' she shouts down to him.

She gets off the bus and looks around her. Where is she? He said it was Bethnal Green and it looks familiar in a way but at the same time she does not recognise anything. Then she sees the sign of the 'Prince Albert', swinging eerily from the single remaining wall of the pub and she knows where she is. The sight chills her. The Prince Albert was always such a lively place. Whenever she had walked past it she had heard music coming from the out-of-tune piano that was in the public bar and there was the sound of laughter and raucous voices. Now it's silent; all she can hear is the creaking of the pub sign.

Nevertheless it has given her her bearings and she turns round and sets off in the direction of her home. It's not easy; she has to pick her way through piles of rocks and rubble. There are volunteers out clearing the road so that the traffic can get through but they are just piling it up on the pavements, great mounds of bricks and concrete where once rows of terraced houses stood. How could anyone survive this she asks herself again and again.

Before she reaches her house she already knows what she will find. It's impossible that her house alone could still be standing when all the rest have been flattened. Yet still she hopes for a miracle and, even when she sees the wreckage that was once her home, she still cannot believe it. She stops and stares. She does not cry or scream or shout; she just feels numb. Her mind seems to have shut down; she cannot comprehend the enormity of what is before her. Her entire world is collapsing around her.

'Irene, is that you?'

She feels an arm go round her shoulders.

'Are you all right? Irene?'

She looks uncomprehendingly at the man. Does she know him? He looks familiar.

'It's me, it's Fred, Fred Ford.'

'Yes, of course. Hello Fred. How's your Dad?' she asks automatically.

'Are you sure you're all right?'

'Yes, yes, I'm fine.'

She sits down on a pile of rocks.

'It's quite a shock, isn't it,' he says. 'The whole area's been hit really bad. We've been digging people out of the rubble for days.'

'Where are they?' she asks.

'Sorry?'

'Where are my children? They were supposed to be with Kate. Where are they?'

'Sorry I don't know anything about no children. There was a little blonde girl copped it down Arlington Street last night but I haven't heard nothing about your kids.'

'Do you know where Kate is?'

She sees him shuffle uncomfortably.

'Kate got caught up in a raid last week. She was trying to get home but never made it. She was running down Hanbury Road when the bomb fell. Poor woman, never knew what hit her.'

Kate was dead. Kate. Dead. She looks up at him.

'She can't be.'

He nodded.

'I'm so sorry. She caught the full impact.'

She starts to cry. Poor Kate.

'She was looking after my kids. What's happened to them? Were they with her? Were they hurt?' she asks.

'Looking after your kids was she? That must've been why she wouldn't go in the shelter with the others. Rose Brown said she tried to get her to go down into the Underground with her but she said she had to get home. She must've been thinking about your kids.'

She found herself nodding at him. Yes, that sounded just like Kate.

'So where are they?' she asked. 'My kids, where are they?'

'I'm sorry Irene, I don't know anything about them. Look why don't you come with me down to the WVS and we'll get you a nice cup of tea. Maybe someone down there can help you,' he says.

She knows it's pointless; he knows nothing about her children. Nevertheless, she allows herself to be led down the road, past the ruined houses and piles of rubble, past the volunteers shovelling rubbish out of the street, past people she vaguely recognises that are desperately trying to salvage something of their old lives from the wreckage, past burnt-out lorries and vans, until they reach the WVS centre. She watches as Fred goes across to one of the women and speaks to her. They come towards her. She watches as though she is floating above them, as though this has nothing to do with her.

'Hello there Irene. Sorry to hear about your house. But at least you're all right, that's the main thing. How's the baby?' the woman says briskly.

She nods towards Irene's flat stomach. It's Kate's friend, Rose.

'Hello Rose. The baby's still in the hospital; he's not too good.'

'I'm sorry to hear that. Like a cuppa?'

Irene nods. She sits down on a wooden bench.

'Look Irene I've got to go now. There were quite a few incendiary bombs last night and some are still burning. They need every man out there. Now, if you need anything, you know where to find me,' Fred tells her, picking up his cap.

'You just stay here for a bit, until you're feeling better,' he adds.

Irene smiles at him weakly. He is a kind man even if he does look a bit pompous in his Home Guard uniform. Not a real soldier, like Ronnie.

'Thanks, Fred,' she says. 'Remember me to your Dad.'

Rose returns with a cup of steaming tea and, despite her anxiety, Irene drinks it gratefully.

'Fred had to go,' she explains. 'He said that you were with Kate just before she died.'

'Yes, we were on the bus. I'd been to see my Betty. Now she's got her hands full with that family of hers. They've never got enough to eat and ...'

Irene is not in the mood for a gossip, so she interrupts:

'Tell me about Kate.'

'Kate? There's not a lot to tell. She said she'd been to see you and the baby and she was on her way home to make tea for your kids. We'd just got off the bus when the air-raid siren went off. Right by Bethnal Green tube station we were. I made straight for it but Kate wouldn't come with me. I tried to persuade her but she said she'd be all right.'

Rose obviously does not enjoy thinking about it. She sniffs and blows her nose loudly into a large, white handkerchief.

'She should've listened to me,' she continues as a tear trickles down her cheek.

'Did she say where the children were?' asks Irene.

'Yes, she said they were at Sunday School.'

'Do you know what happened to them?'

Rose shakes her head.

'Why don't you ask at the church. Or, better still, come back this afternoon, Olive Staunton helps in the afternoons. You know Olive, she takes one of the Sunday School classes. She'll be able to tell you.'

'Yes, I know who you mean, quite young, with blonde hair.'

'That's the one. She'll be here around two o'clock.'

'I'll do that.'

'You feeling all right now?'

'Yes, thanks. That tea did the trick.'

She does feel better; she is getting a clearer picture of what happened. Her children were not at home when the bombs dropped. Now she just has to find out where they have gone.

There are two hours until Olive comes on duty, so Irene decides to make some enquiries at the school. It takes her only a few minutes to reach the school gates and she is pleased to see that the school looks unharmed. She lets herself in and goes in search of the head teacher. Miss Bentley is sitting in her office with a mound of paperwork in front of her.

'Ah, Mrs Smith, I was going to get in touch with you. Your children haven't been to school for over a week. I realise that things are difficult for you at the moment but we would appreciate knowing if you have made other arrangements for them. The situation is chaotic enough, what with the evacuations and the bombing; it really is hard to keep track of them all.'

She pauses and looks at Irene over her spectacles. Irene feels like crying. All at once she is a small child again being reprimanded by her teacher.

'I've been in hospital,' she says.

'Yes, so I heard.'

She looks at her expectantly. This is obviously not a good enough excuse in her book.

'May I sit down?' Irene asks.

The headmistress nods towards a chair.

'Well?'

'The thing is,' she hesitates. 'Well, I don't know where the children are. I thought you would know.'

'Me? Why should I know?'

'I thought that maybe one of the teachers was looking after them.'

'I think you'd better explain to me exactly what has been happening, from the beginning.'

Irene relates the events of the past two weeks, in so far as she can.

'Let me see, the last time anyone saw these children was midday on Sunday, when your friend made them lunch? That's over a week ago.'

'Yes, as far as I know. I'm going to talk to the Sunday school teacher to see if she knows anything more.'

'I'm sorry I can't help you. It makes sense though, the last time they attended school was ...'

She checks the register.

'Friday 6th September.'

The headmistress looks harassed. Her normally tidy hair has struggled loose from its grips and gives her a bedraggled look.

'Well, Mrs Smith, I hope you track down your children,' she says. 'When you do, please let me know so that I can complete the paperwork.'

She sighs and makes a feeble attempt to collect the wayward greying hair in one of her grips.

'It's very difficult to keep track of all the children these days. It's not surprising that some of them go missing,' she repeats. 'I shouldn't worry. Someone will be looking after them.'

Irene stands up. Does nobody know where her children are?

'Thank you anyway, Miss Bentley. If you hear anything will you let me know?'

'Of course I will. Where will you be living? I heard that the Hanbury Road area has been virtually razed to the ground.'

Her question makes Irene stop. Where is she going to live? Her home has gone. There is only one possibility.

'I'll be staying at my Mum's in Islington.'

She takes a scrap of paper off the desk and scribbles down her mother's address.

'Fine, I'll let you know if I have any news.'

The headmistress opens a folder and pulls out some papers. Irene recognises this as the signal for her to leave.

Before she returns to the WVS centre Irene decides to visit the centre for evacuees. She has never been there before but she remembers Maggie talking about it. It's not far from their house; she wonders if it's still standing.

Not only is it still standing but it looks impregnable. A young woman is busy copying out name labels from a list, another woman is checking gas masks.

'Can I help you?' the woman with the gas masks asks.

'Yes, I'm trying to trace three children. I wondered if they might have been evacuated.'

The other woman looks up.

'What are their names?'

'Maggie Smith, William Smith and Grace Smith.'

She runs her finger down the list.

'There's a Richard Smith, aged nine.'

'No.'

'Angela and Sheila Smith, they're twins, aged six.'

'No.'

'Sorry then, they're not on this list.'

'Could they be on a different list?' Irene asks.

'When do you think they were evacuated?'

'Last week, sometime after the 8th.'

'In that case, no, the previous batch of evacuees went from here on 2nd September. We haven't sent any since then. This is the next batch.'

She waves the list at Irene.

'Are you sure?' asks Irene.

Surely someone knows where they are. They can't just disappear off the face of the earth.

'Positive. You could try some of the other evacuation centres. Maybe they've heard of them.'

'Thank you.'

'Sorry we can't help,' the woman with the gas masks calls after her.

Irene walks back to the WVS centre. She is tired and her breasts ache. She will see what Olive has to say and then she will get the bus to Mum's. Maybe her mother knows something.

Olive Staunton is busy in the kitchen making an enormous pot of soup. Her hair is tied up in a brown headscarf. When she sees Irene she turns down the gas and comes across to talk to her.

'Hello, Rose said you wanted to speak to me,' she says, wiping her hands on her apron.

'Yes. It's about my children.'

'That's Maggie and Billy, isn't it?'

'Yes, and I've got a younger one, Grace.'

'Yes, I remember her; she's a real sweetie. So what's happened?'

'I just wanted to know where they went after the air raid.'

'Oh, I remember that, the Sunday before last. We were all terrified. We stayed in the crypt until the all-clear then we sent all the children home.'

'Is that all? Didn't they say where they were going or anything?'

'No, I assumed they were going home as they usually do. Why, has something happened to them?'

Irene takes a deep breath and explains that she was in hospital at the time and when she came back their house had been bombed and there was no sign of the children. She tries not to cry.

'So you see, they seem to have disappeared.'

'I'm really sorry, but I can't tell you anything else. As far as I knew they were going home. Although now you mention it, Billy did say something about a neighbour. Maybe they went there.'

'Kate Kelly?'

'Yes, I think that was her name, Mrs Kelly.'

'She was looking after them while I was in hospital.'

'So what does she say?'

'She was killed in the air raid.'

'My God, that's awful. Well, I don't know what I can say. They were definitely with me until the all-clear sounded, so they weren't caught up in the air-raid. When they didn't turn up last Sunday I wasn't really surprised, most of our children have already been evacuated; there's only a handful left now.'

Irene feels that there is an enormous weight pressing down on her chest; she can hardly breathe. She says goodbye to the Sunday school teacher and heads for the bus stop. There is nothing else she can do; she does not know who else to ask. She feels the need to see her mother; she will help her.

It's mid afternoon by the time she arrives in Islington and it's already getting dark. Her mother opens the door and looks at her in surprise.

'Hello Irene, well I wasn't expecting to see you today. My goodness child, whatever is the matter. Now, now, there's no need to carry on so. Come in off the step and tell me what's wrong. Is it the baby? Has something happened to the baby?'

Irene wipes her eyes and steps into the familiar hallway. It's such a relief to see her mother. For the second time that day she feels like a child again.

'Come and sit down. You just get your breath back while I make us a nice cup of tea.'

Her mother bustles off to the kitchen. She hears her calling up the stairs to Dad.

'Les, our Irene's here. Come on down.'

Irene follows her mother into the kitchen. The sight of the old cooking range and the familiar tea pot are strangely comforting.

'He's been having a lie down,' her mother explains. 'He's not too good at the moment, I'm afraid. His ticker has been playing up again.'

She puts her arm around Irene's shoulders and asks:

'So what is it pet? What's happened to upset you? Is it the baby? Has something happened to the baby?' her mother repeats.

'Is it the kids? Where are they anyway? Didn't they come with you?'

'Leslie's fine. He has to stay in the hospital though, until they operate on him. I expect Kate told you about his heart.'

'Yes, she did. Oh the poor little scrap. No wonder you're worried. Here drink this, it's fresh.'

She means the tea leaves have not been used before. She hands a cup of the tea to Irene. It's hot and very strong. Her mother has put some sugar in it. That's her remedy for all life's ills: a cup of hot, sweet tea. Irene sips it slowly; she knows she must tell her mother the news but she does not know where to start.

'Kate has been killed in an air raid,' she says at last.

'Oh no, poor Kate. Oh dear Lord, that's awful, that's terrible. I can't believe it. Kate. Oh, I shall miss her,' her mother says.

She pulls out a handkerchief and blows her nose.

'We've been friends for years,' she says, the tears trickling down her worn cheeks. 'More years than I can count.'

'What's that Lil? What's happened?' Irene's father asks.

He is a tall man, whom age has diminished by giving him a pronounced stoop. Irene thinks he looks tired; his face is etched with deep lines and there are bluish bags under his eyes. He shuffles into the room in his carpet slippers.

'It's Kate, those bloody Jerries have got her, killed in the bombing,' his wife says through her tears.

She blows her nose again.

'My God, that's dreadful. Poor Kate, never did anyone a bad turn that woman. I wish I were twenty years younger,' he wheezes. 'I'd give the Hun a run for their money, I can tell you. Murdering old women and children, that's all they can manage.'

'Hello Dad,' says Irene, giving her father a kiss on the cheek. 'How are you?'

'Not as good as I'd like to be, girl. So you've come all this way to tell us about Kate, have you? That's kind of you.'

'Well, not exactly.'

Her mother looks up.

'So what else has happened?'

'We've been bombed.'

'Oh my God, not you as well.'

'Bloody Jerries. When was that then?' Dad asks.

'While I was in hospital, the same day Kate was killed.'

'Is it bad?'

'Everything's gone, wiped out, there's nothing left.'

'Nothing? No furniture, clothes, nothing?'

'No nothing at all.'

'Oh dear God,' her mother begins to moan. 'What is this world coming to?'

'Well, you'll all have to come here then,' her father says. 'We can make room. You and the baby can have your old room and we'll put the children in your brother's room.'

Her father has it all worked out.

'Where are the kids by the way?' he asks, looking around as if she has hidden them behind the sofa.

Irene takes a deep breath.

'It's not as simple as that. There's something else,' she says.

'What do you mean, something else? Not more bad news? Irene, where are the children?' her mother asks.

She swallows hard; she doesn't want to upset them. She knows her father's heart is not strong.

'I can't find them.'

'What do you mean, you can't find them? Where are they?' her father asks.

She notices he is breathing heavily and his skin has taken on a grey tinge.

'Sit down Dad, you look all in.'

'I'm all right girl. It's you and them children I'm worried about. What's happened to them?' he replies, but nevertheless sits down heavily on the sofa.

'Kate was looking after them.'

'I told you to bring them over here, we could have managed,' her mother says. 'I told you. They should have been with their Nan and Granddad.'

'It wasn't fair on you and Dad,' Irene protests weakly. 'Any-way Kate wanted to have them.'

'It wasn't right leaving them with her. You should have brought them here,' her mother repeats. 'I'm their grandmother. Now look what's happened.'

'I thought they'd be safe with Kate. After all it was only for a few days.'

'So where are they?' her father persists.

'I don't know,' she says.

She wants to scream at him. Don't they realise what chaos there is out there? Why are they hounding her?

'I don't know. Nobody has any idea where they are. I have asked everywhere I can think of; nobody has seen them. They have just disappeared.'

'Rubbish, they can't have vanished into thin air just like that,' her mother snaps. 'Somebody must know where they are.'

'Were they caught up in the bombing?' her father asks. 'Have you tried the hospitals?'

Irene tries to control herself; she is on the point of breaking down but she feels she must be strong. There is no point taking her fears out on her parents. They are just as worried as she is.

'I don't think so. Their Sunday school teacher said they were with her until the all-clear went.'

'What about the evacuees? Maybe they've been evacuated.'

'I've tried that.'

'They have to be somewhere,' her father insists.

Her mother starts to cry more openly now.

'What about my poor little Gracie? She's just a defenceless wee thing. Oh dear God, out there on her own. God knows what is happening to them.'

She is getting worked up now; her voice is rising. Tears streak her tired face.

'You must have some idea where they are,' her father continues.

'Can't you understand Dad? I don't know what's happened to them. If I knew I'd go and get them.'

It's too much. She collapses onto the sofa beside him and starts to sob, hysterically.

'I have to find them. I can't lose my children as well.'

Her father puts his arm around her. She is a child again.

'Hush now, girl. We'll find them. They can't have gone that far. Don't worry. We'll find them,' he repeats.

His words don't comfort her. Gradually it's dawning on her that her children are actually missing and in all the chaos it might not be that easy to find them.

MAGGIE

June comes to collect them. She checks her papers as she leads her charges below decks and along the narrow passage way.

'Right, the Smith children.'

'Yes, Miss,' replies Maggie.

'You three are in this cabin. Get yourselves organised, unpack your clothes and put them away tidily. Remember, this is a ship; there is not much storage space.'

'Shipshape,' says Billy. 'That's what they call it.'

June smiles.

'That's right, shipshape and Bristol fashion. When you've done that, put on your life jackets and come along to the lounge.'

She peers at her papers again.

'That's on the Upper Deck.'

'Aye aye, Miss.'

'Billy, behave.'

Maggie gives her brother a gentle push. She is embarrassed but June just smiles and moves on to the next cabin.

'Ruth and Rita Holmes? In here please.'

Maggie can hear her repeat the instructions at each cabin until all her charges are housed. She closes their cabin door and looks around her.

Grace has stopped crying at last and is looking wide-eyed at her new home.

'We going to sleep here, Maggie?'

'Yes. Isn't it nice. All of us together.'

She puts her suitcase on the bunk and opens it. Billy does the same.

'Wow, two of everything,' he says, holding up socks in one hand and underpants in the other.

The WVS has supplied them with new coats, pullovers, shirts, stockings, vests, pyjamas, pants, a cap for Billy and hats for the girls. There are new boots for Billy and shoes for Maggie and Grace.

'I've got some gloves,' says Grace.

She sticks her tiny hands into the navy gloves and waves them about.

'What's this?' asks Billy.

'That's your ID card Billy. You must take good care of that, because that tells people who you are. Here, let's leave it in the bottom of my case for safety.'

She takes it from him. This is a new identity card, it does not have their home address, only the address of St Margaret's Orphanage. Their old ones are probably lying beneath the wreckage of their house. She tucks it into a pocket in the lining of her case, next to the tiny piece of their old door.

'What's that?' Billy asks. 'That blue thing?'

Maggie pulls out the splinter of wood.

'Don't you recognise it?' she asks.

'Is that from our front door?'

His eyes are round with amazement.

'Yes. I brought it to give us some luck.'

He reaches out and touches it.

'Can I have it?' he asks.

'No, you'll lose it.'

'And then we'll have no luck,' says Grace.

She sticks her thumb in her mouth and sucks it, noisily. Maggie is tempted to tell her to stop but decides against it. She places the piece of wood back in the case.

'We've got this, too,' Billy says, pulling at the CORB identity disc around his neck. 'June said we've got to keep it on at all times.'

It has his name in capital letters and the number B2046 beneath it.

'Yes, well you need your ID card as well, so you mustn't lose either of them.'

'And me?'

'Yes, you too Gracie. We all have to keep them. Now let's get organised. You have that bunk Billy. Grace and I'll sleep on this side.'

'Me on the top?' asks Grace.

'Yes, you on the top. Let's hurry and put everything away then we can go and explore.'

'Yes, yes, yes,' says Billy, jumping up and down on his bunk. 'Yeaas!'

Maggie is amazed at how quickly he is regaining his confidence. She wishes she felt the same. She cannot shake off this feeling of dread.

Their cabin, and those of the other children, is on 'B' Deck. June has told them that there are one hundred and thirty children on board, some are, like them, going to Australia and some are going to South Africa.

At first they have great difficulty walking along the passage way. As the motion of the ship tosses them from side to side they grab hold of anything they can to stop themselves falling. Maggie feels queasy; her stomach seems to be moving in one direction and the rest of her body in the other.

'Maggie, I's scared,' whimpers Grace.

Maggie hopes her sister isn't going to be sick. Her face is very pale.

'Are you feeling all right, Gracie?'

'She's got to get her sea-legs,' Billy tells her. 'Then she'll be all right.'

'I's fine,' Grace says.'Don't want sea-legs.'

'Come on, up here,' Billy instructs them, pulling himself up a metal staircase.

They lurch along another passageway until they see some more children, also heading for the ship's lounge and tag along behind them. Nobody speaks until they arrive in the lounge, where a cacophony of childish voices reaches out to greet them.

Maggie feels an overpowering shyness at being among so many people but it does not seem to bother Billy. He soon spots his friend and dashes across to join him. The children drift automatically into their new groups, excitedly chattering about what they have seen so far. Nobody seems to be worried about where they are going. Maggie has met some of the children already, at the school in Liverpool. She recognises one of the girls and moves closer, hoping she will speak to her but, before the girl can say anything, the chief escort claps his hands to get their attention. He has taken up position on a stage at the far end of the lounge, where he can look down at them all.

'Good morning children,' he says, then waits for the chorused reply to die down.

He is an imposing man, tall, with a grey moustache and dark rimmed spectacles; his voice booms out across the room.

'Welcome aboard *SS Orinoco*. My name is Mr Stevens and I am the head escort for this trip. I have a few things I want to tell you and I want you to listen carefully. First of all, you must always remember that you are on board a ship and although we want you to feel free to move about and enjoy your time on board, you must realise that there are places that, for your own safety, you cannot go. In particular, no children are allowed on the top deck at night.'

He looks around him.

'I see you are all wearing your life jackets. Good, make sure that you put your name on them and have them with you at all times. Your lives may depend on them.

You have already met your allocated escorts and know which group you are in. Please stay in that group. Each day, after breakfast, I want you to make your way to the aft deck for morning prayers. After prayers your escorts will tell you the plans for the day, which will include a daily boat drill. Remember your escorts are here to look after you and have your safety and well-being at heart, so please do as they say.'

He emphasises the last two words then nods towards the escorts, who are lined up behind him. They all look nice, she thinks, but June looks the nicest. They are wearing their normal clothes but each has a CORB armband so that they can be distinguished from the other adults on board. She counts them, there are fifteen, six men and nine women. All, except the head escort and the chaplain, are young.

'We also have Doctor O'Neill on board to help you if you get sick.'

Maggie can see Billy out of the corner of her eye; he is sticking his finger in his mouth and pretending to be sick. The boy with him is giggling.

Mr Stevens indicates a man in a naval uniform, standing to his right. He has a big bushy beard.

'And his assistant, Nurse Herries, and of course, our chaplain,' he continues.

These two are standing beside the doctor.

'I know this is an exciting time for you all and maybe for some it's a bit frightening, but, nevertheless, I want you to behave yourselves and do as your escorts instruct you. This is a long voyage. For some it will take almost three months to reach your new homes. We will try to keep you all occupied in useful activities during the voyage and I hope you will take this opportunity to get to know your fellow passengers and learn something about the countries you are going to visit. But children, never forget one thing, our country is at war. You are very fortunate indeed to be going somewhere safe.'

He stares meaningfully at them. Maggie sees that Billy and his new friend are trying hard not to giggle.

'Now remember children, the escorts are always available to help you if you have any problems,' he continues.

Then he sits down and, like a sudden swarm of bees, the hum of childish voices starts up again.

This is the start of, what Maggie will later come to think upon, as the happiest two and a half months of her life. It's like being on an extended holiday; even the lessons they have are fun. For a while at least she does not have to worry; she can let the responsibility for her brother and sister fall on June's willing shoulders. It's only at night, when she is lying in bed in the dark that she thinks of Mum and feels sad. She still cannot believe that Mum is dead, so when she thinks of her it's as she was before, sitting in their kitchen drinking tea with Mrs Kelly or she imagines her with the new baby. She wonders what he is like and whether he is better now.

One day June announces that she is going to form a children's choir. She tells them that she was a music teacher in Cardiff before the War. All the children, even Billy and Grace, have singing lessons once a week, usually in the ballroom, where June can accompany them on the ship's piano. Now she wants to choose the ones with the right voices for the choir. She has made a list of the possible candidates and asks them to come to the ballroom after breakfast. Maggie is both terrified and delighted to be invited to join them. She loves singing but the thought of standing up in front of other people makes her knees tremble.

'She didn't ask me,' Billy complains. 'Nor Grace.'

'Grace is too young; she couldn't learn all the words,' Maggie explains. 'There's a lot to learn.'

Poor little Gracie, at first she could not stop crying for her mother and Maggie did not know what to do to comfort her but even she has become happier lately, more like the cheerful little girl she was before.

'But I could. I can sing,' he insists and starts up with '*Good King Wencelas*'.

He is completely out of key and Maggie laughs.

'Do you want me to ask June if you can join?' she asks, knowing exactly what his answer will be.

'Nah, it's daft girl's stuff.'

June is already sitting at the piano when Maggie arrives. Some of the other children are grouped around her. Maggie feels herself blushing; she hopes she is not late.

'Sorry Miss,' she mumbles and slips into a seat near the back.

'That's all right, we're still waiting for a few more. Come closer, sit here in the front row where I can see you.'

She is not cross; she beams at Maggie and the others. Maggie watches her sort through a pile of music then lift the lid of the piano and play a few notes. The last of the children arrive and they are ready to begin. June plays a loud chord to bring the choir to attention then says:

'All right children, I think we'll start with a few popular ballads, songs you already know from school'

She turns to the piano and plays the opening notes to 'Greensleeves'.

'On a count of four.'

The music starts and the children begin to sing this old favourite. Then it's 'My Bonnie lies over the Ocean', followed by 'It was a Lover and his Lass'. Maggie enjoys singing them. She closes her eyes and for a moment she is back in her school classroom, with Miss Bentley hammering away on the piano and Mum at home waiting for her.

'That was lovely,' June says.

Maggie opens her eyes. Nothing has changed. She is still here on the ship and they say that Mum is dead. A big lump forms in her throat and she thinks she is going to cry.

'Now that we are all loosened up,' June continues, 'we are going to look at something new.'

She smiles and hands round some song sheets.

'I'm sure you all liked the film 'Pinocchio' so I thought we'd sing some of the songs from it. Some of you may already know them.'

There is a buzz of excitement. They all know and love 'Pinocchio'. It's one of Maggie's favourites; Mum took them to see it at the cinema. Even Grace enjoyed it although she kept asking questions all the time and fell asleep on Mum's knee at one point. She thinks of Mum again and how pleased she would be if she knew that Maggie was chosen for the choir but that makes her sad and she pushes the thought to the back of her mind for another time.

'How many of you know 'Hi-Diddle- Dee-Dee'?' June asks and plays the opening bars.

A dozen hands shoot in the air. Everybody does.

When the practice is over Maggie goes up onto the deck. She needs some fresh air. She enjoys singing but it reminds her so much of Mum that she feels unbearably sad. Mum was always singing. There is a hollow feeling within her whenever she thinks of her mother. She walks to the bow and looks back, towards England. All trace of her homeland has disappeared from sight; the ship is surrounded by a heaving sea the colour of pewter and above her the sky is leaden. Even the convoy of ships, that has been with them since they sailed, has disappeared. They are completely alone. For the first time since they left Liverpool Maggie feels frightened and her hand moves instinctively to her life vest.

IRENE

They are all there. Grace is running into the scullery shouting:
    'Mummy, come quick. Billy's got blue paint all over him.'

She follows her outside into the street. There they stand, Maggie and Billy watching their father paint the door. Billy has paint on his knees and down his shirt. How has he managed that? Surely he hasn't been kneeling in it, the little devil. Ronnie has his back to her; he is wearing his brown work overalls and he's applying the paint in long, smooth strokes.

    'Won't be long now, dear,' he says, without turning round. 'Almost finished.'

    'Billy's naughty, isn't he, Mummy?' Grace says with that little lisp she uses when she is being coy.

She looks up at her mother and smiles. Her blonde curls have shaken free from her ribbons and golden strands of hair shine in the morning sunlight. Irene reaches out to pick up her little daughter and ... wakes. It's not real. It has been nothing more than a dream. A dream. Yet she can still feel their presence; she can still smell the paint. The sun still feels warm on her face. She closes her eyes and sobs. Please God, let it be more than a dream.

She turns over; her pillow is wet with tears.

It has been almost six weeks and still Irene does not know what has happened to her children. Each morning she wakes to the despair of not knowing; each morning she faces the reality that they are still missing. She has been back to the bomb site re-peatedly and questioned everyone she could but no-one remembers seeing the children that day; everyone was busy looking after their own families. The pain in her chest has dulled to a constant ache, as though she is carrying their suffering around with her. Worse than anything she cannot shake off the feelings of guilt. Her head tells her that there was nothing else she could have done, that it's wartime, but her heart says she should never have left them. She knows she will never get over this; she will never be able to forgive herself, never.

The bus pulls up outside the hospital. Today is the day they are operating on Leslie. They wanted to leave it until he was at least six months old but he has been so weak lately that they have decided to go ahead with it.

She pushes open the swing doors and heads for the Babies' ward. She has the bottles of breast milk with her, even though they are not needed today.

'Mrs Smith, you're early, Doctor has not finished yet.'

'I know. I just couldn't sit at home waiting.'

'Of course. Look why don't I get you a nice cup of tea?'

'Thank you Sister.'

She sits down in the waiting room and takes out her knitting; she is making a matinee coat for Leslie. The clicking of the knitting needles is soothing and by the time the nurse returns with the tea she is more composed.

'Will the operation take very long?' she asks.

'It depends,' the nurse replies.

'Will he be all right? He is so tiny.'

'He'll be fine. Mr Cardew is a wonderful surgeon.'

'But he is so small.'

'He has put on two pounds since he came in,' she reminds Irene. 'He's not as small as he was.'

She smiles at Irene and says:

'Come on now, drink up your tea. I'll let you know when I have any news.'

He is like a doll, so small and perfectly formed; his skin is alabaster and his lashes lie like gold on his cheeks. He is so beautiful, a surge of love makes her want to cry and she has to choke back a sob. At least God has granted her this; he has let her keep her baby. As far as the surgeon can tell, the operation has been a complete success. Now they just have to wait to see how Leslie responds. She knows he will get well; that certainty lies deep within her, despite the world of uncertainties in which she is living. Leslie will survive; she is sure of it.

The door to the Babies' ward opens. It's Mr Cardew.

'Mrs Smith, you're still here?'

'Yes, I just wanted to stay with him a little longer. I thought he might open his eyes.'

'No, I don't think so. He'll sleep for a while now. Why don't you come back tomorrow? He'll be awake then.'

'How long will he have to stay in there?' she asks, pointing to the enclosed bubble in which the baby is sleeping.

'A week or so, it really depends on how he progresses. We don't want him to get any infections.'

'No, of course not.'

She puts her hand on the glass fronted incubator, the nearest she can manage to touching her son.

'Bye, bye Leslie, see you tomorrow,' she whispers.

She picks up her coat and her knitting and leaves.

She decides to go to Bethnal Green instead of straight back to her mother's house. She knows it's a waste of time. She was there last week and nothing had changed but, nevertheless, she feels compelled to try again. The bus is not long in arriving and soon she is walking through those familiar streets.

'Irene, Irene, is that you?' a man's voice calls out.

She stops and turns round. It's George Wills.

'George, fancy seeing you here. What are you doing in Bethnal Green?'

'I'm back on a spot of embarkation leave and thought I'd see how you were doing. I was just on my way to your house when I saw all this.'

He waves his hand at the burnt out houses and heaps of rubble that line the once busy street. The sight of her husband's old friend is just too much; her tears start to flow and she cannot stop them.

'Whatever's the matter?'

She is embarrassing him, she is sure, but what can she do? He waits patiently as she struggles to get her emotions under control.

'Here, take this,' he says, thrusting a khaki handkerchief under her nose.

'No, it's OK, I'm all right now.'

She swallows hard and says:

'We were bombed out.'

'I can see you've had it bad here,' he says. 'Didn't realise it was your place too.'

'There's nothing left of the street. It's all gone,' she says. 'Every house, gone.'

'My God. I'm sorry. Come on, let me buy you a cup of tea.'

She nods and says:

'We could go to the WVS shelter; it's just over there.'

Once the tea is on the table in front of them, George asks:

'So where are you living now?'

She is frightened to answer him in case she starts crying again, so she just sips her tea. It's not very strong, but it's hot and sweet. She can feel it reviving her.

'I don't usually have that sort of effect on women,' he says with a smile. 'I'm sorry if I startled you.'

'No, it's me that should apologise. It was the uniform; it reminded me of Ronnie for a minute. I'm sorry.'

He looks at her waist.

'You've had the baby then?'

'Yes, a boy, Leslie, after my Dad.'

'That's nice.'

He drinks some tea.

'So, where is he?'

She looks at him blankly.

'The baby, where is he? At your Mam's?'

'No, he's still in the hospital.'

She explains about Leslie's heart operation.

'So you see, I shouldn't be crying, I should be happy. The doctor said the operation went very well; he'll grow up to be a fine healthy boy after all.'

'That's smashing news. You must be very pleased.'

She gives him a watery smile.

'What about the kids? What do they think about having a baby brother?'

'I don't know,' she replies.

She can see he is perplexed.

'I don't know where they are. Oh George, it's awful, I just can't find them anywhere. I've asked everyone; nobody has any idea what's happened to them. I don't know if they're alive or dead.'

She puts her head in her hands and sighs.

'I'm beside myself with worry.'

She explains to the bewildered soldier what she has discovered about her children's disappearance. He stares at her in disbelief.

'I can't believe it. All three of them? I just can't believe it,' he repeats. 'God, this bloody awful war.'

'When will it end?' she asks.

He puts his hand on top of hers.

'It was dreadful about Ronnie, I know, but he was a soldier; he died fighting for his country, fighting for his children. For his kids to go like that, well it's just not fair,' George says.

She can tell that the news has upset him. He thinks that her children are dead.

'Nothing's fair these days,' she says.

She drinks her tea as they sit in silence for a while. No, she will not accept it; it's not possible that they are all dead.

'So have you been up to see your Mum?' she asks, wanting to break the silence.

'I'm going there tonight. I've got forty-eight hours before we're shipped off to God knows where.'

'So tell me something about yourself, George.'

She wants to change the subject, to think about something else for a bit, to push her worries about her children to the back of her mind, just for a few minutes.

'There's not a lot to tell; I'm twenty-eight, single and before the war I was a motor mechanic.'

'Same as Ronnie?'

'Not quite, I worked for the bus corporation.'

She looks at him, seeing him for the first time as an individual and not just another man in uniform. He is thin and wiry, with dark hair and eyes. She wonders if he has foreign blood in him. He has a warm smile, even if it's a bit lopsided.

'Where were you born?' she asks.

'Whitby, all the family are Yorkshire men. I've got three brothers, all older than me. Two are in the army and one has a reserved occupation; he's a policeman.'

'All boys?'

'Yes, my Mam says it's a nightmare living in a house full of men.'

He chuckles.

'What about your Dad?' she asks.

'He's in the Home Guard. He used to be a bus driver before he retired. That's how I got the job; he put in a word for me with the boss.'

'And your Mum?'

'Mam stays at home and looks after the house. Len, he's the policeman, still lives at home and now she's got evacuees she says she's got no time to go out to work.'

'Evacuees?'

'Yes, some kids from Lewisham, cheeky pair of brats but she's fond of them. They've been with her since the beginning of the war.'

'That's over a year now,' Irene comments. 'Hardly seems possible, does it.'

She is thinking back to before the War, to the happy little family they were then.

'Look Irene, I'm sorry but I've got to go now or I'll miss my train.'

'Yes, of course.'

She finishes her tea.

'Thanks for the cuppa.'

'Where are you staying, with your Mam?' he asks.

'Yes, I've nowhere else to go. Once Leslie's out of hospital I'll see about getting myself a job. I can't manage on the war widow's pension.'

'Give me the address and I'll look you up next time I'm in London,' he says and smiles his lopsided smile at her again.

She hunts in her shopping bag for a pencil and a scrap of paper and scribbles down her mother's address.

'It would be nice to keep in touch,' she says.

She feels a closeness to George that she knows is because of his friendship with Ronnie. How strange that he should come looking for her today.

He folds the paper carefully and places it in his wallet.

'I'll write and let you know where I am,' he says. 'If that's all right with you?'

'Yes, of course.'

She knows from what Ronnie told her that soldiers live for their letters from home. It's the least she can do for this man who has showed her so much sympathy.

'Enjoy your leave,' she says, removing her coat from the back of the chair.

'Let me.'

He takes the coat and helps her to put it on.

'Thanks.'

'Bye then Irene.'

He seems reluctant to leave.

'You'd better hurry.'

'Yes, well goodbye again,' he says.

'Good luck,' she calls after him.

She puts the baby back in his cot and covers him with the blanket. He is already asleep. What a little angel he is. It's almost four months since he came home from the hospital and still she cannot get used to the fact that he is here. He is growing bigger and stronger every day. Treat him like a normal baby, the doctor said, because that is what he is now. She tiptoes from the room and pulls the door so that it's almost closed, but not quite.

'Have you time for some tea?' asks her mother, holding up the familiar brown teapot.

Irene looks at the clock.

'No, not really. The bus comes at five to and it's ten to already.'

'Is Leslie asleep?'

'Yes, I've fed him, changed his nappy and put him down, he'll sleep for an hour at least.'

'I'll look in on him when I've done your Dad's breakfast then. Here, I've made you some paste sandwiches for your lunch.'

'Thanks, Mum.'

She kisses her mother on the cheek and picks up the bag of sandwiches. She does not have much appetite these days, but, if she does not want them, her friend, Sally will eat them. She is always hungry. She tightens the belt on her raincoat. Her mother is right; she has lost a lot of weight since Leslie was born. She knows she should eat more, if only for Leslie's sake. The doctor at the hospital said she should continue breastfeeding as long as she can so she still gives him a feed first thing in the morning and last thing at night. It has become a lot easier lately since he has been taking solids; he is no longer so greedy for her attention.

She can see the bus in the distance and hurries towards the bus stop. She cannot risk being late. The owner of the factory, Mr Levin, has already warned her that the next time she is late he will dock her pay. He pays her a pittance as it is so she cannot afford any censure. She could have earned twice as much in the munitions factory but she is frightened that her milk might become contaminated. Maybe once Leslie is completely weaned she will ask if they have any vacancies, although the tales that she hears are not encouraging. It's dangerous work; only last month there was an explosion and one girl died.

'Hello Irene.'

It's Liz, one of the girls from the factory; she works on the machine next to Irene. They do identical work; this week they are making a batch of naval uniforms. It's an interesting job even if the pay is poor and at least she feels that she is doing something for the war effort.

'Looks as though we just made it.'

The bus pulls up alongside them. It's full but the conductor tells the passengers to move along and Irene and Liz squeeze on.

'You look tired,' says Liz. 'The baby keeping you up?'

'Not really, it's more to do with sleeping in that bloody shelter every night. I'd be happy to risk it in the house, at least I'd get a good night's sleep, but Mum won't hear of it.'

'You should get one of those Morrison shelters; then at least you can stay inside in the warm.'

'Wouldn't make any difference; I'd still have to listen to my Dad's snoring. It's a wonder he doesn't bring the house down with all the blooming noise he makes. I'm thinking of telling the Ministry of Defence about him; I'm sure he could be Britain's answer to the Blitz. He could bring down more houses than a dozen bombs.'

'What about the baby, doesn't he wake him?'

'No, Leslie just sleeps right though it all, air raids, snoring, the lot.'

'Sounds a contented little chap.'

'He is, for now. It might be different once he starts teething. You'll have to come round and see him some time; he's really grown. I can hardly believe he's the same sickly baby that was in the hospital.'

'You're so lucky. I'd love to have a baby.'

Liz is barely twenty-one and her boyfriend is in the air force; they plan to get married once the war is over.

'They're showing "Gone with the Wind" at the Odeon this week. Want to go?' asks Liz.

'I've already seen it four times; I just loved it.'

'Well?'

'I'll see what my Mum says. If she'll watch Leslie then I'll go. Which night were you thinking of?'

'Saturday?'

'Yes, why not; I'm sure Mum won't mind.'

Friday is pay day so she will have some money and anyway it has been a while since she last went to the cinema. She turns to Liz and says with a smile:

'You know everyone thinks I called the baby Leslie after my Dad but really it was after Leslie Howard.'

Liz laughs.

'It could have been worse; you could have called him Clark and people would not have known whether it was after Clark Gable or Clark Kent.'

'Superman you mean?'

'Talking of supermen, have you heard from that friend of yours lately?'

'George?'

'Yes, George. How many men friends do you write to?'

'I had a letter the other week but he doesn't say much. I know they're in North Africa but I learn more from "Pathe Pictorial" than I do from him. Anyway I don't want you to get the wrong idea about me and George; he's just an old friend.'

Liz gives her a wry smile.

'Still it's good to have someone to write to, isn't it.'

BILLY

Billy is hiding inside one of the life boats. He will wait five more minutes and then if he is not found he will go and look for them. Eddie is useless at hide and seek; he is the easiest one of them all to find. He just does silly things like standing behind a pillar and he never looks in the life boats or goes on the top deck.

'We're not allowed to go up there,' he says. 'It's forbidden.'

He does not understand. That is what makes it fun.

Billy's legs are getting cramped so he straightens up to stretch them for a minute. One of the other boys is coming towards the life boats. Billy squats down again hurriedly. He knows he has been spotted and wants to giggle.

'Got you,' shouts the boy, pulling back the tarpaulin. 'Billy's here. I found him. He's over here.'

The others come running up and Billy climbs out of the life boat.

'My turn to hide,' says the boy.

'I'm bored with Hide and Seek. Let's play Cowboys and Indians,' Billy suggests.

'Yeah, good idea,' shouts one of the boys. 'Baggsy me as a cowboy.'

'No, you're an Indian,' Billy tells him. 'You're Sitting Bull.'

'But I'm always an Indian,' he wails. 'I want to be Roy Rogers.'

'Well, you can't, Eddie's Roy Rogers.'

'Let me be Buffalo Bill then.'

Billy ignores him. The boys know that, since he told them that Buffalo Bill was his granddad, he is always Buffalo Bill.

'We need the rope,' he says.

'I'll get it,' says Eddie. 'It's in my cabin.'

He runs off in search of the rope. The rope is essential for this game; they need it to tie up the Indians. One of the escorts, the one who takes them all for PE twice a week, is a wizard at teaching them how to lasso each other and tie knots in rope. They are so good at tying knots now that the other day they could not undo one of the Indians and had to send for an escort to help them. The escort told them off but he did not report them to the Chief Escort, so it was all right in the end.

Billy is enjoying life on the ship. Most of the escorts are good fun; they are not really like teachers at all. At first they were a bit serious but now that they have been at sea for a few weeks everyone is very relaxed, even the soldiers. They like having the children on board and often play football or games of deck tennis with them. One of the soldiers, a spotty faced lad from Cardiff, has become their friend. He sits with them for hours, telling them stories about his life before the war, how he played football for the local team and how his Dad was a miner. Sometimes he pulls out a battered pack of playing cards and teaches them card tricks. He tells Billy that this is his first time away from Wales and his first time on a ship; he is as excited about going abroad as they are. Billy wonders if Dad went on a ship like this. He asks the soldier:

'Is this boat going to France?'

'No, France is miles away.'

'You have to go in a boat to France, don't you? It's across the water isn't it? My Dad was in France.'

He remembers Mum talking about the boats rescuing the soldiers from France.

'Yes, that's right, but not this one. This one's going to Singapore.'

'And Australia,' Billy tells him. 'We're going to Australia.'

When the soldier tells him he is homesick for Wales, Billy understands. He doesn't tell the soldier that some nights he cries into his pillow because he wants to go back to London, to his friends, to his Nan, even to his school and he doesn't tell him how much he misses his Mum. All this he keeps inside himself.

One day the escort tells them that they will have a special treat.

'We will be in Cape Town for a whole day and you will all get the chance to go ashore and look around,' he says.

There is a buzz of excitement in the room. Billy looks across at Maggie for confirmation, does this mean them as well? Are they all going? It seems so. Everyone is going, even the escorts. June is going too, but not with them. She will be with the other escorts. The children are told to gather on the deck and wait for her.

'Now girls and boys, put your sun hats on, turn up your collars and keep your sleeves down. The sun is very hot and I don't want any of you getting sunburnt,' she instructs them.

She waits until they are all ready and then says:

'You see those people on the quayside, they have come to take you out for the day. It's very kind of them to do this so I want you all to be on your best behaviour. Now I know I can rely on you to be polite and do as you are told.'

The children nod in agreement; they are jumping about with excitement. Billy feels as though he has swallowed a bottle of pop and it's all bubbling up inside him.

'Line up in twos, children,' June says. 'Right, well if we are all ready, let's go. Have a lovely day, everyone.'

The crocodile of children marches down the gangplank. Maggie holds Grace by the hand and Billy walks behind them with Eddie. His legs feel strange. He has become so accustomed to the roll of the sea that now that it's gone he thinks he will fall over. He grabs the handrail and looks at Eddie and laughs. Eddie is staggering too. When they get onto dry land June hands them over to an elderly couple with a small dog.

'This is Mr and Mrs Van Huut. They have kindly offered to show you around Cape Town for the day.'

Maggie looks worried and Grace is squeezing her hand so tightly that Billy is surprised that she does not cry out.

'Hello, I'm Billy,' he says, 'and this is my big sister Maggie and my baby sister Grace.'

'Hello Billy, nice to meet you and you too Maggie, and Grace,' the lady says, she speaks English but with a funny accent.

'Right, well I'll see you later,' says June. 'Six o'clock?'

The couple nod and June takes the next group of children to meet their hosts for the day.

'Is that your dog?' Billy asks.

'Yes. His name is Toby.'

'Does he bite?'

The lady laughs and the man says:

'Only little boys.'

Billy knows he is joking. The dog is pleased to see them and jumps up and tries to lick his face.

'Well, children, what would you like to do?' Mrs Van Huut asks.

Even Billy does not know what to reply to this question. This is so different from anywhere he has ever been.

'How about a picnic on the beach?' Mr Van Huut suggests.

'Yeah. A picnic. That's brilliant.'

'Yes, we'd like that,' Maggie says shyly.

'Good, then that's what we'll do,' Mrs Van Huut says. 'We'll have a little walk around the town first, then we'll go to the beach.'

The town is hot and crowded. Mrs Van Huut explains that it's market day and lots of people have come to do their shopping. Billy knows it's rude to stare but he can't help it; the people are so different from London. They wear brightly coloured clothes and most of them are black. Billy has not seen any black people before but he is not surprised. The escort has told them that all the black people come from Africa and he knows that Cape Town is in Africa. He has been teaching them about all the countries that they will visit on their way to Australia. The women have big, bright scarves tied around their heads and no shoes; they wear tablecloths wrapped around their bodies and some of them have baskets balanced on top of their heads. The men look poor. Some are leading goats on a string, just like they were dogs. Mr

Van Huut says they are taking them to the market to sell them. Billy holds his nose; it smells here.

Then Mrs Van Huut takes them into a shop to buy some things for the picnic. This is more like home but even here the food on the shelves is different. Billy's mouth waters as he watches her select the fruit: apples, bananas, grapes and some things he has never seen before. There is even more fruit here than on the ship. Mrs Van Huut speaks to the lady behind the counter in a language Billy does not understand and gives her some money.

As they leave, Mr Van Huut points to a big, dark mountain that looms behind the town; it looks just like a table top.

'That's Table Mountain,' he tells them.

'Our teacher told us about it,' Maggie replies. 'He showed us a picture of it.'

'Right, I think we have enough things now,' Mrs Van Huut says, adding a bag of sweets to her shopping. 'Let's go to the beach.'

The beach is wide and long and covered with fine, golden sand; it stretches for miles. It's nothing like the beach at Southend where Mum and Dad took them once. Mr Van Huut explains that if you stand in the sea, just at this spot you will have one foot in the Indian Ocean and one in the Atlantic Ocean. Billy takes off his socks and shoes and runs into the water to try it.

'Just here?' he asks.

'That's it, right about there.'

Billy stretches out his arms. One half of him is in the Indian Ocean and the other is in the Atlantic Ocean. The dog runs in and splashes him; he wants to go swimming with them. He barks and jumps up at Billy.

'He wants to play with you,' says Mr Van Huut.

He takes an old tennis ball from his pocket and throws it along the beach. The dog bounds after it and catches it just before it runs down into the sea. Billy chases after him. He wants to take the ball off the dog and throw it again but the dog will not let him; he runs off and starts to dig in the sand.

'Silly old thing, he's going to bury it now,' says Mrs Van Huut.

She has set a plaid rug on the beach and is busy unpacking the picnic. Billy can see sandwiches and cake as well as the fruit. She takes out a large bottle of lemonade and some plastic cups. Billy sits down beside her and digs his feet into the sand, watching it run between his toes. It's warm and tickles him.

'Why don't we build a sandcastle?' Maggie says to Grace.

She still has her sunhat on. She bends down and starts to scoop a large hole in the sand. Grace has never been to the beach before so she does not understand what Maggie wants her to do.

'Look Gracie, like this,' says Billy.

He helps Maggie mould the sand into a mound.

'We need a bucket,' she says. 'To build the turrets.'

'What about using one of these,' Mrs Van Huut suggests and hands her one of the plastic cups.

It's not very big, but it works well. Before they have even built two turrets Toby has joined them; digging is obviously his favourite pastime.

Maggie tries to pull him off but he just rolls on his back and offers her his tummy to tickle instead.

'Oh, you're so sweet,' she tells him. 'I wish we had a dog. I'd call him Toby, just like you.'

'Come and have something to eat,' Mrs Van Huut says.

Billy is starving. He leaves the sandcastle and sits down next to the woman. He likes Mr and Mrs Van Huut; he would like to stay with them instead of going to Australia. If he can't go back home then he will stay here.

The afternoon goes very quickly and it seems no time before Mr Van Huut is looking at his watch and saying that they have to leave. Billy can feel the disappointment showing in his face so he tries to smile and look happy. He dries his feet on a towel that Mrs Van Huut gives him and pulls on his socks and shoes. Why can't he stay here? He could come to the beach every day and never have to wear shoes and socks. He could learn to swim and teach Toby how to bring the ball back when he caught it.

'Cheer up old chap,' Mr Van Huut says. 'I know what we'll do, we'll go and get some ice creams before you go back to the ship.'

Ice cream. Billy loves ice cream. It was a special treat on Sundays, before the war, when Dad was home. Dad would take them out for a walk after lunch and buy them each an ice cream cornet. Mum preferred a wafer.

Mr Van Huut buys three vanilla cones and when Grace drops hers in the sand and begins to cry, Mr Van Huut does not tell her off; he just buys her another one.

On the way back to the ship Mr and Mrs Van Huut tell them that they have a son who is fighting in North Africa; they say that they miss him very much.

'Our Dad was a soldier,' Maggie says. 'He died in the War.'

'Our Mum is in Heaven,' Billy adds. 'They're in Heaven together.'

'Oh you poor little things,' Mrs Van Huut says and hugs them one by one.

Billy likes being hugged by Mrs Van Huut; she smells nice, of spices and apples.

The day has passed so quickly, Billy can hardly believe that it's six o'clock already and they are back on board the ship, laden with presents of sweets, apples, oranges and books. It's like an early Christmas. Mr and Mrs Van Huut have been very kind to them.

'Maggie?'

'What is it Billy?'

'Why can't we stay here and live with Mr and Mrs Van Huut?'

'Because we're going to Australia.'

'But Mr and Mrs Van Huut haven't got any children, I'm sure they'd like to have us.'

'Yes, Mrs Van Huut says I'm the prettiest little girl she has ever seen,' adds Grace.

'They have a son in the army,' Maggie reminds them.

'But he'll probably get killed,' Billy says, popping a sweet into his mouth. 'Why don't we ask June if we can stay?'

'Because we're going to Australia.'

'I don't want to go to Stralia,' Grace says with a pout.

The ship is already steaming out of the harbour and the outline of Table Mountain blends into the darkening sky. One by one the lights in the town begin to come on.

'Look at that, it's like Fairyland,' Maggie says, 'just like Fairyland.'

MAGGIE

A few days after leaving Colombo, Maggie sees one of the soldiers talking to June. She is listening attentively, nodding her head in agreement to whatever he is saying. Maggie is gripped with curiosity. Why is June talking to him?

She does not have long to wait to discover the reason. The very next day, when the choir are assembled and waiting for June to tell them what they are going to sing, instead of opening the piano as usual, she asks them to sit down. She has something to tell them, she says. They all look at her expectantly. Does this have something to do with the soldier, Maggie wonders.

'I've got some wonderful news, children. We have been asked to take part in a concert.'

She waits for the hum of excited chatter to die down then continues:

'Private Fergusson is putting on a concert for the soldiers before they disembark at Singapore. He has been listening to your singing and would like you to take part.'

'All of us?'

'Yes, the whole choir.'

'Oh Miss, will we have to sing in front of all those soldiers?'

'Yes, Mary, but don't worry, you'll be fine. Now the concert is in two weeks time, so we have to begin practising, right away.'

'What are we going to sing, Miss?'

Most of the children are getting excited at the idea now but Maggie is apprehensive.

'I thought we'd sing them a medley of songs from Pinocchio.'

At this a cheer goes up; the children love the songs and most of them know the words by heart.

'Maggie I'd like you to sing a solo. I thought, maybe, *"When You Wish Upon a Star"*? You like that don't you?'

She cannot believe that June is asking her this.

'But Miss, I couldn't.'

'Of course you can; you sing it all the time.'

'But that's different, Miss, I'm with the others. I just couldn't sing it on my own.'

'Well, we'll practise it together. Don't worry; you'll be all right, you see. Now come on, we'd better get on, we've got a lot of work to do. Let's warm up with *"Hi-Diddle-Dee-Dee"*.'

She lifts the lid of the piano and begins to play the introduction.

The next day Maggie is sitting on the deck, behind one of the life boats when she hears June's voice. She is talking to Mr Stevens, the chief escort. They don't realise that Maggie is there.

'Is it true?' June asks.

She sounds as though she is crying.

'I'm afraid so. It was on the wireless this morning. There are only 158 survivors.'

'I can't believe it. Bloody U-boats.'

'Yes, those poor children, on their way to a better life in Canada. It's unthinkable,' Mr Stevens says. 'I've told the other escorts but I think it'd be best to keep it from the children. We don't want to frighten them.'

'Of course but there aren't any U-boats here, are there?' June asks.

'No. These kids are lucky; the war hasn't touched this part of the ocean yet.'

Maggie feels her stomach tighten with fear. They are talking about sea evacuees, she is certain. She thinks of the huge expanse of sea that surrounds them and imagines what it must be like to fall overboard. Suddenly she feels very alone.

'It's the King's speech at four,' he says. 'Bring your children up for that, will you.'

'Yes, Mr Stevens.'

Maggie waits until she hears them move away and then gets up. She had planned to practice her song but she doesn't feel like it any more. She desperately wants to be home, back with her Mum and the new baby, back with Dad, before the war. If only she could turn the clock back. She wonders if her little brother is still alive. And Mum, where is Mum? It can't be true that she is dead. She won't believe it. One day Mum will come and find them, she knows she will.

As the ship grows closer to Singapore there is a change in the soldiers' attitude; they no longer spend their days lounging on the main deck, smoking and chatting to the children. There is a tension in the air. Everyone knows that the time has come for them to leave and return to what everybody has successfully managed to suspend from their thoughts during the lazy weeks of the cruise. It's time for them to go back to the war.

Maggie has no time to feel sorry for the soldiers; she is far too busy worrying about her solo. The concert is the night before they dock. She has been rehearsing the words of the song until she knows them backwards but still she worries that she will forget them. Her friend, Janet has explained to her about stage-fright.

'Actors and actresses get it. It's when your mind goes completely blank and you can't remember a word. It's awful. Then they let down the curtain and someone has to go out front and make some jokes so that the audience don't get angry.'

Janet's father is a playwright and Janet has been to many of London's West End theatres with her parents. She has an excellent memory and one of the things that Maggie likes about being her friend is that she tells her about the plays she has seen even though they seem a bit dull to Maggie, not at all as exciting as 'Pinocchio' or 'The Wizard of Oz'. She likes to imagine the people going in to watch them, the women in their fur coats and the men in suits and fedoras.

'Well,' Maggie argues. 'There isn't a curtain in the ballroom. So what happens if someone gets stage-fright there?'

'I expect they just pull you off the stage and someone else sings a song.'

'Oh I wish June hadn't asked me to do it,' she wails. 'I know I'm going to be a disaster.'

'Don't be silly. It'll be over in a moment and then everyone will clap and you'll become stage-struck and end up a famous singer in Australia and marry a film-star.'

The girls laugh. Sometimes they allow themselves to dream, to imagine what the future holds in store for them. Janet has her future planned out for her. Once the war is over, her father wants her to go to university and study English and Drama, just as he had done. Most of the other girls want to get married and have lots of babies and there is one who wants to be a vet and work with animals, but Maggie does not really know what she wants to be. At the moment all she can think about is for the war to be over and to be with Mum again.

At last the day of the concert arrives. June takes them through one last rehearsal and declares that they are all excellent.

'You'll knock them dead,' she tells them, with a bigger than usual smile.

Maggie thinks June looks lovely. Her hair, normally twisted into a roll at the back of her neck, is loose and flowing. It's a lovely shade of chestnut brown and reaches to her shoulders. She wears a dress that Maggie has not seen before; it's red, with a red and white collar and a red belt that nips in her waist. Even her lipstick is red. Maggie wishes she had something special to wear. She only has two dresses; one is already a bit small for her but the other, a cotton dress with tiny blue flowers on it, is quite pretty. She is wearing that one.

'All right Maggie? No first-night nerves?' June asks.

Maggie shakes her head. It's too late to back out now. She cannot let June down; that would be awful.

'Good girl. I'll tell you when to go on.'

Maggie sits at the side, with the other members of the choir, waiting for their turn. The ballroom is packed. The children sit on the floor at the front and then, behind them, are the soldiers. The men are all in high spirits, joking and laughing amongst themselves. The ship's captain stands up and welcomes everyone then hands over to the man that Maggie saw talking to June earlier.

'Welcome everyone. We have some very special people in the audience tonight,' he waves towards the children and everyone cheers and claps. 'And some even more special people on the stage.'

He looks towards the choir and again everyone claps. Maggie feels herself blushing. She can see Billy and Grace sitting in the front row.

'But first we're going to start with some old Tommy Handley jokes from our old friend, Corporal Tim Thomas. So, just sit back and enjoy yourselves. Let's have a big hand for Tim Thomas.'

The applause is deafening and a gangly young corporal gets on the stage. Maggie can hardly hear what he is saying for the noise from the soldiers as they laugh and barrack their comrade. Her stomach is churning and making gurgling sounds; she wishes she had eaten her lunch but she had had no appetite. Now she just wants to slip away and hide.

The comedian is followed by a man playing the accordion then two soldiers come on and do, what they call, an 'Astaires and Rogers' routine, which seems to involve a lot of foot tapping and sliding across the stage. Then she sees June stand up. The compère is saying:

'Now for the highlight of the evening, The *Orinoco* Sea Evacuees Choir.'

Amid thunderous applause the choir files onto the stage just as June has instructed them. The compère lifts his hand and the noise dies down. June sits at the piano and they wait for her signal. First they sing '*Give a Little Whistle*' and the soldiers all join in with the whistle and when the choir has to shout 'Pinocchio' or 'Jiminy Cricket', they join in then as well. It's wonderful. Suddenly Maggie is no longer nervous; this is fun. Next they sing '*Hi-Diddle-Dee-Dee*' and again everyone joins in the chorus.

Now it's time for her solo. The rest of the choir sit down on the stage and she stands there alone. She is no longer nervous. She looks down at Billy and Grace. They are waiting for her to begin, wide-eyed, expectant. She takes a deep breath, looks to June for her cue and begins. This time the soldiers are silent. From deep inside her the song swells as the words and the music blend together. Her voice is clear and sweet; it soars up into the night sky and drifts across the ocean. Somewhere, somehow her mother can hear her; she knows it. She is singing for her.

Then it's over. There is silence. At first no-one moves then they are applauding her. Her. They like her. The soldiers are stamping their feet and whistling. Billy and Grace are clapping. June is beaming at her and encouraging her to take a bow. She feels euphoric. This is the most wonderful moment of her life. She never wants it to end but already the choir is getting to its feet and June is playing the introductory bars to '*You Are My Sunshine*'. This time everyone is singing, soldiers, crew members and children.

Afterwards, lying on her bunk, listening to the tiny snores of her sister, she relives every moment of the evening. She never believed it could be so wonderful. June was delighted with them and gave them all a hug; she said they had done a grand job. That was the nicest part of all, when June had put her arms around her and hugged her; she smelled of roses and face powder.

'You have a lovely voice Maggie,' she said. 'You did really well tonight. You looked a real young lady, standing up there, in front of everyone. I'm very proud of you.'

Since Maggie arrived on board the ship her world is expanding in a way she never thought possible; after almost two months, the horrors of London and the orphanage seem to be no more than a bad dream. And yet, in some way, here, far from home, she feels closer to Mum than ever before. Sometimes, like now, even when she is feeling happy, a wave of homesickness sweeps over her and she can see their blue front door, standing so bravely amongst all the brown ones; she can taste her Nan's rock cakes warm from the oven; she can see the twinkle in Mrs Kelly's eye as she jokes with Mum and she can smell again that special mix of lavender and cigarettes that clung to her mother and she wishes with all her heart that Mum was here with them.

Maggie closes her eyes and begins to hum her song to herself. She will do that, every time she sees a star she will wish that Mum comes and takes them home again.

After the soldiers have left, the ship seems empty. At first the children are subdued, but then, gradually, the excitement of approaching their destination grows. They are heading for Fremantle, in Western Australia first.

The teacher teaches them all about Australia. Maggie knows that Fremantle is on the west side of the country and Melbourne, where they are going, is on the east, another two thousand miles away. He names the different parts of the country and the children write them on a map in pencil: Queensland, Victoria, Western Australia, Northern Territory, Southern Australia and New South Wales. He shows them where the deserts are and tells them to colour those areas yellow.

When one boy asks what would happen if they get lost in the desert, he says:

'Well, unless someone finds you very quickly, you will die of thirst.'

This frightens the children but then he explains that the only people who live in the desert are aborigines. They are black people who were the original inhabitants of the land, so they know how to survive in such a hot, dry climate. He assures them that they are not going anywhere near the desert.

At last the day arrives; they are approaching Fremantle. It's very hot; the sun is a bright golden ball in a cloudless sky. All the children who are due to disembark are on deck, their suitcases at their feet and their winter coats over their arms. They are hot and uncomfortable in their English clothes. Maggie feels her vest sticking to her back. The escorts have lined them up near the gangway, but the children cannot keep still; they are stretching on tiptoe to get a glimpse of their new home. Maggie stands back with those who have further to go. Grace and Jenny are on one side and Billy is on the other. The coastline that stretches out before them is wild and rugged; tall, barren cliffs reach down to the sea, where white tipped waves crash against the rocks in a cascade of foam. It looks a frightening, forbidding place. Maggie is glad they are not going to disembark in Fremantle.

Then the unthinkable happens.

'Billy Smith,' Mr Stevens calls out his name. 'Ah, there you are boy. Come along. You should be over there with the other boys. Are you packed ready?'

'No Sir. I don't get off here.'

'We're going to Melbourne,' chips in Maggie.

She still does not realise.

The chief escort looks at his list.

'Yes, that's right, Maggie and Grace Smith. The Sisters of Nazareth are meeting you in Melbourne. But you, my son, are leaving the ship today. You're going to the Christian Brothers in Wadene.'

Billy stares at him in amazement.

'No,' he shouts. 'No, I'm not going. I'm not going anywhere without my sisters. No. That's not fair.'

'Now, now, son. You can't go with your sisters. They're going to a girls' school. You can't go with them. It's not allowed.'

'But I want to.'

'I'm sorry but that's the way it is. Now go and get your suitcase or you'll have to leave without it.'

'But ...'

'Now.'

Billy runs off in the direction of his cabin. Maggie can hear him sobbing all the way.

'Wait here,' she tells Grace. 'I'm going to find June.'

She races off to where she last saw the escort. June is on the top deck, talking to one of her colleagues.

'What on earth is the matter, Maggie?' she asks.

'It's, it's, it's Billy,' she at last manages to spit out. 'They're making him get off the boat. It's too soon. He's supposed to leave when we do. Please stop them.'

June puts her arms around her and hugs her.

'That's right Maggie; that's what it says in the file. You and Grace are to go to the nuns in Melbourne but Billy is going to a farm school in Wadene.'

'But I don't even know where Wadene is,' Maggie blubbers.

She looks accusingly at them. They are supposed to look after them. She thought June was her friend.

'We're supposed to stay together. He's my brother; I have to look after him,' she adds. 'I'm the eldest.'

'I'm sorry, Maggie. It's impossible. They're expecting him in Wadene. Look, don't cry. He'll be all right. There are other boys going there as well. He won't be alone and they will look after him for you.'

'But I'm his sister; I have to look after him. Can't you stop it June, please. Please speak to someone. Please.'

She is desperate now. Why can't June understand that they have to stay together?

June hugs her tighter.

'I'm sorry, Maggie; there's nothing I can do, nothing.'

'Why can't we stay with you?'

She is clutching at straws. Surely there is something June can do to help them?

'I'm going back to England after the children get off in Melbourne. We all are. We have our jobs to do.'

'It's not fair. Just because he's a boy.'

'I know it doesn't seem fair but really it's for the best. He'll have a great time in Wadene. He'll be with lots of other boys.'

June strokes Maggie's hair.

'Now you be a brave girl and go and help him pack his bag. You don't want to miss him getting off, do you?'

Maggie does not know how she manages to get back to their cabin; she walks as if she is in a dream. By the time she arrives, Billy has stuffed his clothes into his case and is trying to close it. She looks at his tearstained face and wants to weep. How will he manage on his own?

'Here let me help you,' she says. 'Have you still got your ID card?'

'Yes, it's where you put it,' he whispers.

'Here, take this.'

She takes the piece of their old door and breaks it in two. She gives one piece to him and puts the other back in her case.

'For luck,' she says.

He puts it in his case but doesn't say anything. All the life seems to have gone out of him. She starts to cry again. Poor Billy. She was supposed to take care of him; she had promised.

'Will you come and see me Maggie?' he asks.

'If I can Billy. If I can.'

How can she promise him anything? If this can happen to Billy, what lies in store for her and Grace?

'I'll write to you. I promise.'

'Will you?'

She nods.

'Every week?'

'Every week.'

'Will you look after Grace?'

'Yes.'

'They won't split you up as well, will they?'

'No, Billy. I think it's just because you're a boy.'

'I don't want to be a boy. I want to go with you.'

She wipes her eyes; she does not want him to remember her crying.

'You'll be all right, you see. Here, put on your coat.'

She helps him button up his coat and puts his cap on his head and straightens it. Then she gives him a big hug.

'Come on now, they're waiting for you.'

She follows him up onto the deck and watches as he joins the other boys walking down the gang plank. She can make out the figures of two priests on the quay; their robes flap in the breeze like black crows. The chief escort is speaking to them. They give him a piece of paper and he looks back towards the line of children and beckons. She sees a small group of boys break away from the other children and go across to him. The chief escort shakes hands with each of the boys then walks away. The boys follow the two priests along the quay. Billy is with them; he is looking back at her. He is calling her name. She continues watching, her eyes aching from the strain, until she can no longer see them. They have disappeared. She looks back at the other children; they are climbing into a waiting bus. She can hear their cheerful chatter. She hears the engine start and the bus drives away. There is no-one left on the dock. It's deserted.

'Maggie, where's Billy gone?' asks Grace.

Maggie cannot speak. The crew are preparing the ship to leave. The gangplank has already been removed and she can hear the heavy clanking of the anchor being raised. It's too late to do anything. He has gone. She begins to sob and tears flow down her cheeks. It's so awful. She thinks her heart will break. This is the worst thing that could have happened to them and she is powerless to do anything about it.

PART TWO
AUSTRALIA
1941-43

'Oh my friends, don't you know
How a long time ago
There were two little children
Whose names I don't know?

They were taken away
On a cold winter's day
And left in the woods
So I heard some folks say.'

'Babes in the Woods' (Traditional Australian song)

BILLY

Billy feels in a daze. He follows the boy in front of him until they are told to stop.

'Wait here,' says the man in the long black cloak.

He is dressed a bit like Father McNally except that he has a hood on his robes. None of the boys speak; they all look frightened. Billy begins to cry again.

'Don't cry,' whispers the boy next to him. 'You'll get into trouble if they see you crying.'

He swallows hard and fights back the tears. How he wishes Maggie was there to help him. He does not know how he will manage without her.

'Right, come along boys, follow me.'

The man has returned; he has some papers in his hand. He tries to smile at them but his face only contorts into a grimace.

'We're going to catch a train; we've a long way to go,' he tells them.

The boys don't reply. They follow in silence.

It does not take long to arrive at the railway station and board the train. There are fifteen boys altogether; Billy's group get into the first carriage with one of the men in black and the rest of the group have the second carriage. The man that is with them looks at them kindly; his face is round and shiny and there are dimples in his chin.

'Put your bags up on the racks, boys and make yourselves comfortable,' he tells them.

They do as he says.

'It's a long way,' he explains, 'almost three hundred miles.'

'When will we arrive?' asks one of the boys.

'Not until tomorrow morning,' he replies.

He sits down and spreads himself out. His gown is stretched tightly across his stomach and he fidgets for a bit until he is comfortable. Then he pulls out a pair of spectacles and looks closely at a list.

'Damon Stuart?'

'That's me, Father.'

'You mustn't call me Father, boy. I am not a priest. You only call the Reverend Mooney Father. You must address all the Brothers by their names; I am Brother Anthony.'

'Yes, Brother Anthony.'

There is a loud whistle and with a shudder the train begins to pull away from the station.

'William Smith?'

'Yes, Brother Anthony.'

He calls out the boys names one by one then, satisfied that all are present, pulls out a book and begins to read.

At first the boys say nothing then Damon leans across and whispers to Billy:

'I saw you on the ship. You were always hanging about with that boy with red hair.'

'Eddie. He's gone to live with his aunty then he's going home to his mum when the war is over.'

'He's lucky; I'm here for good.'

'What do you mean, for good? Aren't you ever going home?'

'No, I don't have no home. I was in an orphanage. Now I'm going to learn to be a farmer.'

'Do you know where we're going?' Billy whispers.

'Course I do; we're going to the Wadene Farm School. It's run by the Christian Brothers. I was in a Christian Brothers' orphanage in Kent,' he adds. 'They decided I should come out here and learn to be a farmer. I might even end up with my own farm.'

He looks pleased at the prospect.

'Will there be animals at the farm school?'

'I should think so, pigs and sheep I expect.'

'Horses?'

'Probably.'

'I like horses. The milkman used to let me ride his horse sometimes.'

Billy thinks of the milkman and his horse. He was a big man and he would swing Billy up onto the horse's back as easily as if he were a feather. He feels the tears coming and blinks rapidly. He must not cry. They will think he is a baby if he cries.

The boy pulls out a packet of sandwiches and begins to eat one.

'Don't you have any sarnies?' he asks.

'No, I didn't know I was getting off the ship. I thought I was staying with my sisters.'

'No way, the Brothers don't like girls; they have to go to the nuns. Anyway they can't do the stuff we boys do.'

'I suppose not.'

'Here, you can have one of these.'

Damon gives him one of his sandwiches; it's cheese and pickle, his favourite. He leans his head against the window. The countryside is flashing past now, fields and fields of nothing but scrubland; the city has been left far behind them. There is little to see from the train window; there are very few trees and a bare and empty landscape stretches out to the horizon. He has never been in the countryside before; it's all so different from London. Where are all the houses? Where do people live? Where are the shops? The train seems to be cutting its way through a barren wilderness. He thinks he will never be able to find his way back and a feeling of panic grabs him.

He wonders what Maggie and Grace are doing. The ship will be well on its way to Melbourne now. This time he cannot help himself and a tear trickles down his cheek. Will he ever see his sisters again? June used to say that everyone would go home when the war was over but he does not have any home to go to. It was bombed. What if they cannot find him? He looks again at the bleak landscape; there are no towns out here. How will Maggie know where to look for him? The train is taking him further and further from her. Even Maggie will not be able to find him here.

'Want to play cards?'

A boy opposite is shuffling some playing cards. It's the same boy who spoke to him in the queue. He looks at him closely; he is very thin, 'needs a good square meal' is what Billy's Nan would say. Billy wipes his eyes on the back of his sleeve and nods.

'My name's Louie. What shall we play?'

'Snap?'

He does not know many card games. Dad taught him how to play Snap and Happy Families but he remembers that you need special cards for Happy Families. He realises he has not thought about Dad in a long time and feels very sad. He wishes he was not dead.

'OK. What about you?'

Louie looks at Damon.

'OK,' is the reply.

They persuade a fourth boy to join them. Billy enjoys the game and the time seems to pass more quickly. At one point they are making so much noise that Brother Anthony looks up from his book and tells them to play more quietly. Before long Billy realises that it's pitch black outside the window and he can see nothing except their own reflections. Brother Anthony closes his book and slips it into the pocket of his soutane.

'I think you boys should try to get some sleep now. We still have a long way to go and I'm sure you want to be fresh and lively when you arrive. Find yourself a space to stretch out and no more chattering.'

He leans back and closes his eyes; it's clear that the card game must end. Billy is quite comfortable in the corner by the window but one boy decides to lie down on the floor and one of the bigger boys swings himself up into the luggage rack and stretches out, his feet dangling above Billy's head.

'Goodnight, Billy,' whispers Louie.

Billy closes his eyes, the motion of the train is comforting and he is soon asleep.

A violent shudder and the screeching of brakes as they pull into the station soon rouse the boys. Billy is stiff; he stands up and stretches his arms upwards. A quick glance through the carriage window tells him it's still dark outside. He shivers. It's bitterly cold.

'Hurry up now boys. We've arrived. Time to get off the train. Get a move on now. Collect up all your things.'

Brother Anthony is standing there holding the carriage door open. Billy grabs his suitcase and stumbles out onto the platform. Where on earth is he? Apart from a wooden hut and an ancient sign that says 'Wadene', there is nothing around them. The darkness stretches away into the distance as far as he can see. The other boys tumble out onto the platform next to him and line up in silence. Everyone is shivering; the cold is eating into their bones. 'Follow me and keep together,' instructs the second Brother.

He leads them to two parked trucks and unhooks the tarpaulin on the back of the first one.

'Right, the first eight boys in here,' he tells them and emphasises his words with a wave of his stick.

One of the boys jumps up into the truck and then the others follow. Billy joins the next group. While they wait for Brother Anthony to undo the tarpaulin on their truck, he looks back at the train. It's pulling away from the siding, its long shiny body like some mythical dragon, dotted with tiny lights and enveloped in a cloud of billowing smoke. It roars and huffs and puffs and then it's gone, lost in the darkness. The only light now is the lamp that swings above the ancient sign. A silence descends on the group. The boys look at each other but nobody speaks. The revving of an engine tells them that one of the trucks is about to leave.

'OK boys, jump up,' Brother Anthony says, pulling back the tarpaulin. 'We'll be late for breakfast if we don't get a move on.'

He helps the smaller children clamber up into the truck but Billy can manage on his own; he jumps up, scraping his knee as he does so. There are some benches in the truck and the boys huddle together on them for warmth. Their truck starts up with a cough and a shudder then moves off; the second part of their journey has begun.

'Is it much further, Brother Anthony?' one of the boys asks.

'About ten miles.'

Ten miles, that sounds a long way, Billy thinks. He is feeling very hungry and cannot stop shivering. He does up all the buttons on his coat and puts his hat on. Suddenly he feels angry with the escort on the ship; he had told them it was hot and sunny in Australia. Nobody had said anything about it being so cold.

'Shall we sing a song?' suggests Louie. 'My mum always let us sing a song when we went on the train.'

'We're not on a train, stupid,' says one of the bigger boys.

'Do you know Ten Green Bottles?' someone else asks. 'We could sing that.'

'What about Brother Anthony? He might tell us off.'

'Don't be daft; he can't hear us when he's driving.'

Nervously at first, the boys begin to sing:

'There are ten green bottles hanging on the wall.

And if one green bottle should accidentally fall ...'

By the time there are only five green bottles left, the boys are laughing and singing as if they have known each other forever. Billy is still cold and hungry but now he is not so frightened.

The sun is just peering over the horizon by the time they arrive. Wadene Farm School is surrounded by a tall wire fence; he wonders if it's to keep people out or to keep them in. They wait by some heavy iron gates while Brother Anthony gets out and laboriously swings them open. The trucks drive in and park alongside an old barn. The boys, happy that they have arrived at last, clamber out and stand in the cold morning light, stamping their feet and chattering.

'Here we are boys,' says Brother Anthony. 'Just in time for breakfast.'

He rubs his eyes.

'Ah, here's your welcoming committee.'

Billy turns to where Brother Anthony is pointing. A dozen or so of the most raggedy boys he has ever seen are running to greet them. None of them is wearing shoes and all have the most awful haircuts. They don't look very friendly.

'They will take you along to the refectory for a nice cup of warm cocoa,' adds Brother Anthony. 'Then they will show you your new home.'

The new boys stand back nervously; this is not what they were expecting.

'What are you boys waiting for? Get a move on, and the rest of you get about your business. What do you think this is, a public holiday?' a sharp voice says.

It's the one who Billy now knows is called Brother Dermot. Obediently they pick up their suitcases and traipse after the raggedy boys. They pass a number of wooden buildings with corrugated iron roofs; the largest of these has a veranda covered with honeysuckle and its smell is sweet in the cold air.

The refectory is situated in a low brick building, where a number of long wooden tables covered with lino have been set with metal bowls and spoons. The new boys are directed to sit down at one of the tables and wait. Billy feels nervous; the farm boys are regarding the newcomers with interest as they wait for their breakfast but nobody says anything.

'Ah, the new boys have arrived. Come in boys. Sit down,' says one of the Brothers sitting at the top table.

He looks at one of their little escorts and snaps:

'Willis, get the cocoa and be sharp about it.'

'Yes, Brother Patrick.'

The boy hurries out and returns almost immediately with a tray of mugs and a huge jug of cocoa. He puts it on the table in front of Billy.

'Well, pour it out boy.'

The cocoa is warm and watery and Billy drinks it down quickly. A bowl of grey porridge is placed in front of each of them. Billy tastes it; it's even worse than the food in the orphanage in London. He thinks back to his last breakfast on the ship: hot muffins with butter and honey and a boiled egg. He looks around him; the other boys are eating their porridge in a greedy silence.

The boy called Willis stops beside him and whispers:
'If you're not going to eat it, I'll have it.'

Billy picks up his spoon and begins to eat but, before he has time to finish, a bell rings and the bowls are being cleared away. The boys stand up and file out of the refectory.

'Hurry up,' Willis says. 'I'll show you your room.'

He leads them across the yard and into another building that appears identical to the first. The walls are of unpainted wood and the floor is bare. Billy is in the same room as Louie. There are six iron-framed beds on each side of the room and Billy and Louie have the two at the end next to an open window. Billy sits down on his bed; the mattress is lumpy and the single blanket is threadbare.

'You have to take off your clothes and put them in your case then you put these on,' Willis tells them. 'I'll be back as soon as I've taken the others to their dorm. Wait here for me.'

He disappears down the passage with the remainder of their group.

Billy looks at the clothes laid out on the bed, the shorts and shirt are khaki, as is the pullover. He starts undressing.

'We'll look like soldiers,' he says to Louie and pulls the shirt over his head.

It has a hole in the sleeve but it's clean.

'And yer undies,' a voice instructs them.

It's one of the older boys.

'You're not allowed to wear underwear here, not until you're twelve,' he explains.

'Not even my underpants?' Louie gasps.

'No, put it all in your case and leave the case at the end of your bed.'

The boy is about twelve years old. He is very brown and thin but Billy thinks he looks strong.

'You don't need your socks either.'

The boy is barefoot.

'What about our shoes? Can we keep those?'

'If you want, but after a while you won't want to wear them. Nobody does. They'll get too small for you anyway.'

Billy takes off his socks but replaces his shoes; he does not want to go barefoot no matter what the boy says.

'My name's O'Malley by the way. I'm in charge of this dorm, so if you have any questions come to me.'

Billy smiles. He has so many questions he does not know where to start.

'Why can't we wear our own clothes?'

'It's the rule, everybody has to wear the uniform.'

'But what happens to our clothes?'

The boy shrugs.

'Ah, Willis, there you are.'

'Yes, O'Malley.'

'Take these two over to the school when they're ready. And don't be all day about it.'

Billy opens his case and places his clothes inside then, when he is sure no-one is looking at him, he reaches in and takes out his ID card and the piece of wood that Maggie gave him. Maggie said he must not lose it; he will hide it somewhere as soon as he can. In the meantime he slips them both into the pocket of his shorts, along with his CORB disc. It's important that he hangs onto something from before. He has a feeling that everything is going to change from now on.

A boy is standing at the front of the class reciting something and all the others are watching him. He falters and makes a mistake. Billy is horrified to see the brother lean across and hit him across the legs with a stick but the boy does not cry out, instead he continues with his recitation. They wait until he is finished and then Willis says:

'Please, Brother Dermot, these are two of the new boys.'

He leaves them standing there and scurries away to sit at his desk.

'About time too Willis, now get out your catechism,' the brother replies.

He turns and looks at Billy and Louie. He narrows his eyes as though he cannot see them very well; they are cold eyes and seem to look straight through them. He pulls out a handkerchief and wipes a drip from his long, thin nose then says:

'Names?'

'William Smith.'

'Louie Brown.'

'Ah yes, Brown, you're from St Patrick's.'

'Yes, Brother Dermot.'

'And you Smith, where are you from?'

'Bethnal Green, sir, uh Brother Dermot.'

'Bethnal Green? What's the name of the orphanage, boy?'

'St Margaret's, me and my sisters were staying with the nuns.'

'I see. Well, Smith, how old are you?'

'Ten, Brother Dermot.'

'Do you know your catechism boy?'

'I don't think so Brother Dermot.'

'You don't think so?'

Billy is aware that everyone is staring at him. He has done something wrong but he does not know what it is.

'What sort of an answer is that?' Brother Dermot continues. 'You either do or you don't.'

'Yes, Brother Dermot.'

'Well, do you know it or not?'

'No, Brother Dermot. I don't know what it is. I'm not a Catholic.'

The silence in the room is dreadful. He hopes Brother Dermot is not going to hit him like he hit the other boy. He can feel his knees shaking and does not know if it's because of the cold or because he is so frightened.

'We will see about that. Sit down.'

He turns to the rest of the class and says:

'Put your books away and get out your slates ready for Brother Lucius.'

As he is about to leave he stops at Billy's desk.

'You will come to me after vespers every day until you catch up.'

'Yes, Brother Dermot.'

When the door closes behind him the boys are on their feet; they crowd around the newcomers.

'Where you from then?' asks one.

'Got any grub?' asks another.

Billy shakes his head.

'What, nothing?'

'We're from London,' says Louie.

'What's yer names?'

'All right boys, that's enough now. Back in your seats and get out your slates.'

Another brother has come in; this one is tall and thin and has a bald patch on the back of his head. He walks to the front of the room and regards them with a kindly smile.

'It's Brother Lucius,' whispers Willis. 'He's OK; he hardly ever uses the strap.'

Despite his confident words, Willis slips back into his seat and takes out his slate.

Brother Lucius looks at the new boys but says nothing. He turns and begins writing something on the board. It's a list of sums.

'You have ten minutes to complete these sums. Begin.'

The boys do as they are told. The room is quiet; all Billy can hear is the squeaking of the chalk as it skitters across the slate. He likes sums. The first ones are quite easy. He does them quickly. The next one is more difficult; he copies it down carefully and looks at it for a moment. The chalk is old and is hard to write with. He wonders why they cannot use pencils; he has not used chalk since he was in the First Year. The memory of his old school comes flooding back to him with such force that he wants to cry out. He bites his lip and concentrates on the sums.

'Stop,' says Brother Lucius.

He looks straight at Billy.

'You, the new boy, what is your name?'

'William Smith, Brother Lucius.'

'Well, Smith, what is the answer to 145 + 209?'

'Three hundred and fifty-four, Brother Lucius.'

'Correct.'

'Barnes, 623+578?'

'One thousand, one hundred and one, Brother Lucius.'

'Wrong.'

A dozen hands shoot up in the air.

'You, the other new boy.'

'Brown, Brother Lucius, one thousand two hundred and one.'

'Correct.'

Billy has six sums correct. He is worried that Brother Lucius will beat him for getting some wrong but instead he explains where Billy has made mistakes. Plenty of the boys have made mistakes but Brother Lucius does not cane any of them. Billy decides he likes Brother Lucius.

When the lesson ends Willis comes over to them. Billy knows that Willis has got almost all his sums wrong.

'That's school over for today,' he says. 'Come with me; I'll show you where you have to work.'

'Work?'

Billy is surprised but Louie just shrugs.

'All us boys have to work,' Willis explains. 'This is a farm.'

'I don't know anything about farm work,' Billy protests. 'I've never been on a farm. I've never even been in the country before. I'm from London.'

'Don't worry, you don't have to do farm work. You have to help carry the stones for the convent, like me. Hurry up. We'll be in trouble if we're late.'

He starts to run and Louie and Billy follow him. They pass more dormitories and a big, stone chapel.

'We built that,' Willis says proudly. 'I didn't do much because I'd only just arrived here then, but I helped mix the cement.'

Billy looks at him; he is small for his age but he must be very strong, he thinks, if he can build something like that.

'Here we are. I'll get Richards; he's in charge.'

They are standing on a building site. The land has been cleared and flattened and the walls of a building are being constructed by a gang of small boys. The walls are not very high, not much higher than Billy.

'You the new boys then?'

Willis has returned with one of the older boys; he is wiry and his skin is the colour of a nutmeg.

Billy nods.

'Good. What're your names?'

'Smith.'

'Brown.'

Well, Smith and Brown, this is what I want you to do today. See that pile of stones over there? Bring them over here so that the boys can use them.'

Billy looks to where he is pointing. In the distance he can see a group of bigger boys breaking up some rocks with sledgehammers and piling them into a heap beside them. It's this enormous pile of stones that he and Louie have to move.

'Come on lads, get moving.'

'What are you building?' asks Billy, tentatively.

'It's a convent or something,' replies the boy in charge. 'Now get on with it before Brother Dermot catches us standing around.'

Brother Dermot, Billy remembers him and his cruel eyes. He walks across to the makeshift quarry quickly. Thank goodness he kept his shoes on; the ground is hard and covered with sharp stones. He cannot understand how all the boys are able to run around barefoot. Don't their feet hurt them?

The boys breaking the rocks look up when they arrive but they say nothing and don't stop what they are doing. Billy can see the sweat running down their foreheads and dripping onto the ground. It's not cold now; the sun is overhead and beating down on them. He bends down and picks up a stone; it's heavy and the sharp edges cut his hand. He can hardly stand up straight but he manages to stagger across the building site and deposits his load next to Richards.

'That's it, good lad. Pick the smaller stones first until you get used to it. It won't take you long; you'll soon be running back and forwards, you see.'

He smiles at him and turns back to building the wall.

They have to be in bed as soon as it is dark. Billy lies on his back looking up at the window. There is a moon and its eerie light fills the room. He can hear the night cries of some animal and the hooting of an owl. He shivers: it's all so strange, nothing like London. Louie is very still; Billy thinks he is already asleep. But Billy cannot sleep, his back hurts and he has cuts and blisters on his hands. Willis says that that is good, the blisters will harden his hands and then they will not hurt anymore. He hopes he is right. Willis made him bathe his hands in cold salt water and held them in there for five minutes, even though they stung. He tells them that they are lucky because at the moment they only have to work in the afternoons. Once they are eleven years old they will have to work all day; there will be no more school. Willis says he likes going to school because it's easier than breaking rocks, even though he gets caned most days. Billy shudders when he remembers the dark red wheals on the backs of Willis's legs.

He closes his eyes; it's important to sleep because Willis says they have to get up early in order to do their chores before breakfast. But sleep won't come. For the first time that day he thinks of his sisters. Where are they now? Have they arrived at their orphanage? Are they as frightened as he is? He feels the tears pricking at the back of his eyelids and squeezes his eyes tightly; he does not want to cry. He must be brave and then one day he will go and look for them.

MAGGIE

Maggie stands on the deck until she can no longer see land, her face is stinging from her tears. She feels helpless, surely there was something she could have done to help her brother. Poor Billy, how is he going to manage on his own? She has let him down.

'Maggie, I'm cold. Can we go below now?' asks Grace.

Maggie looks at her little sister; she is clinging to Maggie's skirt and her face too is streaked with tears.

'Of course we can Gracie. Let's go and see what's for lunch, shall we?'

The child's face brightens at the prospect of food but Maggie is not hungry; all she can think about is Billy.

As they make their way down to the lower decks they meet June.

'Right girls, I've been looking for you. Everyone has to have a medical examination before they disembark in Melbourne. Maggie can you and Grace go along to see Doctor O'Neill at 3 o'clock? It's nothing to worry about, just a routine examination.'

'Yes, June.'

'Are you all right? Have you been crying again?'

Maggie nods and her eyes fill up with tears once more.

'Now that's silly. Your brother will be fine. They will take good care of him and when the war is over you will all be together again.'

She takes a handkerchief out of her pocket and hands it to Maggie.

'Here, wipe your eyes.'

'But how will we find him when the war is over?' Maggie snivels.

She does not want to be comforted. This is her fault; she deserves to suffer. She should have protected him.

'We have all the records you know; we know where every child is going. He won't get lost, I can assure you. Now blow your nose and no more tears, there's a good girl.'

Maggie does as she says but she is not convinced. She does not understand why they are in Australia in the first place and not still in London; it does not make sense. She wants Mum. Mum would know what to do

'Run along now; they are just about to serve lunch.'

She smiles at them.

'And it smells like fish and chips to me.'

Grace beams at her.

'That's my favourite,' she says.

Maggie looks at her; her little face is all smiles now. Thank goodness she does not really understand what is happening to them. Maggie takes her hand and smiles. She must be brave for Grace's sake.

'Come on then, let's go and have some lunch,' she says.

In almost no time at all they are steaming into Melbourne harbour. A flotilla of small boats has sailed out to greet them; people are shouting and waving flags. There is excitement in the air.

This time they are prepared; they have their bags packed and June has given them both their school reports and a report on their behaviour. She has told Maggie that the reports are excellent. Maggie is pleased. She puts them safely in her suitcase with her identity card. She carries both suitcases and Grace carries the sandwiches. They line up ready to disembark. It has been a tearful morning; all the children are sad to be leaving their new friends. Maggie too is very sad to be leaving her friends, especially Janet. Janet is going on by train to Sydney, to live with her uncle and aunt. There is only one girl, Nora, who is going to the Poor Sisters of Nazareth with them.

The captain sounds the ship's siren. The ship has dropped anchor, the hawsers are tightened and the ship has moored safely alongside the quay. On the quayside she can see crowds of people and a military band. The strains of '*Waltzing Matilda*' float up towards them. The children crane their necks to see what is happening and a buzz of excitement runs through the line. Some children break away to lean over the rail and get a better view but Maggie stays where she is. June has explained that there will be a civic reception for all the children so she is not surprised when they file off the ship and are led across to a raised wooden stage, decorated with flags; there are the Union Jack, the Australian flag and some she does not recognise. When they are all assembled, almost a hundred expectant children with bright, shiny faces, the mayor of the city climbs onto the stage and addresses them:

'Welcome to Melbourne children, welcome. We are so pleased to see you here and to know that you have at last arrived safely in our beautiful country. Here you will all be safe from the terrible war that is ravaging your own country, no more bombs, no more air raids. You will be safe here in Australia,' he repeats. 'Now I know that some of you will be moving on to other parts of the country but I can assure you that, wherever you go, the people of Australia will welcome you with open arms. You are our hope for the future. Welcome to Australia.'

He steps down and the band begins to play '*God Save the King*'. The children all stand to attention and sing along. Maggie knows the words because they learnt them in school. A woman is passing amongst the children handing out sweets and someone else gives them an orange. She feels very important; everyone is smiling at her and the other children. But what do they do now? She does not have long to wait before she finds out. June is by their side, with Nora close behind her.

'Follow me girls, I'll introduce you to the ladies who have come to collect you and take you to your new home.'

Maggie turns just in time to see Janet being swept into the air by a man with the same red hair as her. It must be her uncle. Janet is laughing and chattering excitedly. Maggie looks away;

she wishes there was someone like that waiting for her. She can see the nuns standing patiently in the distance; they look like witches in their long black robes. All they need are broomsticks and tall hats. They start walking towards them. Her legs feel like lead. She does not want to go. She does not want to live in this country no matter what the mayor says. She wants to get back on the ship; she wants to go back to England with June; she wants things to be as they were but then she remembers Billy and she knows that even if she had the choice she would have to stay here.

'Good morning Sisters. These are the girls for The Poor Sisters of Nazareth orphanage in Pardy Creek,' June says.

'Good morning,' the witches chorus.

It's sad saying goodbye to June. Maggie clings to her in desperation, wanting to extend their time together if only for a few more moments but in the end the nuns are tutting and fidgeting so much that it's clear that they have to leave.

The nuns have arrived in a battered old van, which the younger of them drives. The children are instructed to climb in the back. Nora has little to say and Grace is tired, so the girls sit in silence contemplating their future and looking at the passing countryside.

Maggie feels more comfortable being in a city, even though Melbourne does not resemble London in any way; there are fewer people and hardly any cars. All the buildings are bright and clean, many of them built of shuttered wood or stone, with wide verandas. There are no bombed streets, no piles of rubble; the streets are broad and the houses more widely spaced. She sees no soldiers and no fire wardens; there are no blackout curtains hanging at the windows and the gardens are planted with flowers, not turnips. They pass a park where some boys are playing football and she thinks of Billy and swallows hard. It's true what June said, there is no war in Australia; they will be safe here. The Germans will not be able to drop bombs on their new home.

Soon they are leaving the city behind them and driving through tree covered hills, where gullies carved from the land lead back down to a sparkling sea in the distance. Is the ship still moored in the harbour or has it already left? There will be no children on it now. She imagines June and the other escorts lounging on the deck, with nothing to do and nobody to look after. There is a sinking sensation in her stomach when she finally realises that they are now on their own. There is no Mum, no Nan, no June, no Billy, just the two of them, her and Grace. She looks at her little sister, sleeping peacefully beside her. She will have to be her mother now.

'Do you think it's far?' asks Nora.

She has a strong Irish accent and sometimes Maggie has trouble understanding her.

'I don't know,' she replies.

'Is it much further?' the girl leans forward and asks the nun.

'You'll know soon enough when you get there,' is the reply.

The nun continues to stare ahead of her; she does not speak to her companion. She is an old woman. Maggie thinks she is almost as old as Nan. Her face is criss-crossed with fine lines and there are two deep grooves between her eyebrows. Mum used to call those frown lines. She remembers Mum standing in front of her dressing table mirror and smoothing them away with face cream.

'If you keep frowning like that, my girl, you'll get them too,' she would say to her.

Maggie knows she has a habit of frowning when she is concentrating. She runs her finger between her eyebrows; she cannot feel any lines there.

'Is your mammy dead?' asks Nora.

'I don't know. They told me she was dead but I don't believe them.'

'Why don't you believe them? Why would they say it, if it wasn't true?'

'I don't know. It's just, well my Dad died and I know what it feels like when someone dies.'

She remembers the hollow feeling inside her when the telegram arrived.

'I don't feel like that about my Mum,' she adds. 'I keep thinking she's back there looking for us.'

'My mammy died. I went to the church to say goodbye to her.'

She thinks Nora is going to cry but instead she sniffs and says:

'That's why my aunty sent me to the orphanage.'

The bus is driving through fields of wheat now; Maggie has never seen such a wide expanse of land before. It's like a sea of rippling gold, unbroken and never ending. Then she notices a winding road, weaving its way between the swaying crops. It's just like in 'The Wizard of Oz'. She hums a little bit of '*The Yellow Brick Road*' to herself. Nora looks at her and smiles. The motion of the bus is making her feel sleepy now so she puts her arm around Grace and closes her eyes.

Something is disturbing her dream; she is walking through the fields with Tin Man and the Lion. They are looking for Billy. The Lion says he has seen Billy in the desert.

'We're here, wake up.'

It's Nora shaking her arm.

'We're here,' she repeats.

Her voice is quavering. Maggie is not sure if her companion is frightened or excited. She rubs her eyes and sits up just as the van lurches to a halt. Grace is already awake; she is playing with her teddy bear.

'This is Australia,' Grace tells the bear. 'You'll like it here; the sun shines all the time and there are horses. Now you mustn't be frightened of the horses because they are all good horses; they won't bite you or kick you. And there're lots of nice things to eat, like chocolate and bananas.'

The bear stares back at her blankly.

'Come on girls, out you get,' instructs the nun.

She does not smile at them. Maggie notices that she has no laughter lines around her eyes. Maybe she never smiles; maybe she cannot smile; maybe it's against the rules to smile.

'The Mother Superior is waiting to see you.'

They climb down from the bus and stand, blinking in the bright sunlight. Before them is a big, stone house; there are steps leading up to a veranda that runs all along the front of it. Behind the house are a number of low, wooden buildings, linked by covered walkways. This is the orphanage. This is their new home.

'Come along girls, follow me,' the nun says.

Her companion waits until they have all got off and then drives the van away.

They follow the nun up the steps. The cases are heavy and Maggie would like to leave them on the steps but she is frightened that they will lose them.

'Hurry up now, don't dawdle.'

She tugs at the bell-pull and after a minute or two the door is opened by a young girl in a faded blue dress. Her face is thin and pinched and her dress is too big and hangs loosely on her slender frame.

'About time, Hawes, we don't have all day,' she says to the girl.

'No, Sister,' the girl replies.

'Is the Mother Superior in her study?'

'Yes, Sister.'

The girl disappears into the shadows and the newcomers step into the hall. The nun knocks gently on one of the doors.

'Come in,' a disembodied voice says.

Maggie thinks back to when they were in St Margaret's Orphanage. Is this going to be the same? The nun pushes them into the room. The Mother Superior sits behind a polished wooden desk. Behind her, hanging on the wall is a crucifix.

'Well, you must be the Smith girls,' she says.

The Mother Superior has an Irish accent, just like Nora. Maggie does not know what colour her hair is because it's hidden under her white cap but her eyebrows are black and bushy, like a man's. She wears a pair of rimless glasses which look as though they are about to slip off the end of her nose. She does not smile at them.

'Yes, Mother Superior. I'm Margaret and this is Grace.'

'She's very young,' she says, peering over her glasses at Grace.

'I's 'free',' Grace says.

'Indeed. Well, she will have to go into the babies' section,' she says and writes something down on her pad.

'And you, girl, how old are you?'

'Twelve, Mother Superior.'

'Good. Do you know how to cook?'

Maggie shakes her head.

'Sew?'

Again Maggie shakes her head.

'Goodness me. Well, I suppose you'll soon learn.'

She turns to Nora and says:

'And you are Lynch, I take it?'

Nora nods.

'I have your report from the orphanage in England. You are due to take your first communion, it says. Excellent.'

She picks up a handbell and shakes it. Almost immediately the door opens and the nun comes in.

'Sister Angelica, take these two away. The little one can go to the babies' section and the others to Sister Agnes.'

'Yes, Mother Superior.'

Sister Agnes is the nun who met them at the port; Maggie hates her already. They follow Sister Angelica to their dormitory, a large room with an open quadrangle in the middle.

'Mother Superior says these girls are to sleep in here,' she tells Sister Agnes. 'The little one comes with me.'

She takes Grace's hand.

'Come along child,' she says.

'No. Don't want to,' Grace says, stamping her feet.

'We'll soon see about that,' Sister Agnes says.

She moves towards Grace.

'No, it's all right. She's just frightened,' Maggie says. 'She doesn't understand.'

She bends down and whispers to her sister:

'It's all right Grace. You go along with Sister Angelica; she'll look after you now. I've got to stay here with the big girls.'

'Don't want to.'

'You'll be fine, honestly. I'll just be here, not far away. I'll see you all the time. Now be a good girl and take care of Teddy.'

Grace hugs her teddy bear closer to her and starts to cry.

'Don't cry, sweetheart. I'll see you every day. It's just that the big girls have to sleep in here and you'll be in another room with lots of nice girls, your own age. It'll be fine. You'll see. Just make sure that Teddy behaves himself.'

She is terrified that Sister Agnes will be cross with Grace for making a fuss. But Grace is now more concerned about Teddy and meekly follows Sister Angelica out.

'That girl will have to learn that she can't have her own way all the time,' Sister Agnes grunts. 'Now, you two, strip off all those clothes. Then into the shower with you.'

They run into the shower together while Sister Agnes stands watching them. She will not let them come out until she is satisfied that they are clean. The water is freezing. Maggie tried to tell her that they had all had a warm shower that morning on the ship but she just told her to be quiet, to speak only when she was spoken to.

'Your clothes are on your beds,' she says. 'You can put the things you came with in your suitcases. You won't be needing them.'

Maggie looks at the new clothes; they are dreadful. The shoes are too big and they have not given her any socks. She wonders if she can take some socks out of the case but she is frightened that the nun will punish her. The dress is the same faded blue as the one Hawes was wearing; the vest is holey and the knickers are baggy. She sighs. What is going to happen to her lovely new clothes? Why can't she wear them? She feels resentful. Why are the nuns treating them like this? Why have they split up her and Grace? How can she look after Grace if they are in two separate buildings? It's so cruel. She remembers the look on Grace's face; she was so frightened. Poor little Grace, she is too small for all this.

She waits until Sister Agnes is saying something to Nora and hurriedly takes her ID card and the remnant of blue-painted wood out of the case and slips them under the mattress. She has a feeling that she might not see this case again.

Sister Agnes has told Nora to go with her so Maggie sits on the bed alone and surveys her new home. All the beds have iron frames and flock mattresses. Her bed has a single sheet that is more grey than white and a dark grey blanket. Some of the beds have pillows but there is not one on her's. The walls had been painted a light shade of grey many years ago and now are grubby with finger prints and scuff marks. There are no pictures, only a large crucifix at the end of the room. It's a dreary room and as she studies it she wants to cry. How long will she have to stay here?

The door opens and Nora comes back in; her face is wet from crying. Her pigtails have gone. Someone has cut off all her hair and what remains, sticks up from her scalp in angry tufts.

'What on earth has happened to you?' Maggie asks.

Nora is sobbing.

'They said I had nits,' she eventually spits out.

She is angry.

'Smell that,' she says and bends down so that Maggie can smell the strong disinfectant that has been applied to her head.

'That's awful. What is it?'

'I don't know but it's making my head sting.'

She runs her hand sadly over her cropped head.

'They said it was sinful to have long hair and that it encourages nits. That's why they cut it off.'

Nora goes to her bed and lies down.

'Sister Agnes says you have to go and see the doctor next.'

Maggie is terrified. Are they going to cut her hair off as well? She hasn't got nits. She pulls at her pigtails nervously.

'It's over there in the next hut. Sister Agnes is there as well,' Nora informs her. 'It was her who cut off my hair. She enjoyed it.'

She has stopped crying now and is tugging a comb through the remaining tufts of hair.

'It'll soon grow,' Maggie tells Nora.

Nora is wrong; it's not Sister Agnes, it's the sister who drove the bus, Sister Bridget. She smiles at Maggie and tells her to take off her dress so that the doctor can examine her. Maggie does as she says. It does not take long. The doctor looks at her hair and teeth then listens to her heart before telling the nun that she is in good health. He scribbles some notes on her file.

'Good. Put your clothes on again child and follow me,' Sister Bridget says.

She takes her into a side room and tells her to sit down.

'I'm sorry Margaret but we have a strict rule here that means that no-one may have long hair. It's for hygienic reasons, you understand,' she explains. 'So I'm going to have to cut off those lovely brown pigtails of yours.'

She looks genuinely sorry as she takes a pair of scissors out of her pocket.

'Turn round.'

Maggie feels the scissors cut through her pigtails, a couple of snips and they are gone. The nun combs the remaining hair into place, and trims off a few stray ends.

'There that's done. It's not too bad at all,' she says with a smile.

'Will they cut my sister's hair too?' Maggie asks.

The nun nods.

'It's orphanage policy,' she says and her smile is sadder this time.

Maggie does not feel like smiling; it's as though yet another piece of her identity has disappeared. She resists the temptation to look at the pigtails which she knows are lying at her feet. June had plaited them for her this morning. What a long time ago that seems now.

BILLY

He is dreaming that he is playing football in the street outside his house. They are all there: Louie, Bob, Damon. He dribbles the ball along the ground and passes it to Louie. Suddenly Brother Dermot is there, he tackles Louie and Louie falls to the ground. Brother Dermot has the ball now; he is running towards the goal. Billy runs after him.

'Foul,' he shouts. 'It's a foul. Stop him. He's not in our team. Stop him. He's in the Devil's team. He's doing the Devil's work.'

A rough hand shakes him awake.

'That's enough Smith.'

O'Malley is standing over him.

'You've been dreaming again,' he says.

He slips his hand into Billy's bed.

'Bloody hell, and you've wet the bed again. Get up. You know what'll happen if Dermot finds out and it won't be just you who's in the shit; I'll be for it as well.'

He pulls Billy out of the bed.

'Hurry up before he gets here. Pull that sheet off and I'll help you turn the mattress over.'

Billy is awake now. His teeth are chattering. He pulls off the sodden sheet and runs into the showers with it. He can't understand it; he hasn't wet the bed since he was a baby. He feels humiliated and is glad Mum is not there to see his shame. The commotion has woken the others and everyone is stretching and moaning at having been woken so early. He turns on the shower and stands under it, holding the sheet in his arms. The water is cold and he can feel himself turning blue. He dries himself hurriedly on a threadbare towel and rings out the wet sheet as best he can. The sun will be up in an hour and then it will dry quickly. All he has to do is make sure that Brother Dermot does not find it first. He folds it up and shoves it in one of the unused lockers.

The first bell sounds.

'What're you up to, Smith?'

It's Barnes. He has been at the farm school for years; Willis says he is not to be trusted.

'Nothing.'

All the boys are up now and crowding into the shower room. Billy pushes past them and goes back to his bed. O'Malley has turned the mattress over and left a new sheet out for him. A dirty brown stain on the mattress tells of an earlier episode, maybe his, maybe someone else's. He covers the bed with the sheet and pulls an old army blanket over it. He hopes that Brother Dermot will not find out.

'Get off to work,' O'Malley says.

He looks cross. Billy pulls on his shorts and shirt and hurries out. His bare feet are silent as he runs over to the hen house. He is early, the second bell has not rung yet. This is his first chore of the day: he has to sweep out the hen house and feed the chickens. At first he was afraid of the chickens because they would rush up to him when he entered the hen house and peck at his legs but now he is used to them and has given each of them a name.

'Chuck, chuck, chuck,' he whispers to them. 'Molly, is that you?'

Molly is a light brown bantam that follows him as he works.

The sun has not risen above the horizon yet but he knows that when it does the land will be flooded with light. The dawn does not approach slowly here, like it did in London. London, he can barely remember it now. Sometimes, like last night, it returns to him in his dreams but it's distorted, changed, a place he no longer recognises.

He picks up the broom and begins to sweep. The chickens don't like this; they flap and screech and huddle together at the far end. Sometimes he lets them out into the yard so that they can scratch at the baked earth, but it's still too dark and the foxes might be about.

Louie used to help him with the chickens but that was before. He shivers when he thinks about Louie. The doctor says he may never walk again after the accident. Accident. Everyone says it was an accident but Billy knows better because he saw it happen. It was almost a month ago. Louie had been preparing for his communion with Brother Dermot. Louie is not very clever; Billy knows that now. Louie had difficulty remembering all the words that he had to say and that made Brother Dermot angry. The angrier Brother Dermot got, the more Louie stuttered and stammered. Every day he got caned on the hands until his palms were red raw and bleeding but still he could not memorise the words. One day Brother Dermot told him to come to his room after class. Louie was very frightened; he begged Billy to go with him. So Billy went with him as far as the door and then waited outside. He could hear everything that was said.

'I am going to beat this laziness out of you my boy. One way or another you will learn your catechism. I would be failing in my duty as a Christian Brother if I could not teach you the words of our Lord. Bend over. Now, repeat after me: "*I believe in God the Father, Almighty, Maker of Heaven and Earth.*"'

Whack. Billy heard the swish as the man's cane descended on Louie and a cry of pain.

'Repeat those words,' shouted Brother Dermot.

Billy heard a sob then Louie said: '*I believe in God the Father, Almighty, Maker of Heaven and Earth.*'

'Good. Now: "*I believe in Jesus Christ, his only Son, our Lord.*"'

Whack. Once again Billy heard the cane and Louie's sobs. He could stand it no longer, he ran. He did not see Louie after that. Brother Anthony told them that Louie was ill and would be staying in the sick bay until he was better.

The second bell rings. He sweeps the chicken manure into a pile outside the door; later he will have to take it to the vegetable garden and spread it on the beds. He opens the sack of meal and plunges his hand inside. This job he likes. The chickens recognise the signals and gather at his feet, clucking excitedly. He extends his arm, scattering the feed across the floor and watches as they dash to and fro, pecking at the seeds.

'Here Molly.'

He bends down and scatters some seed at the bantam's feet. She pecks at it daintily and he strokes the top of her head. He must hurry because he still has to set out the plates in the dining room before the third bell rings for breakfast.

The boys stand as Brother Dermot enters the dining room and silence descends on them. Nobody dares to speak when he is on duty. They bow their heads and repeat the morning grace.

'Begin,' he says.

Billy picks up his spoon and starts to eat his porridge; there is something wriggling in it but he closes his eyes and eats it anyway. O'Malley is sitting opposite. He leans across and whispers:

'He knows.'

Billy feels his stomach turn to water. If Brother Dermot knows that he wet the bed again then it will be a beating for sure. He thinks about Louie. Will Billy end up in the sick bay as well?

'You going to eat that?' whispers Willis.

Billy shakes his head. He is not hungry. Fear is paralysing him. He does not know what to do. It will not be the usual cane across the back of his legs; this time he is sure that Brother Dermot will kill him. He looks across at Barnes; he has a smirk on his face. Willis says he is a sneak. Maybe Barnes told Brother Dermot about the sheet he hid in the locker.

They file into the classroom; Brother Dermot is already there. There is a wet sheet on the desk in front of him. The boys sit down in silence; they all know what is going to happen. Billy thinks he is going to cry. He bites his lip hard. Brother Dermot is looking straight at him.

'Well now, what do you think we have here?' he asks, looking round the class.

At first no-one answers then Barnes puts up his hand.

'A sheet, Brother Dermot,' he says.

'Yes, indeed, a sheet. What sort of sheet may I ask?'

'A wet sheet,' the boy continues.

'Just so. Now you may wonder what I am doing with a wet sheet on my desk.'

One of the boys sniggers nervously.

Brother Dermot glares at him

'Well, I am looking for the owner of this wet sheet.'

He looks around the room, slowly and stares at the boys. Billy realises that he does not yet know that it's his sheet. Brother Dermot picks up the corner of the offending object between his finger and thumb and holds it before him as though it were a live snake about to strike.

'One of the boys in this class owns this sheet and it will not be difficult to discover which one. However,' he pauses, 'I am giving that boy a chance to own up right now. You have until lunchtime to decide. If the culprit has not owned up by then the whole class will be caned.'

A ripple of fear runs round the classroom. Billy sees Barnes staring at him. So he does know. What should he do? Willis is his friend; he does not want him to be caned because of him. And Damon and Bob, they are all his mates. You are supposed to look out for your mates, that is what Dad always said. 'Take your punishment like a man.' But Dad had not said that; it was a character in a cowboy film. Dad never hit him, not once. Billy makes a decision; it's the bravest decision he has ever made.

He raises his hand.

'It's mine,' he says.

His voice is barely a whisper.

Brother Dermot drops the offending sheet on the floor.

'Is it indeed? Right, you, O'Malley, take this over to the laundry room and be quick about it. The rest of you, take out your books and turn to the Ten Commandments,' he says.

Then he looks at Billy. Billy wishes he were a hundred miles away. He prays he does not wet himself again, not here, in front of the class.

'Smith. Out the front.'

Somehow Billy manages to stand and make his way to the front of the class. His knees are trembling. The boys are silent. They know what is about to happen. They have their books open in front of them but no-one is reading.

Brother Dermot takes a chair and places it by his desk then he goes to the cupboard and takes out a leather strap.

'Take your trousers down and bend over that chair,' he says.

His voice is icy. Billy's hands are shaking so much he can hardly undo his buttons. He bends over the chair. This is so much worse than the cane. He knows all the other boys are watching him, looking at his naked butt. He is scarlet with humiliation.

Thwack. The pain is unbearable. A cry escapes from his clenched lips.

'This will teach you not to wet the bed, you disgusting boy.'

Thwack. He cannot hold back his cries now. Again and again, the strap descends; he thinks it will never stop. He loses count of the times that Brother Dermot strikes him. His butt feels as though it's on fire. Suddenly Brother Dermot stops. It's over.

'Get up and go back to your seat,' Brother Dermot says.

Brother Dermot seems calmer; he no longer looks angry. Billy sees him clearly now; the man feels better because he has hurt Billy. This is what it's all about; he enjoys beating them. He enjoys it. It has nothing to do with breaking the rules or wetting the bed; it's just something that Brother Dermot likes to do to them. Billy is angry. He knows that there is nothing they can do about it; Brother Dermot will always find some excuse to beat them because he wants to. As Billy sits gingerly on the edge of his seat he makes his decision; he is going to run away. He tries to focus on the book in front of him but his eyes are still full of tears; he blinks them angrily away. He does not know how he is going to do it or where he will go but he knows he must leave the farm school.

The morning classes drag slowly. Today they have Brother Anthony who teaches them English. Normally Billy likes this class, especially when Brother Anthony reads them a story but today he cannot concentrate because of the pain; his butt is raw and sticking to his shorts. It's handwriting and he cannot make the chalk obey him; his letters are jagged and slope away from him. A plan is forming in his head and the excitement is building up inside him. His eye has started to twitch again. He puts his hand up to stop it. He can feel the little pulse underneath his fingertips, beating away, telling him that he has no time to lose. When the classes finish for the day he will run away. He will ask Willis to tell Richards that he is in the sick bay. That will give him at least three hours before lunchtime. No-one will miss him until then and, by the time they do start looking for him, he will be a long way away.

It's easier than he expected. One of the older boys is taking the truck into Wadene to buy flour. Billy waits until no-one is looking and then jumps up into the back and hides under a pile of sacking. He can hear the boy talking to someone; it's Brother Patrick, who works in the kitchen.

'Make sure it's a full sack, now; last time they short-changed us. And look for any weevils. That man'll pass any old rubbish off on you boys.'

Brother Patrick laughs. Billy can imagine his mouth, hanging slackly open, exposing his rotten teeth. He shivers. None of the boys like him. Billy has heard the older boys talking; they call him a perv. Billy is not sure what that means but he knows there is something not right about the Brother. He has a habit of creeping up behind you and putting his hand on your butt and when he punishes you he does not hit you across the legs with a cane, like the other Brothers, he puts you across his knee and hits you on the bare butt with a strap. Richards warned him to watch out for him.

'He's always playing with his old fellah,' he said. 'And he likes the new boys, especially the blond ones, like you; so you be careful.'

Richards is always looking out for Billy and Willis. He is sixteen; he will be leaving soon. He told them he was going to work for a construction company in Perth as soon as the Brothers let him go. Maybe that is where Billy should head, for Perth. It suddenly dawns on him that he does not know where Perth is, or anywhere else for that matter. Still, wherever he ends up it will be better than staying here and putting up with Brother Dermot's beatings. He pulls the sacks over his head and lies as quietly as he can. He hears the boy climb into the driver's seat and slam the door.

'No going walkabout; I know what you get up to in Wadene, hanging about all day talking to those abo sheilas.'

The boy does not reply. Billy hears him start the engine. At last they are on their way. He waits until he is sure that they are away from the school and then he sits up and looks back. He can make out the farm school in the distance; it's disappearing in the cloud of reddish dust that the truck is trailing behind it. Soon he will no longer be able to see it. Despite the throbbing in his backside a feeling of elation comes over him; he is no longer afraid. He crosses his legs and leans back on the wheel rest. The road is bumpy and full of pot holes. The boy drives fast and Billy is thrown from side to side but he does not mind even though the jolting hurts his butt. This is exciting. There is nothing to see, just the dusty road receding behind him and the occasional gum tree. There has been no rain for two months and the land is baked hard. They pass a clump of wattles, their golden flowers bright in the sunlight. Billy wipes the dust from his eyes and moves further back into the truck. He can hear the driver singing to himself; it's '*Waltzing Matilda*'. Billy wants to join in but he is frightened that the boy will hear him. He does not know what the boy will do if he discovers a stowaway; he might take him straight back to the farm school. So he sits quietly and waits.

After a while he notices that they have passed some ramshackle, wooden huts and he can see the railway line running alongside the road; they must be near the station now. The truck begins to slow down. There is a train coming and the boy has to wait before he can drive over the crossing. This is Billy's chance to get out. He waits until the truck has stopped and the train is thundering past then he jumps down and hides behind some rocks. The crossing gates swing back with a groan and the truck moves away.   He will count to a hundred before he moves just in case the boy looks back and sees him.

'One, two, three ...'

He cannot wait to reach a hundred; he peers round the rock but there is no sign of the truck. Elated he stands up. Only a tiny cloud of dust in the distance tells him that the truck was ever there.

He lets out a whoop of joy.   He can hardly believe it; he is free.

BROTHER LUCIUS

Brother Lucius pushes himself to his feet, his knees hurt from the stone floor but he refuses to use a kneeler. A little pain is nothing compared to what our Lord suffered for us, he thinks. He has been praying for guidance. He tries to be humble and accept the way things are but each day he finds it more difficult. This is not what he expected.

He believes he is a religious man so why is this life so hard to bear? When he was eight years old his parents promised him to the Church. They told him that God would bless their family if they gave one of their sons to Him and he was the chosen one. At first he was resentful at being sent away from his brothers and sisters but with time he became used to the monastic life and entered into the Christian Brotherhood with an open heart. He went to the Christian Brothers University and learned to be a teacher. This is what he has always wanted to do, teach boys who are more unfortunate than himself. This is what being a Christian Brother is all about, providing religious and secular education for the poor unfortunates of this world. At least, that is what he thought; that is why he volunteered to come out to the Wadene Farm School, but now he is not so sure. It's so frustrating. He has tried speaking to Father Mooney but it gets him nowhere.

'You must not put yourself above your brothers,' Father Mooney said. 'Remember they have not had the benefit of a university education like you; they are pure, simple souls, trying their best to do God's work.'

Even when he tried to tell him how Brother Patrick took one of the new boys to his room every night all he said was:

'Brother Lucius I hope we don't have a Judas amongst us,' and would not listen to anything more.

He shudders when he recalls the fear in the boy's big blue eyes. He was a pretty child when he arrived but days of hard work and nightly abuse at the hands of Brother Patrick have turned him into a frightened shadow that trembles at the slightest sound. Each night when Brother Lucius kneels to pray he prays that God will help Brother Patrick and show him the error of his ways.

He takes out his lessons for the day. He likes to prepare the work before he goes into the classroom although it's not really necessary as the level is very low. Even the Third Year boys have not got beyond simple addition and subtraction. A couple of the new boys seem to be quite bright; it will be good if he can maintain their interest but experience makes him doubt it.

He hears the bell for breakfast and straightens his cassock. He runs his hand over his tonsure; it's still tender from where he has recently shaved it. He feels a sense of guilty pride; he is the only brother that is allowed to wear a tonsure. That is the problem, he thinks; the rest are just a crowd of illiterate bogtrotters. They should not be teaching children at all; they are lay Brothers trained only for domestic and agricultural work. In the early days almost all of his colleagues were teaching Brothers but now they let anyone take charge of a class. He has tried to explain to the other Brothers that beating a child across the legs will not make him learn any faster but no-one listens to him. And why should they? All the Brothers are encouraged to use corporal punishment; it's the first thing they are taught when they arrive in Wadene. What can he do to change things? Beside which, the lay Brothers work for nothing. Who else would they get to do the work? Father Mooney is right. They are not scholars; they have had no training. What else are they supposed they do? Even he has to admit that some of the boys are hard to control; they are a mixed bag, mostly abandoned or illegitimate and almost all unruly. Never having known love, they don't seek it nor expect it but that does not excuse the severity with which some of his colleagues treat them. He sighs. There is nothing he can do about it except pray to God to give them enlightenment.

His colleagues are all sitting at the table when he arrives in the refectory.

'We have been waiting, Brother Lucius,' says Brother Dermot.

'I am sorry. I was delayed,' he replies.

Brother Dermot stands and recites the grace. There is a clatter of noise as the boys sit down and begin eating.

'How are you today, Brother Lucius?' asks Brother Anthony, forking a slice of bacon into his mouth.

'I am well thank you.'

He does not feel like conversation. Something is happening to him; he cannot shake off these negative thoughts. Is he having a crisis of faith or is it just being here in Wadene? He looks at his companion. Brother Anthony is a good man; he used to be a baker before he got the call from God. And yet yesterday he saw him beating a child with a strap just because his writing was not straight enough. But then, who is he to judge? Father Mooney's words come back to him:

'Judge not, lest ye be judged.'

'Coffee Lucius?'

'Thank you, Brother Dermot.'

He looks at the man's hard face; he cannot see a grain of Christian charity in it. He knows that Brother Dermot is in constant pain from the arthritis in his knees but he should welcome that pain as Jesus welcomed his pain on the cross. No Brother Dermot has been here too long; he has steeped himself in cruelty and now he is not aware of what he does.

'You have heard about the boy?' Brother Anthony asks.

Brother Lucius shakes his head.

'Which boy?'

'Smith. He's run away.'

He knows Smith, a quiet boy. He is one of his better pupils, a newish boy.

'How did that happen?'

'Nobody knows but he hasn't been seen since Sunday. He told Richards he was sick and nobody has seen him since.'

'Where can he have gone?'

'Wherever he is we'll find him. Someone will come across him and send him back to us and, when they do, that boy will wish he'd never been born,' says Brother Dermot.

'He's been here almost six months, hasn't he? Why has he run away now?'

Usually the new boys took some time to settle in but once they had, they got on with things like everyone else. No-one had run away for years The last one to do so was Hopkins. He remembers him clearly. A boy with tow coloured hair and the face of a girl. They found his body on the railway line; his leg had been severed and he had bled to death before the dingoes got to him. He shudders at the memory.

'Who knows what goes on in these kids' heads. Anyway he'll soon wish he hadn't bothered,' adds Brother Dermot.

'Has anybody been out to look for him? Have the police been informed?' Brother Lucius asks.

'Father Mooney rang them this morning,' Brother Anthony tells him.

'What if he's lost? He could die out there in this heat.'

'God will look after him,' Brother Patrick assures them.

'Ungrateful child,' Brother Dermot mutters, pushing himself up with his stick so that he can get a better view of the boys. 'If I hear another sound there will be no breakfast tomorrow, for any of you,' he bellows.

Brother Lucius can see that his arthritis is particularly painful this morning.

The room is quiet.

'They're all talking about Smith,' explains Brother Anthony. 'They're frightened.'

'I'll give them something to be frightened about,' replies Brother Dermot. 'When I say silence, I mean silence.'

The Brothers know not to contradict their colleague.

'Has anyone questioned the boys to see if they know where he's gone?' Brother Lucius asks. 'What about his friends?'

'Yes, he's always hanging about with Willis. Has anyone spoken to Willis?' Brother Anthony adds.

'I have questioned them all and I am certain that they don't know of his whereabouts.'

Brother Lucius has no doubt about that; he does not want to think about Brother Dermot's interrogation methods.

After breakfast he walks across to the chapel. His first class is not for another hour, so he can spend some time in quiet contemplation. Maybe an hour of prayer will cleanse his heart of all these doubts. He sees the boys heading for the classrooms and his thoughts return to the runaway. What possessed the boy to run away like that? He seemed settled in his new life. True he was very quiet but he worked hard and never got into any trouble, as far as he was aware. Why would he risk his life by running away? Wadene was miles from anywhere; it would be very easy for him to wander into the bush and get totally lost. The boy would never survive on his own. Unless he was found very soon he would die of thirst and heat stroke. Poor child, he would say a special prayer for him.

WILLIS

Willis waits until he sees Brother Dermot enter one of the classrooms then he runs across to the sick bay. He peers in the window. Nobody seems to be there. He knows where Louie is, in the bed at the end. He opens the door and creeps in. Brother Dermot has forbidden the boys to visit Louie. He said he was too ill for visitors but Willis does not believe him.

He can see Louie; he is lying very still and his eyes are closed.

'Louie,' he whispers. 'Are you awake?'

Louie's eyes open but he does not move.

'Hello Willis? Is that you?'

'Yeah, I've come to tell you something but I can't stay long because old Faggot Face'll kill me if he catches me here.'

'What is it?'

Louie's voice is weak, as though he is in pain.

'You all right?'

'My back hurts.'

'Why don't you sit up?'

'I can't. I can't move my legs. That's why they won't let me go back to school.'

'That's good, isn't it? I wish I was in here. I wouldn't mind lying in bed all day.'

Louie looks as though he is going to cry.

'They won't let us visit you,' Willis explains.

'I know. He says I can't see anyone until I've learnt my catechism. He comes every evening to teach me.'

Willis knows who he means.

'Does he still hit you?'

'No, he hasn't laid a hand on me since that night.'

'Bloody bastard.'

'What did you want to tell me?'

'It's about Billy. He's run away.'

'When?'

'Two days ago.'

Louie smiles faintly.

'I hope they don't find him.'

'So do I. Old Faggot Face is on the warpath, lashing out at everyone. He's got out his new strap, you know, the one he uses for special occasions, with the studs at the end. We all got a taste of it on Monday when he realised Billy was not there.'

There is a noise in the back room.

'I've got to go. Just wanted to let you know the news.'

'Thanks Willis.'

Louie closes his eyes. He looks as though he is sleeping. Willis hears the door open and a voice asks:

'Is someone there?'

Willis ducks behind the screen and edges his way to the door.

'Hello Louie, just woken up have you?'

It's Brother Anthony; he has come to read Louie a story.

Willis slips out before the Brother notices him; he can still hear his voice droning on as he crosses the courtyard. He must hurry or he will be late. Richards is not too bad; he will moan at him but he won't report him. He cannot stop thinking about Billy; he cannot believe that he would do that. They are bound to find him and then it will be worse than ever for him.

'Oh, there you are. I thought you'd decided to run away as well,' says Richards.

He is leaving in a few weeks and is always smiling these days. Willis wishes it was his turn to leave but where would he go? He has no family that he knows about and does not even remember anything about the time before he came to Wadene. This is his home; he has never known anywhere else.

'Nah, somebody has to do the work now that you're going,' he replies with a grin.

'Right, well let's get on with it.'

'What do you think'll happen to Billy when they catch him?' he asks, picking up a shovel.

'If they catch him, you mean.'

'What, do you think he'll get away then?'

The idea has never occurred to Willis that someone could just walk away from the Brothers.

'We'll have to see, won't we. Now come on, you're over there with the others.'

MAGGIE

Maggie is woken by the sound of the bell ringing angrily. She sits up automatically and feels for her shoes. They fit quite well now but she wonders what will happen if her feet continue to grow. Will they give her some new ones? She sits staring at her scuffed toes. She seems to have been here forever. The others are moving around, pulling on their shifts or running into the shower; everyone likes to get in and out of the shower as quickly as possible, before Sister Agnes arrives. She looks along the dormitory; Sister Agnes is at the far end talking to one of the new girls. Maggie slips into the bathroom and splashes cold water on her head, she does not want to shower today. If she is quick Sister Agnes will never know the difference. She combs her wet hair into place and pulls her dress over her head. It too is getting tight, especially across the chest. She hates having to take her clothes off in front of everyone else, but worse than that she hates the way Sister Agnes stares at her naked body. There is nowhere she can hide from those prying eyes.

'Get a move on girls, those cows aren't going to milk themselves, now are they,' Sister Agnes shouts down the room.

The nun wanders into the showers but today she is too late; almost all the girls are dressed and about to leave.

Maggie likes milking the cows. At first she was afraid of them but she soon learnt how to handle them. All the girls have their favourites; Maggie's is a big, brown and white cow called Daisy. She talks to her all the time she is milking her. Sister Bridget told her that a contented cow gives sweeter milk. She hopes it's true. She never shouts at Daisy, like some of the others do and sometimes she strokes her back and sits with her face pressed against her warm flanks.

As she is walking across to the cow sheds she sees Grace for the first time in over a week. She breaks away from the other milkmaids and goes across to speak to her; her sister is covered in patches of violet paint.

'What's that Gracie?' she asks, pointing to the paint.

'It's 'petigo. I've got 'petigo.'

'Come here, let me give you a hug.'

'No, I'm 'tagious. You mustn't touch me.'

'OK, I'll just hug the good bits.'

She puts her arms around Grace's body and hugs her. It's so good to feel her little body in her arms.

'Does it hurt?' she asks.

Grace shakes her head.

'Teddy has it too but Sister Angelica won't put any violet stuff on him and now he won't get better,' she whines.

Maggie is surprised that she still has her teddy bear. They tried to separate her from it once and Grace had become very upset. She had wet the bed repeatedly and, even though Sister Angelica had made her stand with the wet sheet over her head all morning, it had not cured her. It was not until Sister Bridget had suggested that they return the teddy bear to her that she improved. Sister Bridget is kind; she never shouts at them and never smacks them across the legs like the others do.

'I don't expect he has it as bad as you Gracie, that's why. Did you ask Teddy if it hurt him?'

'Yes, he says it itches.'

'Does yours itch?'

'A bit.'

'You mustn't scratch it now; you know that don't you?'

Grace nods her head.

'And don't let Teddy scratch his either.'

Grace nods again, more vigorously.

'Where are you off to?'

'Sister Angelica says I'm well enough to feed the chooks today but Teddy is afraid of them. I told Sister Angelica that they keep pecking at Teddy's legs so she said I should leave him in my room.'

'Margaret Smith, what are you doing?'

It's Sister Agnes.

'Got to go, Gracie. I'll see you later. Love you.'

'Love you, Maggie.'

Maggie hurries after the others; she does not want to upset Sister Agnes. The nun's favourite punishment is to deprive the girls of their lunch and make them spend the lunch hour kneeling in the chapel asking God for forgiveness.

Maggie has no exact idea how long they have been at the orphanage; it must be almost a year, she reckons. The only way she can tell the passing of the months is by counting the religious festivals; there has been one Christmas, one Easter and soon it will be the second Harvest Festival. She thinks of Billy and sighs. How is he getting on? Has he made any friends? Is his life just like theirs or is it worse? She cannot imagine that it's better but she hopes it's no worse.

She swats at a mosquito with her hand and rolls onto her side. Some of the girls have been allowed to sleep on the veranda tonight because it's so hot. She is the only one still awake; she can hear the gentle snores of her companions mingling with harsh chirping of the crickets and in the distance the occasional howl of the dingoes. She feels very alone and wishes Mum would come and take them home; she misses London. She has tried to adapt to living in the countryside but it has not been easy. There are so many scary things. A bullfrog calls to its mate and a moment later she hears its croaky reply; they are down by the marshy pond where she goes to collect the water for the animals. She sits up and peers through the mesh screen at the night. The kerosine lamps that hang in the porch have been extinguished and although it's a cloudless night the light from the stars is not strong enough to illuminate anything. There is no moon but she does not need moonlight to know what is out there; the grass is burnt a dusty brown and everything is covered in a fine red powder. Until the rains come, it will stay like that. The night is still. Large birds roost in the gum tree and when the sun comes up they will stretch their wings and fly away in search of food, cawing and screeching as they go and making such a clatter of noise that it will wake everyone. A sudden movement makes her start but it's only a lizard that has ventured up from beneath the veranda. All sorts of creatures live down there, goannas, spiders, geckos, toads and snakes. She hates snakes. There are no snakes in London, except in the zoo of course. A tear trickles down her cheek as she thinks about her trip to the zoo; that was in a different life and she was a different girl then. She was only a couple of years older than Grace is now and she remembers how they had to keep together, in a crocodile, each child holding hands with one other. Ann was her best friend and they clung to each other's hands all afternoon, as they filed past the animals in their cages, squealing and giggling whenever they saw anything that frightened them, like the baboons with their sharp teeth and their big red bottoms. Miss Jenkins escorted them that day and when they returned to school she made them draw their favourite animal. Maggie had drawn a brown bear because it looked like one Dad had given her for her birthday. She lies down once more and closes her eyes; she must be up at sunrise.

She is not tired. Her mind is racing and she cannot conjure up that soporific state that she needs in order to be able to sleep. Normally she has no trouble sleeping; she is usually dead tired from all the hard work that she has to do each day after school but tonight is different. She is worried about Grace. Her sister is not settling in very well and has made few friends. The nuns are not unkind to her but they are strict and Grace has trouble under-standing what it is she is supposed to do. She spends more time talking to her teddy bear than she does to anyone else. Maggie has tried speaking to Sister Angelica about her, suggesting that if Grace moved into their dormitory to be with her she could look after her. Sister Angelica was very understanding and said she would see what she could do but in the end the nuns decided that until Grace was five she would have to stay where she is. That means another year at least.

What is going to happen to her when Maggie leaves? Sister Bridget has already told her that when she is fourteen she will have to find a job. She must do something to help her sister before that happens.

The next morning after breakfast she goes straight to see the Mother Superior. The girls are not allowed to enter this part of the orphanage; it's for the nuns alone. She can feel her knees trembling as she makes her way down the corridor. The Mother Superior's room is at the end on the right. She hesitates for a moment then knocks lightly on the door.

'Come in.'

Maggie opens the door and steps inside. The Mother Superior is writing something at her desk.

'Yes?' she asks without looking up.

'Excuse me Reverend Mother,' Maggie begins.

The nun looks up in surprise.

'What are you doing here child? Who sent you?'

'Nobody, Reverend Mother.'

'Nobody?'

The Mother Superior sits back and removes her glasses; she stares at Maggie for a moment.

'Smith, isn't it?'

'Yes, Reverend Mother, Margaret Smith.'

'Well, Margaret Smith, what can I do for you?'

'Please Reverend Mother, I want to speak to you about my sister Grace.'

'Ah, yes, Grace Smith. I know who you mean; the little quiet one. So what about her?'

'She's unhappy, Reverend Mother. She was only little when we came here and she still has not settled down with the other girls.'

'I see, so what do you want me to do about it?'

'If she were in the same dormitory as me, I could look after her; she wouldn't be so afraid.'

'Afraid? What does she have to be afraid of?'

'She misses Mum. She's never been away from her before.'

'Your mother is dead if I recall correctly.'

'That's what they told us,' Maggie replies, rather too firmly.

She sees the Mother Superior stiffen.

'Maybe you are reading too much into this, child. Your sister has been here for a year; she must be used to the orphanage by now. Perhaps she is just seeking attention; young girls often do that.'

'But she wets the bed and she never did that at home.'

'It's been a big change for her. I'm sure that given time she will settle in, like all the other girls.'

'But ...'

'No more buts, child. It's time you went to your class. Next time if you have something that concerns you about your sister, you must speak to Sister Angelica.'

The Mother Superior replaces her glasses and picks up a piece of paper from her desk.

'Yes, Reverend Mother.'

Maggie hesitates then says:

'It's her birthday soon; she'll be five in just a few days,' she adds. 'Sister Angelica said that she could move up when she was five.'

The Mother Superior looks at her in exasperation.

'You are a very persistent young lady, Margaret Smith. Well, if your sister is about to have her fifth birthday then I will speak to Sister Angelica about it, but I cannot promise anything. It will depend on how much space there is in your dormitory. Now run along before I lose patience with you.'

'Thank you, Reverend Mother.'

Maggie hurries out of the room before the Mother Superior can change her mind. Now she has to speak to Grace before they find out that she has lied about her sister's age.

BILLY

Billy thinks of the day he arrived in Australia. He knows they landed in Fremantle. He tries to remember what the escort told them about Australia. He closes his eyes and concentrates until he can see the map before him. Fremantle was at the bottom, he remembers, that must mean it's south. He has to go south but which way is south? What was it the escort said? The sun sets in the west. He said if you stood with the setting sun on your right then south was straight ahead. Billy looks up at the sun; it's directly overhead and blinds him. He will not be able to tell which way is south until later but there is no time to wait for the sun to set; he must leave now before they miss him. He has made his plan. He will follow the railway tracks until he reaches Fremantle. He reasons that the train has just arrived from there so all he has to do is walk in the opposite direction.

He looks around him cautiously. There is no-one to be seen only an old dog stretched out in the shade of a gum tree. He pulls his hat down over his eyes to shade them from the harsh light and sets off alongside the track. The grass has been burnt to a grey-brown straw but it's softer under his feet than the road. He walks for what seems hours and still sees no-one and nothing. The tracks wind endlessly on into the distance. He is tired now and thirsty but his fear drives him on; he will soon be there he tells himself. He is beginning to realise that he should have made better preparations. He needs water and food. And where will he sleep tonight? He has not considered these things. A snake slithers towards him. Billy stops; he must not move. It's best to stay completely still; that is what Willis told him. The snake does not see him and carries on its way. Billy waits to see if there is a second one; they are often in pairs. When none appears he moves on. He is not too worried by snakes; Willis told him that they will only attack you if you bother them first. What he hates are the spiders; there seem to be so many of them in Australia. There were spiders back in London; he remembers them well but they were tiny creatures that scurried away and hid in the corners of the cupboards or under the sofa, not these great hairy things that live in the gum trees. Even the spiders in Mrs Kelly's air raid shelter were not as bad as those. Some are even poisonous according to Willis. The worst one is the Red-Back spider; that can kill you in ten-seconds. It's only small, so small that you don't always notice it but if you stand on it, it will bite you. He looks at the ground carefully. He has not had any shoes for two months now; the ones he arrived with soon became too small for him and although he cut out the toes, they were more painful to wear than going barefoot. And anyway, none of the other boys wore shoes and he soon felt conspicuous wearing them. His feet are now tanned a dark brown and the soles are tough, like leather but would that be enough to stop a spider bite? He is not sure.

Billy checks the position of the sun; it has moved across the sky and is dipping towards the earth. He is going the right way after all. This realisation pleases him so much that he feels a new burst of energy. He has no idea how long it will take him to get to Fremantle but he will continue walking until it's dark. The more distance he can put between himself and the farm school, the better.

It seems impossible that it can be any hotter but it's; he feels that his blood is boiling and he can hardly put one foot in front of the other. He is so tired and so very thirsty. His body aches all over and his foot is bleeding from where he stepped on a stone. He wants to cry but he cannot even do that; his eyes are dry and itchy. The railway tracks seem to go on forever, no sign of a station, no houses, nothing. Not even a train has passed him. There is a haze on the horizon ahead of him and he thinks he can make out the outline of some houses. It cannot be far now. Maybe it's a town. Maybe it's Fremantle; even if it's not Fremantle there will be water and food there. He staggers on but the town seems just as far away as ever. Maybe it's just a mirage; he has read about mirages. They can drive people mad.

At last he sees a clump of gum trees in the distance and abandons the tracks to collapse in their shade. As his body hits the ground he is asleep almost immediately and his head fills with dreams.

Billy dreams that he is on board ship and they are heading for England. Willis is with him. He tells Willis that he will like it in England, that his sister will look after them. They are standing on the deck, looking at the sea and a boat is heading towards them. He can see its name painted on the hull, '*Wadene*'. He cannot move. It's coming closer and closer; it's coming for him and Willis. His legs feel like lead. He cannot move. The figures on deck become clearer; they are tall men in black robes. He does not want to see their faces but he already knows that one of them is Brother Dermot. He carries a jug of water and he offers it to Billy but Billy is too frightened to take it. It could be poisoned. He sees a tiny spider running around the rim. 'Drink, drink,' the brother urges him.

Something wakes him. He jumps up, frightened. He wants to scream but no sound comes from his parched throat. There is an old man squatting beside him. He is the blackest man that Billy has ever seen. His skin is so dark that it's sucking in all the light around him. Billy stares. The man is completely naked except for a small pouch covering his old fellah; his hair is grey and frizzy and he looks at Billy from eyes that are as black as night. His face is a web of deep wrinkles. Billy is frozen with fear. He does not know what to do. He has heard tales of the aborigines. They are wild people, savages, the Brothers call them; some are even cannibals. The man has a spear made of blackthorn by his side. Is he going to kill him?

The aborigine holds out a billycan. Billy hesitates; his dream lingers in his mind, still too strong, but at last his thirst overpowers him and he reaches out and takes the billycan. The water is warm and tastes of iron but it's good. He gulps it down greedily.

'Thank you,' he says.

His voice surprises him; it's nothing more than a whisper.

The aborigine pulls a small piece of dried meat out of his pouch. Billy takes it gratefully. It's like chewing leather. He wonders what it is, some dead animal, dingo maybe. He looks at the sky; the sun is moving towards the horizon. He has been asleep for hours; it will be dark soon and he still has a long way to go. He is worried. He does not want to walk through the night in case he gets lost but he knows that he cannot stay here on his own. He knows there are wild dingoes around; sometimes he could hear them from the farm school. How will he protect himself?

The aborigine stands up and picks up his spear. He is leaving. Billy watches him walk away. He is not heading south; he is going west, into the setting sun, away from the railway tracks. Billy hesitates. If he follows him he might never find his way back to the tracks but, if he stays, he will be alone. The thought of a night alone in the bush galvanises him into action; he jumps up and runs after the man. The aborigine does not turn and look at him. He just keeps walking.

They walk until the sky turns crimson and the sun sinks out of sight then the aborigine stops by a mound of rocks. Billy sits down on the ground; his butt still hurts from the beating that Brother Dermot gave him and his feet are sore from walking. He watches the black man dig into the soil beneath a rock with his spear. He digs until he has a deep hole then he bends down and drinks, cupping the water in his hands. He motions for Billy to do the same. There is water bubbling up at the bottom of the hole; it's muddy but it's cool water. Billy scoops some into his hands and drinks. Then the man lifts up one of the smaller rocks. Billy sees some ants scurrying to escape but before they can do so, the man picks one up and pops it into his mouth then motions for Billy to do the same. Billy is hungry but does not want to eat ants, not live ants. He imagines them wriggling about in the old man's mouth. He shakes his head, no, not ants. The man squats down on his haunches and helps himself to some more, trapping them with one hand and delicately lifting them to his mouth with the other, as though they are the greatest delicacy. He looks at Billy and smiles. His teeth are big and jagged; they gleam white in the dwindling light. He is enjoying his meal and seems in no hurry to move on.

Just when Billy thinks they are going to spend the night by these rocks, the aborigine gets up and starts walking again. Billy has no option but to follow him; he realises now that he is completely lost. He keeps as close to the man as he can as they trek on through the bush. The aborigine seems to know exactly where he is going but Billy cannot make out any landmarks; by now it's far too dark. The night is full of strange sounds and Billy wonders how the aborigine will protect them if they are attacked by wild animals; his spear does not look all that efficient. Desperately he tries to remember what the escort told them on the boat. There are dingoes in Australia, certainly, but what else? He wonders if there any lions or tigers or was that in Africa? A noise, like a muffled roar makes him start; it sounds just like a lion. He looks at the aborigine; if he has heard it, he makes no sign and continues to move forward in the darkness.

After what seems a very long time, they come to a clearing. The moon has just begun its ascent and by its watery light Billy can make out a few makeshift huts; they are humpies, nothing more than windbreaks made from thorn branches. Sitting on the ground outside these crude dwellings are more black people. Billy hesitates as the man goes up to one of the humpies and squats down beside an aborigine woman. He says something and points at Billy. Billy feels afraid. Maybe they are cannibals after all; maybe he has brought him here to kill him and eat him. His teeth start to chatter and he stops, too frightened to go any further.

The woman comes across to him. She says something and touches him on the cheek then she laughs and pulls at his blond hair. He tries not to stare at her; her skin is not as black as the man's but she too looks old. She is naked and when she bends over her breasts hang loosely against her stomach. He has never seen a naked woman before and feels himself flush with embarrassment. The man has curled up on the ground inside the humpy. He says something to the woman and she takes Billy's hand and leads him to another smaller windbreak. She points inside and smiles. Four dun coloured dogs are curled up asleep in there. Billy understands. He can sleep with the dogs. He hesitates. Will they bite him? He has heard that dogs know if you are afraid of them. Gingerly he creeps up next to them; one growls slightly, but the others don't care. The smell of the dogs is strong but it's warm in there and Billy feels surprisingly safe. He is not used to dogs; the only dog he knows is old Mr Ford's dog and he is nearly as old as Mr Ford. Mum promised that they could have a dog when the war was over but he does not think that that is going to happen now. He lays his head against the nearest dog's flanks and soon he is fast asleep. Tonight he does not dream.

Billy is woken as soon as it is light. The dogs are up and jumping around excitedly; one of them comes across and licks his face. It's a wet, salty lick and smells of something rotten. Billy crawls out of the humpy. The aborigine has his spear in his hand and is talking to a group of other men. They are going hunting. Billy jumps up and starts to follow him but the woman stops him. She shakes her head and motions for him to sit down. Then she gives him a piece of honeycomb. It's very sweet and good but it does not fill him up; he licks the honey off his fingers and watches her. She goes over to the other women and says something; they all look at him and he feels embarrassed again.

The men and the dogs are leaving. Billy hopes that the aborigine will remember him and invite him to go with them but he does not even look his way. A boy of about five years old comes across with a puppy the same colour as the hunting dogs and sits down beside him. The puppy is very fat and it wriggles out of the boy's grasp and jumps into Billy's lap. At first Billy is unsure what to do with the puppy but the animal has its own ideas and begins to chew the edge of Billy's shirt. He strokes it carefully, gently trying to disentangle it from his clothing but now the puppy wants to play; it takes Billy's arm into its mouth and tugs at it. The puppy's teeth are like tiny razors, fine and sharp.

'Hey, that hurts,' he says, laughing.

The aborigine boy laughs too and tries to talk to Billy but Billy cannot understand a word he says. In the end the boy gives up and takes hold of Billy's shirt, tugging at it until Billy stands up and follows him. They leave the puppy playing with an old bone and head for a grove of eucalyptus trees where there is a waterfall cascading into a small pool. On the rocks above a purple heron watches the boys.

The little boy pulls at Billy's arm once more, trying to tell him something then he turns and jumps into the pool with a squeal of pleasure. For a moment Billy hesitates. This must be what the boy wants to say; he wants him to go swimming with him. The sun is already climbing into the sky and Billy knows it will soon be very hot. He runs towards the water and jumps. The icy water makes him gasp and he can feel his skin tingling. At first his butt stings but the water soon numbs the pain and he jumps up and down, splashing and shouting. This is good. He feels good. He is free. The heron lets out a cry and flaps lazily away, the dull beat of its large wings lost in the boys' merriment.

Once the men have gone hunting, the women set off in separate directions, foraging for food. Billy, the boy and the woman set off towards a rocky outcrop to begin their search. First of all the woman shows Billy how to move the rocks carefully so that he can catch the insects before they scurry away out of the sunlight.

She lifts up a rock and finds some spiky looking insects then looks at Billy and mimes 'good to eat', by popping one in her mouth and rubbing her stomach and smiling. Billy wants to laugh but he does not want to offend her and he knows he must pay attention; this could save him from starvation. At first he is nervous about touching the insects in case they bite but he watches the boy carefully as he shows him how to grasp them correctly. The boy and the woman look at him, waiting for him to try. He lifts a rock and picks one up. It wriggles in his fingers and he thinks he will drop it. The woman says something and points to his mouth. She wants him to eat it. He does not know what to do. At last he closes his eyes and puts the insect into his mouth; it's like eating dry grass, crisp and crunchy. When he opens his eyes they are both smiling at him. Most of the insects they collect that morning are eaten straight away but some get popped into the woman's pouch of leaves to take home.

It does not take him long to realise that although the insects are considered a tasty snack, what they really want to find are grubs. They move towards a clump of eucalyptus trees and begin to search around the roots and on the trunks of the trees. He is worried that there may be some spiders there, so is very careful what he touches.

A cry from the boy alerts his mother to his discovery and Billy goes across to investigate. Under a pile of mouldering leaves there are some fat, white maggots. The woman is delighted; she puts one in her mouth and beams at her son then puts the rest in her pouch. These will be very welcome at home.

They spend the whole day looking under rocks and in the trunks of the eucalyptus trees for things to eat. Billy tries to help as much as he can but he still does not know which grubs are good to eat and which are not. When he picks up something she sometimes takes it from him and pops it into her pouch of leaves and sometimes she shakes her head, miming 'not good to eat' and puts it back. He cannot tell the difference; to him they look the same.

When the pouch is full they turn and head for home. Billy is still hungry. He hopes the men have had a good day hunting; he is tired of eating little wriggling creatures. Then he sees them, some small berries which look like the tomatoes they ate on the ship, only smaller and greener. These look good to eat so he picks one and takes it to the woman. She is very pleased with this find and comes over to help him pick them. They have picked about a dozen of the little fruits when there is a rustling sound and a large, brown snake slithers out from under a rock. Billy lets out a yell and leaps back. The woman puts a restraining hand on Billy's arm and shakes her head. What does she mean? Not good to eat? He starts to laugh hysterically as they watch the snake slither away.

By the time the men return, it's nightfall and Billy is really hungry. All he has eaten, since the honeycomb that morning, are a few grubs, some insects and some sort of root that had a bitter taste. The men are pleased with themselves; they have speared a kangaroo and an emu. They drag the carcasses into the clearing where the rest of the tribe are waiting. Billy and the boy are told to build a fire of brushwood while the women set about skinning, plucking and cleaning the catch.   The hunting dogs lie down, patiently waiting for the women to throw them some scraps then, snarling and sniping at each other, devour their share as quickly as they can.

The fire is burning fiercely so one of the men puts some grass on it to dampen it down before they hang the meat over it to char. Soon the smell of roasting meat is mingling with the wood smoke. Billy is ravenous; he has never smelled anything so good in his whole life. Maybe life won't be so bad living with the aborigines.

MAGGIE

Grace's bed is at the end of the room, next to the window; it's the bed that Maggie slept in when she first arrived at the orphanage. Now she sleeps near the door, a privilege for being one of the older girls. She wants Grace to sleep next to her but Sister Agnes will not hear of it. She was very annoyed when she was told that Grace was joining them. Now Maggie has to be careful or she will find herself in trouble for the slightest misdemeanour but she does not mind; the important thing is that Grace is much happier. Once the lights are out and the doors shut, the little girl scampers up to Maggie's bed and climbs in beside her and there she stays until morning.

Maggie hears the cock crow and shakes her sister awake.

'Time to get up Gracie, hurry up now.'

Grace knows the routine; she hurries back to her own cold bed and starts to get ready for the day.

'Smith One,' Sister Agnes barks as she comes into the dormitory. 'Get over to the kitchen as soon as you're ready. Sister Bridget wants some help loading up the honey.'

'Yes, Sister,' Maggie replies.

She is 'Smith One' and her sister is 'Smith Two'.

It takes her only a few minutes to pull on her dress and run across to the kitchen. This is the day when the man comes up from the village to collect the honey that the nuns make. It will be her job to load the jars onto his wagon. She has to be careful because if they tip over and any of the honey spills the man will not pay the nuns for it.

The wagon is already in the yard and the man's horse is tied up at the rail near the cow shed. She knows the man will be sitting in the kitchen chatting to Sister Bridget and drinking tea from his old tin mug.

'There you are Smith, just in time. Help Bruce load up the jars, will you. I've got a treat for you today,' she adds. 'We're going into town.'

A visit to the town. Maggie can hardly believe her luck. She has never been chosen to go with Sister Bridget before. She picks up one of the stone jars and takes it out to the wagon. There are already about twenty empty jars on the back, waiting for her to collect them and stack them in the kitchen. Even empty they are still heavy and she cannot manage more than one at a time. It takes her quite a while to empty and reload the wagon but eventually it's finished and she goes into the kitchen to tell Sister Bridget. Her hands are sticky and smell of the sweet honey. She puts her finger in her mouth and sucks it. Delicious. She likes honey but the girls never get to eat any of it; what the nuns don't use, goes to the market and is sold.

Sister Bridget has her parasol and sits up front next to Bruce. Maggie is instructed to jump up behind and squeeze in next to the honey jars. It's barely light but already the flies are buzzing around the sticky pots; Maggie picks up a leaf and tries to fan them away. The man hitches up his horse and for a moment the flies swarm across to the horse but soon give up and return to the honey pots.

'Hurrup,' the man cries and flicks his whip across the horse's rump.

The wagon rumbles off and they are on their way. Even the flies don't bother Maggie today; she is so excited. She has never been away from the orphanage since the day she arrived; she has no idea what lies beyond these gates but she knows they are not heading towards Melbourne. They are going to the market town that lies due north of them. Soon the wagon leaves the stony track and drives along a tarmac road through fields and fields of nothing but burnt grass; the countryside is unchanging, endless miles of dried up pasture. She leans back against the honey jars and dozes in the warm sun. There is a strong breeze and soon it will be unbearably hot. She is glad she has brought her sunhat with her.

The jolt, as the wagon comes to a halt, wakes her and she looks around to see that they have arrived in a small town. A few stalls line the side of the road and people are setting out their vegetables and fruit. So this is the market. She feels a bitter disappointment. It's nothing like the bustling, rowdy markets of the East End. Once again a wave of homesickness threatens to engulf her and she swallows hard.

'Down you get, young lady. Let's get these honey pots unloaded before the flies devour them.'

She jumps down and helps Bruce unload the wagon. Once the jars are neatly stacked on the stall and Sister Bridget has collected her money, she turns to Maggie and says:

'I need to buy some groceries and then we will see about getting a lift back to the orphanage. Stay close to me; I need you to carry the shopping.'

'Yes, Sister.'

There are not many shops as far as Maggie can see: a butcher's, a post office and a corner shop, that is all. Consequently, it does not take Sister Bridget long to make her purchases and persuade the local postman that he can take them back to the orphanage in his van.

'I'll have to make a few stops on the way,' he explains, 'but it won't take long.'

He has a strong accent and Maggie finds it hard to follow what he is saying.

'That's fine,' Sister Bridget says, climbing into the seat next to him and directing Maggie to the back of the van.

This journey is not as comfortable; there are no windows in the back of the postman's van and the floor is cold and hard. She sits on top of a sack of mail and wedges herself against the seat behind the nun. The postman chats happily to Sister Bridget; he seems to be glad of the company.

'Got to drive over to Biddy Jameson's with some medicine from the doc,' he explains.

'What's the matter with her now?' asks Sister Bridget.

'No idea; the usual I expect. She's as thin as a drover's dog; I know that. Doc just asked me to drop it off for him.'

'That's over by Rainy Creek, isn't it?'

'Yes, a bit out of your way, but it won't take long.'

Maggie hears the nun tut-tut with irritation; she knows she is thinking about the lunch she has to prepare when she gets back.

They soon leave the town behind them and rattle along the road; the van travels a lot faster than the horse drawn wagon and Maggie feels that she is flying.

'Can you smell that?' the postman asks, suddenly slowing down. 'Smoke.'

Maggie leans forward and peers out of the window. She can see a pall of black smoke on the horizon. It's coming towards them.

'Bush fire,' he says. 'Good God, what're we going to do?'

'There's no need to blaspheme,' Sister Bridget says, tartly.

The van pulls to a halt and the postman gets out; Maggie and the nun follow him.

'Yeah, bush fire,' he says and points to the fields.

Maggie can see them now. The kangaroos are fleeing from the fire; they bound across the parched fields, desperate to outrun the flames. A flock of birds has the same idea and flies overhead. The sky darkens as they pass; the beating of their wings and their frantic cries fill the air.

'What will we do?' cries the nun. 'We can't stay here.'

'We'll have to go back to town. It's OK, not to worry; the wind is taking the flames northwards. We'll skirt round it and soon be out of harm's way,' he says but does not look convinced.

Maggie is not so sure; the cloud of smoke is thicker and blacker now and she sees flashes of red and gold flames, leaping towards the sky. She coughs; the air has a bitter, acrid taste.

'Well, one thing's for sure; we can't stay here. This road isn't going to last long,' he adds.

The tarmac is already hot and bursting into tiny bubbles. She stamps her foot down hard and it leaves an imprint in the bitumen; tiny dribbles of tar stick to her sole.

'Hey, girl, get back in the van,' he tells her.

She knows he is frightened; his voice gives him away. He reverses quickly and turns the van round. Soon they are heading back the way they came. His fear is infectious and she realises she is shaking.

'I need to get back to the orphanage,' Sister Bridget complains. 'I have the lunch to see to. Can't you just drive straight there?'

'Sorry Sister, we have no choice. I'd be as mad as a cut snake if I drove you through that. Somebody else will have to cook the lunch today.'

The van hurtles down the road, throwing Maggie from side to side. She clings to the back of the seats and prays that the fire will not catch them. Sister Bridget has stopped complaining now and is praying aloud:

'*Heavenly Father, who art in Heaven* ...'

Maggie is exhilarated; she does not know if it's fear or excitement that is making her heart race.

'I knew this was going to happen,' the postman mutters. 'Just needed a spark for it all to go up. Been as dry as a tinder box, for weeks. Just knew it was going to happen.'

The nun continues to pray, her eyes closed and her hands clasped together in supplication.

A fat bodied aeroplane flies over them. It's low in the sky and Maggie knows it's about to douse the fire in water.

'Good on ya, lads' the postman says. 'Didn't take you long to get out here.'

She can hear the relief in his voice. A fire engine hurtles past them, followed by two trucks filled with local men carrying some makeshift tools.

'Soon be under control now,' he says to his passengers.

She hopes he is right. The excitement is waning now and she is feeling frightened. It's unbearably hot in the van; the postman has wound down all the windows and there is no escape from the scorching air. Bits of dry straw blow into the van and they are soon covered in dust and soot. She is worried that they will not reach the town in time.

'Please God it's not going to be another one like Black Friday,' the postman continues.

'What's Black Friday?' Maggie asks, her curiosity overcoming her shyness.

'The worst bush fire in living memory,' he replies. 'Two million hectares of land destroyed, nearly four thousand homes burnt and seventy people dead. We don't want another one like that.'

The nun continues to pray, this time with renewed vigour.

By the time they arrive, the news has already reached the town and everything is in disarray; the market stalls have been dismantled and people are boarding up their homes and dousing them with whatever water they can find.

'Stay here,' the postman instructs them. 'I'll find out if the road is clear for you to get back to the orphanage.'

Maggie and the nun get out of the van and stand in the shade of a giant gum tree to wait for him.

'Don't be frightened, child; God will look after us,' the nun reassures her but Maggie does not really believe her.

Maggie knows that even good people die in the bush fires. The townspeople are worried but there is no sign of panic; they are used to these occurrences. Most of the men have gone to tackle the blaze and it has been left to the women and the children to protect their homes. They may not be scared but their animals are. The horses in particular are getting nervous; they whinny and neigh their concerns and try to pull themselves free from their harnesses. Maggie sees the man who bought the honey; he is reloading his wagon with the jars, while all the time his horse is kicking up its heels and trying to get away.

'Whooah there ole mate,' he says. 'Just a minute now and we'll be off. Take it easy, now.'

The horse is not convinced. At last the man has his wagon loaded and gingerly unties the horse and takes the reins; the horse rears up and Maggie thinks the wagon is going to capsize but the man is ready for him and his hand is on the animal's neck, stroking him and calming him. At last he is able to lead the horse away and they set off in the opposite direction to the fire.

'Sister Bridget, why don't we ask the honey man if we can go with him?' she says.

The nun looks up from her meditations. The wagon is heading in the direction of the orphanage.

'Run after him child and see if he can take us.'

'Hey mister, mister,' Maggie calls. 'Wait a minute.'

The honey man stops and looks back at her.

'Are you still here? I thought I saw you leave in the postie's van.'

'We did, but when he saw the fire he wanted to come back. Sister Bridget wants to know if you can give us a lift back to the orphanage?'

'Of course, but you'll have to hurry. I don't want to get stuck here all night if they don't get that fire under control.'

'Sister Bridget, he says yes,' Maggie shouts, waving at the nun. 'Sister Bridget.'

Sister Bridget picks up the shopping and waddles across to them.

'There's no need to behave like a hooligan, child.'

She turns to the man.

'It's very good of you, Bruce. God bless you.'

She hands Maggie the shopping.

'Now help me up child and you get in the back.'

Once more Maggie is in the back of the wagon amongst the honey pots.

The return journey is considerably swifter than their outward one. Maggie feels sorry for the horse. He is trotting full out but the driver does not need to encourage him with his whip this time; the horse knows in which direction lies safety. The road is busier now; those people with farms are all hurrying back to protect them.

The driver has little conversation; he is concentrating on the road and Sister Bridget has resumed her prayers. Maggie looks around her; the land here is unchanged but the sky behind them is black with smoke and she can still smell the burning vegetation. The flies have disappeared. Maybe they too know something is happening and have flown off to safety. She dips her finger into a tiny pool of honey that the man spilled when he was reloading the wagon. It's sweet and delicious. For a moment the taste transports her back to her childhood. She imagines she is a honey bear, like Winnie the Pooh. When she was little, her teacher used to read them stories about Winnie the Pooh, every afternoon just before it was time to go home. Home, she has no home now; the bombs destroyed everything and the only stories the nuns tell them are Bible stories.

They are almost there. With the briefest of goodbyes, Bruce drops them off at the top of the lane that leads to the orphanage.

'I must get back to my farm,' he explains, 'to make sure the sheep are safe.'

All the farmers are worried about their livestock; if the wind changes direction who knows what may happen. Maggie has heard talk of animals getting caught in the blaze and being burnt alive. She shudders at the thought.

'Thank you Bruce, you are a good man. God bless you,' Sister Bridget says.

'Hurrup,' he calls to the horse and they move off, the sound of the horse's hooves, reverberating on the metalled road.

Maggie picks up the shopping and follows the nun along the lane. The heat is blistering and she can feel the sweat trickling down her back.

Sister Angelica is waiting by the gate for them.

'Oh thank God you are both safe,' she cries, clasping her hands together and looking heavenward. 'The postman telephoned to tell us what happened. He says we're not to worry; they have the fire almost under control.'

'The lunch, what's been done about the lunch?' Sister Bridget asks.

'It's all right; we got some of the older girls to give a hand. Everyone's in the refectory now.'

Sister Bridget turns to Maggie.

'Well child, you'd better run along or there'll be nothing left. Leave the bag, I can manage that now.'

Maggie puts down the shopping and runs across to the refectory. The normal dry, sandy ground is wet; they have been soaking the sides of the buildings.

BILLY

The man opens the door and stares at the aborigine.

'Who is it, Henry?' his wife calls from the kitchen.

'It's that old abo I told you about, you know, the one we see out by the watering hole sometimes. He's got a boy with him.'

'What's that?'

The woman comes to the door to see what is happening. She wipes her hands carelessly on the front of her pinny leaving floury streaks across the green and pink stripes.

'Well I'll be stuffed, what's that little chap doing here?'

'What's this all about then, mate?   Where's the boy come from?   What are you doing with him?' the man asks the aborigine.

The aborigine looks at him; his face gives nothing away. Then he turns and walks back towards the bush leaving Billy standing on the doorstep. Billy does not know what to do. It's clear that the aborigines don't want him to stay with them anymore. They are packing up their camp to move on and he does not know where they will go.   He looks at the elderly couple nervously.   Will they send him back to the farm school? Should he run after the aborigine?

'What's your name lad?' the man asks.

He hesitates; maybe it's best to say nothing for now.

'Don't fret the boy now, not on the doorstep. Come in lad, come in. My, my, look at the state of him; he's a right little savage.   Hasn't had a wash in weeks I'd say.   And hungry too, no doubt. Come on lad, don't be shy. He won't bite you. He looks fierce but he's all heart is my Henry.'

The woman smiles, a big, warm smile which sends little crinkly lines running up her cheeks and around her eyes.

'Come into the kitchen and you can tell us all about yourself. I've just taken some fresh buns out of the oven. You could eat one of those couldn't you?'

Billy does not reply but he does not refuse the warm bun spread with butter and honey that she sets before him.

'He must be famished. That hardly touched the sides, did it now. Would you like another one?' she asks.

Billy nods; he is feeling better already. The man she refers to as Henry sits opposite him.

'Well now lad, it's time you told us something about yourself.'

Billy looks at the woman.

'Later Henry. Look, when he's finished this you take him out to the pump and get him cleaned up and I'll see if I can find any of our Jack's old clothes for him.'

She gives Billy a mug of milk and another bun. As Billy picks it up he becomes aware just how dirty his hands are; there is thick red mud under his fingernails and the skin is engrained with dust. He suddenly thinks of Mum; she would be so ashamed of him. If he closes his eyes he is back in their kitchen and he can hear her telling him to go and wash his hands. A tear trickles down his face.

'There, there now, son, don't take on; you can tell us all about yourself later. Come on, eat up and we'll get some of that muck off you,' says Henry.

'And put some of that stuff on his hair, you know the stuff the vet gave you for the sheep. '

Billy gulps down the last of his milk and follows Henry into the yard.

He knows he must say something soon. They are nice people. The woman has given him an old pair of trousers and a plaid shirt; the trousers are a bit big but she gave him some braces to hold them up. Best of all she has given him some cotton under-pants and a pair of old boots. The boots feel very strange. He has not worn anything on his feet for ages. He decides to wear them only for special occasions and leaves them on the porch.

'Right then my lad, it's time you and me had a chinwag,' Henry says.

Billy follows him out onto the veranda. Henry sits in a rickety swing seat and motions for Billy to sit on a bench opposite him. The man swings gently to and fro in silence. He has lit a pipe and sucks at it lazily. He seems to be in no hurry to start his interrogation. He looks at the boy and nods appreciatively.

'You've scrubbed up quite well mate.'

Billy does not know what to say. Henry continues:

'This is a great place to sit, you know, when you want a smoke. It's a bit hot right now but come the evening it's fair dinkum.'

He puffs contentedly on his pipe.

'So I've been saying to myself that lad's got a good yarn to tell. Am I right?'

He smiles at Billy.

'How did you come by that abo for a start? He's not your usual abo, you know; his lot are a bunch of naked savages. Pintupi, that's what their tribe is called. Live out in the bush and eat grubs and things. Can't make stockmen out of them; they don't have any time for the white men. They're wanderers, they are. Always moving from place to place.'

He pauses and looks at Billy.

'That's what's so strange you being with him.'

He waits.

'I got lost,' Billy says at last.

'Ah so you can speak. For a minute there I thought you were a bloody wombat. So what's your name then mate?'

'Billy.'

'Billy. Anything else?'

'Smith.'

'Billy Smith. So where are you from Billy?'

His stomach sinks; this is it. They will find out about the farm school and send him back to the Brothers.

'Don't send me back,' he cries. 'Please don't send me back; he'll kill me.'

'Whoaa there, how can I send you back when I don't know where you're from?'

He peers at him then asks:

'You a Pom?'

Billy nods.

'One of them war refugees?'

Again Billy nods. His stomach has cramps. He knows that he will be sent back to the farm school.

'Geeze, how on earth did you get out here? We're miles from anywhere. The only people we ever see around here are those abos when they're passing by and the odd crazy swagman looking for a job.'

'I got lost,' Billy repeats. 'The black man found me and took me with him.'

'Well you can think yourself lucky he decided to bring you to us. That's no life for a white boy out there in the bush.'

He doesn't ask Billy where he was before he met the aborigine.

The brassy sound of a gong is summoning them to eat.

'That's Sarah,' he explains. 'Grub's up.'

He taps his pipe against his boot and slips it into his top pocket.

'Come on mate.'

There are five of them for dinner. Besides Henry and Sarah, there is an old man with a grey beard and next to him is a black man, another aborigine. This aborigine is not like the one that brought Billy to the homestead; this one is wearing blue overalls and a wide brimmed hat that he removes and places on the ground beside him.

'You sit here son,' the woman tells him.

'He's called Billy,' her husband tells her.

'Billy. That's nice. Well Billy this here is Arthur.'

The old man grunts and continues to spoon his soup into his mouth. It has dripped onto his beard and the man wipes it away with the back of his sleeve.

'And this young fellah is John Tjapanangka. You can call him John T.'

The aborigine smiles a wide, toothy smile at Billy.

The woman pours some of the hot soup into Billy's bowl. He looks at it; it smells nice.

'Roo soup,' the woman explains.

She hands Billy a hunk of bread. Instinctively he looks for the weevils. There are none.The soup is delicious. He eats it quickly then wipes out his bowl with the bread.

'Hey, where's the fire?' Henry asks with a laugh.

'Leave the lad alone; he's hungry that's all.'

'Hungry? Famished I'd say. Want some more, sport?'

Billy nods. This time he tries to eat more slowly.

Once Arthur and John T have finished their food and gone out into the yard for a smoke, Henry turns to his wife and says:

'He's one of those war refugees.'

'Oh the poor little lamb, how on earth did he get out here?'

'Beats me. He says the abo brought him.'

'You from London then?' she asks Billy.

'Yes, Bethnal Green.'

'Right. So where are your parents? They still in London?'

'My parents are dead.'

'So you're a poor little orphan,' she says.

Billy nods his head. What will they do with him now?

'So how old are you Billy?' she asks gently.

Billy thinks hard. He remembers he was ten when he arrived in Australia but how many months have passed since then? Every day is the same, some are hotter, some are colder, but the routine at Wadene is always the same. Only at Christmas did things change. The boys got invited to the homes of Catholic families and had a proper Christmas dinner. Last Christmas, his first in Australia, he and Louie went on the train to spend the day with Mr and Mrs Connor. They gave them turkey and sweets and put them on the train again in the evening. That had been such a lovely day.

'Ten,' he replies. 'Or maybe eleven now.'

'You're not very big for ten,' she comments, almost to herself.

'You'd better show him where to sleep,' Henry says.

'He can have Jack's room.'

'Is Jack your son?' Billy asks.

The soup has made him feel confident.

The woman looks sad.

'Yes lad, he's in the army.'

'He enlisted back in '39, one of the first to go,' adds Henry.

'My Dad was in the army,' Billy tells them. 'He was in France, but he got shot.'

The woman pulls a handkerchief out of her apron pocket and blows her nose noisily.

'Come on I'll take you to your room.'

Billy's room is at the back of the house. It's small and narrow but there is a bed and a washstand in it.

'You get the water from the pump,' she tells him, 'and the dunny's out the back. Hop into bed now and we'll talk about what we're going to do with you in the morning.'

Billy climbs into the bed. There is a big wooden cross on the wall above the bed.

'Are you Catholic?' he asks, nervously.

'Goodness me no child, honest to God Methodists we are. Not that we get to chapel that often. Sometimes the minister rides by to see us but even he doesn't come much these days, not since the war started.'

Billy closes his eyes; he is very tired. The bed feels soft and comfortable. He is asleep in no time.

SARAH

Henry is still sitting at the table when Sarah returns.

'All right?' her husband asks.

'Yes, the poor little lamb could hardly keep his eyes open. He was asleep as soon as his head touched the pillow.'

'So?'

'So what?'

'So what do we do with him?'

Sarah does not answer her husband; instead she busies herself with clearing the table. She stacks the plates in the sink and goes out to the pump to draw some water. Henry follows her.

'He's a refugee. Somebody must be looking for him,' he says. 'Maybe we should contact the police.'

She remembers the fear in Billy's face when he begged not to be sent back. Sent back, but to where? There were no other homesteads around here and no schools either.

'Did you see those wheals on the back of his legs? Someone's been walloping him with a stick or something,' Sarah says.

'Yes and it looks as though someone's been beating the hell out of his butt too.'

'Who can have done that? Not the abos?'

'No. Maybe he's been in one of those orphanages,' her husband replies.

He takes the bucket of water from her.

'I could drive in to Maroo and see if Bert knows anything about a missing boy.'

'We don't want the police snooping about,' she says. 'Why don't we just wait a bit to see if anyone's looking for him?'

'And what happens if they are?'

'We'll worry about that when we know more about what's happened to the child.'

'Well I can tell you one thing, something's not right there. A young Pommy boy wandering about with the Pintupis, I reckon that's strange.'

'Let him stay here a bit, at least until we find out what's been going on,' says Sarah. 'He could help you around the farm.'

Henry puts the bucket down on the kitchen floor and returns to his seat by the table.

'God knows I could do with some help since Jack went. Arthur's getting past it these days and that John T is a useless string of beans.'

He pulls out his pipe and busies himself with tapping down the tobacco and trying to light it.

'Well?' Sarah asks, splashing the water into the sink in her impatience.

'He could help with the yard work.'

'And the chooks.'

Henry nods. The pipe is lit now and he puffs contentedly.

'We could let him stay for a while, if you want. See how he settles down.'

'Good.'

She washes the last of the plates and stacks it with the others. It will be nice to have a youngster about the place.

MAGGIE

The smell of the mince boiling away on the stove makes her feel ill; it's always the same. Peas and mince, peas and mince, they serve it every day and she eats it because by lunchtime she is usually starving; she would eat anything. If only there was a potato to go with it. She pops the last of the peas from their pod and takes the pot over to Sister Bridget.

'Put it down over there,' she tells her. 'And go and get me some more water.'

Maggie picks up the bucket and goes out to the pump; she hates getting the water. The ground is wet and muddy around the pump and full of frogs. They jump away when she appears but still she does not like them. Worse than that, she has often seen snakes by the pump. She is terrified of snakes. Sister Bridget has told her that if she sees a snake she must stand quite still and shout 'snake' at the top of her voice then someone will come and rescue her. The first time she did that no-one came. She stood, shaking with fear, and watched the snake slither across the path in front of her and disappear down a hole in the ground. Now she does not bother to shout; she keeps still and waits until the danger is over.

She fills the bucket and carries it back to the kitchen, trying not to splash too much on the ground. If it's not full to the top the Sister will make her go back and fill it again.

'Smith, the Mother Superior wants to speak to you. Put that bucket down and get over to her office right away,' says Sister Bridget.

'But, I've got the laundry to do,' Maggie protests.

'You'll have to do that later. Hurry up now.'

Maggie pours the water into the sink and wipes her hands. She hopes the Mother Superior is going to tell her that she can leave. She is fourteen now; all the other girls of that age have already left to go to work. Maybe this is her turn. Her heart beats excitedly at the prospect. If she goes to work she will be able to save some money and then she can take Grace away from here.

The Mother Superior's office is in the main building, right next to the chapel. The last time she was there was when she went to see her about Grace. She wonders what it's about. She is pretty sure that she has not broken any rules, so it must be about leaving. One part of her is excited and desperately wants to escape from the orphanage but the other is worried about Grace. She does not want to leave her on her own.

She knocks timidly on the door.

'Come in.'

The Mother Superior is sitting at her desk; she is dressed in her usual black habit, with a white cowl and wimple. Her spectacles balance precariously on the end of her nose as she reads the papers on the desk in front of her. When she looks up Maggie's eyes are drawn immediately to her chin, where some dozen or so grey hairs have sprouted. She looks more like a witch than ever.

'Smith?'

She glances back at her papers.

'Yes, Reverend Mother.'

The Mother Superior beams at her, revealing an incomplete set of yellowish teeth. Maggie looks down at the ground; it's rude to stare.

'Today is your last day at the orphanage. I have decided that it's time that you left and went to work. After all you are a young woman now. We have found a family in Ballarat that needs a reliable domestic servant; they have offered to give you a job.'

She consults her papers once more and continues:

'Yes, a good job. They will pay you £1.17s.6d a week plus your keep. More than generous if you ask me.'

Maggie continues to stare at the floor. It sounds a lot of money; she will surely be able to save some of it and then she and Grace can be reunited.

'Well girl? What have you to say?'

'Thank you Reverend Mother.'

'You will catch the bus in Pardy Creek; Sister Bridget will drive you to the bus stop. Here is your fare.'

She places the money on the desk in front of her.

'When do I leave?' Maggie asks.

'Straight after lunch.'

'Please may I go to the Lower School and say goodbye to my sister?'

'Your sister?'

'Grace Smith.'

The Mother Superior sighs and looks as though she is about to refuse but then she changes her mind and says:

'Why not. Tell Sister Agnes that I have given you permission to speak to your sister.'

'Thank you, Reverend Mother.'

'Now run along and get ready; you have an exciting journey ahead of you. And before you go I want you to go into the chapel and thank God for your good fortune.'

'Yes, Reverend Mother.'

She settles herself in a seat by the window; her stomach is churning with a mixture of excitement and fear. Her bag is on the luggage rack above her head. It weighs next to nothing. All she has are the clothes that she is wearing and a change of underwear. She never did find out what happened to her lovely new clothes. She sighs. Well they would not fit her now anyway, even the ones she is wearing are feeling tight.

The bus is only half full, mostly people from the outlying farms going into Maroona, the woman sitting next to her explains. Today is market day. Maggie tells her that she is going to Ballarat to work. The woman wants to know more about Maggie but Maggie is reluctant to talk about the orphanage. What can she tell her? That the nuns beat you for the slightest thing: dropping a plate, having a hole in your threadbare skirt, forgetting the words of a prayer? Should she tell her how they eat ant-infested bread for supper and tasteless gruel for breakfast? How if you are late for breakfast because you have been up since five a.m. praying in the chapel and then doing your chores, you go hungry? Will she understand if Maggie says she does not like the way Sister Agnes stands and watches the naked girls having a shower? Will she think it right that the nun flicks their bare buttocks with a wet towel as they come out? Should she tell her that until today her life has been an endless round of work, prayer and sleep? The woman is smiling at her, waiting to hear of her wonderful life with the nuns.

'My sister is still there,' Maggie says at last. 'Her name is Grace.'

'Oh that must have been nice for you, my dear. Not so lonely for you with your sister there.'

Maggie smiles.

'When I've saved some money my sister is going to come and live with me.'

'Well that'll be very nice for you both. You from England?'

Maggie is surprised at this question, she thinks that her English accent has disappeared.

'Yes.'

The woman smiles; she looks pleased with herself.

'I thought so. One of those poor little war refugees?'

Maggie nods. The woman turns to talk to her friend across the aisle and leaves Maggie to stare out of the window. The corn has been cut and the fields are now mile upon mile of dry stubble. They pass tall haystacks and a horse-drawn plough cutting long, brown swathes through the dusty earth. She thinks of London and its busy streets, with double decker buses and trams, people hurrying to and fro, on their way to work or queuing up for food, the market traders shouting out their wares, hectoring passers-by to buy from them, the old men in their Home Guard uniforms on parade, and soldiers on leave, running to catch trains that will take them to see their families. A kaleidoscope of re-membered images flashes before her eyes. She remembers the stink from the tanning factory; once again she is crouching in Mrs Kelly's Anderson shelter, breathing in the damp smell of earth and cordite. Now she is walking to school with Billy and the sounds of her friends' voices come to her over the years: '*Mother, mother, I feel sick, send for the doctor, quick, quick, quick,*' the girls chant.

The bus is entering the town and the women bustle about, collecting their possessions around them, all conversations sus-pended while they get themselves organised. They pull into the bus station and the bus stops with a shuddering groan. The bus driver, an old man with a grizzled beard, gets down to help his passengers alight.

'Goodbye my dear,' the woman says, picking up her shopping basket and smiling at Maggie. 'Good luck with the job.'

'Goodbye,' Maggie replies.

The women file off, each one with a smile and a joke for their driver. Maggie looks back down the bus; a couple of young men in overalls and a smartly dressed woman remain in their seats.

'Any more for Maroona?' the bus driver calls down the bus.

Nobody moves.

'OK, next stop, Ballarat.'

Just as Sister Bridget promised, Mrs Brookes is there to meet her at the bus station. She is a tall woman with dark hair that she has pulled back from her face with two tortoiseshell combs and she is wearing lots of make-up. Maggie thinks she is pretty; she re-minds her of June.

'You must be Margaret?' the woman says.

She has an Australian accent but it's much posher than Mag-gie has heard before. She nods at her and tries to smile but she is very nervous. Her stomach is in knots.

'This is my daughter Annabel,' the woman continues, pushing a lanky, young teenager forward.

'Hello,' the girl says.

She has her mother's dark hair and eyes and the same, slow refined accent.

'Come along then.'

She looks at Maggie's battered bag.

'Is that all the luggage you've got?' she asks.

'Yes. I've grown out of most of my clothes,' Maggie replies.

'Well, never mind, you'll be wearing a uniform most of the time, anyway.'

She strides off and the two girls hurry to keep up with her.

'Is it far to your house?' Maggie asks the girl.

Annabel shakes her head, she appears to be rather shy.

The house is large; there are a lot of rooms to clean. Maggie has her own room on the top floor, overlooking the back garden; it's lovely. She sits on the bed and looks around her. The room is simply furnished in blue and white. There is a narrow chest of drawers for her clothes and a table and chair where she can sit and write to Grace. Someone has put a small vase of yellow daisies on the table. But the best thing is the bed; she cannot resist the urge to bounce up and down on it for a moment, to feel the lovely springiness of the mattress and to bury her head in the soft pillow. This is heaven. She lays back and looks up at the ceiling. She has the whole room to herself; she no longer has to share with twenty other girls. At last, now she will be able to get on with her plan: she is going to save up enough money so that Grace can come and live with her and then she is going to find Billy. June said that they had records of where everyone went, so it shouldn't be too hard to trace him. She will get a better job and they will all live together until they can get back to England. A gentle knock at the door wakes her from her reverie. She sits up in surprise; she is quite unused to privacy.

'May I come in?'

It's Annabel.

'Yes, please do.'

Maggie gets off the bed and smooths the counterpane with her hand.

'Mummy has to go out but she says that you don't have to start work until tomorrow. She wants me to show you over the house and tell you what has to be cleaned,' Annabel tells her.

'All right.'

'Can you cook?' she asks.

'Not very well, I know how to prepare the vegetables though.'

She thinks of the mince and peas that her friends will have eaten for lunch today. She is not going to mention that.

'Mummy usually does the cooking but sometimes she needs some help in the kitchen,' Annabel explains. 'Peeling the potatoes and things.'

She is standing in the doorway, shifting her weight nervously from one foot to the other.

'Don't you help your Mum?' Maggie asks.

'No, I'm still at school.'

'Do you want me to come with you now?' Maggie suggests.

Annabel smiles.

'Yes please, let's do it before Mummy and Daddy get back.'

Maggie follows the girl down to the kitchen. She is so happy to be out of the orphanage; even the fact that she is here alone, without her brother and sister, does not spoil it. It's going to be much easier now to help both Billy and Grace than it was before. For the first time since she left London, she feels free. She has a job and somewhere to live. That is enough for now. She will work hard and save as much money as she can. Then she will look for something better.

BILLY

Billy and Henry walk out to join John T at the sheep pens; it's shearing time and Henry wants him to learn how to shear the sheep. Last year all he was allowed to do was collect up the fleeces and take them to the shed for washing.

'I expect you'll have your own place one day, son, so you need to learn all you can,' Henry says.

Billy likes it when Henry calls him son; it makes him feel part of the family. It's over a year since he arrived and he enjoys working on the farm; the idea of having his own spread appeals to him. He remembers what his friend Damon said to him that day on the train, how he wanted to be a farmer and have his own farm. Damon had not learned a lot about farming at the orphanage; he spent most of his days like Billy, carting stones and mixing cement. He wonders what he is doing now, probably still building that bloody convent.

'Hi Billy. Over here.'

John T is bent over; one of the ewes is between his legs, bleating angrily. The shears are in his hand. Half the ewe is already shorn and a pile of dirty fleece lies at his feet.

'You do the next one,' he says, not looking up until he has finished.

He releases the animal and the ewe bounds to her feet and runs to the end of the pen; she looks bald and pink without her thick coat.

'Doesn't it hurt them?' Billy asks Henry.

'No, they like to have their coats off, especially in the summer.'

'Just like us,' Billy jokes.

He feels nervous. He does not want to cut the sheep by mistake.

'I like to get them done before lambing then there's time for their coats to grow a bit before the lambs are born,' Henry continues.

'Show me once again,' Billy tells John T.

'OK.'

He grabs another ewe and begins. Billy concentrates; John T makes it look so easy.

'Right, now you have a go,' says Henry. 'Remember to get a good hold of her before you start and don't be nervous. The sheep will stay still if you are confident.'

'OK, Boss.'

He likes calling Henry boss, even though he knows he can call him Henry. It makes him feel grown up. He grabs one of the ewes and turns her on her back, tucking her head between his legs. She bleats pathetically.

'That's it.'

John T hands him a pair of shears.

'Now cut the fleece as close to the skin as you can without stabbing her, and don't hurry, take your time,' Henry instructs him.

Billy starts snipping the fleece near the stomach and then moves out towards the back, just as he saw John T do.

'That's good. Try to keep the fleece in one piece.'

He does not look up. He is concentrating on his work and the sweat is running down his back with the effort.

'Don't rush it. Keep a steady rythmn.'

His hand slips and he nicks the sheep's skin.

'Oh, I'm sorry,' he says.

The sheep bleats in surprise and tries to struggle to her feet.

'Grab hold of her Billy; don't let her go.'

He grabs at the animal's fleece and wrests her back into position.

'Good, now carry on from where you left off,' Henry tells him.

He resumes clipping and before long he has the whole fleece lying at his feet and lets the ewe up to rejoin the flock.

'Pretty good for a first time, lad. We'll soon make a sheep-man out of you, I can see.'

Billy works all through the morning with John T; he shears another four sheep then the stockman tells him to take a break. He slumps down in the shade of the lean-to and watches John T. He is so quick the ewes hardly have time to realise what is happening. Billy rubs his back. It aches from bending over and there is a blister forming on his right hand. John T sees him examining it.

'You'll soon get used to it, mate. Here collect up the fleeces and put them in the shed then we'll go and have some tucker.'

As usual they all sit around the table in the yard. Sarah has made a rabbit stew and ladles him out a generous helping.

'How'd it go, Billy?' Sarah asks, passing him a hunk of bread.

'OK. I think.'

He looks at Henry for affirmation.

'Yes, you didn't do bad, son. Give him a few more to do this afternoon, John T,' he says. 'You'll probably get them all done by the end of the week, with Billy to help.'

John T does not look convinced but he grunts:

'OK Boss.'

Arthur belches.

'That was right good tucker, Missus.'

Sarah nods and smiles at him.

'I'll go out and look at that watering hole this afternoon, Boss, see if I can clean it up a bit,' the old man says.

'Good idea, Arthur. Billy can run you out there in the truck when you've finished.'

Billy looks up in surprise. He almost chokes on his food and that makes Henry laugh.

'Don't you want to take the truck?' Henry asks him.

'Yes, Boss. I'll run him out there.'

'That's a good lad.'

Henry has never let him take the truck out on his own before. He taught him how to drive it not long after Billy arrived on the farm but so far Billy has only driven when Henry wanted a rest or if he needed him to back it up to offload something. This is the first time he has trusted him on his own with it. He gobbles down the rest of his food as quickly as he can.

'Ready when you are, Arthur,' he says.

'Hold your horses, young un. I want some of Sarah's apple pie before I go back to work.'

'Will you have a piece, Billy?' Sarah asks, placing a steaming apple pie on the table.

It's straight from the oven and smells of cinnamon and nutmeg. He nods.

'Yes please.'

Sarah's apple pie is not something you turn down, no matter what else is on offer.

Henry has asked Billy to help John T with the lambs; six have been born already and John T tells him that there are at least another twenty to come. Normally Henry and John T manage alone but this year Henry has problems with his back so he wants Billy to take his place.

One of the ewes has died unexpectedly so Sarah has asked him feed its lamb with an old baby's bottle; he has got up extra early every morning to do it before he starts on his other chores. He has named the lamb Snowy because it's so white and fluffy; he can push his fingers deep into her soft coat and feel her heart beating. Once the lamb is strong enough to stand on its own feet he has to put it back in the flock with another ewe; a surrogate mother Henry calls it. That is what Sarah is to him, Billy thinks, a surrogate mother. He is very fond of Sarah and Henry; they treat him like their own son.

At first he was always on edge that they would find out about the orphanage and send him back there, but they never did. It does not seem to matter to them where he has come from; they accept him as he is.

'Why don't we ever see the Pintupi round here?' he asks John T.

The stockman looks at him. They are out looking for one of the ewes; she is due to give birth any day and she has gone missing. Henry thinks a dingo might have got her.

'Pintupi never come near the white fellah,' he says.

He is chewing on a piece of grass.

'So where are they?' asks Billy.

John T waves his arm.

'North, south, who knows? They go long distances. Following the song lines.'

Billy looks across the wide expanse of scrubby grassland; there is nothing to see except the sheep grazing as best they can.

'What're song lines?' he asks.

'All aborigines have song lines,' John T explains. 'They are our ancestral pathways; they link us to our past. They're how we find our way around.'

'Do you have song lines?'

He is thinking of the Pintupi aborigines that looked after him; they were always singing strange songs and making weird music. He also remembers how the man led him through the bush with no hesitation, as though there were signposts all the way.

The stockman shrugs. He whistles for the dogs.

'Why do you live here John T?' Billy asks.

'This is my home.'

'But where is your family?'

He shrugs again.

'Did you live with your family when you were a little boy?'

John T stops and hunkers down in the shade of some wattle trees. Billy squats down beside him. The stockman pulls out a flask of water and offers it to him.

'When I was a kid these men came, took me away from my family. I was only so big.'

He holds out his hand to show Billy how small he had been.

'I was in the bush with my mother and my brother, hunting for goannas. The white men drove up in a big jeep, grabbed me and my brother and drove off. They said it was for our own good, that we would go to school and learn stuff. Grow up like the white fellahs. We went to live in a children's home with other aborigine kids.'

'What happened to your brother?'

John T shrugs.

'Doing the same as me somewhere, I expect.'

'Don't you ever see him?'

He shakes his head.

'Did you see your mum again?' Billy asks.

'No. Don't know where she is now. Long time ago.'

'Perhaps she's following the song lines,' suggests Billy.

John T looks at him and snorts. He pulls out a packet of cigarettes and lights one.

'Give us a fag?' Billy says.

The stockman hands him one and laughs as Billy struggles to light it. Billy sucks at the cigarette; the smoke is raw and burns his throat but he perseveres. He tries to control the smoke and blow rings in the air like John T does but he coughs and the smoke escapes in a sudden burst.

So John T has no family either.

'Why did they do that, John T?' he asks. 'Why did they take you away from your family?'

'I don't know.'

'What did your mother do?'

'She couldn't do nothing; the white men were too strong for her. They waited until my father was off hunting with the other men, so it would be easier for them. I watched her running behind the truck calling to us, but she couldn't keep up. We left her behind and we never saw her again.'

Billy thinks about the days he went hunting for grubs with the aborigine woman and her son; if someone had come along and grabbed him and the boy, the woman could not have protected them.

'Come on, we've got to find that bloody sheep before the dingoes do,' John T says.

They get up and move out into the hot sun. The dog sits watching them, waiting for its instructions.

'Do you miss your family?' Billy asks.

'What do you think?'

'Why don't you try to find them?'

John T does not answer. Maybe it's too late. He wonders how old John T is, twenty maybe, thirty. It's hard to tell.

'What about your family?' the stockman asks. 'Where are they?'

Billy does not reply. No-one here knows that he ran away from the orphanage.

MAGGIE

Maggie has been working for the Brookes for six months. She works hard and her employer has not had any reason to complain. In fact she tells Maggie that she is very pleased with her and is going to write to the Mother Superior and tell her so.

Maggie is content, she has already saved three pounds from her wages. She would have saved more but she needed to buy some new shoes and a dress to wear on her afternoon off. She enjoys having some money to spend. She would like to buy something nice for Grace but she knows it's not worth sending her anything because they will just take it from her. She will wait and buy her a lovely pink dress when she leaves the orphanage.

Maggie gets on well with Mrs Brookes, who is a fair employer and she likes Annabel. Annabel is still at school but she is the same age as Maggie and they get on well, although sometimes Maggie wonders if there is something bothering Annabel. She is very nervy when she is at home and speaks very little. She behaves like the girls in the orphanage, as though she is frightened of something; she jumps at the slightest sound and does not look at you directly but sits with her head down. Maggie does not understand it. What could be frightening her? She never hears Mrs Brookes shouting at her and she did not even punish her when she dropped Mrs Brooke's favourite china vase and broke it. All her mother said was:

'Try not to be so clumsy Annabel.'

And then:

'You'd better sweep it up; don't leave it for Margaret to do.'

Sunday is Maggie's afternoon off and at first she used to stay in her room or go for a walk alone, in the park. Then one day Annabel suggested she meet up with her and her friends and go to the cinema. Now she sees them regularly. There is Sandra, who goes to school with Annabel, and Barbara and her twin brother, Greg, who live next door. Maggie likes Greg; he reminds her of Billy and makes her laugh. Annabel is a different person when she is out of the house, laughing and chattering like any other fourteen-year-old.

Maggie sees very little of Mr Brookes, except when she brings him his breakfast in the garden room. He usually rises early and likes to eat before his wife and daughter have woken. Today, however, he comes into the kitchen just as she is making his toast.

'Good morning Mr Brookes,' she says with a smile.

'Good morning Margaret.'

'I'll be right out with your toast,' she says. 'It won't be a moment.'

She has already laid the table with butter and marmalade.

'There's no rush,' he says. 'Why don't you sit down a minute?'

She looks at him in surprise.

'Won't you be late for work?' she asks.

Normally he is in a rush and constantly looking at his watch. Sometimes he makes her think of the Mad Hatter in 'Alice and Wonderland'.

'I'm not going in today. Sit down and tell me how you are settling in.'

She does not know what to do; she cannot disobey him but she has so much to do this morning. It's Monday and there are the beds to strip and the sheets to wash and iron besides all the usual chores like cleaning the bathrooms and putting the Hoover round the lounge. Reluctantly she sits down at the table beside him.

'That's better.'

She does not know what to say.

'You are a very pretty girl, Margaret. Do you know that?'

She shakes her head.

'Well you are.'

He reaches across and pushes a stray hair away from her cheek; she feels his fingers linger on her skin. Unconsciously she edges her chair back from the table.

'So Margaret, are you happy working here?' he asks.

'Yes, sir,' she replies.

Her voice is no more than a whisper. She does not like the way he is looking at her.

'My wife treats you well I hope?'

'Oh yes sir, Mrs Brookes is very kind to me.'

'That's good.'

He is staring at her. His eyes are sad, but his lips are smiling. He reaches across and before she can remove it, he takes her hand in his.

'If there is anything you ever need Margaret, you can come to me. You know that don't you?'

She nods. She can feel herself blushing with embarrassment. She wants to remove her hand but does not know how to do so without offending him. He is stroking it gently with his thumb. His nails are neatly manicured and the back of his hand is covered with dark hairs.

'How old are you Margaret?' he asks.

'Fourteen.'

He sighs.

'Fourteen, what a lovely age, so fresh, so young,' he murmurs to himself.

'Sir, your toast will be cold,' she says. 'Shall I make you some fresh?'

'What? Yes, OK.'

He stands up abruptly; he too can hear the sounds of his family moving around. Soon they will be down for breakfast.

'No, tell you what, leave it. I'll join my wife for breakfast this morning.'

'Very well sir.'

When he leaves the kitchen Maggie sits down again; her knees are shaking. What was the matter with him this morning?

At one point he looked as though he was about to cry. What a good job Mrs Brookes did not see him holding her hand like that. She would have sacked her immediately.

Maggie does not see Mr Brookes again until dinner time when she takes the hotpot into the dining room.

'Thank you Margaret. When you've brought in the vegetables you can go and eat your supper. There's no dessert this evening,' Mrs Brookes tells her.

She turns to her husband.

'It's my bridge evening tonight,' she adds.

'What time will you be home?' he asks.

'Not late, about nine I expect.'

Mr Brookes helps himself to the hotpot; he does not look at Maggie.

'I'm not hungry, Mum. Can I be excused?' asks Annabel.

She is very pale.

'You have to eat darling. Just try a little.'

'Maybe I'll have something later. I'll ask Margaret to put some on a plate for me.'

'OK, if that's what you want.'

Mrs Brookes looks at Maggie, who nods in agreement. Something is wrong with Annabel; she is as pale as a ghost.

It's always a simple meal on Monday's, usually leftovers from the weekend, so there will not be too much washing-up to do. After that she is free for the evening. She thinks she might go for a walk and post the letter she has written to Grace; it's a lovely cool evening. She goes upstairs to wash her face and comb her hair.

'Are you going out Margaret? Can I come with you?'

It's Annabel.

'Of course.'

The girls take the long route to the park so that Maggie can post her letter. They walk side by side in silence for a while.

'Is it nice having a sister?' Annabel asks.

Maggie looks at her; she has never considered this before.

'Yes, I suppose it is, but it's a lot of responsibility,' she adds thinking of Grace all alone in the orphanage.

'I've only ever had brothers. Tom's the eldest. He's nice. I was a bridesmaid at his wedding and I wore a lovely dress. It was blue with pink rosebuds round the neck.'

'I've got a brother too,' Maggie says. 'He's ...'

She pauses and calculates Billy's age in her head.

'He's twelve.'

'Is he still in England?'

'No, he's somewhere here in Australia, but I don't know exactly where.'

She feels like crying but instead she takes a deep breath and tells Annabel the story of how they became separated.

'Oh, that's awful,' Annabel says and Maggie can see that she really means it.

Annabel takes Maggie's hand in hers and squeezes it.

'You must have been so frightened.'

'I was. We all were. When I've got enough money I'm going to take Grace away from the orphanage and then we're going to look for Billy,' she tells her.

'As soon as I'm old enough I'm going to Melbourne to live with my brother,' Annabel says.

This news surprises Maggie. Why would she want to leave her Mum and Dad and their lovely house? She waits for Annabel to tell her more but instead she says:

'I'm on holiday now, six weeks off school.'

She does not look particularly happy at the prospect.

'I think it's time we went back,' Maggie tells her.

'Oh let's stay a bit longer; we haven't been on the swings yet. Anyway Mummy won't be back until nine.'

'OK, just a bit longer.'

If asked, Maggie would say that she is too old to be going on the swings but once she sits on that hard, wooden seat and pushes herself away from the ground she just wants to go higher and higher. It's exhilarating. She feels her worries slip away from her; with every thrust of her legs they fall away, one by one. She closes her eyes and imagines that she is flying through the air, the wind against her face.

'You girls, be careful, you could fall. You're a bit big for those swings,' a voice says.

She opens her eyes. An old man with a black and white dog on a lead is watching them. She looks at Annabel and they both begin to laugh.

'Come on,' she says. 'I think it's time we were going.'

When they arrive home there is a light on in the lounge but there is no car in the drive.

'Mummy's not back yet,' says Annabel.

She looks disappointed.

'Well I expect your Dad's in.'

Annabel does not reply; her face has resumed its tight, closed look. Her 'indoor look' Maggie calls it. She thinks how much prettier she is when she is outdoors, smiling and chattering like the other girls. They close the front door quietly behind them.

'Annabel, is that you?' Mr Brookes calls from the lounge.

'Yes, Daddy. I'm off to bed.'

'Come and give your old Dad a kiss goodnight then.'

Annabel looks at Maggie and sighs.

'See you tomorrow, Maggie.'

Maggie goes into the kitchen to make sure she has left everything tidy for the morning. When she comes back, the lounge door is shut but she can hear the murmur of voices. She is tired, she climbs the stairs and is soon in bed and fast asleep.

She is dreaming that she is flying through the clouds. She can look down and see everything below her like a world in miniature. Now she will be able to find Billy and Mum; all she has to do is fly through the sky until she sees them.

Suddenly she is awake. There is someone in her room. She sits up straight, clutching the bed covers to her chest.

'Who's there?' she asks.

Her voice is hoarse.

'Ssh. It's only me, Margaret. I thought I heard you cry out and came in to see if you were all right.'

She begins to tremble. It's Mr Brookes. Why is he in her room? What does he want?

'I'm fine, Mr Brookes. Thank you.'

She pulls the bed covers more tightly to her. As her eyes become accustomed to the gloom she can see that he is wearing his pyjamas. He sits on the bed. She can feel his weight pulling down on the covers. He smells of whisky. A faint light from the street lamp falls across the counterpane. She cannot move. The man is looking at her and smiling.

'Don't be afraid, Margaret.'

Slowly he takes the sheets from her hands and pulls it back. She is terrified. She wants to get up and run away but she cannot move.

'You are a pretty girl, Margaret. A very pretty girl.'

He reaches out and touches her cheek. His fingers linger for a moment and then move down her neck until they come to rest on the buttons of her nightdress. He gently undoes the first button, then the next one, then a third. She watches in horror. What is he doing?

'Such a pretty child and such a tease.'

His hand slips inside her nightdress and she feels his fingers on her breast; they close on it tightly and squeeze. She wants to cry out but the sensation is not unpleasant. She does not know what is happening to her.

'There, do you like that, my child? He asks, rubbing her nipple.

She does not reply. Her body is a cauldron of mixed emotions.

He moves his hand across and begins caressing her other breast.

'Yes, I know you like it, my pretty tease.'

He leans closer and begins to kiss her. His breath is foul, tasting of whisky and cigarettes. His moustache scratches her skin. All the while his hand continues to massage her breasts. He begins to groan softly. Is he in pain? He takes her hand and pulls it towards him.

'Come on, you know what to do, my pretty,' he says.

What does he want? He pushes her hand down towards the opening in his pyjamas. She can feel something hard.

Suddenly she hears footsteps. There is a tap at her door.

'Maggie, is everything all right?'

It's Annabel.

Mr Brookes pulls away from her and stands up. He leans over her and places his hand on her mouth. She cannot breathe.

'Don't say a word,' he whispers.

'Maggie? Are you awake?'

They hear the door handle turn, but he has locked it. Now Maggie is even more frightened. What will happen if they find Mr Brookes in her room? They will dismiss her instantly. They will send her back to the orphanage. She is frozen in terror. Neither of them moves until they hear Annabel's footsteps retreating then he slowly removes his hand from her mouth.

'Don't breathe a word of this to anyone,' he says. 'This will be our little secret.'

He bends down and kisses her again.

'Lie down now and go to sleep,' he says.

Maggie does as he says but she knows she will not sleep. As soon as he has gone she gets up and locks the door behind him then she drags the chest of drawers across and pushes it against the door. He is not coming back into her room, not tonight nor any other night.

She climbs back into bed and lies there shaking. What was he doing, touching her like that? She cannot bear to think what would have happened if Annabel had not come along and saved her. She pulls the covers tightly around her. It's not fair. It's just not fair. She starts to cry and buries her head in the pillow to stifle the sound of her sobs. Is there nowhere she will be safe?

She likes it here; she has made friends and begun to have a normal life again. She likes Mrs Brookes; she is very kind to her and she likes Annabel too but she knows she cannot stay here any longer. She must find somewhere else to live, somewhere where no-one can hurt her.

The next morning Maggie stays in bed until she hears the front door slam and Mr Brookes leave for work. She does not care that he has had to get his own breakfast today; she is sure that he will not complain to his wife about her. For a moment she experiences a feeling of power over her employers but it quickly dissipates. She has decided what she will do; she will leave and go to Melbourne and look for another job. She feels bad about letting Mrs Brookes down but it's impossible to stay here now. She cannot even warn her that she is leaving. What excuse could she give? She is sure that Mrs Brookes would not believe her if she told her about her husband's behaviour and her instinct tells her that even if she were believed it would somehow be blamed on her.

She hurriedly gets dressed and goes down to the kitchen just as she hears Mrs Brookes go into the bathroom. She will make their breakfast, tidy the lounge and then when Mrs Brookes goes out to do the shopping she will leave. Her plan clearly established in her head she sets about making the coffee.

'Good morning Margaret.'

'Good morning Mrs Brookes.'

'Just a cup of coffee for me today. I'm meeting some friends in town and we're sure to have elevenses.'

She pats her flat stomach and grimaces. Maggie smiles. She does not understand why Mrs Brookes is always going on about her weight; she is very slim.

'Annabel?'

'A boiled egg please, Maggie.'

Maggie does not look at her.

As soon as breakfast is over and she has done her chores she goes to her room and drags her bag from under the bed. She folds her clothes carefully, lays them in the bag and zips it shut. Although she has twice as many possessions as when she arrived they still don't fill her bag. She puts it back under the bed then she sits down and writes a note to Mrs Brookes. She does not want her to think that anything bad has happened to her so she writes:

'Dear Mrs Brooks

I am sorry but I am going away to find another job. Please don't look for me; I shall be all right. Thank you for everything.

Margaret'

She folds it and places in an envelope. She hears her employer say something to Annabel and then the door shuts. She waits until she hears the car pull out of the drive then picks up her bag and the envelope and creeps downstairs. She does not want to bump into Annabel.

'Maggie, where are you going?'

Annabel is standing in the kitchen; she has been waiting for her. Maggie feels herself blush.

'You're not leaving are you?'

The girl looks horrified. Maggie is frightened that she is going to cry.

'Is it because of Daddy? It is isn't it? He was in your room last night, wasn't he? I knew it. Oh, how could he? Oh, Maggie, I'm so sorry.'

'I've got to go,' Maggie says. 'I can't stay here any longer; I have to look for my brother.'

It's a weak excuse but what else can she say?

'But you can't leave, not yet. You've only just got here. Please don't leave.'

Maggie walks past her and props the envelope against the kettle where Mrs Brookes will find it when she returns.

'I'm sorry.'

She doesn't know what else to say to her. She understands now why Annabel is always so nervous; her father has probably been going into her room at night, too. She hesitates then asks:

'Why did the girl before me leave? Did he touch her too?'

'I don't know. Honestly. She wasn't here very long, only a few months then one day she said she had to leave.'

'So it could have been because of him.'

Annabel nods; she is close to tears.

'Let me come with you,' she pleads. 'Please, take me with you.'

'No, how can I? You have to go back to school. And anyway your parents will find you and bring you back. They will tell the police and then I'll be in trouble.'

'But I can't stay here now,' she wails.

'Tell your mother about him,' Maggie says.

'How can I? She won't believe me.'

Maggie puts her bag down and pours out a glass of water.

'Here, drink this,' she says handing it to Annabel.

She feels sorry for Annabel but there is no way she can take her with her; she does not want the police looking for her and sending her back to the orphanage.

'Lock your door at night,' she instructs her.

'I do. That's why he went to you.'

'Well then, threaten to tell your mother if he doesn't stop.'

'He'll just say it was my fault,' Annabel sobs. 'He's always calling me a teasing minx. It's not true. I don't do anything.'

'Look, wipe your tears.'

Maggie hands her a handkerchief.

'You've only got a few more years to go then you can leave school and get a job somewhere,' she adds. 'You could go and live with your brother.'

Annabel brightens a little at this suggestion.

'Yes, but what do I do in the meantime?'

'Why don't you ask your mother if you can spend the holidays there, at your brother's house.'

'That's a good idea; I could stay there until I have to go back to school in September.'

Arrabel drinks some of the water and Maggie can see that she is much calmer now.

'Where are you planning to go Maggie? Are you going to Melbourne?' she asks.

Maggie nods.

'Do you have anywhere to stay?'

'Not yet. I'll find somewhere when I get there.'

'Go to my brother's. His wife is very nice; I'm sure they will help you if I ask them.'

Suddenly Maggie sees a different side to Annabel. She is no longer a weepy teenager; she is someone who wants to help her friend.

'Wait here. I'll write him a letter and you can take it to him. I'll tell him that I am coming to stay for a few weeks as well.'

She goes into her father's study and takes some paper from his desk.

'It'll be all right, you'll see. He may even be able to help you find your brother. He's very clever you know.'

'I don't know about that. What if he doesn't want me there? What if he gets in touch with your Dad?' Maggie says.

'He won't do that; he doesn't speak to Daddy. They had a terrible row about something last Christmas,' she adds.

She finishes the letter with a row of 'x's and puts it in an en-velope.

'Look, this is his address. You'll have no trouble finding it.'

She is smiling now.

'It'll be great; we'll be together all summer,' she says.

Maggie takes the envelope from her. This would certainly make life easier but she is not sure if it's a wise move. She does not know these people. What if they decide to inform the orphanage that she has run away.

'Annabel, you know that I have to find a job first. I won't be on holiday like you.'

'Yes, I know, but my sister-in-law will help you; she knows everybody in Melbourne,' she says, beaming at her.

Her confidence in her brother and his wife is infectious.

'Look, I have to go now. Your mother will be back soon,' Maggie says. 'I have to be gone before that.'

She wants to be as far away as possible when Mrs Brookes returns from shopping.

'I'll walk to the bus stop with you,' Annabel offers.

She is more cheerful now and bends down and picks up Mag-gie's bag.

'I'm going to miss you, Maggie,' she says, her eyes filling with tears again.

'I'll miss you too, Annabel but we'll see each other again soon. I'll write to you and tell you what happens.'

'Yes and I'll come to visit you.'

'Now, come on, we've got to go.'

As the door shuts behind them Maggie no longer feels frightened; she feels elated. This is just another step in her life and it's going to take her closer to reuniting her family, she is sure.

MAGGIE

Maggie cannot believe her good fortune. Annabel's brother, Tom and his wife, Alice live in a quiet urbanisation on the outskirts of Melbourne. When she knocked at their door she was sure they would read Annabel's note and then tell her politely that they could not help but instead they welcomed her into their home and within a few days had helped her find a job in a local factory and a room in the house of a widow who was taking in lodgers in order to make ends meet.

'Maggie, there's someone at the door for you,' Mrs Robinson, her landlady, calls up the stairs.

Maggie puts down her pen and hurries downstairs. It has to be Annabel; Tom promised he would tell her where Maggie was staying as soon as she arrived.

'Annabel.'

'Hi Maggie.'

The two girls embrace. It's three weeks since they last saw each other.

'Come in. Come up to my room.'

She leads the way up two flights of stairs until they reach her bedroom; it's small but it's comfortable and cheap.

'I thought you were never coming,' Maggie says.

'Mum said I had to wait until she got some more help.'

'So what happened?'

Maggie is desperate to know how Mrs Brookes reacted to her disappearance.

'Well she was very upset that you'd gone. She read your note and said she didn't understand it. She wanted to go to the police but Daddy persuaded her not to. He said that it was not a matter for the police and if you wanted to leave it was up to you.'

'Is that all?'

'Well she went round the house to see if you'd taken anything but when she found that nothing was missing she calmed down.'

Maggie feels her stomach tighten. How could Mrs Brookes think she was a thief? She feels disappointed with her ex-employer.

'And she didn't mind you coming to stay with Tom?'

'No, but it's only for two weeks then I have to go home.'

'What about your father?'

'He didn't want me to come but Mummy persuaded him.'

'And the other thing?'

She does not want to ask directly about the abuse.

Annabel looks down, avoiding her gaze.

'It's OK now,' she mumbles. 'I keep my door locked.'

Maggie hopes this is true but it's obvious that Annabel is not going to tell her any more; she is too embarrassed to talk about it.

'Tom says he will help me find out if my mother is still alive,' Maggie tells her. 'He has a friend in the government who knows about these things.'

'Does that mean you'll go back to England?'

'Maybe. I don't know. I can't go anywhere without Billy and Grace.'

She dare not think so far ahead but her heart beats faster at the prospect.

'Well at least you know where Grace is.'

Maggie nods.

'But not Billy.'

'Don't worry, someone will help you find him,' Annabel reassures her. 'Now tell me all about your new job. Have you made any friends? Are there any nice boys there?'

The girls giggle. Maggie thinks how nice it's to see Annabel again; she has missed her. There are lots of women working in the factory but so far she has not got to know any girls her own age. The women sit and chat during their lunch break while they eat their sandwiches but usually it's about their children or their husbands. Maggie has nothing to contribute. Anyway she does not want to talk about the orphanage or why she has moved to Melbourne so she usually sits in silence.

Maggie arrives back at her lodgings at six o'clock; she is exhausted. The job is very tiring and so repetitive but the money is good. She earns three times what Mrs Brookes paid her. It's noisy and smelly and she stands there, all day long, packing tins into boxes as they come off the production line. Sometimes they are tins of peas, sometimes of beans, mostly she does not notice, her mind is elsewhere, usually thinking about how she can get back to London.

'Hello, Maggie. Had a hard day? You look whacked.'

'No, I'm fine thank you Mrs Robinson.'

'How's that friend of yours, Annabel?'

'I'm going round to see her tonight; she's leaving on Sunday.'

'That's a shame. You seem to get on so well,' Mrs Robinson says as she bends down and takes a shepherd's pie out of the oven.

'That looks good. I'm starving,' says Maggie.

'Well go and sit down with the others. I'm just about to dish up.'

There are four lodgers living in Mrs Robinson's house; Maggie is the only girl. The other three are already sitting at the dining room table, waiting for their meal. She sits next to Fred Barrett, a middle aged salesman who has been living there since Mrs Robinson first started taking in lodgers. Opposite her are a young soldier, who was injured in the war and a New Zealander. The soldier has something wrong with his jaw and hardly ever speaks to anyone and the New Zealander is a newcomer. The four sit in an uneasy silence until Mrs Robinson appears with the pie.

'My, that's a beaut,' says Fred. 'I'm starved.'

'You're right there mate,' says the New Zealander. 'That's a nice bit of tucker.'

Mrs Robinson beams with pleasure. She hands a plate to each of them.

'Veggies?' she asks.

'Sure, pile them on,' says Fred.

He is a corpulent man with a ginger moustache. Maggie likes him; he is always joking with Mrs Robinson and once Maggie saw him pat her on the bottom. Maggie thought Mrs Robinson would be angry but she just laughed and said:

'You keep those big mitts to yourself, Fred Barrett or I'll have the law on you.'

Mrs Robinson always joins them for the evening meal although she eats very little; she just sits smiling at everyone and sipping a glass of beer.

'Any more Maggie?' she asks.

'No thank you.'

Maggie finishes the last of her shepherd's pie and pushes her plate to one side.

'I think I'll go round to Tom's now,' she says.

'OK, my dear, off you go.'

'Nice to be young and fancy free,' says Fred with a chuckle. 'That right Mrs R?'

'Too long ago for me to remember,' replies the landlady, drinking back her beer and smiling coquettishly at Fred.

'I won't be late,' Maggie says.

'OK dear, mind you're back by nine; you're too young to be wandering about at night,' she tells her before turning back to the others and asking: 'Now who's for strawberry tart?'

Alice is in the kitchen washing up and Tom is sprawled on the sofa reading the paper when Maggie arrives.

'Hi there kid, I thought you'd come round tonight,' Tom says.

'Is Annabel in?'

'She's washing her hair. Annabel,' he shouts. 'Maggie's here.'

Maggie takes off her coat and sits down on the sofa. She feels very much at home here.

'Have you found anything about my mum?' she asks Tom. 'Or Billy?'

He shakes his head.

'Sorry kid, nothing so far. They can't seem to find any trace of your mum. You know since you left London, the Germans have bombed the place to smithereens. I imagine that what records there are, are in a hell of a mess. You need to face up to the fact that your mother could really be dead. Is there anyone else we could get in touch with?'

She shakes her head. No Mum is not dead. She will not believe it. It doesn't feel right. She is convinced that Mum is still alive. She does not know why she believes it; she just knows that it does not feel the same as when she was told that Dad was dead. Then it was a certainty. Nobody has actually witnessed Mum's death. It could all be a mistake.

'What about my Nan? Maybe you could find her.'

'Do you think your Nan is still alive?' Tom asks.

'She could be.'

'So what's her name?'

'Lil.'

'Lil what?'

'Lil Rogers, and my Granddad is Les Rogers. I know that because Mrs Kelly told me that Mum was calling the baby after granddad. The baby's name is Leslie.'

Tom wrote down the names.

'Right, is there anything else you can tell me? Anything you can remember about where you lived or where your Nan lived?'

'We lived in Bethnal Green, but our house was bombed.'

She thinks hard for a minute.

'The street was called Stanlet Street.'

'And your Nan?'

She shakes her head.

'I know it was in Islington somewhere.'

'Well that's something to go on. Do you remember where you were staying before you left England? Were you with a family?'

'No, we were with the nuns.'

'Nuns? Are you Catholics then?'

'No. Father McNally took us to St Margaret's when Mrs Kelly died.'

She sees Tom frown. The story sounds complicated she knows; she hopes he believes her.

'Mrs Kelly was our neighbour; she was looking after us while Mum was in hospital but she got killed in the bombing.'

'God, you poor kids,' says Alice, who has joined them in the sitting room.

'Well I'll see what I can do. I'm meeting my mate tomorrow for a pint, I'll have another chat to him about it. He works in the Department of Immigration and Intercultural Affairs, so he might be able to help us.'

'Phil?' asks Alice.

'Yes, if anybody can help, he can.'

'I've got this,' Maggie says and hands him her CORB identity disc. 'Would this help?'

'Is this how you came here, with CORB?' he asks.

'What's CORB?' Alice asks, taking the disc from him.

'It's the Children's Overseas Reception Board. They sent a lot of kids out to Australia. So, that's how you got here then?'

'Yes, they sent us on a ship.'

'Well that gives me something to work on.'

He looks at his wife who smiles at him and says:

'That would be wonderful Tom. Maybe someone can track down her grandparents.'

'Well I'll see what I can do, Maggie, but don't hold your breath. Remember it's wartime; lots of records go missing or get destroyed.'

'And Billy?' she asks.

'He came on the same ship?'

'Yes, we were all together but then they made him get off at Fremantle. Some men in black cloaks took him; they looked like priests.'

'Now that might be easier. I'll get someone to check the orphanages in the area and see if he was sent to one of them.'

'Oh would you? That would be wonderful.'

Maggie cannot believe her luck. Tom is being so helpful. She is bound to find her brother now.

'I'll see what I can find out. But even if they have a record of him, it's not certain that he'll still be there and then if he is there I don't know what we can do about it.'

'Hi Maggie.'

Annabel is hanging over the banister, her wet hair caught up in a white bath towel.

'Go on up, Maggie,' says Alice. 'I've just made a big jug of fresh lemonade. I'll bring some up for you.'

Maggie bounces up the stairs. How wonderful it would be if Tom's friend can find Billy. Then he could come and stay with her in Melbourne; she is sure Mrs Robinson would find a room for him.

She has telephoned the orphanage to ask them how Grace is and if she can go to see her. Much to her surprise they say that she can. As it is almost Christmas she is allowed to make one short visit. She decides to write to Grace first and warn her that she is coming:

'*My dear Gracie,*' she begins.

'*I hope you are well. I have lots of things to tell you since I last wrote. I am living in Melbourne now at the house of a nice lady called Mrs Robinson and I have a new job. I am working in a factory packing tins of peas! Yuk! You know how I hate peas. It makes me think of the orphanage. Next time you have peas and mince for dinner you can think of me standing there all day packing them.*

Mrs Robinson has a boarding house and I have a room to myself. The food is nice and we have toast for breakfast and sometimes we have homemade ice cream. It's quite cheap and I am saving up some money for when we can be together again.

I have written to the Mother Superior and she says that I can come to see you at Christmas. That's in just a few weeks. So that will be fun. You can tell me all about what you've been doing. It will be so nice to see you again. I have missed you, Gracie. See you soon,

With lots of love from your sister
Maggie xxxxxxxxxxx

PS A kiss for Teddy too x'

She folds the letter carefully and slips it into an envelope. She hopes she is not making a mistake going back to the orphanage. For a moment she is seized with the irrational fear that they will make her stay there.

Christmas Day is on a Saturday. The factory is closed for three days and she has told Mrs Robinson that she is going to see Grace. There is nothing to stop her. She has bought some presents for Grace: some chocolate biscuits, bananas, a picture book about kangaroos and a little silver locket. She is not sure if the locket was a good idea but she wants to give Grace something that she can hold on to and remember her by. She gets up early, before it's properly light and boards a bus in the centre of Melbourne. The driver wishes her a Happy Christmas and tells her that the bus goes straight through the tiny town of Pardy Creek; no need to change. The bus is almost empty at this hour but an old lady sitting across the aisle tells her that it will be full on the way back, with people going to visit their families.

The bus driver drops her as near to the orphanage as he can. Nothing has changed; the road is still a dusty track and the landscape in the pale morning light looks bleak and desolate. A shiver runs through her. She thought she would never come back here again but here she is. She trudges along the road until she sees the low, grey buildings of the orphanage in the distance and behind them the menacing stone building that houses the nuns. Her heart begins to race. Maybe she should not have come here. She is overwhelmed with the desire to turn round and go back but she makes herself pause and take a deep breath; the nuns cannot do anything to her now, she tells herself.

She walks up to the main building and knocks on the door. Sister Bridget opens it.

'Well Margaret. The Reverend Mother said you were coming today. To see your little sister, is it?'

'Yes, Sister Bridget. I've brought her a couple of small presents.'

The nun nods. She does not seem to have changed at all in the time that Maggie has been away.

'Follow me. They have just come out of the chapel. I expect Grace is feeding the chickens,' she says.

Of course, they will still have to work, even though it's Christmas Day. There are no days off at the orphanage. A girl comes running up to them.

'Sister Bridget, Sister Agnes wants you in the kitchen,' she says.

The nun looks at Maggie.

'You'll be all right on your own?' she asks. 'You remember where the chicken coops are?'

'Yes, I'll be fine,' Maggie says.

How could she forget? She feels as though she has never been away; every building, every blade of grass, every desolate patch of ground is engraved on her mind for ever. She'll never be able to wipe her memory clean.

'Good. Well nice to see you again, Margaret.'

The nun looks relieved to be rid of her and scurries after the girl.

Maggie follows the path until she comes to the chicken coops. She can see Grace. She is so small she can still climb inside with the chickens. She is talking to them in a low voice as she scatters the corn.

'Grace, it's me; it's Maggie.'

The girl drops the bowl of corn and turns round. It's her sister, without a doubt but she has changed in the time since Maggie left. Her face is thinner and there is no bounce in her step.

'Maggie,' she cries and clambers under the wire and out into Maggie's open arms.

She hugs the frail child against her, unable to speak for the emotion that is swelling up into her throat.

'Is it Christmas today?' Grace asks.

'Yes, darling, it's Christmas Day. That's why I have come to see you.'

'Do the nuns know?' she asks, looking around her, nervously.

'Yes, it's all right. I have permission. Look, I've brought you some presents.'

Grace's eyes light up then she says:

'But I have to do my jobs.'

'I understand, but I'm sure we can go somewhere and talk for a little while first. Why don't we go behind the chapel?'

Grace smiles. This is the place everyone goes to get away from the nuns. There is a big old gum tree there and if you climb up into its branches, no-one can see you. Maggie herself, went there to hide, many times.

It doesn't take long for Grace to clamber up the tree. They sit there, side by side as Grace opens her presents.

'It's lovely,' Grace says as she opens the box with the locket inside.

She looks worried.

'I know you won't be able to wear it but I thought maybe you could hide it somewhere. Look it's got a picture of me inside,' Maggie tells her.

She opens the locket and shows her. She would have liked to put in one of Billy as well but she doesn't have one.

'I'll keep it with my letters,' Grace says. 'Under my bed with Teddy. Teddy will guard it for me. He guards my letters. I read them to him every night.'

'That sounds a good idea.'

She watches as Grace takes a chocolate biscuit and eats it hurriedly. Although she has been writing to Grace every month she has not been sure if Grace could read her letters or not. She only has school in the mornings and, as Maggie remembers well, most of that time is taken up learning the catechism.

'Do you show the letters to anyone else?' she asks.

'Susie. She reads them to me,' she says.

'Who's Susie? Is she your friend?'

'No. She's a big girl. She's in charge of our dormitory.'

'That's kind of her. Is she nice to the girls?'

Grace nods and eats another biscuit.

'I'm going to keep some of these for Freda and Teddy,' she says.

'Is Freda your friend?' Maggie asks.

'Yes. Freda and I do the washing together. We do the mangling. And the ironing.'

Maggie remembers what that was like. Grace does not look strong enough to handle those wet sheets and towels. She thinks back to the days when she used to help Mum with the mangling; it had seemed fun then. But Mum did not have to wash and iron for one hundred and fifty girls, plus ten nuns.

'Freda never gets any letters,' says Grace. 'No-one writes to her.'

'That's sad. But she's got you for a friend, hasn't she.'

Grace nods vigorously and takes another biscuit.

'Are you really going to take me back to England?' she whispers.

'Yes, one day. We have to find Billy first but I have someone helping me with that. It won't be long; I promise you.'

'I miss Billy,' Grace says and a tear trickles down her face.

'Hey now, no crying today. It's Christmas Day.'

'Father Christmas didn't come,' she says with a sob.

'Well I expect he has lost your address.'

'We're all lost now, aren't we, Maggie?'

'No, silly you're not lost. You're here with me and as soon as I can manage it, you will leave here and come to live with me.'

Grace brightens at this.

'And Teddy?'

Of course.

'Do you remember Mum, Gracie?' Maggie asks.

Grace looks at her and shakes her head.

'What about England, do you remember England?'

'I remember the bombs and going on the ship,' she says. 'I liked the ship; there was a nice lady there.'

'That's right, June.'

Maybe it's just as well that Grace does not remember very much then she won't be so unhappy. She won't be tormented with memories of Mum and spend her time wondering if she is alive or dead, like Maggie does.

'I have to go and do my work now,' Grace says. 'Freda says I've got to do the ironing today; it's my turn. She won't be my friend if I don't go.'

'Of course darling. I'll come with you.'

They climb out of the tree and make for the laundry room. Freda is already there. She is taller than Grace but just as skinny. Her hands are red and raw from the washing soda that they use to wash the clothes.

'This is my sister,' Grace tells Freda.

Freda smiles shyly but doesn't answer. She takes the irons from the rack and places them on the stove to heat. Maggie knows they will need at least fifteen minutes to heat up. She will stay a while longer.

'Hello Freda. Grace has been telling me all about you.'

She has a long time to wait for the bus but at last it arrives. She would have liked to stay longer but Sister Agnes said that it was not a good idea; it was upsetting the other girls as they did not have any visitors. She sits near the front, next to the driver.

'And where are you off to, young lady?' he asks.

'Home,' she says and feels happy to think that Mrs Robinson will be waiting for her.

The turkey will be in the oven and her landlady will be bending over the stove, her cheeks red and shiny.

'No place like home,' he continues. 'Especially at Christmas.'

Poor Grace, if only she could have come back with her even if it was for only one night. She sits back in her seat and stares at the passing countryside. Tears blur her vision. She must make more effort to get her family reunited.

PART THREE
1945 - 1946

'Click go the shears boys, click, click, click,
Wide is his blow and his hands move quick,
The ringer looks around and is beaten by a blow,
And he curses the old snagger with the blue-bellied joe.'

"Click Go the Shears", traditional Australian song

MAGGIE

Today she is busy packing tins of lamb stew. There is a picture of a young lamb on the label that is so sweet and cuddly she is sure she could not eat the stew even if she were starving. Mrs Robinson says she is too sensitive about these things.

Her mind drifts back to Grace. She has been to see her twice now. She would like to go more but it's impossible. Whenever she suggests it, the nuns say it's disruptive for Grace and the other girls if she goes too often but they allow her to visit each Christmas. She wanted to bring her back to Mrs Robinson's with her last time but they would not allow it. She sighs. Her plans are taking a long time to come to fruition. She still has not located Billy and the nuns won't hear about Grace leaving the orphanage.

Suddenly the music on the factory loudspeakers is interrupted by the ringing of church bells and the sound of people cheering. Everyone stops and looks at each other. The factory conveyor belt shudders to a halt. Then a voice announces:

'*This is the BBC World Service. London calling. The war in Europe is over. The German Armed Forces High Command has surrendered unconditionally to the Allies.*'

There is a moment's pause while they take in this momentous news then everyone is cheering and someone has set off the factory hooter. It's bedlam.

'Quieten down there, mates; it's Churchill,' says their manager.

The workers stop to listen to the words of the British Prime Minister:

'*God Bless you all. This is your victory. Victory of the cause of freedom in every land. In all our long history we have never seen a greater day than this ...*'

But they can't listen any longer; this is too exciting. No-one can keep quiet. The women are crying with joy and the men go round clapping each other on the back and shaking hands. The war is over at last. After five long years, it's over. Now all they want to know is when their soldiers will be coming home. Maggie's friend, Helen, grabs her by the waist and swings her round and round. She is laughing and Maggie is laughing too. Now the war is over, now they can all go home.

The manager tells them he is closing the factory early and lets them go home. Nobody, not even he, is in the mood for working today.

'That's great. We'll go out to celebrate,' says Helen. 'I'll meet you at the pub at five.'

'Yes, I'll be there.'

She walks home in a daze. She cannot believe it's all over. Now their lives will change. Now they will find out if Mum is still alive and, if she isn't then Maggie will set up home for Grace and Billy. She has plenty of money saved now and if she keeps doing regular overtime then she should be able to rent a small flat for them. Billy will be fifteen now. He'll be able to work soon and then they'll have more money to live on. She stops. She is letting her enthusiasm run away with her; first she has to find out where Billy is living. Tom has had no luck with his investigations but he blames it on the war. Now that the war is over he should have more success; she is sure of it.

Helen is already waiting outside the pub when she arrives. She is wearing a new jacket with a velvet trim on the collar. Helen works on the packing line with her and once a week they go to the pictures together.

'Hi, sorry I'm late. Mrs Robinson wanted me to have some tea before I came out.'

'Kylie and Jimmy are inside, getting the drinks in,' she says.

Maggie has met Kylie before; she is Helen's cousin and often comes to the cinema with them. She has never heard her mention Jimmy.

'Who's Jimmy?' she asks. 'Is he your cousin's boyfriend?'

Helen gives a great hoot of laughter.

'Hell no. He's my big brother. He's just moved back home; he's been working in the shipyards in Perth.'

She links her arm through Maggie's and they go into the pub. It's packed. All of Melbourne seems to have squashed itself into this tiny, smokey pub. It's a typical, raucous Aussie celebration and the beer is flowing fast.

'Hi there, sprog,' says a young man, as he bends down and kisses Helen.

It has to be Jimmy. He looks a couple of years older than Maggie and is very handsome. Like Helen he has tight curly, black hair and neat even features. But where Helen is tiny, he is tall and rangy. As he turns to her to speak she can see he has the same easy-going mannerisms as his sister and she feels instantly at her ease.

'Hi, so you're Maggie?' he says. 'I've heard a lot about you.'

Maggie can't help blushing at this and even though Helen laughs and gives her brother a poke in the arm, she is embarrassed.

'Pleased to meet you,' she says and she means it.

Maggie is late; there was some unexpected overtime today. She hopes that Mrs Robinson has not served dinner yet. As she opens the front door she can catches the smell of something tasty floating from the kitchen. Through the glass door she can see Fred already seated at the table; the soldier is next to him, in his usual place.

'Hello Mrs R,' she calls. 'Sorry I'm late.'

She walks into the kitchen first, to borrow Mrs Robinson's newspaper; she likes to check for any news about the war children being repatriated.

'There's nothing in there today,' her landlady tells her. 'But they were saying on the wireless that some of the war refugees will be going back at the end of the month. One of the Ministries is handling it.'

'Do you know which one?' Maggie asks.

'No, I didn't catch what they said. Maybe that friend of yours will know more about it.'

Mrs Robinson straightens up. She is taking something out of the oven and her face is flushed with the heat.

'What's that? Smells lovely.'

Mrs Robinson smiles and taps her nose.

'It's a rabbit pie,' she says with a wink. 'But don't tell the others. I'm going to let them think it's chicken.'

'Whatever it's, it looks great. Gosh I'm starving.'

'Go on with you. I've never known such a girl for eating. If you carry on like this you'll be fatter than me by the time you're twenty.'

Maggie laughs. Mrs Robinson is what Mum used to call matronly. She has fat, rosy cheeks and at least three chins; her stomach stretches in front of her like a cushion and there are dimples in her pudgy arms. Her backside is so broad that she likes to perch on the edge of the chair rather than sit back in it. Maggie can never imagine becoming as fat as Mrs Robinson, even if she ate rabbit pie every day.

'There was a problem at work,' she tells her. 'We all had to work an extra half hour.'

'Well that'll be some extra money for you.'

She ladles the mashed potatoes into a serving dish.

'Here, take this in for me, will you? Oh, by the way, that sister-in-law of your friend called round earlier. She says her husband has some news for you. Something about your brother.'

Maggie thinks she is going to drop the dish; carefully she puts it back on the table.

'Did she say what it was?'

'No, just that you should go round later this evening, when her husband is home.'

Maggie feels her stomach tighten. Suddenly she has lost her appetite.

'Go on, take in the spuds before they get cold.'

Obediently she carries the potatoes into the dining room.

'What's the matter with you, little Miss Muffet?' asks Fred. 'You're as white as a sheet.'

'She thinks they may have found her brother,' Mrs Robinson explains as she places the pie on the table.

She takes up a big knife and begins to cut it into generous wedges.

'Well that's a grand bit of tucker,' says Fred. 'That's what I call a real bloke's dinner.'

Maggie watches him pile the potatoes on his plate.

'Maggie?'

She nods. Mrs Robinson takes it as a personal insult if anyone refuses her food. She hopes she does not give her too much. Her throat is tight with worry and she does not think she can swallow.

'Just a small helping to start?' Mrs Robinson asks with a smile.

She understands how Maggie feels.

'Just a little,' she replies.

She likes Mrs Robinson; she is a jolly woman and always nice to her. She realises that she has never felt so much at home since she left England.

'Thank you,' she says and she knows Mrs Robinson understands that she is not just talking about the rabbit pie.

Alice opens the door. She is smiling so it must be good news.

'Come in. Tom's just got home. He's in the kitchen,' she tells her.

The excitement is dancing around Maggie's stomach like caged butterflies.

'Hi Maggie,' he says.

She stands in the doorway, frightened to speak.

'Don't look so worried; it's not bad news.'

He grins.

'Not that brilliant either. We've managed, at last, to find out where they sent Billy but he's not there anymore.'

She tries not to look too disappointed.

'It's OK,' he says. 'One step at a time.'

'What happened to him?'

'Well I got in touch with the Christian Brothers Farm School in Wadene, Western Australia. God knows what they get up to at that place but they certainly took their time getting back to me. It turns out that Billy was there. But he was only there for six months and then he ran away.'

'But didn't they try to find him?'

'They tried but he had just disappeared. They say they had the police out looking for him but there was no trace of him anywhere.'

'So nobody knows where he is?'

'It's a big area and a lot of it's desert. He could be anywhere.'

She thinks her heart will break at the thought of Billy alone out there in the bush. He could even be dead.

'Cheer up, we haven't finished yet. We'll keep looking. Oh and another thing, my mate has seen the lists of the kids they are sending back to England and your name's not on any of them.'

Disappointment gnaws at Maggie's stomach.

'What about my brother and sister? His name's William you know, not Billy.'

'I know, you told me that. No, none of you are on the lists. But he did find your names on the manifesto leaving England; he says that you were down as orphans and were sent to Catholic orphanages.'

'I told you that; Billy went to that Wadene place and Grace and I were sent to the Sisters of Nazareth.'

She feels frustrated.

'Look I'm sorry kid, there are no plans to send you or your brother and sister back to England. If you're orphans there's nowhere to send you except to another orphanage and I imagine that they're all full. You would be all right but there'd be no-one to look after your brother and sister; they're better off staying here. You wouldn't want them to go into another orphanage, now would you?'

'I could look after them.'

Tom shakes his head.

'It doesn't work like that, I'm afraid.'

It's impossible. Every way she turns there's a blank wall. Even though the war is over there seems to be no way to find her brother or to get back to England.

'Don't worry Maggie; something will turn up. Tom will keep looking; won't you, Tom?' Alice says, looking at her husband.

'Of course I will. Chin up, kid.'

'How about a glass of lemonade?' Alice asks.

'No, thanks, I have to get back.'

Her feet feel leaden as she trudges back to her lodgings. She hopes that there will be nobody at home; she just wants to creep upstairs and go to bed. But the light is on in the living room and she can hear voices. She closes the door quietly behind her.

'Is that you Maggie?' Mrs Robinson calls out.

'Yes, Mrs Robinson.'

'Come in here dear and tell us what happened.'

Mrs Robinson and Fred Barrett are enjoying a glass of beer together; they have the wireless on and are listening to some dance music. They turn to look at her expectantly. It's too much; she cannot hold back her tears any longer.

'Oh, you poor little mite. What on earth has happened?' Mrs Robinson says, getting up and enfolding her into her enormous bosom.

Maggie takes a deep breath and tells them what Tom told her.

'So you don't have no idea where he could be then?' she asks.

Maggie shakes her head.

'Here, blow your nose. There's no good'll come of all this crying. Let me get you a nice cup of tea.'

'Something stronger'd be better,' adds Fred.

'No, nothing, thanks. I'm going to bed.'

'There must be something we can do,' says Mrs Robinson.

She sips slowly at her beer.

'Didn't you tell me you have some family out that way Fred?' she says at last.

'A brother,' he replies. 'In the police force, actually.'

'Well there you are then, I bet he could help us find that Billy of yours,' she says, smiling at Maggie.

'Could well do. When did you say he went missing?' Fred asks.

'Some time in '41,' Maggie says.

'That's four years ago. A hell of a lot can happen to a young fellah in four years.'

'But it's worth trying, isn't it?' Mrs Robinson insists.

Maggie sees Fred look at his landlady; he knows she is not going to let this go.

'I'll do what I can, but no promises mind, young lady. I'll telephone his station tomorrow. You'd better give me all the details.'

Mrs Robinson rummages in the drawer for a piece of paper and a pencil.

'His name's William Smith, Billy,' Maggie begins and tells him all she has found out about her brother's last whereabouts.

Mrs Robinson writes it all down carefully.

'He has curly, blond hair and blue eyes,' she continues.

'How long is it since you last saw him?' Fred asks.

'Four years, five months.'

'Well I expect he'll have changed quite a bit since then,' Mrs Robinson says with a laugh. 'He won't be the same little boy you knew.'

Maggie has never considered that. She always imagines Billy as he was when they were all together. She might not even recognise him now.

'Don't take on, Maggie. I'm sure he won't have changed that much,' Mrs Robinson reassures her. 'I was just joking.'

She puts her arm around her again and gives her a hug.

'You just leave it to Fred and his brother; they'll find him for you.'

Maggie thinks Fred looks doubtful at this burst of optimism from his landlady but she says:

'Thank you Mr Barrett, I really appreciate your help.'

'Fred my dear, call me Fred.'

'You run off to bed now Maggie and we'll see you in the morning,' Mrs Robinson says.

She turns to Fred.

'Another cold one?'

'Don't mind if I do.'

'Goodnight,' says Maggie.

She feels a little more optimistic now.   Like Tom says, one step at a time; maybe Fred's brother will be able to find Billy for her.

BILLY

At first all Billy can see is a cloud of yellow dust snaking its way along the horizon; he thinks it's a willy-willy but then he remembers this is not the season for tornados. He can hear the drone of the engine before he can see the car but he has already decided who it is. Ever since she knew that the war was over Sarah has been waiting for this day. Then the letter arrived. Billy does not remember ever seeing her so happy. He hammers the last few nails into the plank he is fixing to the side of the stables and collects up his tools. All he has to do now is rub down the rough edges and give it a coat of creosote. He will do that later. The car is getting closer. He can see that it's Ralph Carey's old Ford. He hurries towards the house.

Sarah is in the kitchen plucking the chicken that Henry killed that morning; the smell of fresh Damper bread hangs cloyingly in the air. Sarah has been cleaning and baking frantically. All her storage tins are filled with Jack's favourites: pumpkin scones, chocolate covered Lamingtons and bite sized Bush Brownies. Billy feels his mouth watering when he thinks of them.

'He's coming,' he says.

It's hard to keep the excitement out of his voice. The whole farm has been in a state of turmoil since they received the news that Jack had been demobbed. It's like V-J Day all over again.

Henry wanted to drive to Fremantle and meet him but Jack was very specific in his letter; he had to stay with the others for a bit for debriefing or something, he said. He promised to come out to the homestead as soon as he was able; that was three weeks ago. Henry was disappointed, Billy knew that, but all he said was:

'Thank God he's safe. Thank God he got through this bloody awful war in one piece.'

Then he folded the letter carefully and placed it on the mantlepiece next to Jack's photo.

Sarah drops the chicken on the table; she has only removed half the feathers.

'Oh mercy, I'm nowhere near ready,' she moans.

She wipes her hands on her apron and rushes out the back to the pump. She splashes some water over her face and smoothes her hair into place then she turns and looks at Billy. He smiles.

'You look fine,' he says. 'Shall I go and look for the boss?'

'Yes, do that. Tell Henry that Jack'll be here any minute. Run over to the paddock; I think he's with the horses.'

She ruffles his hair.

'You're a good boy, Billy.'

By the time the car wheezes to a stop outside the house, they are all assembled; even Arthur has hobbled over to join the welcoming party. There is a moment when time seems to hold its breath as they wait for the car door to open and the hot, dry air presses down on them, heavy with anticipation then Henry strides forward and is there helping his son get out of the car and John T is taking his kit bag from the driver and throwing it over his shoulder. Father and son embrace; Billy can see the tears in Henry's eyes.

'Welcome home son. Thank the Lord you're back safe and sound. We've prayed for this moment every day since you left.'

He pulls back and holds his son at arm's length. He looks at him without speaking and Billy can see the horror in Henry's eyes even though he is still smiling.

'Where's Mum?' Henry's son asks.

And Jack turns to look for his mother. She has not moved. She is frozen to the spot. Tears stream down her face as she looks at this emaciated skeleton in front of her. Billy cannot believe his eyes. Is this really their son? Jack is twenty-seven. Sarah told him so the last time they celebrated his birthday with one of his favourite cakes. This man looks about sixty; he looks older than Arthur.

She waits for him to envelope her in his arms; she cannot speak.

'Well Mam, haven't you anything to say to your long lost son? Aren't you pleased to see me?'

He smiles at his mother and Billy notices that some of his teeth are missing.

'Of course I am darling; it's just been so long.'

She hugs him again and the tears stream down her face.

'Come in and have a beer mate,' Henry tells the taxi driver. 'Bloody hot weather we're having.'

'Reckon you're right, it's a hot one all right,' says the man.

He follows him on to the veranda. Sarah is still clinging to her son. She is whispering something in his ear.

'Right then Sarah, let the lad go. You'll wear him out. Come on son, what you need is a nice cool beer.'

'I certainly do, Dad.'

His voice is deep and pleasant. He turns to Billy and smiles. When he removes his cap Billy can see the outline of his skull shining through his shaven scalp; his cheeks are sunken and the skin hangs in loose folds from his bones. He holds out a skeletal hand for Billy to shake.

'Nice to meet you mate; you must be Billy.'

'Welcome home,' Billy says, clasping the hand gingerly, frightened that it will disintegrate under his pressure.

Billy's voice is cracking. This is not what he expected. He thought Jack would be like the man in the photograph on the mantlepiece. This man looks as though he does not have long to live.

'You must be starving son. I'll bring you something to eat,' says Sarah.

'Just the beer for now, Mam. Maybe later.'

'You've lost some weight lad,' Henry remarks, vocalising what everyone else is thinking.

Jack looks down at himself and says:

'This is good. You should have seen me when they picked us up. Most of us were so weak we couldn't stand.'

Billy thinks he still looks very frail as he uses the hand rail to pull himself up the veranda steps. He wants to help him but instinct tells him that Jack does not want any assistance.

'Here, get this down you,' says Henry, handing his son a beer.

He passes one to the taxi driver and takes one for himself. He looks at Billy.

'Want one?'

Billy nods.

'Here you are then, but just one.'

Billy sees Sarah look disapprovingly at her husband but he just shrugs and says:

'Special occasion.'

'So, what kept you lad? We read in the papers that your lot had got back in January.'

'Had a spell in the hospital, that's all Dad.'

'All right now?'

'Yeah, they say I'll be all right.'

'Well once we get some of your Mam's home cooking down you, you'll soon be on the mend.'

'I reckon so.'

Sarah returns with a plate of the Bush Brownies.

'Well missus they look fair dinkum,' says the taxi driver.

'Help yourself,' she says.

She looks at Billy.

'You too Billy.'

Billy does not need to be told twice. He loves Sarah's cooking. The spicy cake crumbles in his mouth. It's gone in a moment. He licks the crumbs off his lips, savouring the taste then washes it down with the last of his beer. The beer is strong and makes his head spin but he does not tell Henry in case he laughs at him.

'Did you mend the hole in the stable wall?' Henry asks him.

'Yes, I've just got to paint it now.'

'Well get along and do it now then it'll be finished before nightfall.'

'OK Boss.'

'See you later Billy,' says Jack.

Billy nods. John T has already gone back to the horses and Arthur has returned to his bunkhouse. Although he works as hard as John T, Sarah and Henry treat him like one of the family. Until this week he has been sleeping in Jack's room. Now of course Jack has to have it back; he understands that. Sarah was very embarrassed when she told him he would have to move out.

'I'm sorry Billy, but you understand, don't you? I have to let Jack have his old room back. There's a spare bed in the bunk house with Arthur and John T; you can sleep there.'

But then Henry had a better idea.

'You're too young to sleep in the bunk house with those two,' he told Billy. 'What would you think if we made you a room over the stables? It won't take much to fix it up and then you'll have your own space.'

Billy is pleased with this arrangement, even though it has meant him working extra hours for the last three weeks to get it ready in time. Fixing the hole in the wall was the last major repair, so now it's almost finished. Henry helped him move the spare bed out of the bunk house and Sarah has made him a patchwork cover for it and given him a rag rug for the floor. The room smells of horses but he does not mind that. In fact he does not even notice it now.

He collects the pot of creosote and a brush and climbs up the ladder to paint the new plank. It does not take long and then he goes across to the pump to wash up for supper. The creosote has stained his fingers and he scrubs them hard but it will not come off. He can smell the chicken roasting and realises how hungry he is. He can visualise the meal already: Sarah will have cooked the potatoes with the chicken and they will be brown and crispy; there will be dishes of sweet corn, swimming in butter and mashed pumpkin and peas. Then for pudding he is sure she will have made a trifle and maybe a plum pudding with cold custard as well.

He stops. Something suddenly occurs to him that he has not thought about before. Henry and Sarah are not very well off; he often hears Henry complaining about the cost of things. What if they cannot afford for him to stay here now that Jack has returned? Arthur is so old now that all he can do are the light jobs, the ones that Billy used to do, like feeding the chickens and sweeping the yard. Henry has been glad of Billy's help; he told him so. But now with both Jack and John T to work on the farm maybe Henry will not want Billy to stay. What will happen to him? Where will he go? For the first time in four years he is frightened.

IRENE

Irene looks at the clock; it's almost three o'clock. She will have to leave soon to collect Leslie from school. She pours some more water into the teapot and stirs the tea with a spoon; she can almost see through it, it's so weak. Things seem to be worse than ever since the war ended; there is nothing in the shops and even when there is you need coupons to buy it. Rationing will have to continue for the foreseeable future their new Prime Minster tells them; we must continue to pull together, he says. That is all very well, she thinks, but what about the likes of her and her mother? They are both widows and now she is unemployed as well. She can understand why they want to give the jobs to the soldiers returning from the war but what about the women that have been holding the country together all this time? Nobody cares about them. She could not believe it when Mr Levin told her she had to leave; he dismissed six women that day. She had protested but it was no use.

'We can't let our boys down,' he said. 'Not after all they've been through, risking their lives for our country. After all, they're the breadwinners; they need the jobs.'

It was useless to protest that she was also the breadwinner in their house since her father had died trying to put out a fire in Reddish Street. Her poor father, he had wanted to do his bit for the country he said, but really he was too old and too weak to be of much use. When he heard that the bomb had landed in Reddish Street he had put on his fire warden's uniform and gone straight there. According to his colleagues the building had suffered a direct hit but he had not hesitated and gone in to check that there was nobody still inside. The roof had collapsed on him, minutes later. So now there are just the three of them: her Mum, Leslie and her. She realises all the other women have similar reasons to want to keep their jobs but it does not make it any easier to accept. Mr Levin is not going to make any exception for her. She does not know what she can do; she will have to find some work soon.

She joins the other mothers waiting outside the school. Her friend Liz is standing near the gate, smoking.

'You're late; they're just coming out,' Liz says, stubbing out her cigarette on the heel of her shoe.

Irene notices she is wearing new nylons. Liz has a job as a typist now, at a company making wrist watches in Clerkenwell. Irene had gone along too, hoping to get a job in the factory. She thought they might favour women because their fingers were more nimble than men's but it was the same story: they had to keep the jobs for the boys returning home from the war.

Liz is married now and has a daughter, Janice. She is only five, a year younger than Leslie, and her grandmother brings her to school in the mornings while Liz is at work. Irene sees Leslie running towards her, with Janice trotting along behind.

'Here they are, last as usual.'

'Hello Mum; got anything to eat?' her son asks as soon as he sees her.

She hands him a jam sandwich.

'Always hungry, that boy,' she says affectionately.

'Well he's a growing lad,' Liz replies.

As usual they walk down the road together, each holding their offspring by the hand.

'Any work yet?' Liz asks.

'No, nothing. All the factory jobs are either taken or reserved for demobbed soldiers.'

'Why don't you try to get something in an office or a shop?'

'I'd love to, but how could I? I'm not posh like you.'

She laughs at her friend, rolls her eyes and quotes, in a perfect copy of Celia Johnson, from the film they saw that weekend.

Liz laughs.

'Brief Encounter' is Irene's favourite film; she has sat through it countless times since its release the previous year and each time has shed tears for the lovelorn couple. She imagines meeting someone like the hero, Alec but if she ever does, she tells herself, she will not let him go, like Celia Johnson does in the film.

'Seriously, I'm sure you could get work if you dressed yourself up and put on a posh accent. You could try one of those shops down West.'

'But it'd take me all day to get there. And anyway what could I do in an office? I can't type.'

'Well I could teach you.'

She looks at Liz.

'Really?'

'Yes of course, I've got an old Remington typewriter at home; you could borrow that. It's a bit battered but it works. You'd pick it up in no time.'

Irene smiles.

'*Well I suppose I could give it a try, darling*' she says with a faultless English accent.

Liz laughs again.

'Right come round to my place this evening and we'll make a start.'

'What, tonight?'

'There's no time like the present. If you want to get a job then we need to get started.'

'All right. I'll give it a go.'

They reach the corner shop.

'I've got to get some flour; if there is any that is. Mum's promised Leslie that she'll make him some fairy cakes for tea,' Irene explains.

'OK, see you tonight then. Bye.'

Irene's head is in a whirl. Is she being too ambitious thinking about office work? Liz does not seem to think so. She says she'll pick up the typing easily enough. Well there is nothing to lose by having a go at it; she has to do something, she reminds herself for the hundredth time.

Her mother is sitting by the wireless drinking a cup of tea. She looks tired, tired and old; her hair is completely white now and she sits slumped forward, as if she does not have the energy to sit up straight.

'Everything all right Mum?'

'They've been talking about the evacuees,' she says. 'How they're sending them all home.'

'What evacuees? I thought they'd all come back by now.'

'No. Seems they sent some kids out to Canada and Australia, right at the start of the war. Now they're coming home again. There have been complaints about it taking so long.'

She looks at Irene. They are thinking the same thing. Irene feels her throat go dry.

'Do you think...?' she asks.

'What?'

'The kids? Maybe that's what happened to them?'

'Well doesn't make sense, does it? Five years and no sign of them. Not even a trace of their bodies. Even dead people turn up eventually.'

'I've never believed they were dead,' Irene says defiantly. 'Never.'

'Well where are they then?' her mother persists. 'Can't just have vanished off the face of the earth.'

'Well they have, haven't they? Anyway who is it that's sending these kids back?'

'Don't know. They did say but I couldn't catch it. Maybe it'll be on later at six o'clock. Did you get the flour?'

'Yes, but he'd only let me have half a pound.'

'That's enough for a few fairy cakes and maybe a couple of scones. What do you say Les?'

She turns to her grandson and smiles.

'Were you a good boy at school today?'

'Yes Nan.'

The child does not look up from his drawing. He is a quiet child; Irene thinks it's probably because of his heart condition. He hardly ever goes outside to play, preferring to sit quietly inside and draw pictures with his crayons. She cannot help but compare this gentle young son of hers with the rumbustious Billy. She feels a pang of longing for her older son and his sisters. Where can they be? She knows they are alive somewhere. But where? She is convinced that if anything had happened to them she would know. Her mother's instinct would tell her, she is sure.

'I'm just going for a lie down, Mum. I don't feel too good.'

'OK, I'll bring you up a cup of tea later.'

Irene needs some time to think. It's as though she is in a state of limbo; she cannot settle to anything. She needs to find a job; that is the most important item on her list otherwise she cannot provide for Leslie and her Mum. They are her responsibility now but hanging over her, shadowing her every step is the need to find her children. She has asked everyone she can think of if they know anything but each time she draws a blank. Her friends tell her that it's useless; the children are dead, yet more, tiny casualties of the bloody war. But she cannot accept it. Even when she tries to face up to this possibility a faint voice inside her is saying 'No, they are alive'. Sometimes she thinks it would be better if they were dead. She remembers how her friend received a telegram from the War Office about her husband. 'Missing, presumed dead' it had said. Missing, presumed dead. What a sentence to hang over you. Not to know, to be always hoping, praying for a miracle, jumping at every knock on the door. Better to know one way or the other. 'Killed in action' is what her telegram read. Oh Ronnie, if only you were here now to help me.

Her eyes, that have been dry for so long, begin to fill with tears. He had not been perfect, what husband was, but he had loved them. Her body aches, just thinking of him. She thought they would grow old together, see their children grow up and marry, have grandchildren to look after but all that has been snatched away from them. Her Ronnie lies somewhere on a French beach, his bones tossed about by the tide. He died fighting for his country, she tells herself, fighting for her and the children but it's of little comfort.

There is a tap on the door.

'Mum, are you all right?'

It's Leslie. She sits up and wipes her eyes.

'What is it, sweetheart?'

'Nan says she's made some fresh tea and there's someone on the wireless talking about the evacuees.'

'I'll be right down, tell her.'

Her mother is sitting by the wireless, a pencil and piece of paper in her hands.

'It's called the Dominions' Office,' she says. 'That's who they are.'

'The people sending the children home?'

'Yes, that's them. Listen.'

'*The children evacuated to the safety of our colonial friends during the war are returning home to their families. This week excited children will be reunited with their loved ones. What a lot of adventures they will have to relate about life in the colonies. Welcome back kids.*'

'So that's it then? They don't give out any names?'

Her mother shook her head.

'That's all, same as they said before. But you could go and ask about that Office, couldn't you?'

'Yes, Mum. Here give me the paper. I'll go down to the police station now and see what they can do to help.'

'What PC Higgins? He won't do nothing. No, you need to go to someone higher up; go to the Town Hall. They must know how you can get in touch with these people.'

'I'll go tomorrow, after I've taken Leslie to school.'

She goes into the scullery and takes her brown skirt out of the ironing basket. She wants to look smart tomorrow. She smoothes the skirt out and holds it against herself. Maybe she will take Liz's advice and pretend to be a bit more la-di-dah. Poor but genteel, that is the look she will go for. She puts the iron on the stove to heat up.

'You going out?' her mother asks.

'Yes, I'm going round to Liz's; she's going to teach me to type.'

'Well I never.'

'Can't be that difficult, can it?'

JEREMY ACTON-DUNN

Jeremy Acton-Dunn runs a hand through his thinning hair; the pile of paperwork on his desk never seems to get any less. Because he had been with the Children's Overseas Reception Board since its inception somebody up there thought it was good idea for him to be the one to tie up all the loose ends when they shut down the Board in 1944. Since then, and especially since the war has ended he has been inundated with requests from anxious parents, desperate to get their children back. He can understand their impatience. He had missed his own boys very much while they were in South Africa. Now they are home, grown and changed in many ways it's true, but safely home. He wonders if they resent the fact they were sent away for five years of their young lives. He knows his wife resents it; she has missed seeing them grow up and never stops telling him so. She accepted his decision at the time but she never really agreed with him, he knows that now. Still she has them back at last.

'Jeremy, sorry to bother you. There's a woman to see you.'

He looks up. Victoria is peering round the door, anxiously.

'It's a Mrs Smith. She is looking for three of her children; they went missing in 1940.'

Not another woman looking for missing members of her family; he cannot keep track of them all.

'Why does she think we can help her?'

'She heard something about us on the wireless. I think she's just grabbing at straws.'

'But all our evacuees are back now, aren't they?'

'All who want to come back.'

'You deal with her. I'm snowed under here.'

She pulls a face.

'All right, I'll speak to her,' he agrees reluctantly. She goes out and he can hear her asking the woman to accompany her. He looks at the photograph on his desk. It's of his wife with her arms around each of her sons; they are all smiling at the camera. He took it just after they arrived home. The boys are tanned and fit. He sighs. Yes, he is very lucky to still have his family intact.

The door opens and a woman enters; she is attractive in a genteel sort of way, with a pleasant smile that contrasts with the sadness in her eyes. It's hard to place her; she looks an educated woman, but her coat is a bit shabby and the soft, brown hat that sits elegantly on her wavy, brown hair looks as though it has seen better days. A woman who has fallen on hard times perhaps.

'Good morning, Mrs Smith. Please take a seat.'

The woman sits down opposite him and crosses her legs, carefully adjusting her skirt, so that he has but the barest glimpse of her nylon stockings. She smiles demurely at him.

'Thank you.'

He smiles encouragingly and asks:

'So how can I help?'

The woman wearily explains about the disappearance of her children and how she has been searching for them for five years. He has the sensation that she has said this many times.

'I can't find out anything about them, where they've gone, who they were with, nothing at all. Then, when I heard that some children had been seen out to Canada, I wondered if that was what had happened to my children.'

'I see. Well it's unlikely but I suppose it's possible. Why don't you give me all the particulars, names, ages, when you last saw them, etcetera and I'll see what I can find out.'

He writes down the details on a sheet of paper then says:

'Right. Is there anything else you can tell me? What about this Mrs Kelly? Have you any more information about her? Could she have left the children with a relative for example?'

'No I don't think so. She had lived next door ever since I can remember. I don't think she had any relatives in London, only her friends at the church.'

'Which church was that?'

'Our Lady of the Assumption.'

'And that's in Bethnal Green?'

'Yes.'

'She was a Catholic?'

'Yes.'

'And you?'

'No, we're C of E.'

'Fine. Well I think I've got enough to go on. I'll be in touch if I come up with anything.'

'Shall I come back tomorrow?'

He looks at her in surprise.

'No, I think that's a bit soon. Why not call back next week and I'll tell you how I'm getting on.'

She bites her lip and he sees her struggling to retain her composure then she smiles at him.

'Next week then.'

He holds out his hand and she grasps it gratefully.

'We will do our best for you, Mrs Smith,' he says and, when she leaves, he goes into his assistant's office.

'Victoria, this is the information on the missing Smith children. Open a file for them, will you and see what else you can round up about them. There must be a record of their whereabouts, somewhere.'

'OK Jeremy, will do.'

The truth is that he feels sorry for this woman. What if it had been his own children who had disappeared? How would his wife have coped? How would he have coped?

BILLY

Billy hitches the horses up to the hay wagon. Henry is taking a load of hay across to their neighbours' farm; he will be gone most of the day and he wants Jack to go with him. He wants his son to meet their neighbour's daughter, Emily. Billy knows this although Jack is unaware of his parents' plans for him; Billy heard them talking about it in the kitchen. Sarah said that it would do Jack good to meet some people his own age and especially Emily because she is such a sweet girl. Billy has not met Emily before but she sounds nice. He imagines that she is like his sister Maggie, with a soft voice and a warm smile.

The sound of sawing wood stops abruptly and silence hangs briefly in the hot air. Jack appears from behind the barn, his arms laden with logs. Billy cannot believe how much he has changed in the last six months; he bears no resemblance to the half-dead soldier that arrived back from the war. At first Jack was not strong enough to do much work around the farm and even when he offered to help with something simple, like bringing in fresh water or feeding the chickens, Sarah would not allow it. Gradually his strength has returned and with the help of Sarah's cooking his weight has increased. Now, apart from the pain and horror that can still be seen in his eyes, he is once again the man in the photograph on the mantelpiece.

'Jack, get yourself cleaned up; we're going over to the Cartwrights' place with the hay,' Henry says.

Jack looks at him in surprise.

'So why do I need to get cleaned up then?' he asks.

'Well ...'

Henry does not know what to say.

'Because there's a pretty sheila over there,' Billy says.

Henry gives him one of his looks.

'A sheila? So what?'

'They'll probably ask us to stay and eat with them,' his father says, looking embarrassed that his subterfuge has been dis-covered.

'Well I'm sure they've got a pump; I'll scrub up there.'

He looks at his father.

'You don't need to come Dad; I can manage on my own.'

'Well ...'

Henry hesitates. Billy knows the boss hates leaving the farm these days; he prefers to stay on his own spread.

'OK, that'd be good. There's plenty I can do here. Billy, you go with him. It'll be easier to stack the hay if there're two of you.'

Billy is delighted; he has not been anywhere since the day he turned up, hungry and frightened on their doorstep. He jumps up onto the wagon and takes the reins.

'I'll be with you in a minute, Billy. I'll just get my hat,' says Jack.

Sarah comes out with a canteen of water.

'Don't forget this,' she says passing it up to Billy.

She leans over and whispers:

'Take care of him Billy, won't you.'

Billy smiles; he knows how much she worries about her son. He feels very important to be the one in charge. The initial wor-ries he had when Jack returned have gone now; Henry seems to need him as much as ever and he knows Sarah's heart is big enough to love him as well as Jack. He likes her son; he treats Billy like a man and he never questions why he is living here with Henry and Sarah .

They drive along in silence for a while; the heat is oppressive and the flies buzz constantly around them. Billy amuses himself by trying to flick them off the horses' backs with the tip of the whip but only succeeds in irritating the animals. Jack seems to be lost in his own thoughts.

'Were you in France?' Billy asks at last.

Jack has never spoken to him about his experiences in the war; Billy is curious to know what happened.

'No.'

'My Dad was in France,' says Billy. 'He was shot by the Germans.'

He wishes he knew more about what had happened to his Dad. At the time it had been sufficient to know that he was dead and not coming back again. Now there is no-one to ask.

'I'm sorry to hear that. We were supposed to go there but by the time our training was over and we were ready to ship out, France had already surrendered. They sent us to North Africa instead.'

'Is that where you were a prisoner, in North Africa?' Billy asks.

'No, that was much later.'

He lights a cigarette and takes a leisurely puff. Billy wonders if he can ask him for one then decides against it. He might tell his mother and the last thing Billy wants to do is be in trouble with Sarah.

'Were the Germans in North Africa then?' Billy asks.

His knowledge of the war is very sketchy; it's mostly gleaned from what the other boys on the ship told him.

'And the Italians. We were fighting the Italians, not Germans.'

'And we won, didn't we,' adds Billy. 'The Allies won.'

That much he knows for certain. There had been an announcement on the wireless and Henry and Sarah had been really happy. Sarah had baked a special celebration cake and they had all drunk a toast to the Allies.

'Eventually. But that was later and by then we had moved out. They brought us back to defend Australia.'

Billy is confused. What was the point of that? There was no war in Australia. That was why they'd been sent here, to get away from the war.

'My outfit was sent to Singapore to fight the Japs,' Jack continues.

'I've been to Singapore,' Billy blurts out before he remembers that no-one knows where he has come from.

Jack looks at him but does not say anything.   He brushes away a fly from his face and waits for Billy to continue.

'Well I haven't actually been there,' Billy explains.   'The ship stopped there when we came from England but we didn't get off. Sometimes they let us get off, but not that time.   That was when all the soldiers left.'

He looks at Jack; he is smoking and staring at the road ahead.

'One of the soldiers was my friend; his name was Owen and he was from Wales.   He used to show us card tricks.   I can still remember some of them; if I had some cards I'd show you,' Billy continues.

Jack smiles.

'I think we've got a pack of cards at home somewhere.   I'll have a look for them when we get back then you can teach me too.'

'Maybe you met Owen?' says Billy.   'If you were in Singapore as well.'

Jack laughs.

'No mate, I don't remember any Owen.   There was a Taffy and a Jock and a few other hundred thousand Poms but I don't remember an Owen.'

'So was it the Japs that made you a prisoner?'

'Yes, that's right, mate.   It was at the end of '41, right after Pearl Harbour when they sent us to Singapore.'

He looks at Billy to see if he knows what he is talking about. Billy nods; he heard them talking about it on the wireless.   The Japs bombed Pearl Harbour and Henry said now the Americans would have to join the war.

'We were only there a couple of months before Singapore surrendered.   The Japs were everywhere; they took fifteen thousand Aussie soldiers prisoner, me included.'

'Did they put you in a jail?'

Billy's curiosity is up.

'Sort of, but not the usual sort of prison. They put us in prisoner-of-war camps and made us work.'

Billy waits but Jack's face has tightened up and he puffs angrily at his cigarette. At last he says:

'They made us build a bloody great road.'

Billy realises that he is not going to tell him any more about the war. He knows Jack had a hard time in the prisoner of war camp; his emaciated body told its own story when he returned. The things he has overheard him telling Henry make life in the orphanage seem easy.

They drive in silence for a while and then he asks:

'How far is it to the Cartwrights' place?'

'Another half hour. Why? Hungry?'

Billy nods.

'Here, eat this.'

Jack takes an apple out of his pocket and tosses it to him.

Billy has met Mr Cartwright before because he sometimes comes to Henry's farm to borrow things. He usually brings a few bottles of his home-brewed beer with him and he and Henry sit on the veranda chatting for hours until Sarah comes out to send him on his way.

Today he is in the paddock with his horses. He has at least a dozen mares and two young stallions and he is very proud of them. Henry says that he has the best horses for miles around.

'Hello there, Mr Cartwright,' Billy says. 'We've brought the hay.'

'Good on ya, lads. I was just thinking of riding over to see Henry about another load. You've saved me the journey.'

'Dad said you'd be running low,' Jack says and swings himself down from the wagon. 'Where do you want it?'

'Follow me. You can unload it straight into the barn.'

Billy flicks the reins and the horses walk slowly forward. He pulls them up by the open barn doors.

According to Sarah, Joe Cartwright is younger than Henry although his boss always denies it. He is a tall, beefy man with a back as broad as a barn door. His face has weathered to the same colour as the reddish-brown soil that surrounds his farmstead and his hair, which straggles out from below his wide, bushman's hat, is iron grey.

'Over there, in that corner, will do just fine. Then, when you're done, come in and have a bite of tucker with us,' he says.

'Will do, Joe. Thanks,' says Jack.

They all eat in the Cartwrights' big, airy kitchen: the farm hands, Joe, his wife Bella, their three daughters and Jack and Billy. There are more than a dozen of them round the table and every-one seems to be talking at once. There is a moment's hush while Joe says grace and then the hubbub starts up again. The food is good: some kind of meat and vegetable hot pot with beans, but not as good as Sarah's. As he eats, Billy finds it hard to keep his eyes off the Cartwright girls. It's a long time since he has seen a girl; there were none in the orphanage, nor are there any on the farm. The only people who come to visit are friends of Henry, usually old men. He particularly likes the younger sister, Adaline; she is like an older version of his little sister, Grace. She has the same yellow curls and round blue eyes. He tries not to stare at her. The other girls are also pretty but not as pretty as Adaline. Emily is a serious girl, with grey eyes and a pretty, smiling mouth; she is not very tall and only comes up to Jack's shoulder. The middle daughter, Julie, takes after her father and is a big, strong girl. Mr Cartwright says she is his main help with the horses; she can ride better than any man. He is obviously very proud of his daughters.

'Beer?' he asks and both Billy and Jack nod.

It's his home brew and it's strong. After the first mouthful Billy can feel his head swimming. He takes a hunk of bread and dunks it in his stew. He likes the Cartwrights; he is glad he came with Jack. He looks at him; he is talking to Emily and smiling. She is telling him about the local town fair. He wonders if Jack will be going. Maybe he will ask him to go along as well. That would be nice and then he might see Adaline again.

IRENE

It's a month since she spoke to Jeremy Acton-Dunn; each week she goes back to see if he has any more news and each week she is disappointed. It's not all bad though; now she is more convinced than ever that her children are alive. He has found their names on the passenger list of *HMS Orinoco*. They were sent to Australia under a scheme run by the Children's Overseas Reception Board. She still cannot believe it. Sent to the other side of the world, without her permission. How on earth could something like that happen? She has challenged Jeremy about it but he cannot explain.

'It was wartime,' he said. 'Things happen in wartime. I expect they thought they were doing it for the good of the children. They had them down as orphans.'

She felt herself turn cold at this. But there was no point arguing with him; it was not his fault. He had only been doing his job. They have become quite friendly towards her in the office. One day Victoria invited her to have a cup of tea with her. Irene told her about Ronnie and how he had died at Dunkirk.

Today she is not going to the office; she is meeting Victoria in the Lyons Corner House. As she gets off the bus she can see her sitting by the window.

'Hello Irene.'

'I'm sorry I'm late; I had to wait ages for the bus.'

'Tea?'

'Please.'

She waits while Victoria orders a fresh pot of tea.

'So any news?' she asks.

She shakes his head.

'Not really. We're trying to trace the list of addresses where the children were sent. The paperwork's a mess.'

'But it must be there somewhere?' she asks.

'Yes, it'll turn up, I'm sure.'

'You'll keep looking?'

'Of course.'

She knows Victoria's boss thinks she is spending too much time on her case; she prays she does not give up.

'Have you found any work yet?' Victoria asks.

'Nothing.'

'Well, in that case, I might have something for you.'

She passes Irene a slip of paper.

'A friend of my mother's owns a bookshop in Finsbury. That's not too far from where you live is it?'

'No, it's quite close.'

'Well he's looking for someone to work in the shop but also to help catalogue the books. You said you could type, didn't you?'

'Yes. That sounds perfect.'

'Well go round there and say that Molly Bell's daughter sent you. Don't leave it too long, though.'

'No, I'll go this afternoon.'

'Ah, here's the tea. Do you want to pour?'

Irene nods. She looks at the slip of paper in her hand and for the first time in a long while she feels hopeful. Maybe things are going to improve from now on.

'Thanks, Victoria.'

Irene is waiting at the bus stop. At first she does not recognise him in his civilian clothes.

'George? George Wills?'

'That's me,' he says brightly as he jumps off the bus. 'Irene, I didn't recognise you; you look different.'

She blushes and her hand automatically smooths down her pleated skirt. She is on her way home from work.

'What're you doing here? I thought you were still in the army,' she asks.

'Come on you lot; you getting off, on or what?' the bus conductor asks impatiently.

'It's all right, I'll get the next one,' Irene tells him. 'I've got plenty of time.'

'Suit yourself, dear.'

She looks at George; it's lovely to see him. She feels an unexpected warmth for this lanky soldier who, stripped of his uniform, looks more in need of a square meal than ever.

'I've been demobbed at last.'

'That's great news.'

But George does not look very cheerful about the prospect of civilian life.

'So what are you doing here?' she repeats. 'Why aren't you in Yorkshire?'

She hopes he will say he has come to see her but instead he says:

'Like all us out of work Tommies, looking for a job.'

'But what about the bus corporation? Can't you go back there?'

'No. By the time I got my demob papers there were no jobs left. That's why I've come down to the Big Smoke.'

'Well I'm sure with your skills you'll find something. They must be crying out for mechanics.'

'You'd think so, wouldn't you? I've been three months looking for work. Life on Civvy Street is no joke.'

She notices that he is carrying a kitbag.

'Have you just arrived?' she asks.

'More or less; I spent last night at the Salvation Army.'

'Come back with me; you can sleep on the sofa until you get sorted out. Mum won't mind. There's only the three of us now.'

'Three?'

'Leslie.'

'Of course. So the kids aren't back then?'

She shakes her head sadly.

'So?' she asks.

She doesn't want him to leave. She had written to him every month while he was overseas. Sometimes she was not even sure he received her letters but she still kept writing to him, telling him her news and what life was like at home. Occasionally he sent her a few lines but it was obvious that writing was not really his forte. Now she wants the chance to talk to him. She is frightened that if she gets on the bus without him she will never see him again. She does not want to lose anyone else from her life.

'Why not. I could do with a decent night's sleep,' he says with a grateful smile.

'Here's our bus,' she says.

'So what have you been doing with yourself?' George asks, once they are seated on top.

'I've got a job in a bookshop,' she tells him, scarcely concealing her pride.

'That sounds a bit of all right.'

'It is; I've only been there a couple of weeks but I'm really enjoying it.'

'So what happened to your other job?'

As tactfully as she can, she explains how Mr Levin had got rid of his female workforce.

'And the kids? Is there no news about them? Haven't you heard anything at all about where they could be?'

'They're alive; I'm pretty sure of it. They were sent to Australia by mistake.'

George looks at her in amazement.

'Sent to Australia by mistake?' he echoes. 'What sort of mistake is that?'

'They thought I was dead; they thought the children were orphans.'

She tells him about Victoria and how she has been helping her.

'She thinks they have found out where Grace and Maggie went. She's written to the orphanage to ask what has happened to them. We're waiting for a reply.'

'That's great news.'

'Yes, if they're still there. It's been nearly six years you know.'

She bites her lip. She tries not to hope for too much; she tries to take Victoria's advice and take each day as it comes but it's hard. At least she knows that her children are alive and she knows where they went; the next step is to find out where they are now. But she will find them one day; of that she is certain.

'So that's Grace and Maggie. What about Billy?'

Her eyes fill with tears.

'Nothing. They can't find anything about Billy other than he left the ship at Freemantle.'

George reaches across and pats her hand.

'Don't worry, Irene; he'll turn up, I'm sure.'

'I never imagined he would be all alone. Whenever I've thought about them, I've seen them together, the three of them. I never dreamed they would become separated. How has Billy managed all this time on his own? He was only ten when they took him.'

'I'm sure he's fine,' says George, but his voice is not convincing. 'At least now you know more than you did before.'

'Yes, that's true.'

She clings to this fact; bit by bit she is getting to the truth. She will find her children and bring them home even if it takes her a lifetime.

BILLY

Jack's appetite has returned and apart from the scars that he carries on his back, he looks completely recovered, but Billy knows that he still has nightmares; he heard Sarah talking to Henry about it.

Billy eats the stew slowly. He likes to drag out mealtimes so he can sit and listen to Henry and Sarah talking. Once he has finished he knows he will have to get back to work.

'I was thinking,' Sarah begins.

When she says this Billy knows she is going to say something that Jack or Henry will disagree with.

'I was thinking that it might be a nice idea to invite the Cartwrights over for a bite of tucker one evening, you know be neighbourly and that.'

'Hrmmph,' says Henry.

'Mum, leave it, will you,' says Jack.

They all know she is thinking of him and Emily.

'Sounds a good idea to me,' Billy says with a mischievous glance at Jack.

Jack glares at him.

'Henry?' she asks.

'Up to you, my dear. Come on Billy, eat up; we've got work to do.'

'Right, that's settled then,' Sarah continues. 'Jack maybe you could ride over there and ask them? Next Sunday would be good.'

Jack has turned scarlet. He does not answer his mother, just picks up some bread and wipes it around his plate, mopping up the gravy.

'I can go, if you like, Sarah,' Billy suggests.

'Thank you Billy.'

'Do you want to invite all of them?' he asks her.

He is thinking of Adaline.

'Of course. What did you think, I was just going to ask Emily?' she says with a sideways smile at her son.

Jack does not respond; he is concentrating on his food.

Dilly gobbles down the last of his dinner and sets off to catch up with John T, who is already on his way back to work.

Sometimes he feels a bit jealous of Jack. Sarah obviously loves her son very much. He tries to remember his own mother but increasingly it's difficult to recall her face and each time he tries, it's Sarah's face he sees. Sarah is his mother now; she even said that to him once. This realisation makes him feel guilty. How can he forget his own mother? It does not seem possible but it's so long since she died that she has become nothing more than a faint memory to him.

Later that evening he washes himself down with water from the hose, cleaning off all the sheep's lanolin that is clinging to his arms and chest. He and John T have been shearing the sheep; today he managed thirty. Henry says he'll soon be as quick as John T but he can't ever imagine being as fast as he is; the stockman sheared fifty today. Billy rubs himself dry with the towel and goes up to his room. Jess follows him. Jess is like his shadow; she is always at his side, even though Henry says that she should be out there with the sheep. He claps his hands.

'Off you go, Jess.'

The dog looks at him sorrowfully and turns and heads off towards the sheep pens.

Once he is dry, Billy puts on his best trousers and a clean shirt; he wants to be smart to go to the Cartwrights. He stands in front of the mirror, a lopsided piece of glass that Henry put up for him and looks at his reflection. What does he see?

A lean boy, tall for his age and strong, he flexes his bi-ceps and admires them in the mirror. His hair is bleached blond by the sun and his body is tanned a deep golden brown from working outside. He pulls a comb through his wet hair. Most of his youthful curls have gone now, he is pleased to see; he looks more grown-up with straight hair. He will soon be fifteen, almost a man. He squints at his reflection. There is a line of fuzz on his top lip; he strokes it carefully and wonders if a moustache would suit him.

'Billy, you ready yet?'

It's Jack. In the end he has decided to go with Billy to the Cartwrights.

'Be right down.'

He tightens his belt, flexes his muscles once more, gives a last appreciative look at his reflection and climbs down the ladder. He hopes Adaline will be at home.

The Cartwrights were delighted to receive Sarah's invitation and they are all coming for supper the following Saturday evening. Adaline was there when he arrived and he managed to say hello to her but that was all; her mum sent her off to do her homework. So he went to the stables with Julie for a while to help her groom the horses while Jack sat in the kitchen and drank beer with Mr Cartwright.

He pushes Jess off his bed and lies down. She was waiting outside the barn for him to come home and, as soon as the truck came round the bend, she was there at his side.

'You'll be in trouble, girl, if Henry finds out,' he says, strok-ing her head.

He likes going across to the Cartwright's place. It reminds him of home in a way. He knows it's nothing like their house in Bethnal Green and the Cartwrights are nothing like Mum and Dad but nevertheless it reminds him of all he has lost.

He lies back on the bed and looks at the ceiling. None of this would have happened to them if Dad hadn't been killed. He should have been there to protect them. He feels a forgotten an-ger stir inside him as he thinks back to how they were plucked out of their happy normal lives and thrown into completely new ones, ones they did not choose. He knows he is lucky to be here with Henry and Sarah. His life could be so much worse. He shudders to think what would have happened to him if he had stayed at the farm school or if the Pintupis had not found him. But, however kind Henry and Sarah are to him, they are not really his family. He used to have parents of his own; he had a Nan and two sisters. Now he has no-one. He wonders what has happened to Grace and Maggie? Are they still in the orphanage or have they been as lucky as him? He hopes so. He opens the drawer of his cupboard and takes out a shard of wood. It's the piece that Maggie gave him, the piece that she took from their old blue door, all those years ago in London. The paint has almost flaked off it but the colour is recognisable. He brushes away a tear and says to Jess:

'Come on Jess, we need to get to sleep. Big day tomorrow. I'm going to better my sheep shearing score. What do you think, thirty-five?'

Jess looks at him, unblinking then turns away. Billy tosses the piece of wood back in the drawer.

'Or maybe not.'

JEREMY ACTON-DUNN

The pile of papers on his desk does not seem to be diminishing; every day there is a query from someone about their child's whereabouts.

'Would you like a cup of tea?' Victoria asks.

'Yes, please.'

'Oh and there's a reply from the orphanage on your desk. I put it on the top,' she continues.

'Which orphanage do you mean?' he asks, picking up the letter.

'The one in Melbourne, about the Smith children.'

His heart sinks. That woman has been pestering him every day for weeks now. He has explained that he will contact her when he has some news but it does not satisfy her.

'I hope it's good news.'

'They've found one of them,' she says.

Jeremy picks up the letter and reads it.

'So they had both girls but one has left and they don't know where she is,' he summarises, handing it back to her.

'Yes, so you can give Mrs Smith the good news when she next comes in.'

'Hardly good news, one out of three.'

'It's a start.'

'I think you'd better ring her. There's a number in the file; it's the bookshop where she works.'

'What shall we do about the other one?'

'Write back to the orphanage and ask them to make some enquiries. They must have some idea where she is. Surely they don't just let the girls wander off and disappear.'

'Right.'

'Yes and I had better see how we can get this girl back to England; there's no money in the budget for it. Make an appointment for me with Sir Percy, as soon as possible.'

'At his office?'

'No, better at his Club, he'll be more amenable.'

The Ratan Club seems to be busy this morning; the main lounge area is filled with elderly gentlemen reading newspapers and the air is heavy with cigar smoke. There is a feeling of complacency in the air as if now that the war is over, life can get back to normal. He spots Sir Percy in the far corner, ensconced in a huge, leather armchair. His former boss sees him approach and, putting down his newspaper, rises to greet his ex-deputy.

'Jeremy, good to see you. Sit down, old chap. How's the family?'

'They're well.'

'Good, good.'

He snaps his fingers at the steward and asks Jeremy:

'Drink?'

Jeremy looks at his watch, barely eleven thirty.

'A bit early for me, sir.'

'Ah, right. Whisky, please Tompkins,' he tells the barman then asks:

'Well what's this all about?'

'It's about some children we evacuated in 1940.'

'1940, you say. Right in the middle of it.'

'Yes. Do you remember me telling you about a Mrs Smith? I wrote to you about her, earlier this year; her three children are missing.'

'Vaguely. Didn't you draw a blank there?'

'Yes.'

'So?'

'Well, I know the case was officially closed but just lately some new information has come to light.'

He waits for Sir Percy's reaction.

'Go on.'

'Well, we've found one of the children.'

'Indeed. 1940? That must have been the last lot of sea evacuees sent out there.'

'Yes. They were on the *Orinoco*. But we've looked at the records and they weren't really part of the CORB scheme. I think that's why we can't find any details of them returning to Britain after the war.'

'The *Orinoco*, you say. That was a rush job if I remember; the Prime Minister was about to close things down. He thought it too dangerous to send children overseas without the protection of a convoy but we already had plans for two more ships to leave. Yes, I remember, the *Orinoco* was one of them. So what happened to these Smith children?'

'I asked Victoria if she could remember the details and she thought we had contacted some of the private organisations to see if they had any suitable candidates.'

'And?'

'It turns out the girls were sent to a Catholic orphanage in Melbourne.'

'But you say you've found one of them already?'

'Yes, the youngest; she's still in the orphanage.'

'And the others?'

'Difficult to trace.'

'They always are.'

Sir Percy picks up his newspaper; he seems to be losing interest in what Jeremy has to say.

'So what do you want me to do?' he asks.

'Their mother wants us to repatriate the girl.'

'But she's in an orphanage, you say. We don't usually get involved with children in orphanages, particularly Catholic ones.'

'Yes, but she should never have been put there; she's not an orphan.'

'Well she must have been put there for her own good. Was the mother destitute?'

'No, nothing like that. She was in hospital having a baby. It was all a mistake. To be honest I can't believe that this could happen. You would think the orphanage would have taken steps to ensure that they really were orphans before sending them all that way?'

Sir Percy opens the newspaper.

'We would have taken the word of the person in charge of the orphanage,' he replies without looking up. 'It was not CORB's job to check the background of every child that we evacuated and especially in this case, children from a voluntary society. It sounds to me as though we only took them to make up the numbers.'

'But doesn't the Secretary of State have to approve the emigration of children?'

He puts down the newspaper and looks at Jeremy.

'Not if they are in the care of a voluntary organisation. The Custody of Children's Act 1891 allows any voluntary agency to make arrangements for children they considered to be abandoned.'

'They weren't abandoned; they just got caught up in the Blitz.'

'It probably didn't look like that at the time. Anyway I don't see what we can do about it now. They wouldn't have sent the children to Australia if someone had not thought it was the best thing to do with them. It wasn't our decision remember; we just provided the transport.'

'But surely we can help this woman to get her daughter back?'

'Look, Jeremy, I've seen this before. The mother can't afford to feed her kids and she expects someone else to do it for her. Then when it suits her she wants them back. It doesn't work like that. That girl is the responsibility of the orphanage now. Her mother can't expect us to pay to have her sent home just like that.'

'But we've repatriated hundreds of children.'

'But they went to the colonies knowing that they would eventually return to their families. It's not the same thing at all. Many parents paid for their children to return.'

'But there must be something we can do to help her?

Jeremy struggles to control his temper. Sir Percy can be very inflexible when he wants.

'How old is the child?' he asks.

'She's eight, nearly nine.'

'And she's been there for what, five years? Well have you considered that you might be causing her more harm than good by removing her from a stable environment? What about the mother? Is she married?'

'She's a widow; her husband was killed at Dunkirk.'

'So how could she support the child if we were to get her back? The girl would probably end up in another home.'

Jeremy thinks of Mrs Smith, with her shapely legs and her big, brown eyes; she would never put her children in a home.

'She has a job and she lives with her mother. In fact she is the breadwinner in the family,' he says.

'Nevertheless it sounds to me as though the girl is better off where she is.'

The steward reappears.

'Excuse me Sir Percy, there is a gentleman to see you.'

'Thank you, Tompkins, show him in.'

He folds the newspaper and turns to Jeremy.

'Sorry Jeremy, maybe we can talk about this later although I have to tell you now that I don't hold out much hope; it's not government policy to repatriate these children. Of course the woman is perfectly free to make her own arrangements with the orphanage but my advice to you is to leave the child where she is.'

He knows the conversation is over. Sir Percy will not relent on this one.

'Thank you for seeing me, anyway, Sir Percy.'

'Keep up the good work, Jeremy, but a word of caution, don't get too involved.'

When Jeremy arrives home, his wife is sitting in the lounge, listening to the wireless.

'Hello darling,' she says, inclining her face towards him to be kissed. 'Had a good day?'

'Interesting, I went to see Sir Percy.'

'How is the old buffer?'

He laughs and pours himself a Scotch from the decanter on the sideboard.

'Drink, darling?'

'A sherry would be delightful,' she says.

She pats the cushion next to her.

'Come and sit down and tell me all about it.'

Someone on the wireless is talking about sea evacuees.

'Just a sec, I'd like to listen to this,' he says, turning up the volume.

'*More child evacuees have returned this week. Ships from Canada and South Africa have brought home more of our young people, all with exciting tales to tell about their time in the colonies. Welcome back to Blighty, kids.*'

His wife sips her sherry and smiles at him.

'I'm so happy the war is over,' she says, 'and we have the boys back.'

'Not all the children have come home,' he tells her and explains about the Smith children. 'Their mother is distraught. She contacts us every day to see if we have any news of them.'

His wife nods; he knows she can sympathise with this unknown woman.

'So what are you doing to help her?' she asks.

'It's been difficult but today we were able to give her some good news at last; we've traced her youngest daughter.'

'Oh, that's wonderful. You know I was at the Ladies' Luncheon Club today and one of the speakers was talking about that very thing, evacuees. She said that, in her opinion, it was much better for children to stay with their parents, even when the home conditions were not ideal.'

'Evacuees or institutionalised children?' he asked.

'Both. This idea that a child is better off in an institution rather than living with its own parents is outmoded.'

'Even where the parents are incapable of giving that child a good home?' he asks.

'There are obviously degrees but in general, yes. And I have to agree with her.'

'Attitudes are changing I know, but, at the time of the sea evacuations, we were at war. People did what they thought was best for the children.'

Since meeting Mrs Smith he has begun to have doubts about the wisdom of the scheme but the reality is, no matter what, thousands of children were saved from the ravages of wartime Britain. They may have missed their families, some mistakes may have been made, but at least they survived. And not everyone wanted to return to Britain. Many children had elected to stay in their new homes.

'So, when will the girl get home?' his wife asks. 'When will she see her mother again?'

'Ah, well that's not so clear-cut; nobody wants to foot the bill to repatriate the girl. That's why I went to see Sir Percy; I thought he might authorise it but he doesn't see it as our responsibility.'

'That's awful. What about the Migration Department, can't they help? Or the Secretary of State?'

'No, we've tried them all; they say it's down to the voluntary societies to sort it out and, unfortunately, all they want to do is send children out there, not bring them back.'

'So the poor woman can't get her daughter back, even though she knows where she is?'

'That's how it is at the moment.'

'Well, I think that's shocking.'

She gives him a look which says that he is not trying hard enough to solve this.

BILLY

Billy is in the paddock, brushing Lady's coat; it gleams like clear honey in the sunshine. The mare gives a little whinny of pleasure when she sees Jack coming out of the stables.

'You're doing a good job there, mate. She's a real beaut.'

Billy gives one last brush to her mane and then pats her affectionately on the neck.

'Good girl,' he whispers, brushing his nose against her.

'I'm going to take her over to Joe Cartwright's to pick up some sacks of seed potatoes. Want to come?' asks Jack.

Billy smiles, Jack takes every opportunity to go over to the Cartwrights' place these days. Much to his parents' delight he has fallen in love with Emily, a tiny girl with eyes that seem to always be laughing at you. But he never goes there alone; he always has to have an excuse, like taking over some hay for their horses or borrowing something that Billy knows they already have hidden at the back of the barn. Today it's the seed potatoes.

'Yes, I'll come if the boss says it's OK.'

They both laugh at this. There is nothing Henry would like better than for Jack to settle down with a wife. If it means that Jack needs Billy's support while he is moving towards this goal, so be it. Henry approves of the friendship that has sprung up between this young foundling and his war-damaged son.

They hear a car come up the drive. The horse is nervous; they don't have many visitors on the farm. Billy leads Lady back to her stall while Jack goes over to see who it is.

'Hi there Bert, don't often see you out this way,' he hears Henry say. 'You remember my son Jack?'

'Sure do. How're doing mate? Hear you had a pretty bad time of it.'

'Glad to be home, that's for sure,' Jack replies.

'So what can we do for you?' Henry asks.

'That lad you've got working here, he's a Pom right?'

'Billy? Yes. Why?'

Henry sounds cautious. Billy moves closer to the door of the stables but stays deep in the shadows. It's the police. What are the police doing asking about him after all these years?

'Oh, it's nothing to worry about. Someone wants to get in touch with him, that's all. If it's him, of course; all we've been told is to look for a Pommy boy of about fifteen called Billy. I thought of your lad straight away. You never did say where you came across him.'

'An old abo left him here.'

'So is he here now?'

'Billy?'

'Yes, can I have a word with him?'

'I'd be happier if I knew who sent you.'

'Look mate, I'm just doing a favour for someone. He's got a brother back in Melbourne whose sheila is pressurising him into finding this kid. I said I'd ask around, that's all.'

'Well it could be him.'

'Is he here?'

'Billy,' Henry calls. 'Billy, come out here a minute. There's someone who wants to talk to you.'

Reluctantly Billy moves into the sun-drenched yard. He hopes they are not going to send him away.

'Hello there,' says the policeman.

He takes off his wide brimmed hat and mops his forehead with a spotted handkerchief. He has sandy hair that recedes back from his temples; his cheery face is covered in freckles and burnt red from the sun. For a moment Billy is reminded of Dad.

'OK son, is your name Billy Smith?'

Billy nods.

'You're from England, right?'

He nods again.

'Well now Billy there's a lady in Melbourne, says she's your sister. She's looking for you. Do you have a sister?'

Billy's heart gives a jump.

'Yes sir. I have two, Maggie and Grace. Maggie is the eldest and I'm next. Grace is the baby.'

The policeman looks at Henry.

'Well there you have it then; he's the one. I'll let them know and you can be expecting a letter from this sister of yours.'

'Is that all?' Billy asks.

'That's all son. Quite enough if you ask me, finding your sister again. She's one determined lady by all accounts.'

The policeman brushes the dust from his hat before putting it back on his head. Billy sees Sarah standing at the farmhouse door; she has come out to see who the visitor is.

'Well I never, Bert Parker. Haven't seen you in a long time. Don't stay out here in the sun, come on in and have a beer.'

'Hello there, Sarah. Well I don't mind if I do; it's a real hot one today.'

The policeman follows Sarah and Henry into the house. Billy and Jack look at each other.

'Well that's a turn up for the books, all right,' says Jack. 'I didn't know you had any sisters.'

Billy nods. He does not know what to say. What does it all mean? Is Maggie going to come and take him away from here? Once he used to lie in bed and pray that she would come for him, but not now. He realises that he does not want to leave here. He loves it on the farm. He loves Henry and Sarah. This is his home now. Even with their own son back they still treat him like a second son. A feeling of panic creeps up on him. If Maggie came for him where would they go? The war is over. Maybe Maggie wants to take them home. He tries to remember what it was like in London but he cannot see his old home clearly anymore; everything is blurred and hazy. He remembers the bombing; he remembers the street where he lived; he remembers Mum although he cannot focus on her face. What he conjures up is more of a feeling than an image; he begins to wonder if he would even recognise her again. Then he remembers that Mum is dead and his home is no more. His eyes fill with tears.

'Coming to the Cartwrights?' asks Jack.

'Yes. I'll get Lady,' he says, rubbing his eyes, surreptitiously.

'Then you can tell me all about those sisters of yours.'

Billy nods but he does not really want to talk about his past, not yet, not until he is older and there is no chance that he can be sent back to the orphanage. He feels mean keeping secrets from Jack; he is his mate. When Jack first came back from the war he did not talk very much about what had happened to him but, just lately, he has started opening up. He has told Billy about how the soldiers were made to march for miles and miles into the jungle, how they had no food, no medicine and hardly any water, how many of them died from disease, how their captors set them to work building a road. He told him of the friendships he made and how it felt when he watched his mates die from beatings or malnutrition. He confessed that he thought he would die there, in that camp, and he is sure that it was only the ending of the war that saved him.

Billy can understand his anger. It reminds him of life at the farm school, only a hundred times worse. Maybe he will tell him about Grace and Maggie; there will be no danger in that.

IRENE

She is cataloguing a new delivery of books when the telephone rings. It's Victoria.

'Have you time to speak?' she asks.

'Yes, the shop is empty at the moment,' Irene replies. 'What is it? Have you found something?'

Her stomach starts to churn and she cannot keep the excitement from her voice.

'Maybe. I've had a reply from the orphanage at last. Can you meet me for lunch?'

'Yes, of course.'

'Shall we say one o'clock at the Lyons' Corner House in Piccadilly?'

'Better make it one thirty; I don't get off until one.'

'OK, one thirty. See you later.'

She rings off. Irene replaces the receiver and automatically picks up the next book but she cannot focus. All she can think of is that they have had a reply. They have had a reply. But what was it? Her stomach is in knots. She looks at the clock on the wall; it says eleven thirty. Two hours to wait; it seems a lifetime. She groans.

'These done?'

Patrick Donovan, the owner of the bookshop, picks up a pile of books and looks at her.

'Yes. I've just got these few left. I'll soon be finished.'

'Quiet this morning,' he says, flicking through one of the books.

'It always is on a Wednesday,' she says.

'I think I'll pop round to the bank. You'll be all right on your own?'

'Yes. Will you be back before lunchtime?'

'Probably not. Why?'

'I'm going to meet Victoria Bell; she has some news for me.'

'That's good. Well just lock up when you go. I'll probably have lunch at home and come back in later this afternoon to see to some things.'

'Do you want me back later?'

Wednesday is half-day closing.

'No, you go on home after you've seen her. I'll see you to-morrow.'

He puts the stack of books back on the desk and wanders absentmindedly back into the shop. He is a nice man but not the easiest person to work for. His mind is always elsewhere. She has been used to employers who give clear, curt instructions. Most of the time Patrick expects her to read his mind and this is not easy because his mind is usually deep inside some new literary work. She fears that he is not a very good businessman. It's over a week since the bank manager telephoned asking him to go round to see him. She hopes the shop is not going to close. Apart from a few scholarly regulars they have not being doing a lot of business lately. She slips another card into the typewriter and types the name of the next book.

Victoria is already sitting at a table, eating a spam sandwich, when she arrives.

'Hello Irene. Sorry, I had to start; I'm famished and I've got to be back by two.'

'That's all right. I got here as soon as I could.'

She looks at her expectantly. Now the moment has arrived she is not sure she wants to hear the news.

'Don't look so worried; it's not bad news.'

'Oh, thank God.'

She sits down and takes off her hat and gloves. Her brown hair tumbles down onto her shoulders.

'The orphanage has got back to us at last. We were right; Maggie and Grace were there. They arrived sometime towards the end of 1940. Grace is still with them but Maggie left last year. She went to work as a domestic servant for a woman in Ballarat.'

She looks at Irene. Irene does not say anything; she is waiting to hear it all.

'The nuns wrote to this woman but she says that Maggie has left her employment; she is not sure where she has gone. All she could tell them was that she left and went to work somewhere else; she doesn't know where.'

'So they haven't any idea where she is?'

Victoria shakes her head.

'No, sorry. But Grace is still in the orphanage and she's fine,' she adds.

'Well if Grace is still there then Maggie won't be far away,' Irene says. 'I know my daughter; she wouldn't leave her sister.'

'Well that's good to know. It should make it easier for us to find her.'

'How soon can I get Grace back?' Irene asks.

Victoria hesitates. She looks embarrassed at the question.

'Well I don't think it's as easy as that.'

'What do you mean? They've been sending the other children home. It's been on the wireless all the time.'

'Yes, I know but that's different.'

'How is it different?'

'Well you see your children didn't really go out under a CORB scheme. They were already in the care of the orphanage and it was just as a favour to the Mother Superior that they went on the same ship. It was go then or they would have had to wait until the end of the hostilities. Technically they were child migrants, not sea evacuees.'

Irene does not know what to say. What distinction is Victoria trying to make? Is this all some more bureaucratic red tape?

'You know they've only just resumed sending child migrants out again quite recently,' Victoria adds.

Irene does not understand what she is saying. What is the difference between an evacuee and a migrant? Why are they still sending children to Australia? Whatever for? The war is over.

'Look Irene, I can see you're puzzled; let me try to explain. Your children were being looked after by the Poor Sisters of Nazareth. The nuns thought the children were orphans and decided to send them to one of their orphanages in Australia. They thought they'd have a better life there.'

'But how could they do that without permission? Surely somebody had to give permission for the children to leave the country.'

'Yes, you're right. It was the Mother Superior; she is allowed by law to find homes for the children in her care. She is in *loco parentis*. All she had to do was sign the forms and the children could be sent to Australia.'

'So it's the law?' Irene asks, in a barely audible voice.

She cannot believe it. Is this what Ronnie died for, so that the law could send his children to Australia? With the stroke of a pen a woman she didn't even know, had destroyed her family; she had changed their lives for ever.

'Yes, I'm afraid so. Voluntary agencies can make arrangements for children they considered to be abandoned.'

'Abandoned. I would never abandon my children,' she shouts.

She cannot maintain her composure any longer and bursts into tears. She is aware of Victoria thrusting a handkerchief in her face; she takes it and blows her nose.

'I'm sorry; it's just the thought that anyone could possibly think that I had abandoned my own children.'

She sees Victoria look around nervously; she is embarrassed by Irene's outburst.

'It does happen,' Victoria tells her.

She waits until she is sure that Irene is calmer and adds:

'I'll do what I can to find out where Maggie has gone. I'll write to the orphanage again and ask them to make some enquiries for us.'

But Irene is more interested in Grace's situation. This is far worse, knowing that her daughter is alive, knowing where she is and yet not being able to get her back. Why is life so cruel?

'But you'll tell them Grace is not an orphan, won't you? You'll tell them that I'm alive?'

'Of course.'

'And when they realise she's not an orphan they'll send her home?'

'I don't know, Irene. I'll do what I can but these organisations don't usually have the money to repatriate migrant children.'

'So how will she get back? I haven't got the money to go to Australia,' she says. 'I can't even afford to send her the fare.'

Her voice is rising again. Victoria reaches across the table and pats Irene's hand.

'Look, one thing at a time; let's find out where Maggie is, first.'

A waitress is standing by their table, a pad in her hand.

'Do you want to order?' she asks.

'Just a cup of tea,' Irene replies.

She looks at Victoria.

'My stomach is too upset to eat anything now,' she explains.

'Of course. Bring a pot for two,' she tells the waitress.

'So what happens now?' Irene asks. 'What if we can't find her? At least let's get Gracie home.'

'I think we should wait for a couple more weeks until we have some news about Maggie before trying to get them repatriated,' Victoria replies.

Irene wants to cry again and does not know if it's from joy, rage or frustration.

'We could write to the police,' she suggests. 'Or the British Embassy.'

Victoria nods.

'Yes, we could do all of that. Leave it with me and I'll see what I can do, but remember there were thousands of kids sent out there; I don't know how good their records will be.'

'But you said.'

She sounds like a petulant child.

'I know. I'll do what I can Irene, but don't get your hopes up.'

'At least speak to your boss about Grace,' she begs.

'All right, I'll see what I can do.'

The waitress returns with the tea and she sits back while Victoria pours it out.

Her mother is in the kitchen when she arrives home. She has been baking and a plate of spicy rock cakes are cooling on the table.

'Been busy,' Irene comments.

'You're late,' her mother says. 'Your dinner is on the stove. Careful, the plate is hot.'

Irene takes a cloth and lifts the plate off the saucepan; the food has dried from the steam and looks distinctly unappetising but she knows she must make an effort to eat it.

'I'm not really hungry, Mum,' she says, picking at the potatoes with her fork.

'Rubbish. You need to eat my girl; there's nothing of you.'

'I saw Victoria today. She knows where Grace is.'

Her mother looks at her in amazement.

'Well blessed be to God. I never thought I'd hear those words. I never thought we'd find any of them poor mites again.'

'She's been in an orphanage in Australia all this time.'

'And the others?'

Irene shakes her head.

'So far, nothing.'

She explains how Maisie and Grace had been together but now nobody knew where her elder daughter was.

'But Gracie can come home, can't she?'

Irene has not seen her mother so animated in a long time; her cheeks are glowing and there is a sparkle in her eyes.

'Victoria's looking into it.'

She does not want to say too much to her mother; she wants to save her from possible disappointment.

'It's all good news today,' her mother says.

She goes to the sink in the scullery and fills the kettle, humming to herself. Irene recognises the tune; Maggie used to sing it all the time. Irene starts to softly sing the words and, as the memory of her daughter takes hold, she can no longer keep back her tears. What has happened to her beautiful Maggie? Where is she now?

'You all right, Irene?' her mother asks. 'There's no good crying. I know it's difficult but you've got to keep your chin up. You'll get them back; you see.'

'I know Mum. It's just that sometimes it's jolly hard, not knowing where they are or whether I'll ever see them again.'

'I know, pet.'

The kettle starts to whistle.

'I'll make you a nice cup of tea,' she says and goes back into the scullery.

Irene wipes her eyes. Her mother's right; there's nothing to be gained by crying.

'George was round earlier; he's found a job,' her mother says, coming back with two cups of tea.

'That's good.'

'Over in Hackney Wick at the timber yard. Not what he's been used to, of course, but it's work. He says he'll pop in later to see you.'

George is lodging down the street now at number 26 with the Arnolds, whose son was killed at Tobruk.

'I think I'll have a lie down Mum, then I'll go and pick up Leslie.'

She pushes her half-eaten dinner to one side.

'Have your tea first. And tell me again what that Miss Bell had to say about Grace.'

George is in high spirits when he comes round to see Irene.

'Get your coat, I'm taking you out to the pub,' he says. 'We're going to celebrate.'

'Mum told me you'd got a job.'

'It's not great but it'll do for now, until something better comes along.'

'Go in and say hello to Mum while I put my face on,' she tells him.

She dashes upstairs and sits down at the dressing table. She studies her face in the mirror. It's not too bad considering, but there are shadows under her eyes and the start of a few crows' feet that have more to do with worry than laughter. She dabs at her nose with some face powder, carefully applies her lipstick then she dabs a spot of lipstick on each cheek and rubs it well in. That is better; now she does not look quite so pale. She puts a final comb through her hair and gets up. Why is she going to such trouble just to go down to the pub with George? She catches a glimpse of herself in the mirror and blushes. She has not been out with a man since Ronnie died; there has been no time and no opportunity. Now she feels like a silly teenager on her first date. What started as friendship between them is beginning to grow into something more as far as she is concerned. Seeing George has made her realise how much she misses a man's company and she has become very fond of having him around. She tells herself she is being foolish; why would George be interested in her, a widow with four children? A nice young man like him could get anyone he wanted. He could marry a young girl and have a family of his own.

'Come on Irene; they'll be calling time soon,' he calls up the stairs.

'Be right with you,' she replies.

She slips on her best shoes and puts on her coat. Leslie is already asleep; she leans over his bed and kisses him lightly on the forehead.

BILLY

On Friday morning Henry falls from the ladder to the hay loft and breaks his ankle. They carry him into the house then Jack drives into town to get the doctor. It's not a serious break the doctor tells them but it will take at least a month to heal. He puts the ankle in plaster and tells him to lie with his leg up as much as he can. So Henry lies on the veranda and shouts his orders from there. He is not the most patient of patients as Sarah reminds him repeatedly. Jack, Billy and John T are hard pressed trying to do their own work as well as his.

By the time the letter arrives Billy has almost forgotten about the policeman's visit; he has been too busy to think about it.

'It's the postie,' shouts Henry from his lookout on the veranda. 'Sarah, postie.'

'All right, hang on a minute.'

'I'll get it,' says Billy.

He runs down to meet the post van which is arriving in a billowing cloud of dust. The battered old van lurches to a stop and the postman gets out. He reaches into his bag and carefully selects the mail he wants to give him. Billy waits for him to give the letters his usual scrutiny before handing them over.

'Here we are. Two bills for Henry, that'll be the fertiliser and the seed no doubt,' he adds.

'One from the War Office for Jack and ...' he pauses and looks at Billy. 'And one for a William Smith, from a lady I reckon, by the handwriting.'

He winks and hands the mail to Billy.

'So, got yourself a lady friend, have you, Billy?'

'It's from my sister, I expect,' Billy says.

He can feel himself blushing.

'Sarah says are you coming in for a cuppa?' Billy asks.

'No, not today, got to go over to the Cartwrights' place next, then out to Bladon Creek. Thank Sarah anyway.'

'OK.'

Billy waits until the postman has driven away then takes the letters over to Henry.

'I've got a letter from my sister,' he tells him.

'Have you indeed. You must be fair chuffed about that, Billy.'

'Yes, Boss,' he says and goes to his room to read his letter in peace.

He does not know what he feels about getting a letter from Maggie; his sister and his old life all seem so far away now.

Beth follows him. Beth is a six month old Australian sheepdog and she and Billy are inseparable. When Jess, the sheepdog, had puppies back in the spring, Henry had said that Billy could have one of them so he chose Beth. She was the smallest of the litter but she was the liveliest; she was off exploring long before her brothers and sisters who preferred to stay close to their mother's warm flanks. He does not know why he has called her Beth. It's a name with a sweet, soft sound and seems to suit her. Henry says that he must train her to help with the sheep but she is still too young. First he says Billy has to learn to control the dog, teach her to be patient, to wait for his commands then they can introduce her to the sheep. He says it will be easy; it's the natural instinct for this breed of dog to herd sheep. So Billy spends all his free time with Beth, building up the bond between them.

He sits on his bed and looks at the letter for a long time before he opens it.

'*Dear Billy,*

I hope this gets to you all right. Don't be angry that it's taken so long to write. I have been trying to find you ever since they took you off the boat in Fremantle. I have left the orphanage now and work in a factory. Grace is still in the orphanage but I hope to get her out of there soon. I have some new friends and they have helped me track you down. They are also going to help us all get back to England.   I can't come for you yet but I will as soon as I can.   I hope you are well.

Your loving sister Maggie'

He folds the letter and puts it on the table. Beth is looking at him, expectantly. He stretches across and pats her head. What will happen to Beth if he leaves?

'Come on girl, we've work to do,' he says.

He is pleased that Maggie and Grace are all right, but he does not want to go back to England with them. His life is here now. He wants to have his own farm one day. Maybe he should write to Maggie and try to explain; Sarah will help him, he is sure.

Sarah wants him to turn over the vegetable patch for her; it's too much work for her these days and usually she gets Henry to do it. As he digs into the dry earth he wonders how they will manage if he leaves. The farm is too much for Jack to run alone. There is John T but he spends all his time with the sheep and Arthur died a couple of months ago of a heart attack. They will have to hire someone else if Billy leaves. He does not like the thought of someone taking his place. No this is where he wants to be; he does not want to be homeless again. Maybe he can persuade Maggie and Grace to come and live with him when he is older.

'What'd she say then?' asks Sarah. 'Your sister.'

'Not much. She wants me to go back to England with her.'

Sarah does not say anything to this. She starts to peg out the sheets on the washing line.

'Don't know what to tell her,' he continues. 'Not much good at writing letters.'

'I'll give you a hand if you want,' she says, removing a peg from her mouth.

'OK.'

He pushes the spade into the ground and watches the crumbly earth fall from it.

'After tea?'

'OK.'

'Henry wants to talk to you when you've finished here,' she tells him.

Henry has his eyes shut but Billy knows he is not asleep.

'You wanted something Boss?'

He opens his eyes and looks at him.

'Yes, Billy.'

Billy sits down on the veranda; it's cool there in the shade. He waits for Henry to speak.

'I've had a lot of time to think these last few days, being crooked up like this.'

He points to his leg.

'Bloody stupid thing to do, going up that ladder anyway. You should have heard Sarah. Should have left it to the youngsters, she said. Not a job for an old bugger like you.'

He laughs.

'Truth is Billy we all get old and there're things that we can't do anymore. But the work don't go away, the cow still needs milking, the sheep have to be looked after. There's a lot of bloody work on this farm.'

He sighs and sucks on his pipe. Billy can see it has gone out but Henry sucks on it anyway.

'Want me to get you a light, Boss?' he asks, getting up.

'Later. Let me finish what I want to say.'

He motions for Billy to sit down again.

'I've never asked you this before, Billy,' he begins. 'Probably because I already knew the answer.'

Billy waits.

'We, Sarah and me, that is, want to know if you are happy here?'

'Sure am, Boss. You've been very good to me.'

'Good.'

He sucks on his pipe again.

'The thing is Billy, with me crooked up like this, Jack can't manage all alone. Now I know you have your sisters and I expect you want to see them, family and all that, but the thing is we need you here.'

Billy stares at him.

'That's it, that's all I wanted to say.'

'I ain't going nowhere, Boss. This is my home now.'

He has made his decision. Maggie will be cross with him but he cannot help that. These people need him. They are his family now.

'Is that all Boss?'

'Yes, I've said my piece.'

'Do you want me to try Beth with the sheep this week?' he asks.

'Yes, why not. Talk to John T about it; he'll show you what to do. Take her out there tomorrow; Jack'll manage around here.'

'Right, Boss.'

'And get me the matches, will you.'

'OK, Boss.'

MAGGIE

She has had a letter from Annabel; she is staying with her brother for a few days and wants to see her. She says she has something to tell her. How mysterious. Maggie wonders what it is. Maybe Annabel has a new boyfriend.

After work, instead of going home, Maggie goes straight to Tom and Alice's house. It's Alice that opens the door.

'Right on time,' she says.

She smells of smoke and something savoury and spicy. There is a black smudge on her cheek.

'Come in the garden; we're all out there. Tom's lit the barbie.'

Maggie follows her through the house and out into the garden.

'Maggie.'

Annabel jumps up when she sees her.

'Oh, it's brilliant to be here. You look fantastic,' she gushes. 'So slim and grown up.'

She gives her a hug. The girls have not seen each other since Christmas because Annabel is away at college now. Maggie thinks that her friend too looks older and more confident.

'Hi Tom,' Maggie says, waving across at him.

He is struggling to keep the flames under control; she can smell the meat burning.

'Squirt some beer on it,' says Alice, handing her husband a bottle of beer.

'I got your letter,' Maggie says to Annabel. 'What's the mystery?'

'It's no mystery. I just wanted to tell you in person and it was a good excuse to come over.'

'Well?'

'Don't be so impatient; I told you it's nothing to worry about. It's just that Mummy has received a letter from the orphanage wanting you to get in touch with them. She wrote back saying that you had left and she didn't know where you were. I thought I should tell you.'

'What do you think they want?'

'I've no idea.'

'Could it be something to do with Grace? Do you think something has happened to her?'

'But you'd know wouldn't you? You write to her all the time.'

'Yes, but she never writes back. I have no idea how she is.'

The ridiculousness of the situation hits her. What does she know about Grace's condition? Nothing. She has only seen her a couple of times. She could be ill or dying. How would Maggie ever know?

'So what are you going to do?'

'I don't know. What if it's a trick? What if I'm in trouble for running away from your house?'

'But Mummy never told them that you'd run away. She just said you had a new job. No, it can't be about that.'

'So it has to be about Grace.'

'You'd better write to them.'

'You think so?'

'Yes and give them your address so that they can write back.'

'All right, I will.'

'Now tell me, what else has been happening? How's Jimmy?' Maggie blushes.

'He's fine. He's got a job here in Melbourne now.'

'So he's not going back to Perth?'

'No, now the war's over he's going back to his old job at the factory.'

'Well?'

'Well what?'

Maggie knows Annabel wants some more details about her romance but she is too shy to tell her how much she is in love. They had hit it off from that first night when they met at the pub and have been dating ever since.

'Yes, I'm still seeing him.'

'Serious is it?'

Maggie blushes again; Annabel is so persistent.

'I think so. He said he wouldn't go back to Perth, not without me. But I can't leave here, not now, with Grace still in the orphanage.'

Then Maggie tells her about finding Billy. She can see that her friend is impressed.

'So you'll soon all be together again,' Annabel says. 'Then you can go back to England.'

'I'm not so sure about that; I haven't heard from Billy yet. And anyway, I don't know if I want to go back to London, now. Oh, it's all such a mess. I love Jimmy. I don't want to leave him but I have to look after Grace and Billy.'

She feels like crying as she says it.

'Look, it's not that bad. At least you know where they are. Billy can come to Melbourne and then all you have to do is wait until Grace can leave the orphanage.'

Tom comes up to them with a plate of sausages. They look a bit burnt around the edges.

'What's up?'

'Nothing. Just girls' talk.'

'How're things at home?' he asks his sister.

'Just the same.'

Maggie looks at Annabel. Has something happened?

'It's Daddy, he's had a stroke. He's paralysed down his left side. Mummy has to feed him and everything,' she explains.

'How awful,' Maggie says politely.

'So, he's confined to his room these days,' Annabel adds. 'Mummy has had to get a nurse in to help her. It's dreadful; poor Mummy can't really manage on her own.'

'Can he speak?'

'Hardly. Mummy understands what he says but I can't make anything out. I'm glad I'm away most of the time.'

Maggie picks up a sausage and nibbles it cautiously.

'Good?' asks Tom.

'Mmn,' she agrees.

She has not thought about Mr Brookes in a long time; she does not want to remember what happened that night. Now that she is older she understands exactly what he was after and what a narrow escape she had, thanks to Annabel's intervention. She tries to feel sorry for him but cannot.

The next evening she writes to the Mother Superior. She has talked it over with Mrs Robinson and she agrees with Annabel; it's a good idea to let them know where she is.

'After all dear, someone might be looking for you too,' says Mrs Robinson.

Maggie has not thought about that. She takes out some paper and a rather leaky fountain pen that Mrs Robinson has lent her and begins:

'Dear Mother Superior,

I heard that you were looking for me. I am living with Mrs Robinson in Melbourne. The address is 55, Long Way, Melbourne. I am well and working in a factory. I hope my sister Grace is well.

Margaret Smith'

She hands it to Mrs Robinson to look at.

'That's fine, dear. Doesn't say too much. If they need to get in touch with you, well now they can.'

'You don't think they'll take me back there, do you?'

'No, now why would they want to do that? They have enough poor homeless girls to feed as it is; they're not going to go out looking for more.'

Maggie puts the letter in an envelope and addresses it.

'I think I'll go and post it right away, before I change my mind,' she says.

'Well don't be too long; it'll soon be dinner time.'

'No, I won't. I'm going to the pictures later, with Jimmy.'

'Sounds as if you two are going steady,' Mrs Robinson says, with a wink.

The noise of something boiling over on the stove saves Maggie from any further questions as her landlady hurries into the kitchen. Maggie can hear her swearing quietly to herself. She picks up her hat and opens the door; if she hurries she will be back before dinner is served.

JEREMY ACTON-DUNN

He can hear the tea lady's trolley as it squeaks its way along the landing towards his office; he looks at his watch, ten o'clock already. Mrs Smith has arranged to come in at eleven and he still has no idea what he will say to her.

'Oh by the way, Jeremy, there's a letter here for you from Australia. It's marked Private and Confidential so I haven't opened it,' Victoria says as she brings in his morning cup of tea.

She places an official looking letter on the desk; the envelope is embossed with the seal of the Australian Government and underneath is inscribed 'Department of Immigration and International Affairs'.

'Interesting,' he says, picking it up and opening it. 'We haven't had any contact with the DIIA since before the War.'

He begins to read it then frowns.

'It's from Philip Shepherd. I haven't heard from him in years. What on earth does he want?'

After a few moments he looks up at Victoria and says:

'You'll never believe this; we've found the other one. She's been trying to get in touch with her grandmother.'

'The Smith girl?'

'Yes, Margaret, the older one. She's working in Melbourne; there's even an address. She's been told her mother is dead so she is trying to trace her grandmother.'

'What wonderful news. You'll be able to tell Mrs Smith when she arrives. She'll be so pleased.'

'Apparently a friend of Phil's has taken a particular interest in the case. Asked him to get in touch with someone here in England,' he says. 'No news of the boy, though. Turns out they traced him to a farm school in Western Australia but he ran away; they are not sure where he is now.'

'Well at least she has her daughters.'

'Bring me their file, will you, and show Mrs Smith straight into my office when she arrives. We need to give her copies of all this information, so that she can follow it up.'

'What about financial help? Did Sir Percy suggest anything?' He shakes his head.

'No, it doesn't look as though we will be able to help. As far as we are concerned the case is now closed.'

He sees the look on Victoria's face. Between her, his wife and the mother he has no peace. They all expect him to do miracles. He can't just conjure the money out of thin air.

'We can't do any more. I know you want to help this woman. So do I but we've done all we can. She will have to find her own way of getting them home,' he says.

'Maybe the Australians will pay to send them back,' she suggests.

'I doubt that very much.'

'It wouldn't hurt to ask, would it?' she smiles at him.

'Oh all right. Get me Phil on the phone and I'll see what he has to say.'

'He won't be there. It's nine o'clock at night in Australia. He'll have gone home.'

'Of course. Well send him a telegram and tell him I'll ring tomorrow morning at nine. He can send me his home number if he prefers.'

'At least you'll have covered all the possibilities then.'

'All right, Victoria. No need to go on about it.'

The telephone rings a few times then a deep voice says:

'Shepherd here.'

'Phil? Good evening. It's Jeremy Acton-Dunn from London. I'm sorry to bother you at home but I wanted to talk to you about the Smith girl.'

'Hello Jeremy. Not a problem mate. How can I help?'

'We've located Mrs Smith, the children's mother.'

'Blimey. She's not dead after all. The girl will be over the moon when she hears that. She's always said that it was a mistake, that her mother was alive all the time. And what do you know? She was right. Did she say where she's been all these years?'

'Looking for her children. Apparently she was in hospital having a baby when the bombs dropped. By the time she got home her house had gone and there was no sign of her family. She's been looking for them ever since.'

'Sounds a bit like her daughter, never gives up.'

'Yes, you have to admire her determination.'

Jeremy thinks of the slender woman with the big brown eyes; he has become quite fond of her.

'Naturally the mother wants to be reunited with her children but that's where we have a problem,' he continues.

'Nobody wants to pay,' Phil says.

'Exactly. There is no way we can find the money to repatriate them. I have tried the voluntary agencies, government departments, nobody is interested.'

'So you wondered if we could pay to send them home?' Phil asks.

'Exactly. What are the chances of them getting back to England?'

'Under a government scheme? Zilch. We're more interested in bringing them out here, not sending them back. Good British blood, don't you know. And anyway, it's not just a question of money. There's a new government act.'

'The IGOC Act? Isn't that something to do with the legal guardianship of immigrant children?'

'Yes, they now come under the Minister of Immigration.'

'So what does that mean exactly?' Jeremy asks.

'It's for the benefit of the kids, to protect them. Any kids that come over here in the future will be under the legal guardianship of the Ministry until they reach the age of twenty-one.'

'What about the children that are already there, like Maggie?'

'Yes, her too, all the evacuees.'

'So it's the Ministry that makes all the decisions?'

'In theory. The Ministry has the guardianship of the children but it has delegated some of the responsibility to the State authorities. They in turn have delegated the role of supervision and welfare to private organisations, the Church and charitable organisations mainly.'

'And there're no plans to send any of them back?'

'Not that I know of. It's just the opposite. Now that the war is over the Australian government want as many immigrants as it can get, especially British ones. The children are best, easier to get them to settle in,' Phil says.

'Mould them, more like.'

'I suppose so but it's for their benefit as well. The kids will have a great life here. Most of them are desperate to get away from Britain. We've seen the newsreels about what it's like there at the moment? Bombed cities, rationing, unemployment; it's a hard life for kids.'

'It's a hard life for everyone,' Jeremy tells him. 'We've just spent six years at war.'

'I know, mate.'

'So how does this affect Maggie and her sister? How can they get back to England?' Jeremy asks.

'That's a tough one. When she's twenty-one she can do what she wants but until then she's stuck here.'

'Is there nothing she can do?'

'Well she could always appeal to the Minister. If he gives her written permission she can leave.'

'The younger one as well?'

'In theory. He has to be sure it's not prejudicial to her well being. But even if she got permission to leave, she'd still have to pay her own passage home; the Ministry wouldn't fund that.'

'So it's unlikely we'll get any help from the Australian government to repatriate this family?'

'No. Sorry mate. I wish I could be of more help. Maybe the mother will have to come out here.'

'Well thanks for your help Phil. I appreciate it.'

'No problem Jeremy. Nice talking to you again. As I said, sorry I can't be more positive. If I hear of anything that could help I'll write to you.'

MAGGIE

Maggie cannot believe it. She has found Billy at last. She should be happy but instead she is disappointed; he does not want to leave. She reads his letter again in case she has misunderstood what he is saying. But no, it's quite clear; he wants to make his life in Australia. He wants to be a farmer and have his own farm one day. He is happy he says and he does not want to leave his friends. She reads the last paragraph again:

'I want to see you Maggie but Melbourne is a long way away. One day I'll come and visit you. I promise. Give Grace a big kiss from me, your loving brother Billy.'

A tear drops onto the paper and smudges some of the words. She should be happy for him; he has found what he wants. She tries to be positive but the disappointment is too great. After all these years apart, thinking about him, worrying if he is all right, not knowing where he is and now that she has found him he does not want her. She is angry with him and feels more alone than ever.

'Come on Maggie, at least you know where he's living now,' says Mrs Robinson. 'He sounds as though he's very happy. That's good isn't it?'

Maggie sniffs and nods. Mrs Robinson is right. Maybe it's Maggie who is being selfish. After all it's not as though she knows for certain that Mum is alive. What she is suggesting is that Billy gives up a happy, secure life to come and live with her. And how could she care for him anyway?

'Think of it like this, you've only that wee Grace to worry about now.'

Mrs Robinson is right, but even that is not going to be as easy as she thought. Tom has told her that Grace cannot leave the orphanage until she is fifteen; they will not let her live with Maggie because Maggie is under twenty-one. When she comes of age it may be different but in the meantime Grace is still an orphan and the responsibility of the orphanage. The only way Grace can leave sooner is if Maggie can find either her mother or her grandmother. So that is what she will have to do.

She puts Billy's letter back in its envelope. She will go and give Tom the news after supper.

The orphanage does not reply to her letter. At first she is looking for the post every day but then she realises that nothing is going to come. The weeks go by and winter turns to spring. She stops wondering why they were looking for her in the first place; it was obviously not that important. Now when she writes to Grace she puts her return address on the letter but Grace never replies. She is not surprised. The nuns would not allow such foolishness. She can imagine Sister Agnes's indignation if Grace were to ask her for a stamp to post a letter.

Maggie is settling into her new life in Melbourne. Surprisingly the news that Billy does not want to return to England with them is almost a relief. She is only responsible for Grace now. Billy has found a new home. She writes to him each month and tells him how she is but only occasionally does she get a brief reply. This does not worry her; she is well aware that he does not write the letters himself. As long as he is happy she is content.

She only sees Annabel in the holidays now. Annabel is too busy during term time to visit her and spends what free time she has with her new boyfriend. It's Saturday and she and Jimmy are going to the pictures as usual. She removes the pins from her hair and brushes it carefully so that the waves frame her face. It's only on Saturdays that she goes to such trouble; normally she twists it around an old stocking to form a Liberty roll, just like her mother used to do. She would like to be blonde, like her favourite Hollywood star, Veronica Lake, but Mrs Robinson says it would make her look tarty. Anyway Jimmy says he likes her hair just as it is.

'Maggie, are you up there?'

'Yes, Mrs Robinson.'

'Come down child, there's a letter here for you from England.'

Maggie stops; for a moment she is frozen, the hairbrush suspended above her head. The face that looks back at her in the mirror has an expression that she cannot explain. Her stomach begins to churn. Who can it be from?

'Coming.'

She hurries down to see who has sent the letter, the hairbrush still clutched in her hand.

'It arrived this morning but Fred put it on the mantelshelf and forgot to mention it.'

She scowls disapprovingly at her lodger.

Maggie picks up the letter. Her name is typed neatly on the envelope. It looks official.

'You open it Mrs R,' she says. 'I can't do it.'

'All right, dear. Sit down now, before you fall down.'

She puts on her spectacles and carefully opens the envelope.

'Dear Maggie,' she begins.

'Who's it from?' asks Maggie. 'Who has sent it?'

Who in England calls her Maggie?

Mrs Robinson turns the letter over. She looks at Maggie and smiles.

'It's from your mother, dear. Are you sure you wouldn't like to read it yourself?'

She holds the letter out to her. Maggie cannot move. This is what she has been dreaming of for so long; this is what she has been hoping for. She always knew that Mum was not dead; she knew it.

'I'll take it upstairs,' she says.

She goes back to her room and sits on the bed, clutching the letter. She is faint with excitement. All that she can think is that Mum is alive; her mother is alive. Her hands tremble as she opens the envelope and takes out the letter.

'*Dear Maggie,*

At last I have found you. You can't imagine how long I have been waiting to send you this letter. I have written to you hundreds of times in my head, now at last I can really write to you. I wonder how you are and if you are happy. I hope they looked after you in the orphanage. They tell me you have started work now. I wish I could see you; you must be so grown up, quite a young lady.

I have missed you so much Maggie, not knowing if you and Billy and Grace were alive or dead has been hard to live with. People kept telling me that you had all been killed in the Blitz but I just couldn't believe that.'

Maggie stops and wipes her eyes; she can barely read it for the tears. So Mum felt the same as she did; she never believed they were dead.

'*Please forgive me for not finding you sooner. I did what I could but nobody would tell me anything. Kate was dead (did you know that?) and the house had gone. It was awful, I didn't know what to do. It was chaos here in London, what with the Blitz then the Doodlebugs, I began to believe the war was never going to end. At least I'm thankful that you didn't have to go through all that.*

I have married again, to George. Do you remember George? He was a friend of your Dad's. He has been very good to us and treats Leslie just like his own son. Your Nan died back in March. She was quite old and had a stroke. And Granddad died the year after you disappeared. You remember he was a fire warden. Well he was killed when a roof collapsed on top of him while he was trying to rescue someone. I miss them both.

It's hard, nobody has much money these days, but I earn a bit at my job in the bookshop and George has a job at the bus depot. At first I worked in a factory, making uniforms for the soldiers. It didn't pay much but I felt I was doing something for the war effort. Then when the war ended and the soldiers came home, lots of the women got sacked, including me. I can understand that they wanted to give the jobs back to the men but I needed my job. Anyway I became friends with the mother of one of Leslie's chums and she taught me to type and persuaded me to go for this job in a bookshop in Finsbury. She said I just needed to dress up a bit and put on a posh voice and I'd have no problem. She was right. The owner's a bit lah-de-dah and I was surprised when he offered me the job but I really enjoy it.'

Maggie smiles through her tears. This is so like Mum. Memories of her come flooding back to her: Mum singing, Mum reading them stories and pretending to be all the characters, Mum imitating the headmistress at her school. Yes, she could imagine Mum pretending to be a posh lady.

'Let me tell you about your brother; he's a good boy, doing well at school and he looks just like his Dad. You know, the red hair and all. He still has some problems with his heart, so he can't play football and things like that, but otherwise he leads a normal life. He is very good at drawing and I've sent you one of his pictures. It was hard when he was a baby; I didn't know if he would survive or not, but he's a fighter, just like you Maggie. I don't know what I would have done without him.

Now all I want is to have my family reunited, to have you all together again. I don't know how I'm going to do that but I will try. I write to Grace but she doesn't reply. Perhaps you can let me know how she is. And Billy? Nobody seems to know where he is. My poor Billy. I have spoken to so many government departments about getting you back home, but everyone says it's someone else's responsibility. But I'm not giving up hope. I'll get you back one way or the other.

Please write to me Maggie and tell me how you are. If you have a photograph I would love to see what my darling girl looks like now.

with lots and lots of love from Mum xxxxxxxxxxxx'

Maggie looks at Leslie's drawing; it's of a train, with smoke coming out of the chimneys. He has written *'For Maggie from Leslie xx'*.

Poor Mum does not know about Billy. What will she say when Maggie tells her? Maybe she will write to Billy herself and persuade him to leave. She takes the letter and the drawing downstairs to show Mrs Robinson.

Maggie cannot explain to Helen how happy she is to hear from her mother; it's as though all her prayers have been answered. Helen, who lives in a noisy, chaotic, overcrowded house with her parents, her grandmother, four brothers and two sisters, one of whom is only six months old, cannot understand what it is to be lonely. She constantly complains about her brothers, even Jimmy, and moans when her mother makes her look after the baby; she tells Maggie she wants to move away as soon as she has enough money. Sometimes Maggie tries to tell her what it was like living in the orphanage, how unhappy she had been but she can see that Helen cannot imagine a life like that so she gives up.

At first she cannot reply to Mum's letter; she just keeps taking it out and holding it. She lifts it to her nose and breathes in, hoping for a hint of those familiar smells that she associates with her mother. She tells herself she can smell the scent of her cigarettes, of her face powder, of her hair, of lavender. She closes her eyes and she can see her there before her; the image that has grown cloudy over the years sharpens into focus and there is Mum's smiling face. Then she reads the letter again and rereads it until she has the words engraved on her memory.

God has answered her prayers. He has found their Mum. She is not dead. She is alive and she has been looking for them. Maggie always believed it would happen, that one day they would all be together again. There were days when she had her doubts, when she cried herself to sleep, days when she told herself it was best to forget London and make a life for herself in Australia, days when she doubted whether she would ever see Billy again. Now it's no longer just a dream; it's a reality. They are not reunited yet but that moment is within reach; they are in touch once more. That is the first step.

When she eventually writes to her mother she tells her first of all about Billy, how he is well and happy then she tells her about herself. There is so much to say, she does not know where to start. She tells her about June and the voyage to Australia; she tells her about the orphanage; she tells her about going to work.

She does not mention Mr Brookes or Sister Agnes; she does not want to see those memories written down in black and white. Instead she tells her about her new friends, about Annabel and Tom, about Helen and her brother Jimmy, about Mrs Robinson, who has treated her like a daughter, about Fred and his help in finding Billy. Then, her wrist aching from so much writing, she tells her how she loves and misses her.

'You finished that letter yet?' Mrs Robinson asks.

She has her hat and coat on, a shopping bag hangs over her arm.

'Yes, just finished. Are you going out?'

'I am, down to the shops. Want me to post it for you?'

'Please'

'What about that man, has he found a way of getting you back to England yet?'

'Tom's friend? No, he's been great but even he doesn't know what I can do to get the money.'

'So it's just the money for the fares then?'

'No, not just that. We have to get written permission from the Ministry.'

'But what's it got to do with them?'

'It's because we're migrant children; They have to give us permission to go home.'

'So if you get this permission will they pay for you to go back to England?'

Maggie shakes her head.

'No, I don't think so.'

'So are you going to write to this Ministry anyway?'

'I have done already. I've been waiting for a reply for ages. Tom says not to worry that these ministries are very busy and it takes them a long time to get round to things.'

'Need to get off their backsides and do some real hard work, if you ask me,' says Mrs Robinson. 'Well dear, you just keep writing them letters and one day you'll get the reply you're waiting for. God looks after his own you know.'

Maggie smiles and hands her the letter. She feels as though an enormous weight has been lifted from her shoulders. Yet nothing has really changed. They are still marooned in Australia, thousands of miles from home but at least now she knows that they do have a home and, more importantly, a mother. They just have to find a way of getting back to her.

IRENE

Irene finishes typing the address and pulls the envelope out of the typewriter; she folds the letter and slips it inside. There is a feeling of fatalism about her actions; nothing is going to come of it, she is sure. She has written dozens of letters asking for help to get her children back but the answers are always the same; there is nothing anyone can do. Even Victoria does not get in touch with her as often as before; she too seems to have given up on her. Irene still telephones her but she never has anything to report. Well at least now Irene knows that her children are all alive and even where they are. If only she could get to see them.

She writes to Grace and Maggie each week, telling them she loves them and promising to get them home as soon as she can. She doubts if they believe her; she hardly believes it herself. She needs to win the Football Pools she tells herself.

And then there is Billy; she does not know what to do for the best with Billy. Maggie says he has made a new life and does not want to leave. She can understand that; he has been through a traumatic time and now he feels safe. Of course he does not want to leave his new home. Irene has started to write to him a hundred times and each time has torn the letter up; she does not want to upset him now he is settled, especially, if she is honest with herself, because she has nothing to tell him. How can she promise him that things will return to normal? How can she promise that she will come for him when she does not have the money? Why unsettle him with false promises if in the end he has to stay where he is? It has been six years already. Her eldest daughter will be eighteen soon; Irene has been separated from her for such a lot of her young life. It pains her to think of what she has missed, how much of their growing up she has not been able to share. Well now she wants to be around for them; she wants to make up for lost time. She is not going to give up; there has to be something she can do to reunite her family.

Working with Patrick Donovan in the bookshop has helped; he directs her to newspaper articles on emigration and changes in government policy. She does not always understand what the articles are about but she can see that there has been a change in attitudes to separating children from their parents. Patrick usually advises her if anything is relevant and if it's worth writing to the people concerned. He says that the more people she contacts the more likely she is to shame someone into helping her to get them home. It sounded a good idea when he first said it but it does not seem to be working. That is the trouble with Patrick; he is too much of an idealist. He is a good man and he thinks everyone else is as willing to help as he is; but she knows that they are not.

The replies she receives to her letters range from '*We are very sorry to hear of your plight, but this is a matter for the Migration Department.*' to '*Although the Children's Act 1948 has tightened the control over migration regulations, in practice we have to rely on the expertise of the voluntary organisations.*' Patrick translates these as '*Sorry, can't help you, dear.*' He explained that although the Secretary of State is the one who legally gives the permission for children to be emigrated, in actual fact he leaves the practice and decision making to people like the Catholic Church and Barnados. The most common response she receives is along the lines of: '*We are sorry we cannot help you but we are sure that the migration of your children in 1940 was in their best interests.*' Nobody seems to be interested in bringing children back to Britain. They don't even mention it in their replies; it's as though she is asking for something that is so unheard of that they are sure they have misunderstood her.

'Another letter?' Patrick asks.

'Yes, but a lot of good it'll do.'

'Don't give up hope my dear; something will turn up.'

He says this to her every day and every day she replies:

'I won't ever give up hope.'

'That's the ticket.'

He wanders back into the shop; an old lady has come in. Irene can hear her high pitched voice; she is looking for a copy of 'Rebecca' by Daphne De Maurier.

She puts the cover on her typewriter; it's almost three o'clock. She will have to hurry if she is to get home before Leslie.

The house is empty; an air of desolation hangs over the place. She opens the window in the kitchen to let in some fresh air and switches on the wireless. One of the big bands is playing some dance music. She hums along as she begins to prepare the dinner. It's at times like this that she misses her Mum most; she was always in the kitchen in the afternoons baking. Even when there was little to be had in the shops her mother managed to make something for tea: rock cakes, scones, when she had eggs, a Victoria sponge, if she had a few scraps of cheddar, cheese straws, when there were apples on the tree in the yard, an apple pie. Irene takes a packet of Ginger-nut biscuits out of the cupboard; they will do to satisfy Leslie until his dinner is ready. Irene does not have time to bake even though she is only working part-time now.

'Mum?' a little voice calls.

'In the kitchen, Leslie.'

'Look what I've got, Mum.'

He holds up his exercise book for her to see.

'A gold star. Well done.'

'Miss Wise said it was the best story in the whole class,' he says proudly.

'You're such a clever boy.'

She bends down and kisses his forehead.

'What's to eat?'

She hands him the packet of biscuits.

'Just two mind. Your dinner will be ready soon.'

It's four months since her mother had a stroke; they had taken her straight to the hospital but there was nothing they could do for her. She died the next day. She shudders when she recalls that day; she does not know what she would have done if it had not been for George. He has been wonderful.

She takes the scrag end out of the cold box and begins to cut it into small chunks. It will make a nice stew; she has some potatoes, an onion and carrots. She will let it simmer for a couple of hours and then the meat will be nice and tender. She thinks back to the time when her father dug up his tiny lawn and planted potatoes and onions in it; those vegetables had been a life saver back then. Her mother had tried to keep the vegetable patch going after her husband died but she was not really up to it. Sometimes they gave sixpence to the boy next door to turn it over with the spade but the weeds would soon take over again. Lately George has suggested he digs it up and grows something but neither of them know much about gardening. Better to let it revert to being a lawn she tells him then Leslie can have somewhere to play.

She and George have been married for nearly three months; she twists her new wedding ring round and round, buffing up the shine as she does so. Just an old curtain ring really, she thinks, but what a lot it promises. She never thought he would ask her to marry him; she is four years older than him after all. But he did and they had spent their honeymoon taking Leslie to the zoo.

The stew prepared and simmering on the range, Irene makes herself a cup of tea and sits down. She will write to Grace she thinks and takes her daughter's last letter out of the kitchen drawer. It's a sad letter that tells her very little about her daughter or her life.

'*Dear Mum,*' she reads. '*I am well. God is looking after me. I hope you and the baby are well.*'

She still calls Leslie the baby even though Irene keeps reminding her that he is now five years old.

'*Teddy has been a bad bear and I have had to lock him in the cupboard until he says he is sorry. He must say 100 Hail Marys then God will forgive him.*

Your loving daughter Grace.'

Irene knows about Grace's attachment to her teddy bear because Maggie has told her about it, but she is very worried about her youngest daughter's attitude to poor Teddy. She seems to shower love on him one minute then punish him for no apparent reason the next. Irene wonders where Grace gets such strange ideas. Why lock her teddy bear in the cupboard for example? She does not say what heinous deed Teddy has committed to deserve this; just that he is a bad Teddy. She cannot imagine that her sunny little Grace has grown into a bully.

She picks up her pen and writes:

'My darling Grace,

Thank you for your lovely letter. I am sorry that Teddy has been misbehaving.'

She stops. This is ridiculous; it's a teddy bear after all. Maybe Grace does need a fantasy friend but this is going too far. She crumples up the paper and starts again:

'My darling Grace,

Thank you for your lovely letter. Have you heard from Maggie lately? Does she get to see you? Leslie is well; he got a gold star today for his story. It's all about trains.'

She hesitates; it's difficult to know what to write to Grace. Writing to Maggie is easy because she tells her about her friends and what she has been doing, but Grace does not reveal anything. Maggie has explained that the nuns read everything that Grace writes but she cannot see that this should be a problem. She wrote and told Grace about George but the child has not made a single mention of him in her letters. She wonders if she is angry with her for not being in touch earlier; she has tried to explain to her that she has been looking for her for years but again Grace made no response. She picks up the pen again; she will write about Leslie and what he has been doing. Maybe Grace will be more interested in that. She has not told Grace yet that her Nan has died; she does not want to upset her while she is so far away. She wonders if she even remembers her Nan.

When she finishes the letter she calls up to Leslie:

'Leslie, I'm writing to your sister Grace; do you want to send her one of your drawings?'

A couple of minutes later Leslie comes down, a drawing of the zoo in his hand.

'What about this one?'

'That's lovely; but it's one of your best. Are you sure you want to send her this one?'

He nods.

'That's OK,' he says and goes back upstairs.

Irene folds up the drawing carefully and puts it in the envelope. Tomorrow she will write to Maggie; she only wishes she had some good news to tell her. From her letters it's obvious that Maggie too is desperately trying to get them all back together but, like her, she is not having much success. That old feeling of desperation returns; how on earth is she going to get her children home again?

JEREMY ACTON-DUNN

Victoria places a cup of tea on the desk in front of him.

'Good morning,' she says with a cheery smile. 'Did you speak to Mr Shepherd? Did he have any advice on how we can reunite the Smith family?'

'Yes I did but it wasn't very encouraging. I don't think there's going to be any reunion in the near future. In fact he painted quite a bleak picture of their chances. Nobody wants to help to bring the children back. I told him that we'd tried everything this end: the Church, other voluntary bodies, the Ministry. It's impossible. There are too many children and not enough money to go round. Other things have higher priority than repatriating a couple of British kids. Anyway, as I've said before, and Phil agrees, the Australians want more immigrants, not less.'

'What about the Australian Embassy?'

'I've spoken to the Australian ambassador. He's not interested.'

'If we can't get them back here, why not see if there is some way of getting the mother to go to them,' Victoria suggests.

He sips his tea and looks at her.

'Funny enough, that's what Phil said. It's an interesting idea. Do you think Mrs Smith would consider emigrating?'

'Well the last time I saw her she told me that she had remarried. She's Mrs Wills now. She's married an old friend of her husband, a chap he was in the army with.'

'Ah. That might be a problem. There's the husband to consider. He might not want to emigrate. What does he do now he's in Civvy Street?'

'I'm not sure but according to what she said, he's a skilled man. I'm sure he'd have no problem being accepted,' Victoria says.

'If he wants to go, that is.'

'Yes, he might not want to uproot and emigrate to Australia.'

Jeremy picks up his tea and sips it slowly.

'It's an idea,' he says at last. 'When I talked to Bruce Masterstone the other day, he mentioned that they were setting up an assisted passage scheme to encourage people to emigrate.'

'The Australian ambassador?'

'Yes. You know, this might just be the answer. Let me look into it a bit more and in the meantime, ring her and ask if she can come in to see me.'

'Will do. Anything else?'

'Yes, get me the Australian Embassy on the line.'

Irene Smith, or Mrs Wills as she now is called, is sitting inside his office. Her face is still; sadness pulls at her mouth, causing her delicately curved lips to turn downwards. She looks up as he opens the door and smiles. Her face is transformed and he understands why she has had no problem finding another husband, despite having four children. She is a very attractive woman.

'Mrs Wills. I'm glad you could make it.'

'Is there any news?' she asks eagerly.

'Not the sort you are hoping for, no. I'm sorry.'

'Is it bad news?'

The smile fades from her lips.

'No. No. It's just that I have had an idea on how we can reunite you with your family. I just wanted to see what you think about it.'

She looks at him expectantly.

'Do you think your new husband would consider moving to Australia to live?' he asks.

'To Australia? Well I don't know. We've never thought about it. George has never said anything. Anyway I don't see how we could. If we had the money for the three of us to go to Australia then we'd have enough money to get the girls home. No, it's never been a possibility. Even with the two of us working we barely have enough money to live on.'

'But if we could get you assisted passages, do you think he would consider it?'

'I really don't know.'

'What about you? Would you like to go to Australia?'

'If it means I can see my children again, yes I'd go. I'd go anywhere to have us all back together again.'

'Your husband was a soldier, I believe?'

She nods. A brown curl of hair drops across her forehead and she pushes it away with a gloved hand.

'Which regiment was he in?'

'He was with my Ronnie. They were both sappers.'

'Royal Engineers?'

'Yes, that's right.'

'So what sort of work does he do now, since he was demobbed?'

'He has a job in a timber yard. That's all he could get. But before that he was a motor mechanic. He worked with a bus company up north.'

'So he has a trade?'

'Yes.'

'The Australian government are looking for skilled men. I think you'd have a good chance of going out on this new scheme.'

'Well I'll talk to him about it but I don't know what he'll say. After all he's got a steady job now. It's not what he's been used to doing but the money's regular and it pays the bills.'

She looks doubtful.

'Talk to him about it,' Jeremy says.

He hands her a poster. It has 'AUSTRALIA, LAND OF TOMORROW' blazoned across the top and underneath there are drawings of horses, sheep and tractors. A big yellow sun shines down on it all.

'I don't understand,' she says.

'This is the new recruitment poster. The Australian government want immigrants. It's a big country and they don't have enough people. It's as simple as that. I thought, if you and your husband were eligible for the scheme it would be a good way of reuniting you with your family.'

She takes the poster from him and stares at it.

'It's supposed to be a very beautiful country,' he adds. 'Anyway here is some more information about eligibility and how the scheme works. Look through it and see what he thinks. See what you both think.'

'I will.'

'It may be the only way you will get to see your children again,' he reminds her.

As soon as the door shuts behind Mrs Wills, Victoria comes in.

'Well? What did she say?' she asks.

'She's going to talk to her husband about it.'

'Do you think she'll go?'

'I've no idea. I hope she does. It's going to be her only chance. It's a great opportunity for them but in the end it will depend on her husband.'

IRENE

The dinner is on the table when George gets home. Without waiting to take off his jacket, he comes straight across and kisses her.

'Smells good,' he says.

'Me or the food?' she asks.

'Both.'

She wants to tell him the news straight away but she is frightened he will not be as excited about it as she is. The thought of disappointment is bitter in her mouth.

'Leslie, dinner,' she shouts.

She watches George pick up his knife and fork and begin to eat. Maybe she should wait, sound him out first, introduce the idea gradually.

'What is it?' he asks.

'What?'

'You, you've got something to tell me; I can tell. What is it?'

He tries to smile but his mouth is full of potato.

'Hi, Dad,' says Leslie, sitting down beside him.

He has taken to calling George, Dad; she has never asked him to and now sees no reason why not. After all he never knew his real father. All these years he has been one of those boys whose father was killed in the war; now he tells everyone he has a step-father. He is such a quiet boy that she never really knows what is going on in his head but he seems happy that she and George are married. He enjoys having a man in the house.

'Your Mum has something to tell us,' he says. 'Haven't you, Irene?'

He gives her a playful dig in the ribs.

'What is it Mum?'

'Let your Dad eat his dinner in peace?'

'Not until you've told us what you're up to,' George says, putting down his knife and fork and looking at her.

'How would you like to go and live in Australia?' she asks.

'What?'

Her husband looks at her, dumbfounded. Whatever he had been expecting her to say, it was not this.

'Australia?' Leslie gasps. 'That's a long way away. That's the other side of the world. That's where Maggie is, and Grace, and Billy. They're in Australia.'

Irene takes the poster out of the sideboard drawer and puts it in front of them.

'I went to see Mr Acton-Dunn today. He told me about this assisted passage scheme to Australia. They're trying to recruit people to migrate to Australia; they want fit, able-bodied men and their families. He thought it might be the answer to our prayers.'

George picks up his knife and fork and continues to eat his meal.

'Well George, what do you think? Shall we go to Australia?' she asks.

Her stomach is churning with anxiety. What will he say? This could be her only chance of seeing her children again.

'But what do you know about going to Australia?' George asks.

'It's the chance of a new life,' she says weakly.

'You're suggesting we up-sticks and go half-way round the world just because this bloke says it's a good idea. How does he know what's good for this family?'

He is not angry but she can tell he is not as excited at the prospect of emigrating as she is. He looks more worried than angry.

'It's not that he's trying to tell us what to do; he only wants to help. He says if we can't get them to send the kids back to us then we could go to them. It makes sense.'

'To you maybe. But you're asking me to give up my job and go back to job-hunting, only this time in a strange country. I'm not sure I'm ready for that. What if I don't find work? How will we live? It was bad enough when I was demobbed, going from door to door looking for a job, but at least I only had myself to worry about then. Now I have you and Leslie to look after.'

'But they need skilled men in Australia. Mr Acton-Dunn said that you'd have no trouble finding work. You get the job organised before you go. I was talking to Liz about it; her brother is going. He has a job in a furniture factory. Got all the papers and everything; he sails at the end of the month, for Victoria.'

'Victoria? Melbourne's the capital of Victoria,' Leslie says. 'That's where Maggie lives.'

George pours some tea into his mug.

'But what's the difference? We don't have the money either way.'

Her smile is even broader now. She is determined to convince him.

'That's the beauty of it; they pay our fares. It's what they call an assisted passage. We have to pay something, but not much, ten pounds or something. I have all the details here.'

She hands him the leaflets that Mr Acton-Dunn gave her.

'Are you sure I'll be able to get work?' he asks as he flicks through the papers.

'Look George, this is what we've always wanted, to get the kids back. You said yourself that the work prospects here are not good right now. Out there you could get a much better job; they're crying out for engineers. What with your experience in the sappers and with the bus corporation you'll have no problem finding work. We could all have a better life,' she adds.

'You think I could get a job sorted out before we leave?'

'Yes, they advise you on everything.'

'But what about all this?'

He waves his hand around, meaning the furniture.

'We'll just take what we really need: clothes, things that we're really fond of, like photos, stuff like that. We won't need much; we'll rent a furnished place at first until you get on your feet.'

'Can I take my books?' Leslie asks.

'Of course, but only the ones you really want. There's bound to be a limit on weight, I'm sure.'

'What about your job?' he asks.

'I'll get another job if I need one.'

He takes her hand in his. He is warming to the idea.

'Well I never expected this,' he says. 'You've had some hair-brained ideas in your time but this beats everything.'

'So? What do you think?' she asks him. 'It'll be a new life for us.'

'Will we go on a ship?' Leslie asks.

She can see that he, at least, is excited at the prospect of this adventure.

'Yes, a big liner,' she tells him.

'Will we see kangaroos? And koala bears?'

'Yes and yes,' she replies. 'You'll see all that and more.'

'I suppose it's worth thinking about,' George says, looking at her and smiling.

'Yes and I could always find some work out there,' Irene says. 'Although I'll be sad to give up my job at the bookshop.'

'I'm sure you will but they must need typists in Australia as well.'

'So what do you say?' she asks.

'Well it can't hurt to make enquiries, can it?' he says at last.

'I knew you'd agree. You'll see; it'll be great for all of us,' she says, putting her arms around him and hugging him.

'All right then, we'll go and find out about it tomorrow. I'll take an extra hour off and we'll go in my lunch hour.'

She wants to cry. Maybe now she will get to see her children again.

MAGGIE

She cannot wait for Mrs R to come home; she is dying to tell her the news. The sound of the front door opening tells her that she has arrived. Maggie bounds down the stairs to greet her.

'Hello there. What's got into you?' her landlady asks, as she puts her shopping on the kitchen table. 'You seem very excited about something.'

'I've got some news.'

'Good I hope. Put the kettle on, dear, I'm parched.'

'I've had another letter from Mum,' Maggie begins, as she fills the kettle from the tap. 'She's coming to live in Australia, her and Leslie and George.'

'Well, I never. You'd better sit down before you break something and tell me all about it.'

Maggie can hardly contain her excitement.

'They could never have afforded it but there's some special scheme; it's called ...' she pauses and refers to the letter. 'Assisted passage. It's new. They will be the first people to come here on it. George has had to give up his job and he's already had an offer of a new one here.'

'That certainly sounds like good news to me.'

The kettle starts to whistle and Maggie pours the boiling water over the tea leaves.

'She says they want fit, able-bodied men and their families to emigrate to Australia and the Australian government are going to pay their fares.'

She puts the teapot on the table and sits down.

'It's wonderful, isn't it Mrs R.'

'It is indeed, Maggie.'

Maggie takes some cups from the rack.

'What else does your Mum say? Does she know where they'll be going? Australia is a big place,' Mrs Robinson asks.

'Victoria. That's here, isn't it? They're going to rent a place at first for the three of them then look for somewhere where we can all live. Mum says that George can get a much better job here; she says that they are desperate for engineers. He was in the Royal Engineers, you know, like Dad.'

'So you'll get to see your Mum at last.'

'Yes, won't it be wonderful. I can't wait to tell Grace.'

'Does she say when they're coming?'

'They have to wait for all the paperwork to go through but she thinks it will be before Christmas.'

'Quite soon then.'

'Yes, isn't it wonderful news,' she repeats.

She is so excited she cannot keep still.

'So you'll be leaving then?' Mrs Robinson asks.

'When they've found somewhere for us to live.'

Mrs Robinson gives a sigh; she looks sad.

'Why, what's the matter, Mrs R?'

'I'll miss you Maggie, I've got so used to having you about the house, it'll be strange without you. You've become like a daughter to me.'

Maggie leans over and hugs her.

'I'll come back and see you, I promise.'

'Mind you do, now.'

'Shall I pour the tea?'

'Yes, do that dear, and don't drown it in milk this time.'

Maggie is impatient to tell Grace the news. She knows there is no point writing to her; it's best to go and see her sister for herself. She has not let the nuns know that she is coming this time; she is just going to turn up and ask to see her. She remembers how the nuns used to scurry around making the girls clean themselves up before any visitors arrived; she wants to see how Grace really is and, to do that, it's best to arrive unannounced.

As she walks up the familiar dirt road towards the orphanage she hopes her actions are not going to rebound on her sister. She hugs her parcel tightly to her chest and walks on. The gate is open and it's easy to slip inside. She decides to go straight to look for Grace. If the nuns catch her she will say she was looking for Sister Bridget.

The girls are already moving towards the chapel for morning prayers; she hopes she can catch Grace before she goes in. She knows Grace will be in the senior dormitory now so she edges her way along the dormitory wall, hoping that no-one will spot her. She sees Freda, Grace's friend, coming out of the building.

'Freda,' she hisses.

'Maggie. What are you doing here?'

'I want to see Grace. Where is she?'

'She's in the sick bay. She's not well.'

'What's the matter with her?'

'Look I've got to go; Sister Agnes is on the warpath again. She's really got it in for me these days.'

Freda pulls up her dress and shows Maggie the partially healed scars on the backs of her legs.

'Be careful she doesn't catch you,' she warns before scurrying away to the chapel.

Maggie feels sick. Seeing Freda's scarred legs has brought it all back to her; she can feel the pain and humiliation as if it were yesterday. The nuns beat them for the slightest offence: not knowing your tables, getting a spelling wrong and especially for making mistakes with the catechism. She hopes Grace is not in the infirmary because she has been beaten too. She waits in the shadow of the veranda until she sees the last of the girls enter the chapel and the door swing shut then she heads for the sick bay. She knows that none of the nuns will be there until after breakfast.

There are three girls in the infirmary; Grace is in the bed at the far end. She does not look up when Maggie enters.

'Grace.'

Grace turns and looks at her blankly.

'Grace, it's me Maggie.'

She bends down and kisses her.

'Maggie is it really you? What are you doing here?' Grace asks at last.

She looks around the room nervously.

'Does Sister Agnes know you're here?'

'No, nobody knows I'm here.'

'They say I'm not well.'

Grace sits up in the bed. Maggie realises that she has grown a lot since Christmas but she is still very thin. She takes hold of her hand; the bones are like those of a tiny bird and her nails are bitten to the quick. She is wearing a faded nightdress that is much too big for her and this emphasises her frailness. Maggie wants to weep with despair. She strokes her sister's hair; it's dry and brittle like straw. Her golden curls are gone, her hair cut short and burnt by the sun.

'You're very thin Grace. Are you eating enough? I've brought you something. Look, some bananas. You like bananas.'

She realises that although Grace is almost nine years old, she has lapsed into talking to her just as she used to do when she was a toddler.

'Thank you but I'm not hungry.'

Maggie cannot believe what she is hearing. All the girls are half starved. No-one would ever refuse some fresh bananas.

'What's the problem Gracie? Why don't you want to eat?'

Grace shrugs.

'I'm not hungry.'

'Are you ill? Have the nuns said what is the matter with you?'

She shakes her head.

'Well something must be wrong with you, otherwise you wouldn't be in here.'

'I fainted,' Grace admits at last.

'It's probably because you're not eating, darling. You have to eat to keep your strength up.'

Grace nods.

'That's what Sister Bridget said. She brought me some honey from the kitchen.'

'Did she? Was it nice?'

Sister Bridget was the only nun there that didn't go out of her way to make the girls' lives a misery.

'It was sweet. The bees make it.'

'Has Mum written to you?'

'Yes.'

'Did you manage to read her letters all right?'

'Yes, I can read fine now. Susie doesn't have to help me anymore. She's left now.'

'Well that's good isn't it?'

Grace doesn't reply.

'Do you understand that Mum has been looking for us all this time, don't you Gracie? She has been as worried as we have.'

'She doesn't come to see me.'

'Well she can't, not yet. She's still in London. You remember London, don't you? It's a long way away. But we'll see her soon.'

'I want to go home. I don't like it here.'

'You will, darling. You will. I have some very special news for you today. Mum is coming to Australia. She is coming here to live with us. You'll be able to leave the orphanage and go to live with her again.'

'She doesn't want me. She has a new family now,' Grace blurts out.

'What? No, of course she wants you. Don't be silly. She loves us all. That's why she is coming here. They are all coming, George and Leslie too.'

'She has a new family now,' Grace repeats. 'She doesn't love me anymore.'

She won't look at Maggie; her head is down and she sits there twisting her hands together, over and over.

'That's not true Grace, of course she loves you.'

Maggie takes her hand in hers again.

'She's got Leslie,' Grace murmurs.

'Yes, I know, but Leslie is our brother. He's not a new family. He's our little brother.'

'Freda says now that Mum is married again, she will have more babies and then she won't want me anymore.'

'Well Freda is wrong. Freda doesn't know Mum. Mum would never abandon you. I told you she's been searching for us for years. She never gave up. And now she's found us.'

'Then why doesn't she send for me?'

Maggie does not know what to say. How can she explain to her sister that her mother has been doing all she can to get them back? How can she explain about the wall of bureaucracy that she has come up against? How can she explain that nobody except their mother cares whether they go home or not?

'She wanted to, Gracie but in the end she has decided to come here and get you herself.'

Grace looks at her and for a moment a shadow of a smile crosses her face.

'She is coming to get me?'

'Yes.'

'Really?'

'Yes, really. Very soon.'

'She is going to take me away from here?'

'Yes.'

'When? Today?'

'No, sweetheart, not today. She is still in London but soon, very soon. You must be patient, Gracie. She says she will be here before Christmas. Look, I've got a letter from her. Would you like me to read it to you?'

Grace nods.

'My dear Maggie,

I have some wonderful news for you. We will all be together again very soon. As we could find no way of getting you and Grace and Billy back to England we have decided to come to Australia instead. We will be together and you will be able to meet your little brother for the first time ... '

She reads the letter to Grace then reads it again just for the joy of hearing what it says. The nightmare will soon be over. They will be reunited. Even Grace looks a little happier at the news.

'Billy?'

'Yes, Billy. We know where he is now.'

'Is he happy?'

'Yes; he's learning to be a farmer.'

She has not written to Grace about Billy's new life on the farm because she did not want the nuns to find out; she was worried that they would send someone to look for him.

'Does Billy know that I'm here?' Grace asks.

'Yes. I write to him every month.'

'Tell him I miss him,' Grace says and starts to weep.

'Of course I will, darling. Now, don't cry, Gracie. You'll be out of here soon. You must be strong. Please, Gracie, promise me you'll be a strong girl.'

She puts her arms around her sister and hugs her. She can feel her ribs sticking out through the nightdress.

'It'll be all right, you see. Mum will be here soon and then she'll take you home.'

They are both sobbing now.

'We'll all be together again, like before,' Maggie whispers, wiping her eyes surreptitiously.

She does not want Grace to see her upset but it's hard to control her emotions; her sister is no longer the bouncy child that lived in Bethnal Green. What will Mum make of the change in her?

Gradually Grace's sobs stop and she sits back, pulling at the bed sheet. Maggie takes a corner of the sheet in one hand and wipes Grace's eyes with it.

'And you'll eat. Promise me that.'

'Yes.'

She peels back the skin of one of the bananas and hands one to her sister. Tentatively Grace starts to eat it. She has trouble swallowing it.

'Is it good?'

She nods.

'Can I give one to Jilly?' she asks.

Jilly is in the next bed.

'Of course. Here, Jilly, would you like a banana?'

A dark skinned little girl, who has been lying there watching them all this time, stretches out her hand and eagerly takes the fruit. Maggie looks at the third occupant of the sick bay; she is a girl of barely five years old. She is watching and listening to all that is going on.

'Would you like one?' Maggie asks.

'Yes, please.'

'Well that leaves one more for you, Grace, for later. Let's hide it under your pillow,' Maggie says.

A bell rings.

'That's the breakfast bell,' Grace says. 'You have to go.'

She seems a bit brighter now.

'Are you sure you'll be all right?'

'Yes.'

'You get my letters don't you?'

'Yes. I have them all.'

'Well I'll keep writing to you and as soon as I know that Mum is on the boat, I'll let you know. It won't be long now.'

'Please go,' she says.

Grace is becoming agitated. Maggie knows why she is so frightened and it makes her angry but there is nothing she can do about it. If she is caught in the sick bay it will be Grace that is punished.

'OK Gracie. Bye darling. Take care of yourself now and eat.'

'I will. Promise. Bye bye Maggie.'

She slips down beneath the sheets and closes her eyes. Maggie does not want to leave her but she knows she has to; it will only cause more trouble if she is caught in here with her. It's not for much longer, she tells herself. Soon she'll have Grace home. She blinks back the tears in her eyes and hurries out. Everyone is heading for the refectory. Soon someone will bring the breakfast for the girls in the sick bay. She must be gone before that.

It's late afternoon by the time she arrives back in Melbourne. She is due to meet Jimmy at seven o'clock but she decides she must go home first to freshen up; she is hot and sticky and her shoes are covered in yellow dust. The meeting with Grace has worried her. She had not realised until then just how unhappy her sister was and she is puzzled by her behaviour; it's as though she is still five years old. Maggie does not know what she can do to help her. She was tempted to take Grace home with her today, just as she was, nightdress and all, but she knew it would not have worked. They would have sent the police after them and taken her straight back to the orphanage. Thank goodness her mother is coming soon. Poor Grace has been there for nearly six years; she doesn't remember what it was like to have a normal life.

'Hello there, where have you been all day?' asks Mrs Robinson.

'I've been to see my sister,' she replies.

'Well come and have a cup of tea and a Brownie; they're fresh from the oven. Then you can tell me all about it.'

Maggie is pleased to see Mrs Robinson's cheerful face; she has come to rely on her landlady's support. She is going to miss her when she leaves. She gratefully accepts the tea and settles down to relate the events of the day.

'So the poor little mite thinks she's been abandoned,' Mrs Robinson says pouring herself another cup of tea.

'Yes, but she was a bit more cheerful after I read her Mum's letter.'

'Of course she was. You see the time will pass more quickly than you expect and before you know it that mum of yours will be whisking her out of that place and back to a normal life.'

The clock on the mantlepiece strikes five o'clock.

'Oh, is that the time? I'm seeing Jimmy tonight; I'd better hurry.'

'Going to the pictures?' her landlady asks.

'Yes, "Gone With The Wind".'

'Oh, I love that film, that Clark Gable,' she sighs and rolls her eyes towards the ceiling.

Maggie laughs.

'It's one of Mum's favourites as well.'

It's nice. Now she can talk about Mum without feeling sad. She knows for certain that her mother is alive and that she will see her again soon. She just has to be patient.

BILLY

Billy loads the last of his possessions into the hand cart and pushes it towards the house. He is moving back into the farmhouse with Henry and Sarah. They have told him he can have his old room back now that Jack is moving out. He said that he was all right in the stables but Sarah has insisted. It will be warmer in winter and cooler in the summer she told him and there won't be so many flies. It's true, her house is wonderfully cool compared to the room above the stables and the fly screens she has put at every window and door keep the flies from invading the house. Sleeping above the animals can be a nightmare in the hot weather but he has never complained because he enjoys the privilege of having a space to himself.

'Need a hand?' Jack asks.

'No, I'm fine thanks. This is almost the last. There's just the bed. Emily says you want it for the spare room.'

'Yes, that's right.'

'I'll give you a hand to take it over later,' Billy says.

Jack and Emily have just moved into their new house. They were married two weeks earlier. Billy has been helping Jack build the house; they have worked on it every day, cutting the timber and laying the bricks themselves. It has been a slow business trying to do it in between working on the farm but at last it's finished, the last coat of paint barely dry. Each time Billy walks past the new building with its wide, wooden veranda, he feels a burst of pride. Who would have thought he and Jack could build a house like that all on their own. Emily has helped too, in her own way. He has grown very fond of Emily. Before they were married she used to ride over on her old pony and make suggestions and sometimes she would bring Adaline with her. Emily had clear ideas on such things as the size of the windows, how big the kitchen should be and she even insisted on an inside toilet. This was the latest innovation and has caused them the biggest headache but that was what Emily wanted and so that was what Jack had to do. The dimensions of the rooms in the house are identical, with nothing to distinguish one from the other, but it was Emily who decided that their bedroom should be the one facing east so that it received the morning sun and that the lounge should face west. The third room was designated as a guest room until any children came along. He remembers how she blushed when she said that.

Henry is sitting in his usual chair on the porch; Billy can see that he has been dozing. He spends a lot of time dozing these days. It has taken a long time for his broken ankle to heal, much longer than the month the doctor originally estimated and since then Henry has not done as much work on the farm as he used to. These days he is happy to delegate most of the heavy tasks to Jack and Billy.

'Hey, Billy, there's another letter for you,' he calls.

'OK Boss, I'll be right over.'

He trundles the cart up the ramp he has placed on the steps and pushes it into the house.

'Hang on there Billy. You're not bringing that filthy cart through my clean kitchen; just leave it there by the door,' Sarah tells him.

She has a mop in her hand.

'Sorry,' he says, in mock fear.

He unloads the last of his possessions: Beth's bed, some boots, his working clothes and his wood carvings.

'And don't even think that Beth is sleeping in your room. She can sleep on the veranda with the other dogs.'

'But Sarah, she's used to sleeping with me.'

'Maybe, but it won't hurt her to learn that dogs sleep outside.'

Reluctantly he puts her bed down on the veranda.

'She can guard you just as well from there,' she adds.

'Here,' he says. 'I did this for you.'

He hands one of the wood carvings to Sarah. It's a plaque about a foot square and he has engraved the words: 'HOME SWEET HOME' on it.

'Oh Billy, that's lovely. I'll put it right there by the door. Maybe you could knock a nail in for me later?'

He nods. He is pleased that she likes it; it took him quite a while to carve and he had to check the spelling of the words with Jack first. He thinks he might do one for Jack's new house as well.

'Do you like the kangaroo?' he asks.

He has engraved a kangaroo on one side and a bird on the other. He likes engraving animals. John T taught him how to do it but John T does not make things like this; he usually whittles away at sticks, carving strange aboriginal patterns on them. Sometimes Billy copies the designs and John T tells him what they represent.

'I do; it's lovely.'

'The boss says there's another letter for me,' he tells her.

'From your sister, I expect.'

'Probably.'

'Let me know if you want to write a reply,' she says.

She dips her mop back into the bucket.

'Now, move along and let me finish this floor.'

He dumps his things on the bed and goes out to collect his letter.

'Everything moved out now?' asks Henry.

'Yes.'

'So we can store some of the hay up there then?'

'Yes, or the sacks of winter feed.'

Henry hands him the letter. Billy squints at it.

'What's the matter?' asks Henry.

'It's not from Maggie; she doesn't write like that.'

'Well open it and see who it's from.'

Billy pulls open the seal and takes out the letter. He feels apprehensive. Ever since Maggie has been in touch with him he has had this constant feeling of unease, as though something is going to disrupt his well defined life.

'I'm not sure,' he says. 'Here, you read it for me.'

Henry takes the letter from him. He fiddles in his pocket until he finds his reading glasses and puts them on the end of his nose.

'*Dear Billy,*' he begins. '*You will be very surprised to receive this letter I am sure and you may be wondering why it has taken me so long to get in touch with you. It has taken a long time to find out where you were living. For many years I thought that you and your sisters were dead, killed in the Blitz all those years ago. But now I have found you all and I thank God for being so good to me.*'

Henry stops and turns the letter over.

'It's from your mother,' he explains. 'I thought you said your mother was dead.'

'That's what they told us, the nuns. They said she was dead. They said she was in Heaven. Why would they say that if it wasn't true?' Billy asks.

He still can't believe it. Maggie had written and told him that Mum was alive but he hadn't believed her; Maggie was always saying Mum was alive. He had torn up the letter. It didn't make sense. Why would Mum allow them to be taken to Australia if she was alive? Now here was a letter from her. Proof that she didn't die. He doesn't know what to think. It's so wrong. He is angry with her.

'Well that's what it says. Maybe the nuns made a mistake. It was during the war after all,' Henry says.

Billy is confused. He does not know what to think. He had been so sure that his mother was dead, despite what Maggie said. She had always believed that Mum and Leslie were still alive but he hadn't. It does not make sense. If Mum is alive then where has she been all this time? Why has it taken her so long to find them?

'Shall I go on?' asks Henry.

'Yes, Boss.'

'*When Maggie gave me your address, I was so happy and I was going to write to you straight away. But then I was worried that if I wrote it might upset you. The truth is that when Maggie told me how well you had settled in your new home, I didn't know what to do for the best, especially as I could find no way of bringing any of you home. I am so very pleased that you are happy. You are lucky that you have met such nice people.*

I know that the last thing you want is to be uprooted again and have to start afresh but I would so love to see you Billy. I am coming to Australia to live.'

Henry stops.

'Well, that's a turn up for the books,' he says.

'What does she mean, she's coming to Australia?' Billy asks. 'Is she coming here?'

'Hold your horses. Let me finish reading it.'

'I have remarried and we are all emigrating to Australia to be near you. By all, I mean your little brother Leslie and George, my new husband. I don't expect you remember George. He was the soldier who came to tell us how your dad died, all those years ago.'

'Yes, I remember him. He came to our house,' Billy says.

Like a series of photos flashing before his eyes he sees his old home and the street with the brown doors.

'We had a blue front door,' he tells Henry. 'It was the only one in the street.'

Henry smiles at him and continues reading the letter:

'There are lots of forms to fill out and we have to wait for an available passage but I expect we will arrive in Melbourne sometime in December. Then I will get Grace out of that awful orphanage and she will live with us. I do hope we can see you. Please write to me,

Your loving Mum xxxx.'

Henry folds the letter and hands it back to Billy.

'I don't have to go, do I?' Billy asks. 'I won't have to leave here?'

'I don't know son. I don't know much about these things. Better ask Jack.'

'I've got to ride into town now,' Billy tells him. 'Jack needs some things.'

He doesn't want to think about it any more. His head feels muddled.

'Well, before you go, I've got something for you.'

Henry reaches into his pocket and pulls out a wad of money.

'Here, this is your wages. I've been thinking; you do a man's work these days so you deserve a man's wage. Now don't go and spend it all in one go. There's no more until next month.'

Billy does not know what to say. He takes the money and puts it in his back pocket. It's the first money of his own that he has ever had.

'Thanks, Boss.'

'Well you run along then. Ask Sarah if she needs you to get anything for her before you go.'

'OK Boss.'

Later that night he takes the letter out again and looks at it. The writing is very small and neat, not at all like Maggie's untidy scrawl. His mind is in turmoil; he does not know what to do. He would like to go over and talk to Jack but now that Jack's married it's impossible; he spends every evening with Emily. They have both said that Billy can go over to the house whenever he wants but he is too shy to go uninvited. He could speak to John T but he does not think that the stockman will have much to say about it. John T does not say much about anything; 'a man of few words' Sarah calls him. Henry has already made it clear that he does not know what to advise, so that only leaves Sarah. He knows where she will be. Every evening, when the sun is setting and all her work is finished, she sits on the back porch with her knitting. She stays there, her needles clicking in time to the rocking of her chair, until the light has gone and she has to go inside. He tucks the letter in his back pocket and goes out on to the porch.

'Sarah, can I talk to you?'

'Of course Billy, what is it? Is it about that letter from your mother?'

'Yes.'

'Bit of a surprise was it?'

'Yes.'

'Want me to help you write a reply?'

He nods.

Sarah knits on in silence. She is waiting for him to speak.

'I don't know what to say to her,' he confesses at last. 'I don't really remember her.'

'Well that's not surprising; you were only a little lad when you last saw her, after all.'

'But I should remember my Mum, shouldn't I?'

'Well sometimes the memory is a funny thing. Sometimes our minds stop us remembering things that cause us pain. Perhaps your mind shut out the memories of your mother because they made you unhappy.'

'No, I don't think so. I remember being on the ship. I just don't remember much before that.'

'So what's worrying you? The fact that you don't remember what she looks like? You could ask her to send you a photo.'

'It's not just that. She says she wants to see me; she says she's coming to Australia to live.'

'Yes, Henry told me. Well that's good news, isn't it?'

He nods.

'It's only normal that your mother wants to see you after all these years; she must have missed you very much. Remember how much we missed Jack while he was away in the war. I understand how she feels.'

'But I don't know what to do. I don't want to go. I want to see her but I don't want to leave here.'

His voice is trembling now. He cannot face the prospect of leaving the farm. Just the idea of it gives him a pain in his stomach. He is frightened that if he leaves here he will never be able to return.

'Billy, you know you don't have to leave here. Henry's told you that we want you to stay. We need your help. And besides which, we love you,' she adds.

'But what if they make me? What if they say I have to live with my Mum?'

'Who?'

'The police.'

'Now why would they want to do that? You're almost a grown man now. You're fifteen, nearly sixteen.'

'But they might.'

She shakes her head.

'I don't think anyone wants to make you do something you don't want to Billy. Your mother just wants to know that you're all right. She just wants to see you.'

'But where has she been all this time?' he asks, his voice hurt and angry.

'Didn't she say in her letter?'

'She said she's been looking for us. She thought we were dead but she still kept looking.'

'Well, think how awful it has been for her all these years, not knowing if you were alive or dead. She must be so happy to have found you at last.'

Billy wipes a tear away with the sleeve of his shirt.

'Maybe I should go and see her,' he says. 'She is my Mum.'

He is becoming agitated. He does not know which way to turn. He is being pulled between his loyalty to Henry and Sarah and his loyalty to his mother. On top of which he feels guilty for being so happy here.

'Well I thought Henry told me that no-one is able to go anywhere at the moment. Your mother is still in London. Why don't you stop worrying about it until we know when your mother is actually going to arrive?'

'Yes.'

'She says in her letter that she is pleased that you have a found a good home. I don't think she is going to make you go to live with her if you don't want to. She just wants to see you.'

'Yes. I could get the bus and go to see her. I have some money now. Henry gave me some wages,' he tells her.

Sarah laughs.

'You'll be away forever if you go on the bus,' she says. 'No. If you decide to go, Jack will drive you to Perth and you'll get the train. It's a long way you know.'

Sarah puts down her knitting and looks at him.

'Do you still want to write to her?'

'Yes please.'

'So what do you want to tell her?'

'I'll tell her about living here with you and Henry, about Beth, about John T and the sheep and about Lady.'

'That's a good idea. Maybe if she learns more about your life she'll understand why you don't want to leave.'

'And about Jack and Emily and the house,' he continues. 'And that I'll come and see her when she's in Melbourne but I'm coming back here afterwards.'

He is feeling better. Sarah is right; there is no point worrying about things that have not happened yet. That is what John T always says. Only John T never seems to worry about anything. He says that you cannot change your destiny; your life is written in the Dreaming long before you are born.

'All right, we'll make a start on it when I go inside.'

'Do you need anything?' he asks.

'No, I'm fine, I'm just going to stay here a bit longer and watch the sunset.'

'I'll go and check on the horses then.'

Whenever he feels nervous or anxious he goes to see the horses. Jack says he has a special relationship with the horses; they always quieten down when Billy is about and surprisingly they have the same effect on him. Whenever Jed Sparks, the vet, comes over to treat one of them Jack tells Billy to go with him; that way the horse is much calmer. He does not know why it is. He does not do anything special but none of the horses are nervous when he is around. It's as though they trust him to look after them; he understands them and they understand him.

What he would really like, when he is older, he confided once to Jack, is to own a stud farm and breed horses. Jack took him to the races at Longton Creek last year, to see the harness racing; that had been fun. He fancies trying his hand at hitching Lady to a sulky and racing her at Longton one day. Jack says it's a good idea and maybe they should think about entering the Melbourne Cup but Billy knows that Jack is just joking; he is not that interested in horse racing now that he has the house and Emily to think about.

Lady sends up a whinny of greeting when he enters her stall. The other horses shift their feet nervously at first, unsure of what is happening and then settle down once they realise it's only Billy.

'Hello there, girl,' he says, stroking her neck gently. 'How's my beauty today then?'

She pushes her muzzle towards him, nudging him affectionately.

'I suppose you want a carrot, do you?'

He reaches in his pocket and pulls out a carrot that he has pinched from Sarah's store cupboard.

'Here you are then.'

She munches it greedily.

'I've had a letter from my Mum, Lady. She wants me to go and see her,' he tells her.

The horse's brown eyes look at him, waiting for more.

'But I'm not going to leave here. I've made my mind up. No matter what Maggie says or Sarah, I'm staying here. I'll go and visit her, but this is where I belong,' he tells the horse. 'It's like John T says, it's written in the Dreaming.'

He strokes the horse's neck again; her coat is warm and smooth. He cannot leave here. He cannot go away from Lady and Beth. He knows that now. This is his destiny.

MAGGIE

There is a knock on the door.

'Get that, will you Maggie,' Mrs Robinson calls from the kitchen.

She is dishing up the evening meal.

'OK,' Maggie calls.

She opens the door. A youth, wearing a bush hat, is standing there.

'Yes?'

'Is that you, Maggie?' he asks.

'Billy.'

She cannot believe her eyes. Can this be her little brother, this tall, young man? She knew he was coming; he had written that he wanted to see Mum. Is this him, at last?

'Billy, is it really you?' she asks, staring at him.

'Can I come in?'

'Who is it, Maggie?' Mrs Robinson asks, coming into the hall.

'It's Billy.'

'Well let him in then. Don't keep him standing on the door-step. Come in lad. My, you're a sight for sore eyes. You'll never know how much we've wanted this day to arrive.'

Billy steps into the hall and drops his bag on the floor.

'Hello Maggie,' he says.

She cannot speak. Tears are streaming down her face. She reaches up and hugs him, clinging on to him as though she never wants to let go of him again, until Mrs Robinson says:

'Let the poor lad go, Maggie; you're embarrassing him. Well Billy, are you hungry lad?'

'Starved. I've only eaten an apple and a bit of bread all day.'

'Well you've timed it just right. We're just having some dinner. A nice pot of kangaroo stew.'

Billy smiles and Maggie sees the boy he used to be, cheeky and full of fun. He may be older, taller, burnt brown by the sun, his curls may have been shorn but he is still the Billy she knew. The boy that nothing could keep down.

'My favourite. Sarah gave me a hamper full of food for the journey,' he tells them, 'but it soon went. The train ride seemed to go on for ever.'

'How long did it take you to get here?' Maggie asks.

'Almost a week.'

'Goodness me. Were you walking?' Mrs Robinson asks with a laugh.

'Just from the station,' he replies with a wink at Maggie.

'You look as though you could do with a bit of a clean-up. Maggie take him out back and show him where the sink is while I finish dishing up the stew.'

'OK. This way Billy.'

'Then take him through and introduce him to the others.'

Billy is instantly at home and soon is telling them all about his journey and life on the sheep station where he lives. He had slept on the train and, when the hamper of sandwiches and cakes that Sarah had given him had run out, he had lived on what he could buy at the stations. Maggie can hardly eat her dinner; she is too full of happiness. She watches him chattering away ten to the dozen about his new life in the bush. After so many years of not knowing if he was alive or dead, there he is, the same old Billy. She can hardly believe it; she wants to pinch herself to see if she is dreaming. She cannot take her eyes off him. He is so grown-up and handsome; she wonders if he has a girlfriend yet. He talks a lot about the sheep station and the people who live there; he is happy.

She cannot help but feel envious of him. He has had a good life thanks to Henry and Sarah; he was lucky to meet them. But then she too has been lucky. She looks across at Mrs Robinson, laughing and chatting to her lodgers; she gave her a home and more than that, friendship.

'I can't stay too long, Maggie. Maybe a week and then I have to get back,' he tells her as he finishes off the last spoonful of stew from his plate.

'That's not long.'

'I know but you see they rely on me. Henry told me that they need me more than ever now that he's getting old. He can't do the things he used to do.'

'What about the son, Jack? Can't he look after the place for a bit?' she asks, a little peevishly.

'Yes. They'll manage without me for a bit but I want to get back before shearing time.'

She feels cheated. He has only just arrived and already he is itching to get back there. She hopes he will change his mind and stay in Melbourne, but she doubts it.

'What about Mum? She'll be so disappointed if you don't stay.'

She feels she is blackmailing him but she cannot help it. She desperately wants them all to live together again.

'Mum will understand. I wrote to her and told her about Henry and Sarah. She understands how I feel.'

He reaches across and touches her hand.

'It'll be OK, Maggie. She'll have you and Grace and Leslie. I know this is what you wanted but we can't turn the clock back. I'll keep in touch; I promise. But I can't stay. I have to go back. They need me.'

'But we need you,' she says, tears blurring her eyes.

She pulls something out of her pocket and gives it to him. He smiles.

'It's a bit of our old door,' he says. 'You've still got it. Our blue door.'

She thinks he is about to cry as well but instead he takes an identical piece from his pocket.

'You kept it?' she says in amazement.

'Yes. You told me to.'

He places the two shards of wood, side by side.

'I thought as long as I had it we would all be together again one day,' Maggie says.

'And we will be, Maggie but not all the time. I have to go back to the farm.'

He hands the fragment of wood back to her.

'I have looked at that piece of wood, so many times,' he tells her, 'especially when I was in the orphanage. It reminded me that I had a sister and one day she would find me.'

'I've missed you, Billy,' she says. 'I've really missed you.'

'You can come and visit,' he says. 'All of you. It's wonderful there. You'll love it. I have my own room; you can sleep in there and I'll move into the bunk house.'

'Treacle tart for pudding,' Mrs Robinson announces, as she clears away the empty plates. 'That OK Billy?'

'Sounds pretty good to me. It's just like being at home,' he says, as way of a complement.

Maggie realises that Melbourne will never be his home. His heart is back there, in the bush. He doesn't speak about the orphanage and what happened to him. He won't even talk about how he ran away. She understands that; like her, he wants to forget that part of his life. She swallows her disappointment. He is happy. He has found a new life for himself and that is all that matters. He is right, Mum will understand.

She can't sleep. She knows it's only six o'clock but she cannot stay in bed any longer. Already her stomach is dancing with excitement. She thinks of Billy, sleeping downstairs on Mrs Robinson's sofa and cannot believe that it's really happening.

The ship arrives sometime this morning. Jimmy is taking her and Billy down to the Port of Melbourne to meet them. She cannot help smiling when she thinks that today she will be with her mother again. In her last letter, her mother explained that she had written to the orphanage about Grace and she is going to collect her as soon as she arrives. This will be Grace's last day there. She wonders if the nuns have told her yet or if they will wait until the last minute like they did when Maggie was told to leave.

She dresses quickly and makes her way down to the kitchen. Everything is in darkness. She opens the door and steps into the yard. The sky is black, like velvet and is spotted with stars. One, bigger than all the rest, seems to hang right above her. Her mind flies back to June and the concert on the ship. She hums a little of her song. So much has happened since then. Some things are best left forgotten but there are others that have been good: meeting Jimmy for one, then all the friends she has made, Annabel, Alice, Helen, Tom and Mrs R. They have all helped to make this miracle happen, to make her dream come true.

The Only Blue Door

EPILOGUE
MAY 2000

MAGGIE

She glimpses the waves breaking along the coast as the aeroplane takes off then they are climbing and everything is lost in cloud. The flight will take almost four hours then there is at least a two hour drive into the bush. For the first time Maggie realises just how far away Billy lives. Still it does not make her feel any less guilty. Here she is, seventy-two years old and visiting her brother for the first time. She had wanted to, often enough, but something always got in the way. At first there was no money to travel, then, after she married, there were the children, and her husband's job; there was always something to prevent her making the trip.

She wonders what he will be like; she has not seen him since Mum's funeral. She should be able to recognise Billy from the photos he has sent of himself and his family over the years, but what of the person himself? It makes her sad to realise that she has never really known him. They stole her brother away all those years ago and she has never got him back. Yes, he came to Melbourne when he was sixteen to see Mum but that was too brief a visit. All she can really remember of Billy is a cheeky ten-year old who loved to play football. She has been reminded of that boy many times since, whenever her own grandchildren have come to stay; the youngest, in particular, is very like the young Billy.

So many years have passed and still the anger burns within her when she thinks back to those lost years. They have all got on with their lives since then but the scars remain. That is why she has to see Billy again before it's too late.

The seat belt sign goes out and she adjusts her position slightly; she wishes she could have a cigarette. As she does dozens of times a day, she thinks of her husband; if only Jimmy was still here with her. It was the shock of his death that has spurred her on to make this journey, the realisation that the people you love don't live forever.

The whole world knows about the migrant children now. It has been on the television and in all the newspapers; they have made documentaries about them and written books. A reporter had even asked her once if she blamed anyone for what had happened to her.

She, Billy and Grace came here because of the war but now she knows that there were other motives fuelling the migration of children. After the war the numbers of children sent to Australia increased, spurred on by financial incentives to the voluntary organisations and the churches that received them. Australia's need for immigrants was top priority and British children, unencumbered by family and easy to mould, were ideal material. It was believed that the children were being given the very best of opportunities; they were being sent to a land of milk and honey. Now they realise the mistakes that were made, the harm that could occur from separating young children from their families. They admit that the institutions were inadequately monitored and inspected, that many of the staff were badly trained and ill-equipped for their task. There have been apologies and offers of compensation but she has no need for either. She has made her own salvation; Billy too has made a life for himself. Only Grace still carries the scars of those years.

Billy was granted automatic Australian citizenship, married a local girl and realised his dream. Now he owns a thousand acres of farm land and has a reputation for breeding some of the finest horses in Australia. He and his two sons, her nephews, run the farm between them. Yes, Billy has made a life for himself. But Billy does not like to leave his farm. Nothing will tempt him away. She knows that Billy only feels safe in his own environment; the roots he has put down in that part of Western Australia are deep. He has no wish, and indeed no need, to move away.

'Would you like something to drink?' the air stewardess asks her.

'A gin and tonic,' she says.

If nothing else it may make her sleep.

She wrote to Grace, telling her about her trip, hoping that she would agree to come with her, but Grace has a busy life these days. She said she couldn't leave.

As she promised, their mother took Grace out of the orphanage as soon as she arrived in Australia. Poor Grace, of all of them she was the one who suffered most from her experiences. At first their mother tried to get her to go to the local school and later to work but Grace could do neither. She, who had been such a happy, sunny child in London, withdrew more and more into herself and would not leave the house. The doctor diagnosed depression and prescribed a course of valium for her but Grace's progress was slow. She never married, preferring to live with Mum and George in the suburbs of Melbourne. Then when Mum died and George became infirm, she invited Freda, the girl she had been friends with in the orphanage, to move in with them. It was the best thing she could have done. Freda had trained as a nurse and was able to help her care for her step-father. But more importantly, Freda understood; they had shared experiences, experiences that had broken their spirits but were never mentioned.

George left the house to Grace when he died and she and Freda opened a boarding kennel for dogs. At last, after all these years, Grace is happy. Maggie knows that the ghosts sometimes return to haunt her but most of the time she lives a normal, busy life.

Maggie drinks the rest of the gin and tonic and signals to the stewardess to bring her another.

She rarely sees her youngest brother, Leslie; he is back in England. So there they are: Billy on one side of Australia, her and Grace on the other and Leslie working in London. The reporter's words come back to her. Does she want to blame anyone for what happened? Yes, she would like to blame someone but what good would it do now?